## About the Authors

**Pippa Roscoe** lives in Norfolk, near her family, and makes daily promises to herself that this is the day she'll leave the computer to take a long walk in the countryside. She can't remember a time when she wasn't dreaming about handsome heroes and innocent heroines. Totally her mother's fault, of course – she gave Pippa her first romance to read at the age of seven! She is inconceivably happy that she gets to share those daydreams with you. Follow her on Twitter @PippaRoscoe.

Cursed with a poor sense of direction and a propensity to read, **Annie Claydon** spent much of her childhood lost in books. A degree in English Literature followed by a career in computing didn't lead directly to her perfect job – writing romance for Mills & Boon – but she has no regrets in taking the scenic route. She lives in London: a city where getting lost can be a joy.

*USA Today* bestselling author and RITA® nominee, **Sandra Hyatt**, pens passionate, emotional stories laced with gentle humour and compassion. She has lived in several countries but calls New Zealand home.

# Royal Weddings

# Royal Weddings
# A Pretend Proposal

PIPPA ROSCOE

ANNIE CLAYDON

SANDRA HYATT

MILLS & BOON

First Published in Great Britain 2022
by Mills & Boon, an imprint of HarperCollins*Publishers* Ltd,
1 London Bridge Street, London, SE1 9GF

www.harpercollins.co.uk

HarperCollins*Publishers*
1st Floor, Watermarque Building,
Ringsend Road, Dublin 4, Ireland

ROYAL WEDDINGS: A PRETEND PROPOSAL © 2022
Harlequin Enterprises ULC

*Virgin Princess's Marriage Debt* © 2019 Pippa Roscoe
*From Doctor to Princess?* © 2018 Annie Claydon
*Falling for the Princess* © 2011 Sandra Hyatt

ISBN: 978-0-263-30566-1

MIX
Paper from
responsible sources
FSC™ C007454

This book is produced from independently certified FSC™ paper
to ensure responsible forest management.

For more information visit: www.harpercollins.co.uk/green

Printed and Bound in Spain using 100% Renewable electricity at
CPI Black Print, Barcelona

# VIRGIN PRINCESS'S MARRIAGE DEBT

**PIPPA ROSCOE**

For Sharon Kendrick.

Without your amazing, encouraging, supportive advice I would never have finished this book.

You are a true Modern queen!

# PROLOGUE

THEO LOOKED AT his watch again. She was late. This wasn't the first time they'd snuck out of the impossibly expensive Swiss boarding school at night, but this time felt different. She'd said that she had a surprise for him and he couldn't for the life of him figure out what that might have been.

Knowing Sofia, it could be anything. She was like that. Impulsive, reckless, often secretive…and most definitely alluring. It had taken Theo a good long while to believe that she wasn't like the other kids at this school. This school that he hated.

He wasn't naïve. He knew attending a school this reputable was a thing he could not take for granted—even if at every single turn the other students tried to make him believe that he shouldn't be there. It hadn't taken him long to realise that he was not wanted, the poor illegitimate scholarship kid polluting their air. He almost shrugged a shoulder at the train of his thoughts. Why should here be any different to the way he had been brought up in Greece, with his mother's family?

The teachers were hardly any better than the students. If there was something to be blamed, it would be his fault. But they couldn't deny his grades. At seventeen he already had scholarship offers at some of the world's leading universities and there was nothing he'd do to jeopardise that. No, Theo Tersi was going to make damn sure that he never had to return to his mother's family vineyards in the Peloponnese. He would be a banker, something in finance. He wanted an office, like his mother's current employer who had paid for his education here. He would never scrabble around in the dust like his uncles and cousins—the ones who had taunted him since his birth. So, no. He wouldn't fight back against the bullies here. He couldn't. Not without risking everything he'd worked so hard for. Because he wanted more. For his mother, for himself. He wanted never to feel the sting of rejection and shame and hunger... And once he got out of this school, once he finished university, he would make sure that no one would taunt him again.

He looked again at his watch, the round white face gleaming in the moonlight. Where was she? Sofia was usually already waiting for him. He looked around. The night seemed almost unnaturally still, as if it were holding its breath, as if in expectation...

And he felt it too. That anticipation, the moment when he would see Sofia emerging from whatever shrub she was hiding behind. He still had to pinch himself sometimes. Never quite sure if he could really believe that someone like her would really be interested in someone like him. But tonight...he was going to tell her. Tell her that he loved her. That he wanted her to be with him when he left for university...that he wanted the life they had often talked about having in the last six months. Because somehow she'd worked her way through the anger and distrust he'd first met her with, she'd broken down the barriers all the taunts and cruel tricks the other students had thrown his way.

She had been the one bright thing in his days at school

over the last few months. For so long his life had simply been about him and his mother, doing whatever it took to get through the day. He'd hated how his mother was treated by her family...because of him, because of the father he'd never met, and never wanted to. The move from Greece to Switzerland had been a fresh start for them both—the opportunity at this school one almost unimaginable for a housekeeper and her son.

And no matter what people threw at him, Theo was determined to bide his time here, knowing that it would get him to where he wanted to be. But the moment he'd first seen Sofia...the way her oceanic blue eyes had sparkled with mischief, the way his heart had kicked and thrashed, as if for the first time, when her gaze collided with his he had found something more from life than just lessons and determination. And it had never stopped, that heart thumping. He felt that same way every single time he saw her.

She had this air about her, as if nothing bad could ever touch her. And it was addictive. He leant into it every chance he could get. But he worried about her, wanted to protect her from herself even. If the school prankster was caught pulling another stunt, the headmaster had been clear—they would be expelled. He doubted they'd ever guess it was the sweet, innocent-looking blonde angel she appeared to be. But he couldn't deny that it was exactly that strange, thrilling combination of innocence and recklessness that had first drawn him to her.

He wasn't quite sure what it was, but there was also a deep desperation within her. Some kind of urgency that called to him, to his feelings for her...his love. She hadn't said much about her family, dropping little breadcrumbs of information about a loving but strict home that stifled the freedom Sofia loved so much. It certainly didn't sound like something that he would run from. But there would be time to uncover the secrets she held. There would be the rest of their lives.

That he was another of her secrets, he hated… It came far too close to the way he thought his father must have felt in order to flee from their village the same night of his birth. As if there was something about Theo that was shameful or embarrassing somehow.

A noise in the bushes off to his left startled him, his heart racing, knowing that it wouldn't settle until he saw her.

'Tersi. I was told I'd find you here.'

Instead of Sofia's softly accented Iondorran tones, fear sliced through his high hopes as the voice of his headmaster cut into the night.

He didn't move. Not a muscle. His heart dropped, sickness and nausea an instant reaction to being caught doing something he shouldn't be doing. But greater than that was his concern for Sofia.

'What's going on?' Theo ventured to the man who had never liked him.

'What's going on is that I now have my prankster. Did you really think that I would allow my car, *my car*, to be put onto the roof of the sports hall and take no action?'

Theo was shaking his head. 'I don't know anything about that, sir, honestly.'

The grim look of determination on the older man's face told Theo that he wasn't believed. Not for a second. Panic began to set in then.

'Where's Sofia?'

'The princess has returned to Iondorra.'

'Princess? What are you talking about?' Theo demanded, any hesitation overruled by his confusion.

'She didn't tell you?'

'Tell me what? Sir, please—'

'Did you really think that a princess would be interested in…?'

The man must have seen the look on Theo's face, the one he knew had descended as quickly as the fury had whipped within his chest. If there was even a moment of pity, or hesitation from the headmaster, Theo didn't see it.

'Well, it's done. She's gone. And you, skulking around in the shadows waiting to see the effect of your handiwork, will regret the day you pulled this last prank.'

'Mr Templeton, I didn't do anything to your car,' Theo said, desperately trying to hold on to his temper.

'No? Then why is your school scarf wedged underneath the wheel arch of my Mini Cooper?'

'I have no—'

Horror hit Theo hard and fast. The last time he'd seen his scarf he had been looping it around Sofia's neck as she shivered in the cold winter's sun. Sofia had lied to him? She was a princess? It was impossible. But as Theo was marched back to the headmaster's office, his quick mind ran over the images that shifted like a kaleidoscope in his memory. Every interaction, every conversation, every kiss and his stomach turned. Each memory played to the sound of taunts he had never risen to. The cries and jibes of students belittling him for his humble beginnings—ones he had taken because this school had been his ticket out. His way to rise up, no matter what people said or did. But Sofia? She was the one who had wanted to keep their relationship a secret. She was the only one who had known where he would be that night. She was the one who had said she had a surprise for him. She was the one who had been pulling the pranks all this time, and had finally left his scarf at the site of the latest one. Had it all been a ruse? Had she spent the last six months priming him to be the patsy? The fall guy to take the blame for her pranks? Was that why he'd doubted her in the beginning, because somewhere deep down he had known it was all lies? Had she really been the cruellest of them all, to make him fall in love with her, when he should have known better?

He was going to be expelled. He was going to lose everything. Because of her.

# CHAPTER ONE

*Paris...ten years later*

PRINCESS SOFIA DE LORIA of Iondorra looked out across the Parisian skyline as the sun began its slow summer descent over the rooftops and cobbled streets of Europe's reportedly most romantic city. The irony was not lost on her. Tonight she would meet the man she would spend the rest of her life with. Not that romance had anything to do with it. No, that was the domain of Angelique— the practical, determined matchmaker who had been employed for that express purpose.

The hint of jasmine that settled around the room of the luxurious hotel near the Sixth Arrondissement from some invisible air dispenser was nothing like the real thing and Sofia longed to return to her palace in Iondorra. Although she did appreciate the soft white and gold tones of the room and, casting a look to the king-sized bed, her heart lurching, she felt desperate to throw herself amongst the soft pillows and deep comfort offered by the impossibly thick duvet. She had been away too long, immersed in diplomatic duties unruffling more than a few feathers caused by her father's recent and increasing absence from the world's stage. More and more, she found that she just wanted to go home.

She pulled her gaze from the incredible view of the Jardin de Luxembourg and paced towards the larger seating area of the stunning suite. Only yesterday she had been in Prague, two days before that, it had been Istanbul. Her body moved oddly within the costume for that evening's masquerade ball—the full corset holding her back straight and pushing her breasts against the gentle arc of the low, sweeping neckline. She felt confined by it, not that it was an unfamiliar feeling to Sofia. The bustle of material behind her, falling into a wide golden train, made her feel as if she were pulling the weight of more than just her, and Sofia couldn't help but think that it somehow fitted that evening.

The masquerade ball being held to celebrate the birthday of one of Europe's minor royals had presented the perfect opportunity to meet her three would-be suitors without attracting the notice of the world's press, or the intrigue of the very royal and rich society that had been waiting with bated breath to see who the Widow Princess would marry next.

A sliver of pain twisted through her heart as she recalled the description favoured by the international press so much that it had almost become part of her title. Princess Sofia of Iondorra—the Widow Princess.

Every time it was mentioned it was accompanied by images of her in mourning, her pale skin harsh against the depth of the black clothes she had worn to honour her husband. Four years. Antoine had been gone for four years. The familiar sense of grief, softened only slightly over the years, edged around her heart. Theirs might not have been a love match in the truest sense, but Antoine had been her friend, her confidant. He had known about her father's illness and helped shield it from the world. He had supported her through their brief marriage as she adjusted to the reality that she would be queen much sooner than anyone had ever expected.

She missed his quiet support and understanding and once again felt the strange sense of bafflement that had met the news of his shockingly unexpected death at a charity car race. The footage of the six-car pile-up in Le Mans had shocked nations, but only devastated one. Because only Antoine's life had been lost.

But she could not afford to indulge in her grief. Not tonight. Antoine, more than anyone, would understand why she needed to remarry for the good of her country. Her father's illness had deepened in the last few months, and, whether she liked it or not, the council was right. If the news of his illness broke while she was still considered the Widow Princess, then the future of her country would be in serious jeopardy. With a fairly inexperienced prime minister forced into making difficult austerity measures, the monarchy was the only stability and security the people believed in. And the only way Iondorra would survive the impending announcement of her father's diagnosis was if they had some hope for the future—a fairy-tale marriage heralding the next generation of royals.

It hadn't been Antoine's fault that they'd not conceived during their four-year marriage. They had tried a few times, but even Sofia had been forced to admit that neither had been able to bring themselves to actually consummate their marriage. And she knew why. Only once had she experienced a chemistry, an attraction that had been at once all-consuming, that had seemed almost to threaten her very sanity. And it hadn't been with Antoine.

It hadn't taken long before her husband had started to look elsewhere for the pleasure that she simply could not offer him. He'd been so devastatingly discreet and quiet about it all. Every now and then he would disappear for a few days, and return with some impossibly expensive gift, offering it to her with eyes that could never meet her gaze. It hadn't angered her, torn her up inside the way it should have done. Instead, all she'd been able to feel was so very sad for the man she cared for like a friend, like a brother, to be trapped in the same cage she was caught within. Duty. A passionless marriage.

And here she was again, on the brink of yet another one. Wasn't the definition of madness doing the same thing over and over again, expecting a different result?

'Are you ready?' Angelique's voice came from somewhere behind her.

'For the royal equivalent of speed dating?' Sofia asked. 'Yes,' she said, answering her own question, all the while shaking her head to the contrary.

Angelique smiled, the movement softening her features into something more relatable than the fierce businesswoman persona she usually adopted.

'Are you sure this is what you want? We can always cancel, find some other way…'

'Are you trying to do yourself out of a commission? That doesn't seem very wise.'

Angelique cocked her head to one side, quite bird-like. 'My finances are perfectly secure, I assure you, Your Highness. And, as you have requested the utmost secrecy, then so would be my reputation. You *do* have a choice, Sofia.'

But they both knew that was a lie. Sofia looked to the window again, as if it were an exit route, as if she could fly to it and escape from what was about to happen. Because somehow, in some way, Sofia simply couldn't shake the feeling that, after tonight, her life would drastically change.

Yes, she'd have met and chosen the man she would

marry, but it felt bigger than that. It felt as if she were on a precipice but that she couldn't see the edge. And it made her angry. Angry for all the sacrifices she had already made, and the ones she could continue to make in the future. As if a summer thunderstorm had zapped her with a lightning strike, coursing white-hot heat through her veins. But where once she would have vented her anger, her fear, all this impossible-to-express energy, Sofia had to fight it. Princesses didn't get angry. They got married.

'Okay,' Angelique said finally as if, too, sensing there was no going back. 'So, would you like the motivational speech now, Your Highness?'

Sofia couldn't help but smile at the gentle humour in Angelique's tone. It felt like years since someone had laughed with her. It *had* been years.

'What would you like? *Braveheart*-style, Beyoncé *Run the World*, or something *à la* Churchill?'

Sofia let a small, sad laugh escape from her lips. 'I'll forgo the attempt at a Scottish accent, I think. I don't suppose you have anything just for me?' she asked, instantly hating the sense of vulnerability her words evoked.

'I do,' Angelique said, locking serious eyes with hers. 'You will be a great queen. You will care for Iondorra with as great a sense of purpose as any who have gone before you. You will rule her with love and duty and sacrifice, but all of that will ensure Iondorra's longevity amongst the world's greatest nations. And you will do it with a man at your side who will love, honour and protect you in a way that allows *you* to protect *your* country. You, Your Highness, are a force to be reckoned with and my wish for you is that you find a man worthy of that. These three suitors are perfect candidates. They understand your duty, your role in life, and are willing and able to support you in that. And now it is time.'

'To go to the ball, Fairy Godmother?'

'No, Sofia,' Angelique said gently. 'To remove Antoine's ring.'

Sofia's fingers flew to the wedding band around her fourth finger. It felt as sacrilegious to remove it, as much as it was easy for her to do so. Antoine would have understood. She placed the simple wedding band she had worn for eight years on the dressing table and felt a little bit of her past slip away from her grasp.

As Angelique left the room, Sofia returned her watchful gaze to the Parisian rooftops. For just a moment, she had fallen under the spell of the other woman's words, grateful for them, thankful. But that positive determination she had felt fizzing in her veins had disappeared with Angelique's departure. And for the first time in a while, she let the façade drop and allowed the feel of exhaustion to sweep over her. Her father's deterioration had increased in the last few months and propelled the need for the one thing she'd been putting off for several years. The cost of keeping her father's illness a secret had been a great one to pay, but one that she would do again and again. Because the people of Iondorra needed security.

She thought of her little European principality, cradled in between France, Switzerland and northern Italy. The country that she was to rule, protect as if it were her child. The country that, ever since she was seventeen and had been whisked away from her boarding school, she had been trained to protect, ruthlessly sculpted to become the perfect princess.

And then, as always following these moments of weakness, came the inner strength that saw her match even the strongest heads of state at the tables of European negotiations. She, and Iondorra, had no time for selfish, moping thoughts. She'd put those things aside a long time ago. Just as she'd put aside the thoughts of her own happy-ever-after.

*Poor little princess*, an inner voice mocked, sounding very much like that of a young man she'd long ago loved. A young man she'd been forced to leave behind, lie to, and a man she very much refused to think of now.

She glanced at the embossed invitation, smiling at how the gold detail of the lettering matched the soft golden yellows of the corseted Victorian-era dress she wore, the crinoline underskirt as heavy as a crown.

For so long she'd been cast as the Widow Princess, it had begun to feel as if she'd lost herself. Not that it mattered. The only thing of true importance was Iondorra. And attending the masquerade ball was just the next step towards the throne.

Each of the three men had been carefully vetted and would, in their own ways, be perfectly acceptable candidates for their role as husband. So there she was, in Paris, dressed up and ready to find the man she would spend the rest of her life with. And if she'd once thought she already had, then it didn't matter. Such fanciful daydreams were for others. Real princesses didn't have the luxury of Prince Charmings.

Theo Tersi scanned the expanse of the large Parisian ballroom, took a breath and instantly regretted it. Where he had expected to taste the hint of satisfaction at the thought of what tonight would bring, the only thing on his tongue was the cloying and competing scents of the perfume adorning the many women in the room. It was an assault on his olfactory system and he was half tempted to retreat and preserve that much-needed function. When he would think back to this moment in the months to come, he would wonder if it had been some kind of cosmic sign to turn back. To think again.

But right now, there was no turning back for Theo.

'All right, I'm here,' grouched the exiled Duke of Gaeten.

'You don't need to sound so pleased about it,' Theo said absently, still scanning the faces in the ballroom for the one that he wanted. No, *needed*. 'Surely the great Sebastian Rohan de Luen is not bored in the face of all this as yet untouched potential?'

'Hah,' his friend almost spat. 'You think me jaded?'

'No, as I said. Bored. You need someone to challenge you.'

'And you need to walk away from this madness before it gets us all into trouble.'

Theo turned and cast a look over his closest friend, the only person who had been there for him when his world came crashing down for the second time. They had been in the middle of a business meeting—Theo soliciting a deal that would see the wine from his vineyard served at Sebastian's Michelin-starred hotels scattered across the globe—when he had received the call from the hospital informing him of his mother's admittance and diagnosis. The bottom had literally dropped out of his world, and Sebastian? Had chartered a private plane to return him to Greece and, rather than simply letting that be the end of it, had contracted Theo's vineyard to his hotels. It had been the only thing that had saved Theo and his business from the wolves—but more importantly it had provided him with enough capital to pay for his mother's healthcare. Without that contract, he would have lost the vineyard, would have lost the roof over his and his mother's heads, and possibly would have lost his mother. And Theo had never forgotten it, and would never. Their relationship had quickly grown from business to brotherhood and, despite the awful foundation of its start, he wouldn't regret it. It had been his salvation in the years since.

But, throughout that dark time, Theo had only seen one face, one person to blame, one person who had lied to him, set him up to take full blame for her actions, and had singlehandedly ruined his life. Had it not been for her, he would have finished his education—would have attended one of the finest universities the world had to offer, and would have been able to provide his mother with more, with better. He would never have been in a position where he could have lost it all. And that fear, the fear of nearly losing his mother, had changed him, had transformed his DNA. Never again would he be the naïve youth he had once been. Never again would he be that *innocent*.

Sofia was the origin point of the change in the course of his life, one that had only exacerbated his mother's later illness. He hadn't been surprised when the doctor had explained that the stresses of the last few years had taken their toll on his mother's already weak heart. The shock of losing her job after his expulsion, the struggle of the following years... Had he not met Sofia, he would never have lost everything he'd held within his grasp—the opportunities, the chances he had been given to be and do better than either he or his mother could have ever expected. Naïve and foolish, he had believed every single one of Sofia's lies before she disappeared, making a mockery of all those words of love, of a future she would never give him—could never have been able to give—when he finally discovered the truth about her.

Oh, he had thought her to be so different to the cruel students of the international boarding school his mother's employer had sponsored him to attend, but at least they had owned their cruelty. No—Sofia's had been worse, because she had hidden her betrayal until the last moment, she had purposefully set him up to take the blame for her reckless actions and he had been expelled.

And the shame he'd felt when he realised he had lost it all? The anger that had coursed through his veins when he realised her words, her touches had been nothing more than a game to be played by a bored and spoilt princess? It had been nothing compared to the moment where his heart had shattered into a thousand pieces. The moment he'd seen the announcement of her engagement. To be betrayed by someone he had…he could no longer bring himself to say the word. He forced his thoughts fiercely away from reflections that would only see him lose his temper. And if anything was to be lost tonight, it couldn't be that.

'I spent years—*years*—watching and waiting to see if I would lose this…need for vengeance.' He had thrown himself into any willing woman he could find in an attempt to erase the memory of her. He hadn't managed to turn his tastes to the blonde hair that seemed dull and lifeless in comparison to the lustre his memories had endowed *her* with. Blue eyes seemed bland and insipid against the sparkle and shine of the strange combination of intelligence and recklessness that seemed unique only to her. Brunettes were the only way forward through those dark, hedonistic two years as he had tried and failed to satiate the wild, driving need for her…for revenge that had all but consumed him.

'Two years in which you developed a truly debauched reputation,' Sebastian said, cutting through his thoughts.

'You sound jealous.'

'I am. How on earth am I supposed to be the most

notorious playboy in Europe, if you are there competing for that same title?'

Theo couldn't help but smile.

'But,' Sebastian said, his mocking gaze growing serious, 'despite all that, my sister doesn't seem to have realised that she will never have your heart.'

'I don't have a heart to give, Sebastian,' he growled, 'but I will speak to Maria. I had hoped that it might dissipate with time, but—'

'I know you do not encourage it,' Sebastian said, slinging an arm around Theo's shoulders. 'Truly. But she is still very much...'

Clearly unable or unwilling to describe the extent of Maria's infatuation with Theo, Sebastian trailed off.

'It will be done. *Kindly*,' Theo assured him.

He liked Maria, but no matter how much he resisted her somewhat naïve attempts to pursue him, nor how many headlines proclaimed him to be just as debauched as her brother, she had not been put off. Yet. Depending on how tonight would go, it could be the final nail in the coffin of her yearning for him.

Apparently appeased, Sebastian replaced his mask and turned back to the party. Following his lead, Theo took a glass of the prosecco and bit back the curse that Europe's insistence that the masses should drink the alcohol like water had clearly infiltrated this Parisian ballroom too. Yes, he made his money with wine, but his tastes ran to whisky this evening, and right now he'd give someone else's kingdom for one.

Theo took in the glamorous couples, the range of costumes that were everything from the sublime to outrageous, but never ridiculous. The sheer extravagance and money in the room saw to that. His quick mind calculated the cost of such an event. The room hire, the staff, the overpriced and frankly unpalatable alcohol being served, all of it would fund a thousand small businesses well into the next year, a fact probably not even considered by the birthday girl's family.

After he'd spent the first few years of his adult life weighing up every single decision, every single purchase, his ability to price almost anything was ingrained. Deeply. From the moment he had returned to Greece with his mother after his expulsion from school, the shame he had brought to the family who had funded his education there, the termination of his mother's employment, and the return to the people who had rejected them both ever since his conception…he had never lost the taste of bitterness in his mouth, no matter how rich, sweet or satisfying the grape or wine he produced.

After initial notoriety as the young vintner shocking the international wine industry—and his mother's family—with the incredible popularity of his Greek blended wine, he had proved himself time and time again. And despite the almost constant criticism proclaiming his success as a flash in the pan—as if it hadn't taken blood, sweat, his mother's tears—even after eight years in the profession, he was still seen as the most upsetting thing to happen in the wine world since the invention of screwtop caps. That he'd dared to produce an award-winning blended wine rather than that of a pure grape somehow suited his own illegitimate status. That he persevered with blended wines seemed only to infuriate the old-school vintners who sniffed and huffed as he dominated the market, proclaiming him a young upstart. He didn't feel young. Especially as he cast a frowning glance around the fancy frippery of the masked ball in Paris. No. He just felt jaded.

None of these people would have given him the time

of day before he'd found his success, and Theo now returned the favour, ignoring the lascivious glances cast his way. Instead of firing his blood, they only turned him cold. If he was honest, not since he was seventeen had he felt the heat of passion truly stir. Desire? Yes. The arousal of attraction? Of course. But never need. Never passion. And he fiercely reminded himself that he liked it that way. Because the last time he had felt that had heralded the destruction of every hope and dream he and his mother had ever held.

And now he was on the brink of facing his demon, he had to remind himself that he was not a monster. That *he* was not as cruel as she had been. As if sensing his resolve, Sebastian turned to him with a raised eyebrow in query.

'I will give her one chance,' Theo said, forcing his eyes back to the ballroom, back to his prey. 'If she apologises for what she did, then I will walk away, no harm, no foul.' But if she didn't, then Sofia de Loria would rue the day she had crossed him and finally learn the consequences of her actions.

# CHAPTER TWO

As SOFIA STEPPED away from the second of the would-be suitors with a resigned smile, she realised that she was losing hope. Neither he nor the first were right and she couldn't help but feel that she was expecting the impossible. She was the worst Goldilocks ever. But as much as she didn't want to rush into another marriage, she didn't have a choice.

She hung back around the edges of the grand ballroom, thankful that she was hidden amongst the crowds of people watching the figures making their way round the dance floor. She had dismissed her personal assistant in order to speak to the suitors alone, and relished the opportunity for the closest thing to anonymity she'd experienced in almost ten years. The fine golden leaf-like swirls of her mask tickled at the edges of her hair, but she would take that minor discomfort for the concealment it offered. It swept upward, asymmetrically, to one side, and matched the colour of her dress perfectly.

Sofia bit back a laugh as she imagined for a moment that this would be how a wallflower, found between the pages of some historical romance, felt. Both terrified and hopeful of being plucked from obscurity to dance beneath the candlelit chandeliers by the handsome prince. But hers wasn't that kind of story. No, *she* was the royal and it seemed that the second sons, or cousins—like the two previous candidates who had seemed so fine on paper—had quite definitive ideas about *their* place within *her* royal office.

She had never wanted it. Not in truth. As a child, she had hardly been perfect princess material. Her parents had despaired and sent her to boarding school, tired of having to bribe the Iondorran press to silence yet another social faux pas on their daughter's behalf. For security reasons they had all agreed to keep her royal status a secret. But for Sofia it hadn't been about a desire for protection, it had been her last attempt for something normal, to be treated like anyone else. But ultimately that had backfired in the most spectacularly painful way.

She became aware of the feeling of someone watching her. As a princess, she was reluctantly familiar with the sensation, but this was different. This *felt* different. The hairs on her arms lifted beneath the unseen gaze, and her pulse picked up at her neck almost painfully. She couldn't shake the feeling that she was somehow being sought out...*hunted*.

She cast a glance around the room to see if she could identify the source. A sea of vivid masks and incredible costumes greeted her, and she caught herself in the unconscious protective movement she hated as her hand went to soothe the phantom sensitivity at her ribs caused by that awful night a year and a half ago.

She was surrounded by people, all engaged in conversations, bodies pressed closer together by the illicit nature given to the mass by the disguise of masks and costumes, but none seemed to be looking her way.

Discarding the feeling as foolish, much like her earlier impression that somehow her life was going to change irrevocably, she searched for Angelique, who had gone to locate her final suitor, but saw no sign of either of them. As the orchestra picked up the threads of a familiar waltz a feeling of nostalgia swept over her.

She could only hold out hope for this final suitor, because without him her country would be left vulnerable and she couldn't, wouldn't, allow that to happen.

It was not her father's fault that he'd been diagnosed with early-onset dementia. But she couldn't help but feel responsible that she hadn't been ready to assume royal duties earlier to prevent the extreme financial loss her country had experienced under his unstable reign. Feel embarrassed that she had been so carefree and reckless as to need two years of strong, mindful guardianship to ensure that she wouldn't bring further damage to Iondorra as every wilful, mindless frippery was ironed out of her character. Feel that sense of guilt that the necessary secrecy of her father's ill health had continued for so long...the silence almost as painful as the disease itself. For surely if she had been a better princess, a better ruler, they wouldn't have had to indulge in this secrecy?

She thought of her mother, tucked away in the privacy of the smaller holdings of the royal family in Iondorra, imprisoned with her husband and a handful of staff and medical professionals ready to manage and care for whatever latest outpouring of anger, frustration or confusion her father experienced almost daily now.

She knew she needed to accept the grief at the loss of a man who had once been a loving father and a fantastic ruler, but she just couldn't. She had grown to almost resent the days of coherence as much as the ones where all semblance of his sanity was lost. They were the ones that she hated most. When she saw her father once again as the man who had loved her, laughed with her, despite the strict requirements he needed her to adhere to. Of course, that was before the diagnosis and her sudden and shocking departure from the international boarding school. Ever since then her life had become one solely of duty.

A waiter paused by her side, offering her a glass of prosecco. She knew that she needed to keep a clear head for this evening, but she couldn't help but clasp the fine glass stem, relishing the cool liquid as it fizzed and bubbled on her tongue.

She was just about to leave the confines of the crowd around her when the hairs on her neck lifted once again and she felt enveloped by the warmth from a body close behind her. Shocked at the proximity of the unseen figure, she breathed in, ready to turn, when the musky, earthy scent of cologne hit her and held her still. It was unfamiliar amongst the sickly sweet, almost chemical fragrance of many of the men here. He waited, as if allowing her to become familiar with his presence, before sweeping around to stand in front of her and bowing long and low. As he straightened and held a hand out to her, she took in the way the white mask disguised his face and almost smiled as his head cocked to one side towards the dance area. The gesture seeming both inquisitive and vaguely arrogant at the same time. A challenge almost, as if daring her to refuse his request.

A feeling familiar, yet so distant as to almost be heartbreaking, rose in her chest. Defiance, recklessness and something more...something almost tantalising made her reach out, made her place her hand in his, even though no word had been spoken, even though the mask he wore concealed his identity. As his fingers closed over hers and he led her towards the dance area she felt a strange sense of vertigo, reminding her of the precipice she had imagined herself upon earlier that evening.

Her thoughts were sent scattering and fleeing as the

figure released her to bring her whirling around in such a way that she had to press her hand to the man's chest in order to prevent herself from crashing into him and losing her balance and breath in one move.

The warmth that greeted the palm of her hand through the thin shirt burned her, sending tingles and fire bursts across her skin and neck, raising a blush of sudden and shocking heat to her cheeks. But, as she went to pull back, his hand came down against hers, anchoring it in place. She stared at his fingers, unaccountably reluctant to see the face of her captor. The deep tan spoke of sunshine and heat, and her eyes snagged on the roughly calloused skin covering the powerful hand.

As the music began he pulled her hand away from his chest into the traditional hold for the waltz as warmth and something else, something almost dizzying, spun out from his hold at her back. The positioning was wrong— his hand too close to the base of her spine to be appropriate for strangers, almost possessive in a way that fired her blood and sent a thrill through her that settled horrifyingly low within her. But that was madness. Surely she couldn't be feeling the stirrings of desire for a complete stranger?

His hold was firm, commanding, and, God help her, she relished it, welcomed it, the need to give herself over to this one stolen moment, for someone else to take the weight of responsibility and duty that almost crippled her. Hidden by the disguise of her mask, she was convinced that this man had no idea who she was. He couldn't, because surely he wouldn't behave so daringly with a princess? And the freedom that thought offered sang in her veins. That just for this moment she could be something other than the Widow Princess. Simply Sofia—herself, a woman with nothing more on her mind than dancing with a handsome man. For despite the mask he wore, she could tell he *was* handsome. The breadth of him, the smoothness of his skin, the inherent confidence more appealing than any physique she could determine. Her heart kicked within her chest as the stranger guided her into the first steps of the waltz, and she raised her gaze, expecting to find him looking down at her intently.

But he wasn't.

She traced the angle of his neck with her eyes, the fine, straight cord powerful and determined, to a jaw that was stubbled in a way that almost wilfully challenged propriety. Treated only to his profile, she consumed every inch of what she could see, and her body reacted as if it had been starved of the sight of it. Which made no sense.

The turn of his head hid the bare section of the mask she recognised from a well-known musical, concealing much of what she could see. His eyes were focused on some distant point on the other side of the room and the heady scent of him filled her lungs as she breathed through the steps of the dance.

There was something almost cold about the way his head was turned away from her...as if, despite the intimacy of the hold, he was *forcing* himself to touch her. And suddenly she felt nauseous. As if her body had somehow tricked her, fooled her into thinking that... what? That her Prince Charming had finally come for her? As if sensing her sudden resistance, her attempt to flee before it had even registered in her mind, he tightened his embrace, all the while remaining turned away from her.

Realising the futility of escape, she used the time to observe the stranger. He was tall, at least six feet, if not more. His shoulders, though pressed back in a perfect frame for the waltz, somehow managed to crowd her in a way that made her, made *them*, feel isolated from the other couples on the dance floor. He led her almost expertly through the movements of the dance and her body's muscle memory bowed to his command. While her mind raced with outrage and confusion that she would be so ignored, so manhandled, her body soared at the unspoken dominance.

The stranger had yet to say a word to her and somehow that made this moment all the more surreal, as if they had mutually agreed that speaking would break this strange spell that he was weaving around her. She knew she should break it though, she knew she should be outraged, terrified even, but there was something… the breadth of him, the feel of his hand within hers…both strange and familiar.

She felt known by him, even if she did not know him. She began to count down the steps to the end of the dance, recognising the cadence and swell of the music as her pulse beat within her chest in time with the waltz, in time with him.

She didn't know what to expect when the dance came to an end. Would he finally speak? Would he look at her, or would he disappear as easily as he had swept her towards the dance floor? She both longed for and resisted the end to this moment and as he brought their steps to a close, bowed, deep and low, her curtsey only half what it should be, because she had yet to be able to take her gaze from finally seeing who this stranger was.

Only when their eyes met, a sob escaped her mouth as she caught the devastating brown orbs, dark against the pure white of the mask, and she was filled with a fury and anger that stole her breath. She actually felt the single lost heartbeat caused by the jolt of recognition.

Theo Tersi.

* * *

Theo had feared that he might not recognise her here amongst the disguises and outrageous costumes of such rich company. He had lost Sebastian to his own personal pursuits some half an hour before, and had been beginning to lose patience. It had to be tonight. It had to be now. Everything in him had been building to this moment for years. He would not let this chance pass.

In truth, it was his body that had recognised her first. The way his pulse unaccountably hitched in his chest, the way awareness had pulled from him an almost electric current that snapped and hissed across his skin. And when he finally did see her, clinging to the edges of the ballroom, he knew that he shouldn't have doubted himself. Even had he not gone to sleep each night for ten years with her face the last thing he saw, the lies and abused promises on her lips the last thing he heard, he would have known her in the dark surrounded by a thousand people. Because she shone like a beacon of pure golden light and he bitterly noted that it had nothing to do with her costume. She had looked like the stepdaughter in the Mother Holle story told to him by his mother in childhood—the one who passed beneath a waterfall of gold. Yet he knew better. She was the other sister—the one who should have been covered in tar.

He hadn't intended to lead her into the waltz, but the moment the idea struck, it wouldn't loosen its grip on his mind. He knew that she wouldn't recognise him, certainly not if he kept his head turned away from her. She probably hadn't given him a second thought since setting him up to take the fall for her pranks. Or maybe she had, laughing to herself long and hard at how she'd manipulated him, how she'd got him to do her bidding.

Holding her and not looking at her had been a sweet

torture. He'd wanted to bare his gaze to her, bore into her the feelings of anger, pain and betrayal... But when he had finally met her eyes, holding them captive with his own, he'd nearly cursed. Because it was he who consumed every emotion that flickered and sparked in her sapphire-blue eyes.

After all these years he'd thought himself immune to her. He'd thought the consequences of her actions would have made him impenetrable to the insatiable desire for her...but the way her body had melted into his, the flickering of her pulse beneath his hand, mocked him as his body had claimed her in the most primal of ways. Because no matter what had passed between them, his body still wanted her, still craved her touch.

Until the jolt of recognition from Sofia that he felt against his skin, the irrefutable horror that filled her gaze.

*Now* she knew him.

He was about to open his mouth, when her sudden, shocking departure slammed it shut. She had picked up her skirts and was racing away from the ballroom floor, disappearing into the crowd of people. But she would not get away that easily. He saw her at the wide French doors, open to the beckoning darkness of the gardens, and a smile curved the edges of his lips.

Theo Tersi drew out his mobile phone, and as he followed her out into the night he fired off a text to the man he had waiting on standby. If she failed to offer him the apology he so very much deserved, Sofia de Loria would regret the day she had ever thought to play him.

Plunged into the darkness of the Parisian night, he stalked amongst the manicured gardens, expecting to have to hunt much more than he did, and nearly crashed into her.

'What are you doing here?' Sofia demanded, appar-

ently satisfied that there were no longer people to over-
hear them as her raised voice was carried away on the
night air. Her outrage struck him low in the chest.

'Why? Not used to discovering an ill-bred bastard
amongst your high-society companions?'

'What?' He noticed her brow pucker in momentary
confusion. 'That has nothing to do with anything.'

'No? I'd have thought your security teams would have
vetted every single person here, check their DNA for their
blue-blood credentials.'

'Don't be such a snob.'

Now *he* was outraged. 'How dare you accuse me of
being a snob?'

'Just because it's reverse snobbery, it doesn't make it
any less prejudicial.'

'You're speaking nonsense.'

'Because I disagree with you? You never did—'

'Don't. Do not talk to me of what I did or did not do
in the past,' he spat as he lifted his mask away from his
face and cast it aside onto the thick emerald grass of the
gardens.

He watched her almost physically bite her tongue and
he used the moment to take her in. The Sofia he knew
had been breathtaking, but Sofia de Loria the Princess
was obscenely beautiful. Her cheeks had lost some of the
softness, striking cheekbones sculpting her face to perfection. The thick plaits of golden hair wrapped around
her head glowed silver in the starlight of the night sky.
A high brow made even more superior with the arch of
a perfect, rich, honeyed eyebrow peeking out from the
top of the mask, brilliant golden furls glinting in the
moonlight.

And, as always, crystal-blue eyes crackled and sparked
as she tried to repress the anger she clearly felt. An anger

he matched, if not exceeded. Oh, he'd had his share of beautiful women in the last two years, once he'd given himself permission to relish and enjoy the success that all his hard work had reaped. Once he'd lifted his self-imposed embargo on sensual pursuits. But no matter how many times he'd cursed her to hell and back, he'd never been able to deny Sofia's beauty.

But even in that he knew he lied to himself. It wasn't just a simple fact of her beauty. It was as if a chemical reaction had ignited within him, fizzing in his veins, urging him to reach out and touch her. Draw her to him and seek her mouth, her kiss…to feed the burning arousal he had really only ever felt with this woman. He wanted her, needed her, with every ounce of his being. But he fought it. He would *not* give in to the temptation she unconsciously offered.

Sofia felt her chest heave against the confines of the tight corset as her body struggled for an outlet for the anger and pure shock at Theo's appearance. Masked, he was impressive. Unmasked he was undeniable. Age had only honed what were already incredible features. Even in his youth he had stood heads above even the older students, and now she had to crane her neck to look up at his scowling gaze, his deep brown irises swirling like the richest espresso. His clenched jaw was dusted with a fine dark stubble as if, even in that, Theo rejected the same propriety that saw every other man there either clean-shaven or fully bearded. His straight nose created a sense of balance between the downward slashes of his cheekbones, and the night cast his proud jaw in deep shadows.

In obvious frustration he ran his hand through his thick hair and on any other man the result would have looked chaotic, but on Theo? It just made Sofia want to reach out and do the same. He was magnificent and for a second she imagined that she could reach for him, that she could draw him to her. Desire, thick and fast, rose up within her chest, even as she knew that she could not act upon it, should not feel it.

She tried not to flinch at the sound of apparent disgust as he finally turned that lethal focus of his to her, casting the entire length of her body in a glance that was anything but lazy, or accidental. No. There was purpose to this…to make her uncomfortable, and she hated that it was working.

'If you've had your fill and there's nothing else?' She refused to stand there before his assessment and be found wanting. She just couldn't. Not tonight. She still had to meet with Joachim, the third possible suitor, her last hope. She could not stand here caught between the past and her future—it was threatening to tear her apart.

Sofia turned to leave, but his hand snuck out and caught her at her wrist. His hold deceptively gentle. The delicate ring his fingers created around her skin thrummed with repressed tension. He tugged, and she almost fell against his chest and this time she just managed to stop her hand from leaning on his chest for…balance, she told herself. Balance.

With her hand still hovering mid-air between them, she risked a glance at his face. It was so close, angled down at her, lips that once she would have delighted in now cruelly sensual and taunting her with a knowing smile. But the anger in his eyes was easier to read than her own reaction, and she welcomed it, embraced it, used it to fuel her now.

'I'm here for an apology.'

'An apology?' Sofia didn't know how he'd caused her to revert to the stammering seventeen-year-old she'd once been. More than a decade of training, diplomacy, education and learning trade negotiations and she seemed only capable of two words around this man.

She knew she owed Theo an apology…more than that. An explanation at the very least, but before she could summon the words to her lips, he pressed on.

'You doubt it?'

'No, not at all, I—'

'Do you know what I regret most? That even as I waited the first hour for you, the second, hidden amongst that ridiculous shrubbery, I didn't even doubt you. It didn't even cross my mind that you wouldn't show. I waited, like a moon-eyed calf, half drunk on love for you. Even afterwards, when the headmaster came to find me, told me of the trick *you* pulled on his car, my first concern was for you, not for myself. My fear was that something had happened to you.'

She felt shame slash across her cheeks in a dark crimson blush, painful and stinging, as if he had slapped her with his hands rather than his words. And all the wishes, wonderings and dreams of what happened to him that night were painted in stark reality by his words.

'It didn't take me long to realise, though. Realise what you had done that night and in the weeks, months leading up to it. To realise that everything you had told me was lies, *Your Highness.*'

Secrets and lies had come back to haunt her and Sofia turned her head away, but his fingers, once again seemingly gentle, but determined, found her chin, and brought her back round to face him, to see the truth written in his eyes.

'Can you imagine what it was like to realise that I had fallen in love with a fabrication? That everything I'd felt was simply the by-product of the ruse of a bored, pampered princess with nothing more to do with her time than to move people around a chessboard of her own imagination? That I was expelled because of *your* actions?'

Shock reared through her, and she stepped back as if she could distance herself from what he was saying.

'I didn't—'

'You didn't know?' he demanded harshly, his fury palpable, shaking the very air between them. 'You didn't even know?' He cursed harshly. 'You all but ensured it when you left my scarf, *my* scarf, beneath the car. Tell me, did you even think of me when you ran back to your country playing the part of the perfect princess as I was kicked out of school? When I lost the scholarships to every single university I had gained entry to? When my mother was fired and we were forced to return to her family with little more than what we could carry? I thought of you, all the while knowing that everything we had lost, every struggle we experienced, was because of your lies!'

Sofia was struck dumb by the pain his words evoked, and the truth that lay within them. She hadn't known that he had been expelled, she hadn't even remembered that she'd been wearing his scarf when she pulled the prank with the car. Because that night, in between her plan to get revenge against the headmaster and meeting Theo, her parents had come to the school and revealed that her father had been diagnosed with early onset dementia. And in that moment, the bottom had fallen out of her world.

Every thought, hope and dream she'd ever held in her heart since falling in love with Theo had flashed through her mind, while she should have been focusing on the physical and mental sentence that had been handed to her father. That the entire time her parents had patiently tried to explain what that meant, what would happen, how she would have to ascend to the throne much sooner than anyone had ever planned for, all she had thought of was him. Theo. Standing there, waiting for her to come.

She had begged and pleaded with her parents to allow her to speak to Theo. To find him where he waited for her. To tell him what was happening. But her father had been uncompromising—no one could know of his diagnosis. No one. And then they had bundled her into a car, and then a private jet, and the whole time she had felt as if she had left her heart behind.

So, no. She hadn't thought of what had happened to him after that night, because she couldn't. She just couldn't allow herself to go there. Because every time she did, what little remained of her heart fractured and shattered just a little bit more.

But she couldn't explain that to Theo. Not now. Because her father's diagnosis still had the power to rock the already shaky foundations of her precious country. Because this? This moment between them wasn't about her or what she could say to justify what had happened that night. This was about him, and God help her, but she deserved every single word, every single feeling he expressed. She needed to honour that, because it was the only thing she would ever be able to give him.

'Tell me, Sofia, did you mean any of it? The pleas you made, the plans…the future you fabricated, all the while knowing it was impossible? Punctuating lies with kisses? Untruths with touches and caresses? When did you know that you would ruin me, Sofia? Before you first spoke to me, or when you realised how easily manipulated I would be?'

'That is enough,' Sofia commanded, digging through

the hurt to find some kind of strength to ward off the harshness of his words.

'Enough? I've barely even begun. *"Please take me away, Theo, I cannot return to Iondorra, Theo. Help me. Theo."'* The cruel mockery his voice made of her childhood words stung as much as the memory of her desperation to escape the confines of a royal life she had been forced to accept.

Theo knew that he had gone too far. He had said too much. Revealed too much of his own pain and heartbreak. And he hated himself for that. He saw the moment that his words hit home, the shimmer of unshed tears in her eyes more bright than any star that night. He cursed, the breeze carrying it away from them. He steeled himself against the innate sympathy welling within him, knowing better this time than to fall for her games.

'*Christós,* I didn't know you at all, did I?'

Suddenly the cord that had bound them in the past snapped, pinging away under the pressure of a decade of hurt and distance between them. And he watched, half fascinated as that royal mantle settled once more around her shoulders, leaving no trace of the young girl he had once loved. Instead, a fury stood before him, iron will steeling her spine and her body as if no soft movement had ever settled beneath her skin.

'You are right. You did not know me. You knew a child. A girl who was reckless, pulled pranks and gave no heed to the people or things about her. A pampered young woman, who knew nothing of real life, or consequences. I am sorry if that girl hurt you, caused you pain. Truly. But she is gone, living only in your memories and imagination.'

It wasn't enough. It wasn't nearly enough, her half

apology. Pain reared its ugly head. Not for the loss of her, he assured himself, but the years he endured after her. The years his mother endured. They did *not* live solely in his imagination. They were etched across his heart and hands as he had clawed his way to where he stood today.

'Now, if you don't mind—'

'Off to find your next husband?'

She stilled her entire body. It was unusual for her, because everything about her contained a restless energy, its sudden and shocking absence such a stark contrast, and for a moment he could have been forgiven for thinking she'd turned to stone.

'How do you…?'

He huffed out a cynical laugh. 'Still keeping your secrets and lies close to your chest? Well, this time I've made sure that I will not fall for either. Unlike whatever poor bastard you've chosen for your next target.'

'Target?' she sighed, a scoffing sound that grated on his ears. It was too similar to the dismissive gestures of people who had thought themselves better than him. 'You know nothing, Theo. Nothing of duty, of sacrifice. Nothing of what needs to be done as a royal.'

'You think your concerns above those of mine?' he demanded.

'Yes,' she said simply. 'Yes, I do. I have to.'

'You once begged to wear *my* ring,' he said, cursing the moment of weakness that allowed his inner thought to escape his lips. 'And instead you married that insipid—'

'Do not speak of him like that,' she commanded.

'Why not? I saw the pictures. Hell, the world saw the pictures of you together. You might as well have been siblings for all the connection you seemed to share. And after his death? You were the Widow Princess who never cried, for all you may try to profess your love for him.' If it had not been so dark, Theo might have seen how Sofia paled beneath the moonlight, might have seen how much his barb had hit home. 'Tell me, Sofia, did he ever make your pulse race, your body throb with desire? Did you ever crave his touch as you professed to crave mine?'

Theo caught the gasp that fell from Sofia's lips, proving the truth of his words and enflaming the sensual web weaving between them, as if he had conjured the very reaction from her body by his words.

Anger, frustration and desire burned heavily on the air between them, and his eyes caught the rise and fall of her perfect breasts against the curve of the corseted dress she wore. Their argument had drawn them closer together, and he could have sworn he felt the press of her chest against his through the mere inches of air that separated them, thickening his blood and his arousal instantly.

'Do you remember, Sofia? What is was like between us? Or were you faking everything?' he demanded. Because somewhere, deep down, he needed to know. He needed to know if it had all been lies. Before him, Sofia swayed, caught within the same tide of desire that he felt pulling at his entire being.

Her lips parted, shining slightly as if recently slicked with her tongue, and he was desperate to taste, to touch, to consume. He needed to know if this time, with all the knowledge he now had, he would be able to taste the lies on her tongue.

His mind roared against it, but his body closed the distance between them, unable to resist the feel of her, the siren's call she seemed to pull him in with. Surely his memory had exaggerated the way she had made him feel. Surely it could never have been that incredible.

He watched her closely, the way her eyes had widened as he'd moved closer, the way she too struggled with the thick, heavy want wrapping around them both. And he saw the moment she gave in to it. Gave in to the silent demand he hated his body for making.

He gave her the space of one breath, to turn, to flee, to refuse him. He gave himself that time, to turn back, to walk away. But when her pupils widened, that breath she took a sharp inhale, all but begging him to press the advantage, to make good on his unspoken promise, he was lost to the need pulsing in his chest. Lost to the insanity of what had been, what now was, between them.

'Tell me you don't want me, don't want my kiss. Tell me, Sofia, and I'll walk away. *Lie* to me again, Sofia,' he challenged.

'I can't,' she whispered, as if hating herself for the confession.

His arm swept around her small frame, drawing her to him and him into madness as his lips descended on hers with ten years of pent-up frustration, anger and a raging need that even the sweep of her tongue against his could not appease.

Passion and desire crackled in the air as they came together, her touch as bruising as his, the almost painful clash of lips, tongues, the merciful bite of teeth that brought clarity as much as it brought confusion.

He had thought himself lost, but a small part of him whispered instead that he'd been found. Found within her, the scent of her winding around him, pulling him even deeper into the kiss. It was everything he remembered and more. His pulse beat erratically in his ears, as if in warning, but it was drowned out by the gentle, almost pleading moans she made into his mouth. But whether Sofia was begging for more or less, he couldn't tell. And that was what made him pull away.

He wrenched himself back, shocked by the intensity

of what they had shared, Sofia, looking equally stunned, her mouth quickly covered by the back of her wrist, pressing their kiss to her lips or swiping it away, he couldn't tell. He needed to sever whatever hold this madness had on him and quickly.

'Now, there's the Sofia I remember.'

'You bastard,' she cried and ran from the gardens towards the safety of the ballroom.

And he knew that, for possibly the first time in any of her exchanges, she had spoken the truth. He was a bastard. Because even as he had lost himself to the kiss, lost himself to the chaotic emotions storming within his chest, his mind was moving at the speed of light.

Because now, it was too late for her. The moment Sofia had issued that half-mustered apology had sealed her fate as surely as the shutter on the camera of the paparazzo Theo had hired to capture the moment of her compromise.

He let loose a bitter laugh. He had hoped that an image of them in a heated argument would do damage enough, but a kiss? So much better for his plan of revenge.

Yes. Sofia de Loria would very much regret the day she had ever thought to play him the fool.

# CHAPTER THREE

*Widow Princess Caught in Clinch with
Wine Playboy!*

*From Widow Princess to
Scandalous Princess in One Kiss!*

*Widow Princess Tames Bad Boy
of the Wine Industry!*

THE HEADLINES SCREAMED in Sofia's mind, punctuated by
exclamation marks that struck almost physical blows as
she threw down the collection of newspapers unceremoniously handed to her by the royal council earlier that
day. She peered through the window of the car and cast
a glance up and down one of Monaco's most famous
streets. The light illuminating the Plaza del Casino de
Mónaco caused the water feature in the centre to sparkle
in the night like a thousand diamonds.

And each and every glint scratched against her already
frayed nerves and temper.

It wasn't the fact that she had been captured in a
kiss with one of Europe's most notorious playboys, and
splashed across the front pages for the world to see. It
wasn't even the fact that the morning after the party,

Joachim—her third and last hope for a fiancé—had regrettably informed Angelique that he could no longer consider matrimony with Sofia.

It was the fact that Theo Tersi—notorious womaniser—had refused to comment. And he *always* commented. By neither confirming nor denying their speculative questions, he had served only to inflame the rabid press. The Iondorran privy council had further tied her hands and refused to allow a statement to be issued by the royal communications office in a desperate act of blind ignorance, wilfully hoping that it would all 'blow over'.

But she knew better. Because the sneaking suspicion that had begun the first moment she'd seen the awful photographs had grown into a living, breathing belief that Theo Tersi had somehow managed to orchestrate this whole disaster. The birthday party in Paris had been under a strict press embargo, the girl's family having sold the rights for images to *Paris Match*. Furthermore, the only photos surfacing from that night were of them—no other guests—despite the fact that Sofia was aware of at least three front-page headline-worthy incidents. In the last three weeks she had stopped wondering how and instead focused on the why.

She bit back a distinctly unladylike growl as she exited the dark diplomatic-plated sedan, remembering how she had held herself that night as her body trembled after their conversation, after their kiss, as it shook at how he had weakened her. For the hours following, her body left overly sensitised, she had found herself pressing her fingers to her mouth as if in denial or longing, she couldn't tell, and no matter how much she wished it the low, aching throb between her legs and in her chest had both shocked and terrified her. She had allowed herself that night to feel, to ache, to want. But in the morning when she had seen the headlines, something within her had turned to steel. Sofia dismissed the guards she usually travelled with. She did not want an audience for what was about to happen.

She cast a glance up and down the stunning architecture of the buildings gathered around Monaco's famous gambling district. She had never been anywhere like it. People filled the streets, couples holding hands, groups of men stalking the bars and cafes brimming with tourists and celebrities. Their excitement was infectious, but she resisted the instinct to relish in their levity, instead clinging to her incredulity that Theo would do something so…so…

Theo had resisted every single attempt she had made to contact him. Email, telephone, text message…she had dismissed the idea of carrier pigeon as ridiculous. In the last two days he had repeatedly posted images of himself on Twitter at some of the many casinos in Monaco, and finally, just an hour ago, she had located this club as his current place of residence, if the latest Victoria's Secret model to hit the headlines was to be believed.

*Two blondes, two Doms and two Ts. Lol.*

*Lol.* Honestly. Sofia had barely repressed the acidic taste of bile at the back of her throat the moment she saw the accompanying obligatory selfie of two beautiful blondes, two bottles of Dom Perignon and 'TT', aka Theo Tersi, grinning in the background as if he was purposefully taunting Sofia. Which he was.

Clearly less than two hundred and eighty characters were needed to explain the models' ecstasy, and the fact they had snared Theo's legendarily short attention span.

She knew that Theo wasn't naïve or stupid. He must have known that every single indecent headline following the publication of their kiss nearly three weeks ago now would take her down with him. She knew that this was an act of revenge, knew that in his mind she most definitely deserved it. And in a very small, very quiet part of her own mind, she feared that he might be right. But right or wrong had no place here. She needed to get him to issue a denial so that she could do whatever damage limitation was required and press forward with her hopes to find a forgiving fiancé.

Her heartbeat thrummed beneath the thin silk top and jeans she had chosen with the express purpose of blending in. Her aim was to get in, get him to agree and get out, without being spotted. In her youth, she had achieved much greater things under the radar. Surely this would be possible?

Her inner voice mocked her naivety, while her desperation drove her forward.

She reminded herself that no one would be looking for her here. It was the first time in nearly ten years that she'd been outside amongst people without the trappings of her royal status and she was slightly fascinated and slightly sad.

Sofia couldn't help but wonder what her life would have been like had her father not become ill. Yes, she still would have ascended to the throne, but could she have had some time? Time to explore a little fun, or even herself just a little...*more*? Would she have found some enjoyment in life in a way she could never do now? Not that she would ever have been able to fritter away money on a hand of cards, or tweet mindlessly using emojis and take selfies with any number of handsome men.

If her father hadn't come to find her that night, would

she have risked it all and found a way to be with Theo as she had often dreamed? No matter how hard she tried to imagine what would have happened had she met him behind the shrubs at their boarding school, rather than the headmaster who must have been sent by her father, she just couldn't. Was that because it could never have truly happened as she had once told herself? Or because she had spent years repressing those exact thoughts and desires for far too long? She could no longer say.

Still, the Theo that she fell in love with all those years ago was now long gone. There had been no trace of him in the eyes of the man who had mocked her so cruelly. Who had taunted her, teased her into furious, anger-filled words in the Parisian garden just three weeks ago. And if there had been traces of him only in the kiss he stole from her, she chose to ignore it.

The large security guard beside the entrance to the club gave her a cursory glance and allowed her to pass through the doors into the dark, cavernous chamber beyond. Music assaulted her ears, and she blinked against the chaotically strobing light throbbing in time with a baseline she felt buzz through her skin and bone to the soft inside of her.

She shouldn't be doing this. She should just let someone else confront Theo, but she knew—instinctively—that this was what he had wanted. As if he had planned everything down to the finest detail and only her presence would do.

Sofia brushed aside her concerns, her fears, and scanned the chaotic mass of people on the dance floor. No matter how hard she tried, she couldn't imagine Theo amongst the thriving group. No. He was far too voyeuristic for that. She remembered the feel of his gaze upon her skin at the Parisian ballroom. Remembered the feel of being hunted by a predator purposefully choosing when best to strike.

Her gaze finally took in the raised area of the club, an entire glass-fronted section roped off and guarded by another large, dark-suited man. She caught sight of the blonde model she recognised from the tweet, and, sure enough, Theo was sitting with one arm draped around her, the other draped around the thin shoulders of the other, the only difference in the scene being the additional upturned bottle of champagne beside the other two. Either the staff were very slow at tending to the tables in this club, or Theo was enjoying showing off his power and wealth. Sofia very much leaned towards the latter.

She made her way towards the large, suited man, and when she tried to pass he thrust out a meaty arm to block her. Shocked, she very nearly uttered the famously awful words, *Do you know who I am?*, but just managed to prevent herself. She was here incognito and she had not the first idea of how to get around the man. She had no experience in these situations, no idea what was required, as usually her security handled every single small thing… but she had dismissed them. Boarding school had been the last time she'd been allowed her freedom and since her return to Iondorra she hadn't exactly been out 'clubbing'.

Did she offer him money? she wondered, then belatedly realised she didn't have any. And even if she had, Sofia had no idea how much would have been appropriate. She could have given the man a year's salary, or not even enough to buy milk. Suddenly feeling completely out of her depth, she felt the sting of tears pressing against the backs of her eyelids and blamed Theo Tersi wholeheartedly. She had not cried once since the night of the debutante ball when she and her mother had spoken. When she had realised there truly was no other option but to assume the throne and marry her childhood friend, Antoine. But in the three weeks since Theo had stormed into her life and turned it upside down, she felt as if she were only a breath away from it at all times.

Suddenly he appeared at the top of the stairs behind the bouncer, towering over her like an avenging angel, and she hated the way that her pulse instantly kicked at the sight. She pushed away the thoughts of how she had reacted to the kiss that night, with all the wanton, suppressed desire of ten years of need and yearning that she had refused to acknowledge. The photographer had caught the exact moment that she had clung to him as if her life depended on it, and the memory brought a furious blush to her cheeks even now.

She took in the sight of Theo's broad shoulders filled out from youth with powerful masculinity, dark hair artfully messy—or at least she hoped it was by design and not the hands of either of the models he was currently parading about. She bit down on the thread of shocking jealousy unfurling in her chest, and replaced it with anger as Theo growled the phrase, 'Let her come.'

It sounded more like the taunt of a battle cry than permission to enter some private section of a club. He'd turned his back on her before she'd taken the first step, and by the time she'd reached the top of the stairs he was nestled in between the two women once again.

She stood before the three of them, separated by the depth of a table with half-filled glasses and empty champagne bottles.

'Can we talk?' she shouted over the loud music.

He placed a hand to his ear, and simply shrugged

in confusion as if the blasted man hadn't heard what she'd said.

'I said—' she shouted, only to realise that a sudden lull in the music had carried her voice far and wide over the private section of the club.

The two models snickered into their hands and Theo's smirk made her utterly convinced that he'd known that would happen.

'I said,' she tried again, 'can we talk?'

He waved a hand before her in a way more regal than any gesture she'd ever managed to achieve. He still had yet to say a word to her.

'In private?'

'Anything you have to say to me can be said here.'

Sofia wanted to snarl. She felt the deep yearning to be reckless, to act out, to do something so un-princess-like as to throw the remaining contents of the glass on the table all over his proud, defiant face. But ten years of suppressing that wild inner instinct won out. Even though she suspected he knew exactly what she wanted to do, what she would have done in the past. Unconsciously she rubbed at the old ache on her forearm, the other arm wrapping around the long since faded bruise against her ribs, while she chose and discarded what to say next.

'We have…business to discuss.'

'Sit,' he said, knowing full well the only place to sit was beside one of the two women he still had his arms around. And Sofia point-blankly refused to add to the collection of women he'd gathered about himself.

'I'll stand.'

He shrugged, once again as if it were her choice.

One of the girls leaned over and whispered in his ear, producing a high-pitched giggle from the other, and an amused grin and a nod of agreement from him as they both returned their attention to her, making it clear she was the subject of the private discussion.

It was becoming increasingly hard to hold on to the thin thread of her control. She locked her eyes on his, ignoring the two women either side of him, and waited. Because the one thing that no one had been able to remove from her in all her years of royal training was her stubbornness. So she watched and waited. She'd have stood there all night too, but he seemed to realise that, and finally dismissed the two women, who pouted and protested but ultimately removed themselves to a table further away. Not before casting her glances that Sofia was sure would have quelled lesser individuals. She had won that battle, but not the war. Not yet.

Theo called over a waitress and requested a chair for her, which was duly produced, and Sofia finally sat down opposite him.

'I see that you have dressed for the occasion,' Theo said as his gaze covered her once again from head to toe and back to her head again.

She raised an eyebrow and shrugged. 'When in the henhouse...'

'Are you calling me a hen?' he asked, full of mock-horror. 'Pecking and scratching around for any little titbit you'd throw my way? Oh, no. I assure you, Sofia, that is not how this is going to play out.'

'For goodness' sake, Theo. It's the cock in the henhouse. You're the...' A painful blush rose to her cheeks before she could finish the sentence.

'Oh, that's adorable, sweetheart.'

'Don't call me that,' she commanded.

Theo felt the thrill of satisfaction as he watched her crystal-blue eyes storm like a Mediterranean downpour. He'd never failed to find enjoyment in teasing her. But seeing her feathers ruffled, seeing her annoyed and angry, held a bittersweet taste this evening.

Good. He wanted her angry. He wanted her annoyed. He wanted her to feel every single thread of emotion that had wrapped around his heart the moment he'd realised just how artfully she'd played and betrayed him. Because it wasn't just him that her machinations had affected. That his mother had been caught up in the fallout was untenable. So when Sofia failed to issue the apology he knew he deserved, she had sealed her fate. The photographer he had hired had done well and been paid well for his services too. Securing front-page headlines throughout the world had been exactly what Theo had wanted, knowing that it would back her into a corner. Knowing that no other royal would want to go near her after being associated with his debauched reputation. He had ignored her for weeks, knowing that it would only infuriate her more. Until yesterday, when he had begun to leave little breadcrumbs on social media of where she might be able to find him. He wanted her on his turf, he wanted her on the back foot, *needed* her to be. This was only the second step towards his utter and complete revenge. She would know the sting of humiliation, she would know the deep slice of hurt and betrayal—feelings that were so familiar to him it was as if he had been born with them—and she would know, ultimately, that she had brought it on herself.

His gaze ate up the image before him. She was wearing clothes he'd never seen her in, certainly nothing that would ever grace the style magazines she was often lauded in. The tight grey denim riding low on her hips made his mouth water, and the silky white top tucked into them was nowhere near indecent, but as it moulded to her perfect breasts, topped by thin straps, he couldn't imagine that she was wearing a bra. He would have seen the evidence of it. The low heel of the suede nude-coloured heels gave her overall appearance a conservative contrast to the barely dressed women at the club, teetering on almost death-defying stilettos.

He had imagined her monstrous over the years, every heartache added to the list of crimes she had perpetrated against him and his mother. He had imagined her begging and pleading for forgiveness, but in reality he could not deny the effect she had on him and cursed his body's weakness for her. Even now, he had to lean forward to hide the evidence of his arousal, his desire for her. The one thing that had never gone away.

Her pupils dilated at his slow perusal, and the realisation that she too was as beholden to their mutual attraction was the only balm to his ego.

'Theo—'

'Princess Sofia de Loria of Iondorra…'

This time she scowled. More like the youthful woman he had once known, and it struck him in his chest. He slowly exhaled the shock, but took great pleasure as those about them started to produce their smartphones and snap pictures of the two of them—some not even bothering to be discreet. He would not be her dirty little secret. Not this time. This time, he would make it impossible for her to walk away from him.

'You must issue a denial,' she said finally, as she tried to ignore the flashes punctuating the beginning of their exchange.

'A denial of what, Your Highness? That we kissed? I believe that is quite undeniable at this point.'

'That we are in a relationship,' she hissed beneath her breath. 'I can't have the world thinking that…'

'Thinking that you are involved with an illegitimate Greek commoner?'

'I was going to say Greek millionaire playboy.'

'Please,' he scoffed. 'It's *billionaire* playboy to you.'

She artfully raised an eyebrow.

'You can look at my financials if you doubt it,' he replied, unable to keep the heady mixture of pride and arrogance from his voice. Everything he'd achieved, every grape, bottle, vineyard and investment, had been despite her machinations and through his own hard work. She could hardly claim the same.

'I'm not here to debate what names the press call *you*, I'm here to get you to put a stop to the ones they're calling *me*.'

He held back the smile that his lips itched to tease into. Instead, shaking his head and offering her a simple shoulder shrug, he said, '*Óchi*. No. I don't think so.'

'Why not?' she demanded incredulously.

'It doesn't suit my purposes to do so.'

'What do you want, Theo?' Suspicion darkened her eyes to a midnight-blue. A colour he remembered from his past, and he thrust the thought aside.

'I want,' he said, unfurling his large frame from the sofa beneath him, closing the distance between them in order to see the moment she realised that she was helpless, that she had no other choice... 'you to learn the consequences of your actions. I want you to learn that we mere mortals will not be as easily discarded as you seem to think.'

*I want you to learn that you cannot destroy me and everything I hold dear and just walk away,* he concluded silently.

'I want you to pay for the way you set me up—'

'Theo—'

He didn't even register her interruption as the wave of indignation and fury pounded in his veins, competing with the heavy base of the club's music.

'I want what you once promised me, what you once begged me for. I want you to make a truth from your lies. I want you to wear my ring.'

His eyes narrowed as Sofia failed to move a muscle, blink even. This mask that she wore, this impossibly regal poise, was different to the young woman he remembered. He had seen her desire to throw a glass of champagne over him earlier, a fit of female pique. But this? No, this was unacceptable. He didn't want poised. He wanted furious. He wanted her to feel what he felt.

'In fact,' he pressed on, now standing, towering above her, cocking his head to one side in a way that showed only disrespect, 'I don't just want you to agree. You see, your name is now entwined with mine. No one of royal pedigree would attach themselves to you in marriage, no matter how desperate they are. No one would want my seconds, my cast-offs. No one would ever choose you again. It doesn't matter how long you wait. Every time I cause a scandal—and trust me, *agápi mou*, I am more than willing to engage in as many I can find—every time I'm seen out with my next conquest, your name will be dragged down with me. Compared to whatever woman graces my bed, the speculation as to whether your poor, wounded little princess heart is breaking over my latest indiscretion will be on every single front page around the world.

'You should be happy, Sofia. You are now tied to me as securely—if not more so—than you used to pretend you wanted to be. So no, I don't want you to simply agree to be my wife. I want you to *beg*.'

Just like the way his mother had begged her employer

to reconsider. Like the way she had been forced to beg her own family to take them in once again. Just like he had been forced to beg to buy the first piece of neglected land that he'd wanted to develop for his own grapes from his mother's family. So that was what Sofia would have to do now.

*'I want you to beg.'*

The words cut through Sofia like fire and ice.

Surely he had to be joking. There was no way they could marry. Not with all this hurt and anger between them. Not with the events of the past between them.

But she only had to look at him, take in the determined gleam in his eyes, the slightly forward bent of his body, the tense muscles of a predator that had already struck, had already cornered its prey and was now only playing, toying with it, before the poor creature was completely devoured. She was that creature. And she hated it. Hated him.

Still, just like that prey, she sought a way out.

'What do you get out of this?'

'Do you not see how this works? My wine sales will go through the roof. I may even request a royal seal,' he said again with that infuriating shrug.

'You'd tie yourself to me in marriage for the rest of your life, just for sales?' she demanded incredulously.

'Princess, how is that any different than marrying for the good of your country?'

'But what about…' She trailed off.

'Love? Happy-ever-afters? I think we learned that lesson quite some time ago, don't you?'

She wanted to argue, to deny his words, to find some way of reasoning with him.

'You are blackmailing me? I have no choice in this whatsoever,' she said, panic rising from deep within her.

'Of course you have a choice. You can walk away, with your reputation in tatters and never see me again. Or we will marry. Give this little scandal a royal fairy-tale ending.'

Sofia knew that he meant it. Knew that he wouldn't let this go. Knew when she had fled the garden in Paris that she had taunted the lion in its cage.

'I'll need that answer now, Sofia.'

She bit back the curses, because there was definitely more than one ready to fall from her lips. There was too much to take in. He had set her up because he thought *she* had set him up? Was this really just some obscene marketing plan for his vineyard? The thoughts were crashing through her mind at lightning speed, but it was the realisation that he was right that came through loud and clear. There was no way that she would ever *not* be associated with him now. And she knew enough about him to take him at his word. He would make sure of it. No one would go near her now that she was linked with a debauched billionaire playboy. She had run out of time. Her father's recent deterioration had seen to that. The only way forward was the one he was offering. No, demanding. The one he had orchestrated and executed so perfectly.

She hated the smile that unfurled on his lips. The thrum of satisfaction she felt coming off him in waves that lapped her skin so very painfully. Sofia bit her tongue, as if her body was protesting the words that she was being forced to say.

'Theo Tersi, please. Pretty please, with a damn cherry on top. Will you marry me?'

# CHAPTER FOUR

THEO DIDN'T KNOW what he'd expected, and, though it might have had to have been forced out of him with the threat of serious bodily harm, he was impressed.

The power and might of the Iondorran royal mechanisms was something to behold. Within a month of her agreement to his demand, a backstory to their sudden engagement had been constructed, non-disclosure agreements had been signed and an engagement party had been planned.

Only one hour ago, an airtight prenuptial agreement had been delivered to the suites assigned to him and his entourage in Iondorra's impressive castle.

Theo stood in the living area nestled within a turret, looking out through a slender window that displayed a view of the rolling green countryside and the mountains beyond, still snow-capped in the height of summer. He knew that from the other side of the palace could be seen Callier, Iondorra's capital city, almost Swiss in its cleanliness and gleaming, ordered precision. For a country that was primarily agricultural, Theo had been surprised to discover just how much the royal family had focused their energies on generating a strong capital, insisting on the development of a university to keep the next generation's interest, rather than seeing them look elsewhere for centres of learning and jobs.

He had done his research on Sofia long before their engagement—his private investigator having been working overtime for the past year in order to set this up. He'd begun the moment that he'd realised he could not let go. He'd often questioned what it must have taken to smooth out the rough, wayward edges of the reckless, almost wild girl he had once known. And he wondered, not for the first time, whether she missed that part of herself. The very part that had drawn him to her like a moth to a flame. Sofia's freedom, her carefree fire, had been too much for a boy who could never have afforded it for himself.

Maria was sat, bent over something small and silvery by the window seat at the opposite end of the room.

'What do you have there?' he asked, forcing himself to turn away from his thoughts.

She looked up and smiled, her dark hair falling in a cascade over one shoulder. 'It's a piece I created for the exhibition in a few days' time,' she replied, offering up the necklace that fell like a river of silver from her hands. 'You're…you're still coming?' she asked. The way she failed to contain the mixture of hope and hurt in her eyes reminded Theo that they really did need to have that talk.

'You are going to sign this?' Sebastian demanded from behind him.

Theo's attention was called back to Sebastian where he sat reading the prenuptial agreement.

'Theo, you cannot sign this.'

'Of course I can.'

'I mean, I expected a few subclauses from her, but really? Twenty million euros to be paid in the event of your infidelity, scandal, or… Is "tomfoolery" even a legal term?'

'I believe she is trying to put me off. But it won't work.'

'If you sign this, then you are a madman.'

'Perhaps. If I had any intention of actually going through with the wedding.'

Theo turned to find both Sebastian and his sister, Maria, staring up at him in confusion. He wished they could have seen what they looked like, frozen in a tableau of shock. He nearly laughed. He had momentarily forgotten that Maria was there too, but he knew that Sebastian would never have kept his charade from her.

'Theo, what are you doing?'

'I am doing what I had always intended to do,' he said, watching Sebastian with heavy-lidded eyes. 'I am going to ensure that Sofia knows what it feels like to wait. To stand there and wonder, and doubt. To feel the humiliation, to have it marked upon her indelibly. I want her to wait there in front of her wedding guests, her country, at the church alone. To realise that I am not there and that I am not coming. I want her to suffer the consequences of her actions, as my mother and I suffered.'

'So, you don't love her?' Maria's quiet voice cut through the silence of the room.

'I could never love that woman.' *Not again.*

'Have you really thought this through?' Sebastian enquired.

'Every day for ten years.'

'What happens afterwards?'

'I'll release a statement saying that I could not force her into a loveless marriage. The press will lap it up. I will be saving her from herself and a marriage that would have broken her. I'll come out a hero.'

'That is cynical, even for you, my friend.'

Cynical maybe, but necessary. It was time that Sofia de Loria learned that there were consequences to her actions.

* * *

It had been years since Sofia had seen the palace's ballroom draped in such finery and filled with so many people. Her father's deterioration had consigned much of her small family's lives to brief external visits, rarely allowing for the opening of the palace, for outward glances to turn inward upon them. Sofia thought that the last time the ballroom had looked like this might have been her fifteenth birthday, before she'd been sent to boarding school and met the man that had brought this down upon her.

This evening was costing the country money it barely had, but lord knew, everyone loved a royal wedding. It was an investment—for the future of her country. She had to see it as such or she'd curl into a ball in her room and never come out.

She resisted the urge to soothe her brow where the beginnings of a tension headache the size of the San Andreas fault line was gathering. She hated the fact that Theo had blackmailed her, hated that there was no confidant, no friend that she could turn to. Her entire life since leaving that school had been about training, learning the tools that she would need to put the country first. She'd had no time for friends, for people her own age. The last friend she'd thought she had was… Theo. With him, she'd been utterly herself.

It could have been so different, she thought. She'd once dreamed of it being different. The same man, yes. But this? No.

However, part of the future she was securing for her country required children. That thought sent sparks of fire and ice across her skin and down her spine. They hadn't yet discussed that. But she'd made sure to put it into the prenuptial agreement. She could be just as sneaky as he. She'd thought with some small pleasure at how shocked he might be to read the clause that required his contribution to IVF treatment. She had absolutely no intention of sharing her bed with him. And even as she'd had that thought, her inner voice cried *liar*. It brought to mind memories of their kiss…the way her body had sung, had clung to him as desire moved like wildfire through her veins, as her body and soul had yearned for more.

The sudden and shocking thoughts raised a painful blush to her overly heated cheeks, and, cutting off her thoughts, she glanced again at the clock, placing the practised smile on her features to satisfy the eager curiosity of various visiting dignitaries. Where the hell was Theo? Perhaps he *had* seen the clause in the agreement and had decided to punish her temerity.

But that thought was completely overridden by the sense of unease beginning to build. Her father was set to make a royal appearance for only a short allotted time. It was needed for publicity, to soothe potentially ruffled feathers on the Iondorran council for the inappropriateness of her chosen fiancé. Theo didn't need to know that at least two whole weeks had been spent in tense negotiations as she'd lied and cajoled her father's old cronies into accepting Theo. She had extolled his virtues, instead of parading his vices, argued the strength of a true love match, even as the lies had caught in her throat. Unconsciously she had repeated the same pleas she had once made to her father, ten years before as he had tried to extricate her from the boarding school.

She'd been surprised how readily they came to her lips, how easily the same fidelity, emotion, desperation had come to her aid. And the privy council had believed it in a way that her father never had.

And now, when she needed Theo by her side, he was

keeping her waiting, keeping her father waiting. His medication was working for the moment, but she knew better than most how quickly that could change. Once again, she absentmindedly rubbed her forearm, feeling the phantom ache where the accident—as she thought of it now—had fractured the bone there and bruised the ribs beneath. From across the room her mother had caught the unconscious action, and she sent her a reassuring look.

When she finally saw Theo at the top of the grand sixteenth-century staircase, her breath caught in her throat. In the back of her mind she was a little jealous—surely this was the princess's moment, to stand atop the staircase and be admired? But this was no fantasy, and Theo was certainly no prince. Yet admired? Yes. He was.

He stood in between Sebastian Rohan de Luen and a young woman so like him that she must have been his sister. Sofia caught the exiled duke's eye, his gaze held just the fraction of a moment, and she saw something more than speculation towards the woman who was to marry his friend…something foreboding.

Theo's powerful frame unfolded down the stairs into a jog, an *actual* jog, towards her. Sofia's head almost whipped around to search for the long-ago voice calling in her mind—*No running in the Grand Room, Sofia!*

He came towards her so fast, she had no time to react, the expression of joy across his features so shocking to her that she didn't prevent the hands that came to her cheeks and took her face in a warm caress as he placed his lips gently against hers. Instantly he enveloped her senses, the soft, earthy smell of him, the traces of electricity that sparkled beneath the pads of his fingertips against her skin, the heat of his lips and the way her body unconsciously rose to meet him…all gone as suddenly as it came.

'*Kardiá mou*, my tardiness in unforgivable,' he said against her mouth, loudly enough for all about her to hear. Sighs rose up about her from the women and indulgent smiles painted the faces of Iondorra's staunchest male dignitaries.

For a moment, the space of a heartbeat, Sofia had been fooled, had been transported back to a time when his kisses seemed to be her whole world. The way she wanted to sink into the pleasure, the comfort, the... Before her mind could finish the thought, she remembered. Remembered it all. The blackmail, the darkness behind his actions, the belief he held that she had set him up... and in a rash and defiant act, she nipped at his bottom lip with her teeth, quick and hard. He pulled back his head in surprise.

'Let me be the first to draw blood, then, Theo,' she hissed in a voice audible only to him.

'No, Sofia. You did that years ago,' he said darkly, his deft tongue sweeping at the thin trace of crimson on his lip, before a mask descended over his features and he turned to the gathering in the ballroom with a broad smile.

As Iondorra's leading figures lined up to pass on their congratulations to the happy couple Sofia and Theo continued their quiet lines of attack in under-the-breath sentences.

'I thought I was supposed to be the one who was fashionably late,' she whispered.

'Fashion doesn't have to be gender specific.'

'Your ego is impossible.' Sofia broke off to welcome the Minister of Trade and Industry. 'Eugene, lovely to see you.'

'Your Highness, felicitations.' She nodded her acceptance. As her father's trusted advisor trailed off and they waited for the next, Theo took up their conversation.

'It has serviced me well over the years.'

'It's not the only thing that serviced you,' she bit out darkly.

'Come, now, Sofia, jealousy doesn't suit you.' Before she could respond, he pressed on. 'You look ravishing as always,' he said, turning to take her in fully.

'That's what happens when the dress you wear to your engagement party is picked by the privy council after three rounds of rigorous polling.'

'You would have chosen something different?'

'Why?'

'I'd like to know what façade I'm going to get. At least if you had chosen your own it would allow me to draw some conclusion about you.'

'Why do you want to draw a conclusion about me? Surely I'm only here to increase your wine sales,' she hissed as she turned to meet the next guest. 'Lord Chancellor,' Sofia said as she extended a hand to meet the last and final man in the greeting line.

Introductions over and done, they both turned to face the large ballroom. As they stood side by side, it could have been forgiven to see them as the happy couple looking over their guests.

'Your governance is modelled on the British system.'

Sofia shrugged a nonchalant shoulder. 'It worked for them.'

Theo inclined his head in agreement.

Sofia drew a deep breath, reluctantly steeling herself. 'It's time to see the king.'

She felt rather than saw Theo sweep his gaze across the crowded room. 'He's talking to someone—let's have a drink.'

Sofia pressed down on her panic. Her father had been

here for fifteen minutes already and she didn't know how long he'd be able to continue before an episode began.

'Theo, please.' Whether it was the tone in her voice, or the fact her small hand had reached out to his, punctuating the request with a slight trace of desperation, she didn't know, but a low lean of his head gave his agreement.

Her mother met their approach with something like the same relief that Sofia felt. The moment this was done, protocol was met, her mother and father could return to the privacy of their suites.

'Your Majesty,' Sofia called to her father, instantly checking his eyes for signs of clarity or confusion, ready to whisk Theo away should the latter be the case. Her father took in the sight of her, assessment shining in his eyes. It gave nothing else away.

'Mother,' she said, pressing a kiss to each of her delicate cheeks.

'Father, may I present Theo Tersi,' she said, stepping slightly to the side, and suddenly overwhelmed with the fear that Theo would do or say something wrong.

'Your Majesty,' Theo said with a bow from his lean neck, drawing to his full height as each man assessed the other.

Her father cut her a glance, one that took her immediately back to ten years before. Anger, a slight trace of confusion, marred the older man's frowning brow. Sofia bit back a curse. They had waited too long.

'I told you,' he growled, 'that you could not...' He trailed off for just a moment, giving her the only opening she knew she'd get. She remembered those words, too, from that night all those years ago. Was that where her father was in his mind? She forced a smile to her face, hoping that if she and her mother could maintain the farce, they might just get through this.

'That I could not find a better man. I know, Papa.'
Not waiting for any further act that might give away his
deterioration, she pressed kisses to each of his cheeks.
Surprise and brief happiness shone in her father's eyes,
warming the cool place of sadness in her heart. 'He's
perfect, Papa,' she said, turning to Theo, whose quick
mind must have already picked up that something wasn't
quite right. 'And makes me truly happy.' As she said the
words, she felt the now familiar sting of tears pressing
against her eyes.

She saw her mother squeeze her father's arm in a gesture both comforting and grounding.

'I'm glad that you found each other again. It's good.
It's right,' he declared finally and the breath that had
been held universally across the ballroom was exhaled
by all the guests.

Theo bowed once again at the older man before they
exchanged a strong handshake, Theo holding it for perhaps just a moment longer than required.

Released from duty, Sofia had turned, pulling Theo
with her, when her father called her back.

She leaned towards her father to hear his whispered
words.

'*En garde*, Sofia. *En garde*.'

She nodded, feeling his words more truthful than any
she'd heard him speak in the last five years. For just a
moment she felt that her father was back, with her, protecting her and caring for her. Until she heard his next
whispered words.

'And watch out for the German parachutist. Do not
speak to him!'

Without having to look at her mother, who was the
only other person to hear the king's incoherent warning,
she replied, 'I will, Papa. I will.'

\* \* \*

Theo had imagined meeting Sofia's parents many times, under many different circumstances. Ten years ago, he had not thought for a second that she was a royal in disguise. Nothing of what she had told him about her family had indicated any such thing. As an only child, like him, she had spoken of finding ways to amuse herself, spending hours delving into imaginary worlds within books, or running through gardens and woods. He had picked through each and every one of her words since he'd discovered that she was a princess—but, as with all good lies, much of it must have been taken from some thread of the truth. But the exchange with her father was…not what he'd expected.

He hadn't missed the moment of panic shared by the two women, mother and daughter, at the way the king's words hadn't quite fitted the situation. And, though he hadn't heard the last exchange, Theo hadn't missed the raw vulnerability in Sofia's eyes when she had proclaimed her happiness and his perfection.

Were they worried that the older man would rile against his common birth? Was her father furious that she was to wed a commoner? Theo had met much discrimination over the years, for various different reasons. He knew what it looked like, felt like and tasted like. And the king? He was not happy.

But he'd said 'again'. He was glad they'd found each other *again*. Which seemed to indicate that he knew about their relationship in the past, which confused him. He'd been convinced that she had kept him her dirty little secret, but—

'Whisky? We will toast with champagne, but if you wanted…'

His dark look at her must have thrown her as her words

trailed off. Her eyes were overly bright, her words just a little too quick. What was going on? A slight noise behind him drew his gaze to see the retreating figures of the king and queen, discreetly spirited away through a side exit. And once again anger whipped through him.

'Your father isn't sticking around for the toast, then?' he couldn't help but bite out. Couldn't help but be transported back to a time when all he'd wondered was why his own father hadn't stuck around. Couldn't help but remember the way his family had treated his mother and himself because of it. Heat and hurt scorched him in an instant.

'No. He couldn't.' Before the growl could escape his lips, she pressed on. 'He's been…working hard and is tired.'

He was used to reflecting that every single word from her mouth was a lie, but this was different. There was the ring of truth in what she said, but there was also a shimmer of falsehood there too or, if not, then evasion distracting him from his reflections on the past.

The toast was given to them by a man he'd never seen before, but was probably a whole lot more appropriate than what Sebastian might have said to a room full of royals. He felt Maria's gaze on him throughout the evening, and not for the first time wondered whether if it might have been better to have let her believe the falsehood he was weaving through the night. She was young and impressionable and wholly overprotected by her brother.

Within an hour Theo was surprised to find himself on the verge of exhaustion. As a successful businessman and vintner, he was used to heading up million-dollar business meetings, but this constant diplomacy was tiring, yet Sofia showed no signs of fatigue, her fake smile—

for he knew it to be fake—was undimmed and as fresh as the first one she had offered.

'Little Sofia,' said an older man with shocking white hair and a broad purple sash spotted with medals and pins that proclaimed his importance. He felt Sofia bristle beside him at the patronising appellation. Unconsciously his protective instincts rose, and he drew to his full height.

'Theo Tersi,' he said, stretching out his hand to sever whatever connection had sprung between his fiancé and the older man.

'Georges de Fontagne.'

'Monsieur de Fontagne is the Minister of Agriculture,' Sofia said, apparently finally finding her voice.

'Sofia,' greeted the small, birdlike woman standing beside Georges, her diminutive stature only serving to magnify her husband's largess.

'Louisa,' Sofia replied with much more warmth.

When Louisa turned her smiling attention to him, Theo took her hand in his and raised it to his lips in such an old-fashioned move, he nearly surprised himself, satisfied to see that a small blush had risen to the older woman's cheeks as she smiled coyly.

'I wanted to offer my congratulations and beg that you satisfy my curiosity once and for all,' interrupted Georges. 'Please, do share the story of your rather *sudden* courtship.' His voice carried, as did the slight trace of cynicism heavy on his words. 'Do not tell me it was born of that horrifying trend of using matchmakers!'

The man's wife was looking thoroughly mortified at her husband's behaviour and Sofia, for the first time that evening, seemed shocked into silence. It was clear that the man knew something of Sofia's search in Paris six weeks before and was taunting her with it. It was untenable.

Theo might not have been born to this strata of society, but he knew in an instant that he had more manners in his little finger than this man did. It reminded him of the way that his mother's family had treated them, *before* he had turned the little dirt pile he and his mother had bought from her family into an award-winning vineyard. Before he had made enough money to buy out the remaining land his mother's family owned and shuffled them off to some distant part of Greece, only to be pulled out of their exile when he felt like it. Only his *giagiá* had taken pity on them, supported them through that first year and then afterwards when his mother became sick. Theo refused to acknowledge the perverse fact that he felt more than justified in seeking his own revenge, but would not counter an attack against Sofia from another quarter. And as such, all temptation to leave Sofia to stew in a mess of his making disappeared.

'We—' she started, but he squeezed her arm gently to stop her.

'*Agápi mou*, I have heard you tell this story before and your natural instinct towards modesty never does me justice. Allow me?' He watched her eyes widen just a fraction with surprise, and she nodded.

'I am sure that you will have heard something of my slightly *scandalous* reputation,' Theo confided ruefully to the couple. 'And I could not lie and say it is not deserved, as I had never thought to find a woman who could live up to the high standard set by my mother.'

From the corner of his eye, he saw Sofia struggle not to roll her eyes, and Louisa struggle not to sigh contentedly. His charm might not have been broadcast in the press, but it was no less potent a skill than his winemaking abilities and he was determined to use it now to its fullest.

'You see, years ago, when I was a young man, I fell deeply in love. I would have given everything for her, and in some ways did.' He felt Sofia flinch and could have sworn he heard the beat of her heart pick up in confusion as to where he was taking this fabricated story. 'But sadly it was not to be. So I hardened my heart, sure that I would never feel the same way again. And I was right.' He had predicted Louisa's brief gasp of shock, and had not been wrong as he'd imagined Georges' avaricious gaze ready for his next words. 'For when I met Sofia I realised that what I had thought was love was just a pale imitation.' Louisa melted, Georges scowled, and Sofia… he simply couldn't tell.

'From the first moment that I laid eyes on her I knew I was completely ruined…' He paused to see if even this would bring Sofia out of her perfect façade, and, though she paled just slightly, no outward sign of upset showed. 'Ruined for other women for ever,' he concluded. 'I knew that she was the woman that I wanted to spend the rest of my life with. You may dismiss that as pure fantasy. Or something based purely on her beauty. But it wasn't. Every word, movement, decision, enthralled. Her intelligence, her poise and, just as much, her playfulness. Did you know that Sofia has a naughty streak?'

'I remember as much from her childhood,' Georges said critically.

'Ah, but this is what makes Sofia so perfect, for while a country needs an iron-willed ruler, the people need fun and authenticity. And that is what really drew me to Sofia. This I knew in just a moment, but Sofia needed a little more time than I. Oh, she made me work for it, I assure you, Georges,' he said, leaning towards the obese man to intimate confidence, while his skin crawled. 'Over our first lunch together, I produced my finest wine…knowing that I had to seduce her senses as much as her mind and heart. It was a very special bottle of wine for me. There were only three made, from the very first grape of my vineyard in the Peloponnese. The first was for my mother, my child will have the third, but Sofia…she had the second.

'Unbeknownst to me, in the years before we had met, I had created the perfect blend of wine, solely in preparation for her. The playful notes of blueberry and bay leaves grounded in the rich, deep Greek soil were simply…*her.*'

Theo realised, as he had spoken, he had caught her gaze with his, the words casting a spell that had drawn the attention not just of the horrible Georges and his poor wife, but also that of the surrounding courtiers and dignitaries. A pin dropped to the floor could have been heard in the silence.

Sofia's face was upturned to his, only a few inches between them, shock and surprise evident in her eyes. He felt, as much as saw, her draw a deep breath, stealing the air from before him. In the silence everything disappeared. The room, the guests, the past…and he was seventeen all over again, looking at the young Sofia as her unpractised body begged him to take her lips. Need and desire encased them, separating them from the rest of the world. The stark sensuality of her calling to him across the years, the months, days and seconds.

He dipped his head, closing the distance between them, and drank from her lips, tasting all the flavours he had just described. The slight sting from where she had indelicately bitten him earlier making it so much more sweet.

Then she opened for him and he plunged into the soft warmth of her mouth, teasing them both with swift movements of his tongue, delving deep within her and relishing every moment.

The roaring in his ears shifted and morphed into the sound of a hundred hands clapping, and just as many voices cheering. He pulled back, suddenly shocked by his own actions mirrored in Sofia's gaze and kiss-bruised lips.

# CHAPTER FIVE

'WHAT ON EARTH were you thinking?' Sofia demanded the moment she collected herself after *that kiss*, and the moment they were free of Georges and Louisa's attention.

'I was thinking that it would be the only thing that might wipe the insidious smirk from that obnoxious man's face.'

'You think *he* is obnoxious? Really?'

'I do.'

'He is an important man in the ministerial cabinet, Theo, I cannot afford—'

'The girl I once knew didn't give a flying fig for what she could or could not afford, Sofia. Tell me, where has she gone?' he asked, searching her face, 'for I cannot find a trace of her anywhere.'

'People change,' Sofia replied, turning away from his penetrating stare. Everyone changed. Her father, Theo, herself. No one was who they once were.

*But not everything changed*, her inner voice taunted her.

No. The way he had kissed her hadn't changed. The moment his lips had pressed against hers, first in that momentary initial greeting, and then later with *that kiss*, it had felt like…home. Some imaginary place in her mind when it had just been the two of them, all those years

ago, with no concerns other than how soon they could
see each other again. His body had called to hers in the
same way it had done all those years ago, and she hated
him for it. Because he was right. That girl was gone and
she could never come back. Not if she wanted to secure
a future for her country. They needed the royal woman
she had become, regal and poised. So she delved into the
inner strength she had forged from the loss of her hopes
and dreams and became that woman again.

She barely spared Theo another glance as she visited
with dignitaries, accepted their congratulations, agreed
to visit with various countries after the wedding—and if
her heart stuttered over that precise word or moment to
come, then she ignored it as she made plans for a future
she could no longer see.

Despite her attempts to relegate Theo to the sidelines,
he hovered almost constantly by her side, dishing out
the same charm he had drowned Louisa de Fontagne
in, showing a peculiar adroitness in conversation with
the various ministers and members of the privy council. And slowly she began to form an image of the man
to replace that of the boy she had known. One who had
skilfully nurtured an international wine conglomerate
from a small part of Greece, one who seemed to have
lost some of that inner sense of insecurity she had once
recognised as being similar to her own, a sense of not
quite being rich enough, or good enough...

'I must say, I'm impressed,' he said into the air just
above her head. For all the world they would look like a
couple very much in love as she tilted her face towards
his. Only he could read the confusion in her eyes. 'One
could be forgiven for thinking that this was an engagement party rather than an opportunity for you to net-
work. But so far I have seen you organise at least three

potential trade agreements with all the panache of a seasoned CEO.'

'Don't think I didn't miss the mention of your precious wine whilst you were talking to Georges. He was practically begging you for shares in your company once he realised that his wife, along with half the world, would seek out the magical wine blend that tasted *just like me*. It was a nice touch, by the way.'

'It was, wasn't it?' The pleasure was evident in his voice. 'You'll have to add it to the cover story your council made so hastily. Really, Sofia? You thought that the world would believe we had been introduced by a mutual friend? That's akin to saying we met on Tinder. But, as you know well, the best lies always have a hint of the truth.'

He waited until he had caught her gaze once more. 'Why did you not tell them we had met at school? Worried they would dig up my expulsion?' He wanted to look in her eyes as she answered his question. Wanted to see the truth she had somehow been able to hide from him. 'Or were you just worried about the world's press uncovering my low upbringing?'

'I never thought that of you, Theo. You were the only one who did,' she said in softly spoken words, and it was not an accusation, but he felt it as such.

Theo scoffed. 'You really have no idea, do you?' It took nothing to bring to mind a childhood that had felt like death by a thousand cuts, a thousand stares, snide comments and a fair few beatings when his mother wasn't looking. 'Up there, the little princess in the ivory tower.' He jerked his head up through the floors above the grand ballroom towards an unseen turret. 'Did you really not see the stares, or hear the words whispered by teachers and students alike? Do you really not know how the world *works*, Sofia? How the powerful turn on the weak in any attempt to guard their pedestal of superior wealth or position? Is it an accident of your birth, or wilful ignorance? I honestly can't tell any more. Because you were, are, many things, Sofia, but I didn't think that naïve was one of them.'

Her eyes turned the dark blue of an electrical storm. 'Naïve? You know nothing of what I have sacrificed—'

'What have you ever sacrificed, Sofia?'

*You*, the thought screamed silently in her mind. Anger rode her pulse to impossible speeds, her chest heaving against the low cut of her dress. An anger so much like desire—the fire in her blood quick to make the leap from one to the other. She felt the breadth of his shoulders expand beside her, and the way he stood proprietorially seemed to encase her, preventing her from seeing beyond the wall of the toned muscles of his chest, cutting her off from the room beyond. It was too much, the closeness of their bodies, the heat pulsating between them, the way her own body seemed to lean towards him as if wanting to pull rather than push him away.

'I didn't think so,' Theo said in the space of her silence. 'I look around the room, this party, this palace and see numbers. Because after I returned to Greece with my mother, it was all about numbers. The number of universities that retracted their scholarship offers after my expulsion. The number of family members that turned their backs on us, the single digit representing the one person willing to help. The number of euros begged and borrowed to buy that first plot of land, the number of times my mother and I went without food, the number of sleepless nights that wrecked us both as we plunged everything we had into that first grape harvest. The number of bottles we were first able to sell, after the number of failed attempts that preceded it. But do you know what doesn't have a number? How *hard* it was.'

She watched him with large, round eyes, and he imagined the pity there, surely. The way her eyes glinted with compassion just a remnant of what he wanted to see.

'I'm so sorry. Truly. I wish I could have helped.'

'Helped?' he demanded, the word almost getting stuck behind his outrage. 'I'm not talking about the work. I would do that every day for the rest of my life and still be happy. What was hard was the belief that *I* had done this to my mother. That *I* had brought this upon the one person in my life who had ever loved me. That, had I not fallen for your pretty lies, then I would have graduated at the top of my class, I would have attended one of the finest universities in the world with a scholarship. My future and my mother's would have not been filled with struggle and numbers of loss… I could have given her the world. For years I felt the weight of that on my shoulders. Until I realised that I was wrong. It wasn't my fault, it was yours. You laid a trail of pretty little lies like breadcrumbs for me to follow all the way to my destitution. And I believed those lies.

'How ironic that we survived the abandonment of my father, only to be cut down at the knees by a pampered princess. One that, no matter how exhausted I was, how many hours I worked in the dust, the mud, the earth, no matter how much I sweated, gained or lost…was the only thing I could think of each and every night. You.'

But his words had come out wrong. He felt the way they tasted on his tongue, heard the way they hit the air between them. He had meant it as a castigation, as an explanation or excuse for what he felt he had to do, all the things that Sofia didn't yet know of. But even to his own ears it had sounded more like a plea. A plea that he could not allow for, so he pressed on with the cruel taunt he knew would drive his desire for her away like no other.

'Until you married someone else.'

The last blow was too much for Sofia to bear. Each word, each statement filling in the blanks in her knowledge of him, changing and reforming what she had imagined for him in the years since that night ten years ago, had twisted the knife deeper in her breast. Until that final mention of Antoine. Her fingers reached for the comfort of the wedding band that was no longer there. Instead they scraped against the cold cut of the diamond that had been delivered to the palace two weeks before, the unfamiliar shape beneath the tips of her fingers cold and harsh. Another ring, worn from duty rather than desire or love.

She knew that she should tell him what had happened that night, knew that she should explain how she hadn't set him up to take the fall for her foolish actions, make him understand that she'd had no choice that night, or any since. Desperately she wanted to tell him that she had meant every word, every hope she'd ever shared with him, but what would it achieve? One part knew he'd not believe her and the other part knew she could not even if he might. The reason she had left that night was bound in secrecy and desperation, to protect her family from what was now only just around the corner. Did it really matter what he thought of her? Only to Sofia. It didn't change anything. Didn't change the fact she needed to be married, needed to no longer be the Widow Princess when the time came for her to assume the throne.

'I simply cannot fathom why you would have married a man who—'

'What, Theo? Wasn't you?' she demanded, cutting

into his sentence before he could cause even more pain by maligning Antoine. 'For all this talk of vengeance and needing to teach me the consequences of my actions—yes, I *was* paying attention in Paris—what is it really? That I dared to marry another man? Is your ego really that significant to you?'

His head reared back as if he'd been slapped and the thin shred of satisfaction at the sight made her feel both jubilant and petty at the same time.

'What would make you feel better, Theo? To hear that I didn't love him? Well, I did. He was a good, kind man who understood me, understood what I needed. Who also understood what my position meant in a way that you *never* will. I am truly sorry that you've faced such hardships, Theo. I am sorry that you feel responsible for them, I am also sorry that you believe that I caused that, that I did that to you. But if that's what you need to do, then so be it.

'And if you need to hear that Antoine and I didn't have the chemistry you seem to effortlessly taunt me with, then fine. We didn't. Does it please you to know that he took lovers? That it shamed him as much as me? Would that help? Do you need to know that each and every touch left me cold and more alone than I can possibly describe? Because the only person whose touch I had ever craved was you? The only person I had ever imagined sharing that part of myself with, was you? Would that ease your ego?'

Shame and misery sobbed in her chest, and tears that had formed without her knowledge or permission gathered behind the lids of her eyes, casting both Theo and the room about them in a blurry haze. She couldn't stand it any more, couldn't stand here knowing that he had drawn from her a secret that she had shared with no other.

So she fled her engagement party, turning her back on the gathered guests, picking up the skirts of her dress as she almost ran from the ballroom.

There were very few times in his life that Theo could remember being shocked into silence, and each and every one of them involved Sofia. But none of them had hit him with the power of a tsunami. Waves of something he did not want to put a name to crashed against him as he followed in her wake. He didn't care if he drew the curious glances of strangers as he left the ballroom with determined steps. He didn't care if they would have to come up with yet another story to define or excuse their actions and their engagement.

All he cared about was what Sofia had revealed to him, and if it made him want to beat his chest with pride and need, and ego, then so be it, even if it made him a bastard. His pulse raged and he felt the burn in his thighs as he took several steps at once towards her suite, feelings that he relished as he ate up the distance she had tried to put between them.

She had told him many lies in the past, but what she had said about her first husband, what she had said about *him*? That was most definitely the truth, and had somehow worked to lift the self-imposed barrier he had placed between them. Now, though, *now* there was no turning back.

Even as he stalked the palace hallways towards her room he felt the rush of desire, the swelling of arousal in his groin, the thickening of this band of want and need around his chest and throat. It might not have changed his plans for her, no. He would still have his revenge. But perhaps if he gave in to this insane desire burning between them, then he might finally be able to rid himself of the devastating hold she had over him. No, not him. His libido. He was a man of flesh and blood, and he would not deny either of them a taste of their basest desires.

He flexed his hand as it trembled ever so slightly in the space between him and the door to her rooms, and thrust it back by his side. Instead, he pushed the door open and kicked it shut behind him as he stepped over the threshold and drank in the sight of his prey.

She sat at the dressing table, staring off into the distance, looking as alone and isolated as she had claimed to be only moments earlier. Her golden hair, swept back into a chignon, glistened in the dimly lit room, matched only by the sparkle of the diamonds around her neck, dipping towards the V in her chest, and he stood half mesmerised by the sight of the rise and fall of her breasts, the only outward sign of her distress…

For the first time in years he felt an affinity with her, as he recognised that they were both in thrall to the spell of desire wrapping around them in great swathes of need.

'Stop.'

'Stop what?'

'This,' she said, gesturing between them. 'Whatever it is you're doing, just stop.'

'I would if I could, Princess, trust me.'

'You don't even like me,' she said, unable to help the smallness of her voice.

'I don't have to like you to want you,' he growled, the admittance rough on his voice. 'It's as if it's ingrained in me as much as my childhood lessons. When I should have been learning algebra, instead I learned the cosine of your skin, the angle of your chin, the circumference of your waist and the weight and feel of your breast. When I should have been learning French, instead I learned the language of the sighs of your pleasure, the rhythm and cadence of your pulse and your desire—'

'Stop,' she tried again, but failing to hide the pleading tone in her voice. And that plea called to him, taunting him, challenging him.

'No, Sofia. Because while I learned all these things, you seemed only to learn self-denial and how to lie.'

'And you are here to teach me my own body, Theo?' she asked, incredulity clear in her oceanic eyes.

He couldn't help the bitter laugh that left his lips. 'I would teach you how to demand the pleasure you so desperately plead for, beneath your cultured, perfect words. To unearth the truth of what your body craves beneath your mind's barriers. *Theé mou*, the Sofia I knew would have not hesitated.'

*'I don't have to like you to want you.'*

The words echoed in her mind. No, 'like' was too easy a word for what lay between them. He blamed her for every awful thing that had happened to him since that night ten years ago, and she blamed him for blackmailing her into this farce, for stealing her choice, even as he professed to give her a choice over this.

*'I don't have to like you to want you.'*

As if that one true acknowledgement had the power to unlock the cage she had just placed her inner self, her desires and wants into, need escaped as if his voice, his words were the key, twisting again and again within a lock so secure she had thought it never to be opened again.

'You want me?' Sofia said, with a voice raw with desire, turning to stand from the chair and stepping towards him. 'Take me,' she demanded.

He shook his head. Slowly. Not once taking his eyes from hers. 'Oh, no, Sofia. You're going to have to do better than that. You will not be passive in this, I won't allow you to hide behind excuses, proclaiming that I drove you to this. No. If *you* want *me*...then take *me*.'

The spell that had bound her from her wants and needs lifted, the challenge he laid at her feet rose into her accepting hands. Hands that tingled with the need to feel his bare skin beneath them.

Could she? Could she really do this? His words were a call to action, but her insecurities held her back. She wanted this. Wanted him with a need that shocked her, scared her even. But she had never done this before, certainly not with her husband... In truth she'd always dreamed of what it would be like with Theo. Fevered dreams, ones that had left her heated and wanting and unfulfilled.

She crossed the distance between them in shaking strides and when she stood before him, a hair's breadth between them, it was as if she didn't know where to start. She wanted it all. Years of hunger made her body stronger than her indecision. Her fingers trembled as they reached just beneath his perfect suit jacket to slip it from his shoulders, and leave it discarded by their feet.

They were on fire as they went to the silk tie around his neck and fed it through the loop that held it secure. She slid it from the collar of his shirt, focusing on the top button and fumbling slightly.

'Look at me,' he commanded. But she wasn't ready yet. She wasn't ready for him to see the desire and need and...innocence she felt shining from her skin, let alone her eyes. She wasn't ready for him to see the truth of her need for him, because if he did he would know. Know that she hadn't the faintest idea of what she was doing.

She slipped the button through its moorings, her thumb tracing a small pathway over hair-roughened skin, the heat from the contact spreading across the back of her hand, up her elbow and straight to her chest. Another button undone, and another tantalising glimpse of the hard planes of his chest…her hands awkward as they lifted the shirt tails from within the belt of his trousers.

Her fingers slid beneath the white cotton onto his deeply tanned abdomen, rippling beneath her touch, causing her to wonder at the evidence of the effect of her caress. His chin nudged her head to the side as he sought access to her neck. But she pulled away from the reach of his lips. He had told her to take him. So she would.

Unconsciously she arched against his chest like a cat, and when he nudged her thighs apart with his own she nearly cried out loud. The thick muscled thigh rubbing the soft silks of her skirt between her own legs was driving her senses wild. The low thrum that had started at her core now roared to life, pulsing with need for satiation, for his touch, for him.

She pushed him back against the wall, relishing her power, never having guessed that she would feel such a thing in this moment. Their bodies collided as his back pressed against the wall, her breasts aching for him.

She slid the shirt from his shoulders, broad and powerful from hard work and intense labour, and her hands swept behind him as he leant forward, allowing her nails to scratch at the thick, corded muscles, bunched with tension. His head rocked back as she did, a growl on his lips she desperately wanted to silence, because it heightened her own need and pleasure.

A pleasure she sought desperately from him as she learnt the adult body of a boy she had once desired, whilst punishing him by withholding a kiss…because if they kissed she might never find her way back. Instead of seeking his lips, she pressed hers against the suntanned skin of his chest, finding the spot beneath his ribs that caused him to suck in a lungful of air.

His hand came round to grasp her hip, and she brushed it away, refusing to let him share this moment of power she had only just discovered for herself. Within herself. The power that somehow he had given her to finally take what she'd wanted for so, so long.

Her tongue found his hard, flat nipple and flicked, the slight bucking of his body speaking only to the leash of control he was holding so strongly. She hated it, hated that he might have control over something that was almost totally overwhelming her.

Her hands went to his belt and drew the leather apart with a snap. The *hiss* as she undid the zip on his trousers was the only sound other than that of their pleasure, loud in the room.

His hands bunched the silk of her skirt at her thighs, pressing it against her skin as he drew the material higher and higher. Her hand went to his wrist, halting his progress, and a battle of wills ensued, finally drawing her eyes to him. He waited, tension evident in the dark blush against his exquisite cheekbones...waited for her permission to continue, and she marvelled at it. This game of power that was unspoken but clear in every movement, every sigh, every touch.

She released the hold she had on his wrist, and he lifted the skirts of her dress to her waist, one hand pinning the material, the other, pressed between her legs, paused, waiting, allowing the heat from his hand to soothe the ache caused by sheer need.

Sofia couldn't help a blush of embarrassment, as the evidence her desire had dampened the silken thong, and her body rippled as his thumb slid beneath the thin barrier to find her, wet and wanting.

Her head was flung back as the pad of his thumb found her clitoris and he stroked and stroked, ringing a pleasure so acute her legs began to shake. She had no idea that it could be like this, that somehow she had *denied* herself this all these years. She shifted as his hand turned, as his finger plunged into her, the strong, thick cords of his forearm almost holding her in place, holding her where he wanted and where she needed.

'Look at me,' he commanded, and this time she was unable to refuse. The deep brown of his eyes were drowned in pupils so large with desire she lost herself in the dark depths of them.

His lips crashed down upon hers, his tongue prying them open and plunging into her mouth as if he needed to consume her whole. As his tongue delved, so did his fingers, deeper and harder, bringing her to a point she didn't yet want to reach.

Her hands flew back to his trousers, pressing gently at the hard ridge of his arousal, even while her inner sense reeled in shock at her actions, and this time she felt the growl building in the back of his throat. Her fingers reached beneath the waistband of his underwear, desperate for the hot, silken skin covering a steel-like need. A string of Greek curses, too quick for her to decipher, littered the air.

'Bed,' he demanded against her lips.

'No.'

He prised open his eyes to take her in, the fierce look of need and want calling to him in a way he had never imagined, her eyes a shimmering turquoise he had never seen before.

'I need to be very clear on what you are saying no to, Sofia,' he said with a growl.

'The bed, I'm saying no to the bed.'

She glanced at it as if fearful…and perhaps it was not the bed itself but the intimacy it invited. And, while they might be tearing clothes instead of strips off each other, perhaps for her that kind of intimacy between them was not welcome.

'If there is anything else you need to say no to…' He had been called a lot of names in his life, some of which he'd earned, but one thing he would never do was force a woman against her will. There was a special circle in hell reserved for men like that.

He held his breath. It would be hard, but if she asked, he would walk away. Walk away and not look back. He watched as his tone settled about her and she realised the truth of his words.

'I'm saying yes, Theo.'

'You always were contrary,' he growled as he crushed his lips against hers, knowing that there would be no going back. No walking away. Not yet.

# CHAPTER SIX

HE TOOK CONTROL as easily as she had given it away.

Peeling his back from the wall and walking her in his arms backwards towards the daybed, he spun them round and pulled her down with him as he lay back on the large expanse of what was probably an original Louis XVI chaise longue.

She still wore her dress, and he his trousers, but frankly he didn't care. The entire length of her body was pressed against his, and it welcomed the light pressure with a sigh.

He had meant what he said. He didn't have to like her to want her. But maybe, he prayed, if they finally gave in to the power of the sensuality that held them together, it would be over. It would sever its hold. Because no matter what woman had graced his bed until now, it had always been her. Sofia. It was she who had called to him in his most fevered of dreams. But the soft-as-silk skin beneath his touch, the heated flesh that seemed to warm even the coldest depths of him, was not a dream, nor a fantasy. She was here. In his arms. And he couldn't get enough.

He drew a knee upward to secure her, imprison her between his legs. The long length of his thigh encased her hip, and she pressed her hands down onto the seat beneath them, holding herself up on toned arms that were deceptively strong.

He didn't want her above him, he didn't like the way she looked down upon him, but the slender neck exposed by the upsweep of her hair called to him. He could resist no longer. His lips and teeth gently nipped at the exposed sweet flesh there, and he inhaled, deeply drinking her in, the soft blueberry and bay scent, heated by her skin, almost a mirror of the first wine he had produced. *Theos*, had he been consumed by her even then? The story he had woven for the obtuse minister came back to haunt him, as did his proclamation that the greatest lies held a kernel of truth.

But he didn't want to think of the past, nor the future, he only wanted to think of now. Her sigh brought him back to the present as easily as if she were a witch who had summoned him.

She placed a hand on his chest, his heart leaping there beneath it, as if it had finally found a missing piece of itself, and he itched to bat it away. Instead, he took her hand in his and pressed his lips against her palm, and even as his body cried out for quick release from this sensual prison he forced himself to stop and savour her as he would a wine. Surely only when he had identified each of the individual flavours, notes of what was unique to her, he would be satisfied, he would *know*.

He took each of her fingers, one by one, into his mouth, his tongue gently sucking on them, relishing the different sounds that fell from her lips as he did so. With one hand he traced the line of her delicate wrist, up to the elbow joint, around the firm muscles beneath her shoulder, and back up to her neck.

She rubbed against him, cradled in his hips, drawing an arousal so acute, so swift, it was almost painful. Once again the game of power was being played between them as she moved to take what she wanted.

He pulled her into his arms, and turned them so that her back was now against the chaise longue, and he was above her, surrounding her with his shoulders and body, and she knew it from the look that entered her heated aquamarine gaze. There was too much assessment there, too much calculation. He wanted her blind with pleasure, as blind as he was at risk of becoming.

He took her lips with his, pressing against the perfect pink plumpness, lathing it with his tongue, drawing moans of pleasure as he plunged into her hot, wet depths, knowing that they were both imagining his tongue somewhere else on her body.

He wanted skin against skin, he wanted to see the rosy, taut nipple he could feel pressing through the material that separated them. He wanted to taste it, tease it.

The dress was beautiful, but it was in the way. His hands ran down her sides, looking for a zip, something, anything to release her from the wrapping and get to the present of her body beneath. He groaned when he could not find anything.

'Theo?'

'The dress…it's…'

She groaned her own frustration. 'It needed nearly two people to get me into the damn thing.'

He looked down on her, for a moment their shared frustration a shared amusement.

'It will only need me to get you out of it,' he said, giving her one last assessing gaze before he took the bottom of the dress, found the side-seam and tore apart the fabric with his hands.

The squeal, almost guilty in its pleasure, that came from Sofia drew an impossible smile from his lips. A smile that died the moment he took in the body that he had been dying to see, touch, taste for nearly ten years.

She was incredible. Her chest bare to him completely, the perfect rounds of her breasts, full and almost tear-shaped against her torso, only her modesty covered by the thin scrap of lace that he had encountered between her legs. She tried to hide from him, her face turned aside as if she was embarrassed by her own skin. Her knees came together before him, as if she was protecting herself from him. He couldn't help the words of praise that fell against her skin.

'Do not hide from me, Sofia. Not now,' he growled, hating how his voice almost broke under the power of his arousal, of his desire for her. His hands went to her knees, gently levering them apart to make room for him as he leaned over her, finally taking one of her nipples between his lips, lathing it and toying it into perfect hard submission.

Her back arched upwards, against his mouth, the almost sob that fell from her lips the greatest satisfaction. He worked his mouth and lips lower, in open-mouthed kisses, leaving a damp trail that he knew the air would cool, sending shivers of arousal over her skin.

'Theo,' she begged and the sound of his name on her pleasure-filled voice nearly undid him.

'You want me here, Sofia? My touch, my tongue?' he demanded.

'You would make me beg?' Her voice broke.

'I would make you own it, own your pleasure, Sofia.'

Each time he said her name, her pupils dilated with pleasure. He almost couldn't say it enough. She nodded but it wasn't enough. He wanted to hear it, hear her wants, desires…*needs*.

For a moment they simply stared, the war of control ebbing and flowing between them like a tide, as he held himself back from what they both so desperately wanted. Until she said it, until she commanded it, until she gave in to it.

'Yes, Theo. I want—'

Her words were lost to a cry of pleasure as he pulled aside the thin, silken material between her legs, as he uncovered the heart of her with his tongue, as he lathed the length of her and returned again and again to the one place that drew the most exquisite sounds of tormented need from her.

Her hips bucked beneath his ministrations, and he placed a hand low on her abdomen to hold her in place for him, his thumb stroking the silken curls hiding her womanhood.

He took her to the brink of her pleasure again and again, refusing to let her fall. Because when she did, he wanted her to be there with him.

'Theo, please…'

He knew what she wanted, what *he* wanted, for the first time their needs the same.

He reached into the pocket of the trousers he still wore, finding the slim wallet and retrieving the foil packet it contained. He left her body only to discard the trousers, never once taking his eyes from her, as he placed the latex over himself.

'This is the last time I will ask, Sofia. If you have any doubts—'

This time it was she that cut off his words, reaching up to pull him down to her, her hot hand like an anchor at the base of his neck, her legs parting for him as if welcoming him home, her lips barely an inch away from his as she said, 'This is what I want, Theo. That is the last time you will ask me.'

Never had he seen her so regal, so commanding, so powerful in her focus, her intent, her need.

He slid into her, filling her slowly, shifting and…

And the moment he felt her tense, he stopped. Shock and surprise as much in him as it was in her. *Theos*, he hadn't even thought. Hadn't even imagined…

'Sofia—'

'Wait, please…just…'

His body was almost shaking, and he bit back the curse that lay on his tongue. As the implications of her innocence struck him, anger poured through him and he realised the true extent of the lies of her first marriage. She was a virgin and he had not known. And somewhere deep within him that made him both fiercely angry and deeply satisfied. But he held back, because he knew his fury would scare her. *Damn*, her naivety burned him, etching her name on his soul.

As her body relaxed into him, she moved her hips experimentally beneath him.

'Sofia,' he tried again, tried to warn her of what she had already lost.

'I knew what I was asking for, Theo.'

No, she hadn't known. But she would. Soon, she would know and for the first time he hated himself for the path he had set for them both.

She shifted once more against him, his body utterly at her mercy now. All thought fled and, coward that he was, he hid in his body's needs, in Sofia's wants, and finally released the hold he had on his control.

Gently, so gently, he withdrew from her, only to resume a torturously slow return. Subconsciously his body recognised the difference, the change from hurried intent to languorous pleasure, pleasure that was to be all hers.

Theo lost track of time in the sounds of her cries, needful and wanting, he knew only the ripple of her skin, the acres of smooth silk beneath his hands, the warm, luxuriously wet heat of her as he drew them towards the point of completion again and again.

Finally, at Sofia's desperate pleas, he took them into an abyss full of starlight and his last thought was that he was fundamentally changed for ever.

As the water poured over her skin, her heart still racing from what they had shared, still pounding before she'd even lifted her eyes to the scattered stars across the still night sky through the large windows of her room, she marvelled at the stretch of unfamiliar muscles across her body. Languid, but poised, as if already wanting Theo again.

She had meant what she'd said. She *had* known what she was asking for, asking of him. But she had not realised that it would make her feel... She shook her head in the shower, scattering drops of water from her hair. What did she feel? It was too much for words.

But there were words she did know. She knew that they needed to talk. Needed to confront the past...or as much of that night, ten years before, as she would be able to share. Because whether he'd wanted to or not, he *had* given her a moment of choice, of control. And as a result, it had become vital that she explain, vital that he knew that she hadn't had a choice when she'd left that night. That she hadn't purposefully set him up as he clearly believed. She couldn't tell him everything, the secret that locked her heart tight against the truth of her father's diagnosis, the secret that was to protect her country from instability and chaos, one so deep she wasn't sure she'd ever be able to reveal it. But she hoped that she could give him something...give him some sense of resolution about the past. Give him some truth amongst the one lie she still maintained.

She left the shower, wrapping herself in the large towel and retrieving a lightweight trouser suit, readily accepting any armour she could against the conversation that she knew would follow, any protection against Theo's impossibly penetrating gaze.

She dressed and went to sit beside the large windows, peering through the darkness to the elusive shadowscape of her beautiful country. The rolling hills she knew lay beneath the deep night, the mountains in the distance, and all the sleeping inhabitants of Iondorra in between. She heard him stir behind her, the sound of his roughened palm against the smooth silk of the chaise longue, consciously or unconsciously reaching for her, she wondered.

'We should talk.'

'Then I should have coffee.'

She gestured to a coffee machine in the corner of the living suite of her rooms. Soon, she heard the spluttering, juddering sound it made as it filled the air with the fragrant, almost bitter taste of coffee that instantly made her mouth water, and turned to find him standing there in his suit trousers and nothing else. She pushed down the distraction of the smooth planes of sun-darkened skin across his powerful torso. They needed to have this conversation. If there was any hope…

'If we're going to marry—'

'If?'

'*If* we're going to marry, then we need to clear the air. We… I need to tell you about that night.'

Nothing in him moved, not a muscle or a flicker of his eyes. Brooding and powerful. She'd always sensed that ability in him, latent, shimmering beneath the surface, but now? Now it had exploded in a technicolour aura that even the most obtuse would be able to identify. The alpha.

'Would you like to sit?' she said, gesturing to one of the two chairs framing yet another large set of windows.

'I'll stand.'

She nodded, returning her gaze to the panes of glass, but instead only seeing his reflection appearing behind her. Somehow she had always felt his presence, waiting, hovering over her shoulder.

'It may not surprise you to know that I was a wilful child. Stubborn and mischievous. My parents despaired of me. I managed to outwit at least three of the most professional nannies and au pairs Europe had to offer. Two were more than happy to sign non-disclosure agreements protecting their reputations as much as my family's. The last, instead, chose a change in her career path. I believe she is now working with horses.' She paused, taking a breath. Steeling herself against what she was to say. 'It's hard to explain what life was like growing up the only child to two parents whose first and last duty is to their country. Especially when one's own nature seems to run contrary to that sense of duty and self-sacrifice.

'When my parents agreed to enter me at the boarding school with my mother's maiden name, it was excused as being for my protection,' she said, with an absent laugh. 'It may have even been to protect the royal name, in case my wildness ruined that too.'

'In case?' Theo queried, as if the thought of her being anything other than the reckless, wayward teenager was impossible.

'But for me it was my *one* chance. Not to be seen as a royal, not to be the woman who would one day rule a country from beneath her father's long shadow, he the perfect king, and me the improper princess. In truth, we're quite minor royals in the grand scheme of Europe's nobility. It was surprisingly easy, especially given the infamy of many of the other students at the school.

'And at first it *was* easy. Creating the lies that kept my identity secret. They gave me protection from having to join many of the friendship groups my parents thought would help iron out my unsuitable behaviours. It allowed for me to be seen as *me*. And you were such a breath of fresh air to me, and I... I relished it. You didn't treat me as if I would break, or as if I was a disappointment, a failure. You just saw...me. You laughed with me, teased me and I couldn't get enough.

'Rather than bowing and bending to the rules of the school, I struggled against them, seeing it only as another form of constraint, another cage I would eventually swap with a crown.' Sofia took a deep sigh, sore and hurting for the child she had been. 'Much of my behaviour then was selfish and, yes, without thought for the consequences of my actions. I am sorry that I lied to you about who I was but... at the time it was my only comfort. The only light I felt within a bound and trapped existence.'

She watched as Theo shook his head against her words. 'You may excuse your lies as much as you want, but you knew what you were doing, *knew* that it was impossible for you to run away with me as you begged me to.'

She shrugged her shoulders helplessly. 'I think... I think that I believed the story I had told. I wanted so much to go with you, to run away from the school, from my responsibilities, from my future. The hours we spent talking about how it would be, where we would go, they had painted a future so firm in my mind that I...' She had thought she would die if she did not live it. 'Honestly, Theo—of all things, believe that what we shared was what was in my heart. I had no intention of making you take the fall for the prank on the headmaster's car. I had no intention of you being expelled.'

'Then what happened?' he demanded.

'I'd been furious with the headmaster. In design class, I and three others had been assigned a group project, but Anna—one of the group—had needed to return home and failed to pass on her part of the project and the remaining three of us were given detentions by the headmaster for not fulfilling the brief. It seems so petty now, but…then? It had seemed like a great injustice. So we hatched the prank to end all pranks. He loved his Mini Cooper. It was the most precious thing he owned, I think. We realised that if we could put two long planks up against the side of the sports hall, we could get the car onto the roof. Between us, the weight of the car wasn't too much, but the sharp edge of the wheel arch hurt, so I used your scarf to protect my hands and… I must have left it behind.

'I had arranged to meet you, to tell you about it. That was my surprise. I had…been showing off, I suppose. But an hour before I was supposed to meet you that night, there was a knock at my door. When I saw my parents standing there, I thought that they had discovered my part of the prank, I thought that they might have discovered my relationship with you. I was frightened then. For you, for me… So I was confused when…'

And now she began to pick and choose her words. She couldn't reveal her father's diagnosis. They were not yet married, the risk to the country still too great. Perhaps if somehow they managed to pull this marriage off then she could finally unburden herself of her secrets. But not yet. She had already prepared this speech, spent hours of each night in the last month, since he'd forced her hand, trying to work out the best possible threads to share, to unearth, to expose…

'They told me they had come to take me home. Iondorra was in a delicate state politically. There was a trend at the time for the smaller European countries to exchange royal rule for political governance, but our parliament was neither old nor strong enough to assume control. But there was enough talk within the parliament to force my father's hand and have me return in order to assume responsibilities much sooner than intended.'

He had still not moved, and she was still ensnared in his predatory gaze, as if his eyes were gently pressing against her words to find the truth of them.

'That night it was agreed that I would return to the palace, and begin learning what I would need.'

She had thought that at the very least she'd have two years before she would even have to start thinking of assuming royal duties. Two years in which maybe she could come to an understanding with her father...and if her father could just *meet* Theo—see what she saw in him—maybe she could somehow get him to recognise their marriage. Even now, her thoughts showed just how naïve she had truly been then.

In a rush she had told her parents about him. Explained that she was in love, begged and pleaded with them not to do this. Not to take her away from him. She remembered the way she had pulled on her father's lapels with white-knuckled hands, the way her mother had looked at her with both sympathy and pity.

But, as had been made painstakingly clear to her that night, she was their country's future and could no longer entertain a dalliance with 'that Greek', as her father had called him, her father's fear and frustration severing the softness of his affection for her and the freedom he had so often before encouraged.

'Could you not have come to me? Could you not have

explained? Could you not have told me so that when the headmaster discovered me I could defend myself? So that I could make him believe *my* innocence?' His words were quietly spoken, but nonetheless whip-quick and just as painful, and Sofia resisted her body's urge to flinch.

'No and no,' she said sadly, because in truth—she still could not. She knew that the excuses she had presented to him, while very much real, were not the whole story. And she counted on his anger as much as her hope for his understanding—because if he *was* angry he might not see the gaping holes in what she had told him.

'Would you make the same decision again?'

He almost wished he could recall the words the moment that they left his lips. But he knew he needed to hear her answer as much as he needed her to say them. If she said no, then he might try to find a way out of this, to extricate himself from his path of revenge. It was as if there was a tide between them, pushing one way and pulling another. He felt like a man drowning, knowing that one push of the ocean would take him to the depths, one pull could see him back to shore, to safety, to a future he could have only prayed for.

As if Sofia felt that same tide, that same sense of the precipice before them, she turned to him, finally facing him, drawing herself up to her full height, her chin angled up as if to meet an oncoming army.

'There was never a choice. For my country, for my duty, yes. I would do it again in a heartbeat.'

Had she known that was the moment she might have been able to save herself from what was to come, she might have answered differently, he thought. But she hadn't. Instead, she only confirmed the words he needed to hear.

He pressed away the excuses she had given him about

their time together, the slow erosion that had begun against the bedrock of his need for revenge. The image she had woven between them of a young woman trapped within a gilded cage of duty as she battled the natural, sprite-like instinct within her. Of a reckless young girl, ignorant of the consequences of her actions. His determination had begun to give…to loosen its grip around his plans and his feelings for her.

But Sofia's decisions that night had put into motion a chain of events that had led him and his mother to such pain… Had he stayed at the school, gone on to university, his mother would not have had had to work every back-breaking moment of those first five years alongside him, pouring their blood, sweat and tears into the very earth that eventually repaid them. But not without cost. His mother's heart attack could have been prevented. The bright, determined, loving woman he knew had been transformed into a vulnerable, weakened, pallid imitation of herself. And it had only been by nearly losing everything again that he'd been able to fund her treatment. But he could have done better. He could have taken his mother away from that hardship, from that life-or-death battle, had it not been for Sofia.

It took him a moment to realise that the buzzing wasn't just in his ears, but that of a mobile phone nestled on her dressing table.

'Do not answer it,' he commanded darkly. They were not done yet.

He watched her take in the number on the screen.

'I have to.' And for the first time after these ten years of absence he saw fear in her eyes and, speaking into the phone, she asked, 'What's wrong?'

# CHAPTER SEVEN

HE HAD MADE Sofia wait while he quickly showered and changed. When she had insisted she needed to go *now* he had refused, firmly stating that five minutes would do no harm. And she hadn't been able to tell him why he was wrong. Bound by secrets she bitterly resented.

She had tried to walk out, but he had caught her arm and ordered her to take a breath. A breath? Even now she felt she hadn't inhaled once since hearing her mother's desperate pleas on the phone. He had dogged her steps as she had tried to leave without him, leaving muttered words like 'stubborn' and 'pig-headed' in their wake.

She scanned her mind for her father's routine. For something that would perhaps explain what could have happened to make her mother beg for her presence.

*'You need to come here. Now. Please, Sofia.'*

Panic was a feral thing, eating up the small, dark, cramped space of the limousine whisking her away to the small estate where her mother and father lived. Between her fear and Theo's brooding presence, she could barely move. It pressed in around her as she clutched the silk of the trouser suit at her thigh.

'I'll ask again—'

'And I'll say again, Theo, I cannot tell you what's going on. I don't even know.' And she hated the helplessness of her words and the truth in them. As the car drew up to the entrance to her parents' home, she commanded him to stay in the car.

And, for once, he must have seen the seriousness of the situation and listened.

Leaving him leaning against the limousine, the early morning sky barely touched by the light of the sun's rays, Sofia raced through the halls, the bodyguard who had ridden with the driver flanking her side.

One floor down from her parents' living quarters and she could already hear the muffled sounds of her father's anger. Her speed picked up, nearly causing her to stumble at the top of the marble stairs. She rushed through the heavy wooden doors, partly open as if ready for her arrival.

'Get your hands off me. Do you not know who I am?' her father demanded, his face red with anger and frustration.

'Of course they do, Frederick.' Her mother's gentle, soothing tone was doing nothing to calm her father's fury.

The sight of her father's frail old body being restrained by two men was almost enough to bring a cry to Sofia's lips. The skin on his arms loose, as if he were a puppy, still yet to grow into himself. Was this growing old? Sofia wondered. Reverting to a childlike state of tantrums, and folds of paper-thin skin?

'Sofia!' her father cried. 'Make them see. Make them see that they have to let me go. I need to speak to the council. The Prime Minister wants to raise the duty taxes on the…on the…' Becoming even more frustrated with his lack of memory, he growled, pushing and pulling against the two men restraining him.

Sofia didn't know where he was in his mind, but it wasn't now. The Prime Minister had greater things to deal with at the moment than raising duty taxes on any-thing, so it must have been some years ago.

'Papa, it's okay. We'll speak to him later. It's four o'clock in the morning, and he'll still be asleep. There's time, Papa.'

'No, there isn't,' he said, almost succeeding in throw-ing off one of the men. Sofia took a step back instinc-tively, hating the familiarity of the fear thrumming her pulse like a guitarist. Once again she rubbed at her fore-arm, at the place where a similar night had caused her father to accidentally fracture her arm and two ribs. She'd never forget the look of shock and confusion in her fa-ther's eyes as he'd utterly failed to grasp what he had done. It was a terrible thing to fear her own father.

'It's you, isn't it?' he demanded now, bringing her back to the present with a thump.

'What, Papa?'

'*You're* keeping me from him. You only want the throne for yourself. You've been…poisoning me. Whis-pering evil into my courtiers' ears. You want me gone.'

'Papa, that's not true,' Sofia said, gently, knowing that any trace of concern or upset only made him worse. Ev-erything in her cried, *no*. Proclaimed that she had never wanted it. 'This country needs you. *I* need you.'

'You never needed me,' he growled. 'Running around the castle like some pixie. Desperate to run off with that Greek boy and turn your back on us all.'

The stark irony struck home for Sofia, but she tried instead to cling to the quickly changing direction of his chain of thought, so easy to flip between her wanting the throne and wanting to throw it away.

'We should have let you go to him. You will be the death of this country. You were never fit to rule,' he cried as one of the carers administered an anti-psychotic drug.

For them to be doing this now meant that they must have been struggling with him almost since he'd left the engagement party. Sofia knew they would have tried everything else.

'I know, Papa,' she couldn't help but admit as he somehow drew out her greatest fears. 'But I'm trying. I really am.'

As the two men assisting her father settled him gently back into a chair, her mother watched her with large, shimmering eyes.

'Sofia—'

'It's okay, Mama, I know. I know he doesn't mean it,' she lied as she turned away. Fear, sadness, loss, grief, it all pressed against her skin like little pin pricks, drawing blooms of invisible blood that left her feeling drained and exhausted.

Theo was watching the sun rise slowly over the forest surrounding the estate, the scent of pine and earth slowly unfurling from the ground in the gentle heat of the early morning. He relished that almost sappy resin taste and he tried to combine grape lineages in his mind in an attempt to distract himself from Sofia's revelation only an hour before.

He could tell that she had been giving him some truths. There was definitely something she was holding back, but…tiny tendrils of doubt about that night were corroding his fierce belief that she had purposefully set him up. They spread through his chest and tightened around his heart. Because just beneath that erosion was something deeper. Something darker and much more painful. Something that spoke of grief and the acrid taste of loss, one he remembered from years before meeting Sofia. This odd sense that he'd lived with almost all his

life…a barely audible whisper from an inner voice…
*abandoned, again.*

Usually Theo could go for months without thinking of
the man who had run from his mother, run from *him*. But
ever since he had set out on this path of revenge he had
always been a shadow at the periphery of Theo's vision,
hovering, waiting. He remembered thinking as a child
that it was only natural to think of his father and had half
convinced himself that when he became a man, when
he was eighteen, he'd somehow magically stop thinking
of him. And to a certain extent that had been true. But
only because of the damage limitation he'd been forced
into following Sofia's actions. But here, in Iondorra, a
place that—as far as Theo knew—his father had never
set foot, a phantom pain was tingling, burning back into
a life he thought he'd long snuffed out.

The creak of the large doorway at the top of the stone
steps to the estate cut through the early morning air, and
the moment he saw Sofia all thoughts fled his mind.

She looked…devastated. And it was horrible. Because
he recognised that look. It was the look a child wore, no
matter their age, when something truly awful was happening to a parent. He had seen it the moment he'd looked
in the mirror after his mother had been taken to hospital.

He went to take a step towards her but held himself
back. He wanted to take her in his arms, to hold her in the
way that no one had held him that day. But he couldn't.
Whether for her, or himself, he didn't know.

'Sofia?'

She descended the steps as if in a daze, her eyes unsee-
ing, a numbness almost vibrating from her. This woman
who had come alive in his arms, to his touch and his need
only hours ago, was now hollow and absent. She came
to stand before him, her head barely reaching his shoul-

ders, so that he had to bend almost, to try and catch her sightless gaze.

'Sofia…' Her name almost a plea on his lips.

'Take me away, Theo. Please.'

Her request rang out over the years from all that time ago, the one he so desperately wanted to forget. They were words he had thrown back at her outside the Parisian ballroom. As if realising it herself, only after it was too late to recall them, she flinched. And then trembled.

*'Entáxei.'* He nodded. 'Okay,' he repeated for her benefit. 'We will go.'

And then he finally gave in to his desire, and pulled her into an embrace.

He had spoken briefly to the chauffeur of the change in plans and, while settling Sofia into the back of the limousine, Theo started on the phone calls needed. He'd pulled up the contact details for Sofia's personal secretary, ordered her to pack a bag and get it to the airport, and cancelled all Sofia's appointments for a week. He'd messaged Seb to make his apologies to Maria, realising that he'd be unable to make the exhibition he'd assured her he'd attend the night before.

As the limousine ate up the miles of smooth tarmac, he began to doubt his decision. He had never taken a woman back to his winery, to the place where his mother still lived. He wondered what she would make of the young princess and hated that he had once had the same thought, under the same circumstances. Hated the fact that he would introduce Sofia to his mother as his fiancée, only to abandon her at the altar. But he would. He must. Because only then would she realise just how much damage she had caused. Just how much hurt…

But as the limousine passed the castle and carried on,

it failed to draw any kind of response from Sofia. The kind of numbness that she wore about her like a shield began to scare him. He remembered that feeling. That hopelessness that was so very easy to hide in. And he couldn't help the wish, the need, to protect her. To shelter her, even if it ran contrary to his own plans. She needed to get away. She needed to find herself again. And for the first time Theo began to doubt his plan for revenge.

Sofia opened her eyes and frowned in momentary confusion at the unfamiliar sights that met them. And then she remembered. Remembered the short flight on Theo's private jet, the drive to the exclusive marina, remembered the way that Theo had ushered her onto the small, but beautiful and most definitely luxurious, yacht and walked her straight into the cabin and ordered her to sleep.

Smooth mahogany surrounded her, and the gentle, rhythmic sway beneath her called her back to that blissful slumber. Sofia wanted nothing more than to bury herself in the comfortable bedding, but unease told her she couldn't. Instinct, memories, they all crashed about her mind and she felt...it all. The numbness that had settled about her had finally worn off, and everything in her hurt. Ached. Her heart for her father, her head for Theo, and her bones, a deep, low ache—that was for herself.

Untangling herself from the nest of sheets wrapped around her body, she sat up, swung her legs over the side of the bed and saw a bathroom off to the left. Peeling off clothes that felt days old, she turned on the shower, not even giving it time to warm up. The shocking cool jets of water hit her skin like a slap, bringing her round, before the water warmed and comforted like an embrace.

By the time she had emerged from the bathroom, a selection of clothes were laid out on the bed. Someone had been in here while she was in the shower. Unseen hands had placed the clothes on the bed she had only just left, an unseen body had been barely a foot from hers while she was naked in the shower, and instinctively she knew. Theo.

While everything in her wanted to scrabble into the clothes and rush to find him, demand that he take her back to Iondorra, she forced herself to stop. To slow the speeding of her thoughts.

*Take me away, Theo. Please.*

She had asked him for this. She blinked back the tears that pressed against the backs of her eyes. She wouldn't cry. She wouldn't break. But she needed this. She needed him. Perhaps, instead of rushing back to be the princess everyone wanted, she could steal this time away, just for herself. Before duty fell like a tolling bell against her, before there was no turning back.

Dressed in a soft white linen shirt and blue capri trousers, Sofia left the bedroom and followed the small galley to the stairs in front of her. The sun beckoned from where it slanted through the shadows and Sofia realised she had no idea what time it was.

Bare feet took the metal steps up to the deck of the boat, and when she emerged into the light she looked up at the stunning sloping arc of a brilliant white sail against a cloudless azure sky. The yacht was small—as in not one of the monstrosities that many rich Europeans preferred—but long and incredibly beautiful.

She would have stopped at the sight of the sea, stretching out on all sides as far as the eye could see, the magnificence of the aquamarine water melding with the sky at an invisible horizon. She would have stopped to relish the heat of the sun as it drenched her in a comforting warmth, finding even the darkest places of her heart and healing it beneath the touch of the rays. But nothing, *nothing* compared to the sight of Theo at the helm of the boat tall and proud as he directed the wheel with just the palms of his hands, his fingers outstretched, his movements smooth and his gaze on the horizon…until he turned that powerful gaze on her.

The sight of him took her breath away. His dark hair was wind-tousled, and a pair of sunglasses may have masked his eyes, but they did nothing to conceal the proud cheekbones and jut of his strong jaw, a jaw covered in a dark brush of stubble that just cried out to be touched. His white shirt, buttoned low, exposed a chest of defined muscle, dustings of dark swirls hidden then revealed as the linen was shaken by the wind. Dark navy linen trousers hung low on his lean hips, and Sofia bit back a curse or a plea to the gods, she honestly couldn't tell any more. This was not the man-child she had fallen for in her youth, this was something altogether different. Her eyes ate up the changes in his body, the muscles corded in his forearms, the glimpses of the trail of hair leading below the beltline of his trousers, the wide stance of his bare feet planting him securely on the wooden deck, looking for all the world as if he were its ruler.

All these things she had not taken in when they had come together…she had been blinded by passion then, and now? Now he simply stood there bearing the weight of her scrutiny, allowing her to take her fill. It was too much, and she used the excuse of the bright sun to shield her eyes, breaking the connection that had bound them together for a moment.

'There are sunglasses over there. As well as some deck shoes, and in the cooler bag some breakfast.'

He gestured to the bench just across the deck and she found everything he had described.

'You need to use the sunscreen too,' he said as he secured the wheel, and disappeared below deck. She sprayed herself liberally with the lotion and donned the pair of beautiful sunglasses. She was just reaching into the cooler bag for a pastry when the scent of fresh coffee mixed with the sea-salt air. She nearly groaned out loud.

'Still drink coffee like a lifeline?'

'Yes,' she smiled, the feeling on her lips foreign and strange after the last few weeks. 'Can't live without it,' she said, gratefully accepting the mug he offered her. She watched as the sea wind whipped away the steam before it could swirl and dance above the dark liquid. Waiting for it to cool before taking a sip, she turned back to the horizon. 'Where are we?'

'The Ionian Sea.'

'It's beautiful.'

He nodded. And for a moment she was glad that they shared this silence. That he allowed her to listen to the sounds of the waves crashing against the hull of the yacht as it glided through the water, the whip and crack of the sail as it strained against the wind. She knew he had questions, she could feel them emanating from him, but that he had not yet voiced them was a pleasant relief.

'You got your boat,' she said with a sad smile, remembering their youthful plans of some impossible future, the ones made at the Swiss boarding school.

'Eventually,' he said, the word marshalled as if he'd wanted to say more.

Theo resumed his position behind the wheel and she folded her feet beneath her on the bench and sipped at her coffee, savouring the strong hit of caffeine and the smooth, sweet taste of the honey he had added. He remembered. She feared that he remembered everything.

It had been so easy to embrace her anger for him when he was being demanding, blackmailing and ruthless. Even when he had played her body's desires against her, plucking strings between them she had long thought severed. But now? Now she could see glimpses of the youth she had fallen for. His kindness, his acceptance of her, unlike anything she had ever known before then, and not since. Not even with Antoine.

If he had forced her to explain, shouted and demanded, she would have retreated. But in this space he gave her she found herself unfurling, expanding within it in a way that was all about her. Not about duty, or trade negotiations, not about a ring she would wear, or a role she would play for her country, for her family.

She couldn't remember the last time she had found time for silence, for herself and her thoughts. Even as she considered it, she felt the rising panic, the fear that something might be happening and she wouldn't know about it. As much as she hated it, she started to look for her phone.

'Your people have instructions to call me if they need you. They have the number of the yacht's satellite phone. Your mobile wouldn't have signal out here anyway.'

'But the meeting with the Hungarian ambassador—'

'Has been rescheduled.'

'And the interview with the *New York Times*?'

'And with *Paris Match*, the Iondorran prime minister, and the Swiss consulate. Your assistant is nothing if not efficient.'

'Yes,' she said, smiling at the thought of the apparently ruthlessly organised Theo dealing with her imperious assistant.

Instead of panic at the thought of all these important events in her diary, she felt oddly relieved. For so long she had borne the brunt of her duties alone. For the first time it felt as if she had someone with her to share the load. Even if only to make the decision she would have known she had to make, but been incapable of making.

She caught sight of Theo's cocked head as he observed her. 'What?' she asked, feeling around her mouth and chin for flakes of the pastry that might have remained from her breakfast, oddly self-conscious under his scrutiny.

'You don't mind,' Theo stated.

'Mind what?'

'That I rearranged it all. I thought you would be hissing like a cat, threatening to throw me overboard and leave me behind in the sea as you hightailed it back to dry land and the nearest helicopter.'

'That's quite a long chain of thought you had there.'

'You were asleep for quite a while. I had enough time to imagine several possibilities.'

'There was definitely a time that tossing you overboard would have seemed like the right thing to do.' But her words reminded her that that was almost exactly what she had done ten years before. And just like that the dam was lifted on the all the questions and all the curiosity about him she had hidden beneath layers and years of denial about him. About them. 'Can I ask…how did you get here? Your own yacht, a billion-euro wine industry… how did you make it happen?'

It hurt him, scratched at a wound that he had buried deep, that she had never thought to find out what had happened to him after that night. That she had so easily discarded him, even as he had at first stalked the internet to find any trace of news of her, as if knowing what she was doing would make the hurt and betrayal any less... or worse in some masochistic way. He pushed back his bitter thoughts and focused on her question.

'When I returned to my mother, she was already packing our belongings. Moritz, my mother's employer, was understanding, but his wife...not so much. She was furious that I had squandered the opportunity they had so generously provided and was determined that we should not bring further shame to their family name.' He still remembered the woman screeching at him and his mother from the top of the stairs, the way all the servants in the house had gathered to watch and the way, despite all this, his mother had placed her arms around him as if to protect him. He remembered the last look Moritz had cast him before they had left. One of pity, not shame, but full sadness and disappointment. He had never wanted to see such a look ever again.

'We returned to my mother's family because there was nowhere else to go. And it started up almost immediately. The snide comments, the years of resentment. My father's abandonment of his pregnant lover had consigned my mother to a life of shame. And the expulsion from school? Just compounded it.'

He couldn't look at Sofia as he told her this. He didn't want to see her expression, to see the truth of her feelings, so instead he looked out to the horizon as he steered the yacht to some indefinable destination.

'My mother had saved some money. Not a huge amount, but some. Enough to buy some land from her family. They were happy to get rid of it, and us, to the small home nestled in its boundary. The land was hard, dry and difficult and not one of them had ever been able to grow a thing on it. Their small winery was failing and, though they did not welcome her, they welcomed my mother's money, every last, single cent of it.' He couldn't help the bitterness in his tone. He hated them for what they had done to his mother. 'They could just as easily have given it to us because it had never made them any money and they hadn't used it for years, almost two generations. Which, ironically, is why it was much easier for me to work with it.

'For the first six months, I simply cleared the land. Each day, each night, bit by bit.' It was as if the mind-numbing work had been the only thing that had kept him going in those first few months where he'd been so raw it felt as if his very heart was exposed to the elements. The pain, the ache of her betrayal, the humiliation that he'd been taken in by her lies. But now, after all that had happened between them, he began to recognise something else in his feelings… the heartbreak that she had turned her back on him. That she had left him. The jagged, wrenching pain that had made it almost difficult to breathe at times.

'My mother would help.' But only when she was feeling up to it, he now recognised. 'I hadn't realised how much knowledge I'd garnered from working in my mother's family's fields. The soil was good, having been left fallow for so long. I worked to ensure decent irrigation systems were in place to not undo all the work already achieved.

'Nikos, my neighbour, would watch from the seat in front of his home. He and my mother would sometimes share a coffee, and occasionally he'd call out suggestions. Mostly he was calling me several shades of a fool for doing it, but,' Theo said with a smile, 'it just made me more determined.

'Once the land was cleared, the night before I was to

start planting Nikos called me over for dinner. Of course, his idea of food was three-day-old, tough-as-a-boot rabbit stew, but the *raki* was good. And so was a bottle of wine he produced from his cellar.

'He explained that it was his own wine, from a small variety of grape that had been growing on his land for generations. He'd never told my mother's family because in his opinion they were money-grabbing, pious *malakes*—his words—something we both agreed on. We stayed up until about three in the morning that night, drinking the few bottles of wine he'd produced. The problem with his grape was that, while it was hardy, it was also harsh. But it had potential. I think we must have talked about the characteristics of the grape, the barrel, the age, with more detail than scientists discussing genetic testing.

'So the next day, instead of planting pure *malagousia*, I took a risk. Half the land was the *malagousia*, and the other half was Nikos's grape. He didn't know the lineage of it, and his grandfather had probably forgotten the name of it. To Nikos, it was just wine. To me, it was the perfect grape to blend.

'The first two years were terrible.' He huffed out a reluctant laugh. It covered the sheer hours of the day he had spent outside, tending to those damn vines. But he wouldn't have changed it for anything. Those years were ones spent with his mother. Eating together, working together, laughing... Before it was nearly cruelly ripped away from him and he realised the true cost of the land.

Could he really lay the blame of his mother's illness at Sofia's feet? Could he hold to the anger that had driven him over the years and once again the moment she had refused to make a different decision? One that might have prevented his mother from ever having to experience such a devastating attack on her health?

In the silence that had settled between them he re-alised that the wind had picked up and set about secur-ing the lines, considering whether or not he needed to bring down the sail.

'Did you ever think about giving up?'

'Every single hour of every single day,' he replied.

'But you didn't.'

'I wouldn't be standing here today if I had.'

'Do you…?' She paused and it drew his gaze to her. 'Do you ever wonder,' she pressed on, 'what would have happened if I had stayed? If perhaps…we could have had the life we'd hoped for?'

Whether he blamed her for what happened to his mother or not, Sofia had still not learned the conse-quences of her actions. Or she would never have asked that damn question.

'Never,' he bit out.

Her sigh was stolen by the wind, and he stalked the length of the deck, hoping that she would leave the con-versation alone. But his hopes were in vain.

'I do. I thought I hadn't, but… I was just lying to my-self. I did. Especially in those first few months. I'd wake up expecting to see you beside me, expecting to find my reality a dream, and my dream a reality.' The wistfulness in her voice cut him deep and he tried to ignore it, espe-cially as she stood and made her way towards the side of the yacht. 'But perhaps,' she pressed on, 'it wouldn't have worked. It was a childhood fantasy. We couldn't have lived off dreams and desire. Reality would have always been waiting around the corner.'

'We would have made it work,' he said despite him-self, finally looking back at her to find her standing at the side of the yacht, looking out at the sea.

'Really? The princess and…'

'The pauper,' he replied.

'You were never a pauper to me.'

'You were *always* a princess to me.'

The wind cracked the sail, lines creaking and groaning under the sway of the boat. The boom started to move, and terror raced through his veins. He shouted a warning to Sofia, but it was too late—she didn't hear him and, facing the sea, was ignorant of the oncoming danger. As the large wooden boom swung round with speed and weight he launched himself towards her, but was too far away. Sofia turned just in time to raise her hands to take the brunt of the hit, but not enough to avoid it. It caught her across the shoulder and thrust her into the sea.

# CHAPTER EIGHT

THEO HATED HOSPITALS. He felt as if the sterile scent of them carried on the air entered his bloodstream and scratched at him from the inside out. He hadn't been back to this one since he had mortgaged his life to the hilt to fund his mother's operation, and he couldn't stop pacing, desperate to escape its walls, but unable to leave.

Lyssandros, the doctor who had become his personal physician of sorts, had kicked him out of Sofia's room for his assessment. Fear. It was a feral, living thing within him. Had he reached her in time? She hadn't been under the water more than five seconds before he'd dived in to reach her. He'd pulled her out, hauled her onto the deck and secured her as quickly as possible, before he dropped the sail and used the motor to get them back to land, breaking every maritime speed law around the world. A helicopter had met them at the marina, and staff had dealt with the vessel as he and Sofia were brought to the hospital.

He'd fought with Lyssandros not to leave her side, and even during the MRI scan he'd been in the small booth with the older man, ignoring the quiet discussions and assessments going on around him as he'd been unable to take his eyes from Sofia's small frame.

She'd been in and out of consciousness, babbling strange words that had scared him. She seemed to have been having an argument with someone about not wanting to leave. It had taken him a few rounds of the repeated conversation to realise that she wasn't imagining herself on the yacht with him, but at some long-ago point in time as she begged and pleaded to stay. He'd been able to do nothing but soothe and promise her that he wouldn't make her leave, but he doubted Sofia had heard him.

A sound at the door to her private room alerted him, and he spun round to find Lyssandros saying something to a nurse and dismissing her. Finally the older man turned to him.

'She is going to be okay.'

Breath whooshed out of Theo's lungs, and he pinched the bridge of his nose as if it were the only thing holding him together. *Dóxa to Theó.*

'She has a concussion, unsurprisingly, so I want to keep her in overnight at least. Given her…status, it's possible that her people might want to move her—'

'They don't know about it yet.'

'Theo,' the doctor admonished. 'She's a princess, so her people, family, even her country, will want to know about this.'

'I'm not keeping it from them, but she needed this time away and—'

'Okay. It's your call, but if I'm asked—I had no idea who she was, other than your fiancée.'

'That's very ethical of you.'

Lyssandros smiled ruefully, though there was a hint of something in the other man's eyes that made Theo pause.

'What's wrong? You said she was okay,' Theo practically growled.

'She is, Theo. She is,' he said, placing a large hand on Theo's shoulder. 'But…look, I really shouldn't be saying anything, and I wouldn't…but it did give me some concern. It wouldn't have been picked up in a normal assessment, but you asked for every test under the sun, and I did them.' Lyssandros led Theo a little further away from the nurses' station of the private wing Sofia had been brought to.

'I don't know what happened, only Sofia will be able to tell you that, but I've noticed a few injuries that would seem…unusual for a…for someone of her status.'

Theo frowned. 'Injuries? She usually has the reflexes of a cat.' Or at least she had done when they were at school. She had to have had, to get the headmaster's car on top of the sports hall. Except when she was distracted, as she had been on the yacht.

'It looks to have happened about a year, maybe a year and a half, ago, from the healing patterns, but around that time she took what must have been a pretty hard hit.'

'A hit from what?'

Lyssandros shrugged. 'She had a fractured ulna—' he gestured to his forearm '—and several broken ribs. I only mention it because it's uncommon for an adult to fracture only one of the two bones in the forearm, unless they are defending themselves.'

'Could she have done it horse riding?' Theo queried, unable to quite understand how else it could have happened.

'I would have expected more damage, or less, depending.'

'You think it was a person. You think she was attacked.'

The older man nodded. 'As I said, it's only because of her status that I ask.'

Theo clamped his jaw on a million unasked questions, able to voice only one. 'May I?'

'Of course,' Lyssandros said, directing him to the door to Sofia's room.

* * *

Sofia's throat felt as if someone had poured sand down it, and she was half convinced that someone was trying to prise her head open with a jackhammer. When the door opened she managed to force her eyelids up enough to take in a figure wearing blue scrubs, and promptly closed them again. If she never saw another doctor again, it would be too soon. She wanted to go. Where, she wasn't sure. She didn't want to be back in Iondorra yet, and she wondered why Theo hadn't arrived to whisk her away. Had he left her? Had he finally decided that even his wine sales weren't worth this much hassle? The thought rocked her. Is this what he'd felt that night? Tears began to gather behind her closed eyes, but she wouldn't cry. Not in front of some stranger.

'Sofia…'

Her eyes flew open to find Theo coming to sit on the edge of the bed.

'Theo? What are you doing in scrubs?'

The rueful smile on his perfect lips did nothing to hide the fierce concern in his gaze. 'Lyssandros, the doctor, told me that I was getting his medical centre wet, so forced me to change into these,' he said, pulling distastefully at the blue material.

'Why were you wet?'

'Do you not remember? You fell into the sea, and I went in after you.'

'You did?'

'How else would you have got out?'

Sofia sighed. 'I'm surprised you didn't leave me in there,' she grumbled, frustrated with herself for not being able to put the pieces of what had happened together in her own mind. The doctor—Lyssandros—had explained that it was to be expected, and, as long as the confusion was only around the accident, he wasn't too concerned. All her tests had come back fine mostly. A bang to the head from the fall, a decent bruise to her shoulder from where the boom had caught her, but aside from that she'd been lucky.

'I was tempted. But the Greek government might frown at the manslaughter of a princess.'

'It would have been murder if you'd intentionally left me.'

'I'd have got away with it.'

A smile pulled at the corners of her mouth, just as a wave of exhaustion descended. 'When can I get out of here?'

'Tomorrow.'

'I hate hospitals. Can you sneak me out?'

'Lyssandros is as close as a friend, but even he's not taking risks with you.'

*And neither am I.* She felt his words, without him voicing them.

'I want to go,' she said, the words slightly slurred.

'I know. But you're safe here. I'm not going anywhere.'

Sofia tried to shake her head, but that hurt, and whatever she'd been about to say disappeared as she fell into the welcoming arms of sleep.

When she next woke, Sofia was thankful that the light didn't hurt her eyes any more, and she experimentally moved her head from side to side, relishing the fact that the jackhammer seemed to have given up.

She turned to find Theo in the chair beside her, his long legs thrust out in front of him, his head resting awkwardly on his fisted hand, elbow on the arm of the chair, and even in sleep the man looked incredible.

Long, midnight-coloured eyelashes dusted his cheeks, his dark hair tousled as if he'd spent the entire night thrusting his hands through it, and his jawline was now in serious risk of growing a half-decent beard. She kind of liked the look on him. It made him even more…just more.

When a nurse entered, Sofia thrust a finger to her lips, unwilling to wake him. The small, dark-haired woman smiled conspiratorially and came to her side to check the little monitor assessing her vitals.

'How are you feeling?' she whispered.

'Like I was struck off a yacht by a boom.'

She huffed out a small laugh. 'You should be able to go soon. I'll have the doctor sign your discharge papers.'

'Thank you. I can speak to the Iondorran consulate and arrange for payment if—'

'No need. That's all been taken care of.'

At Sofia's frown, the nurse gestured to Theo, still asleep, and Sofia nodded and sighed. Not only had he rescued her from the sea, but also paid for her care. He was hardly getting his money's worth out of this, was he? A thread of sadness began to wind through her. Was that all there was between them or could there ever be more? she wondered. For years she had consigned thoughts and memories of him to a locked box in her heart. But now? She wasn't so sure any more.

It took them about an hour to get out of the hospital, partly because Sofia had wanted to thank everyone who had treated her. She made a mental note to ensure there was a donation to the hospital for their generosity and discretion. She couldn't express how relieved she was that there were no reporters camped out on the steps, that no international incident had been accidentally created. She wasn't naïve enough to think that it was out of respect for her, and could plainly see the adoration for Theo in the faces of most of the medical staff. He seemed to be on first-name terms with half of them, and it went beyond simple patronage, which confused her a little. Surely he had not worked up such strong bonds just in the time of her overnight stay there?

She waited on the steps to the hospital as a man brought round a large black Jeep and handed Theo the keys.

He ushered her into the passenger seat and went round to the driver's side, and got in.

'You're driving yourself?'

'Why? Did you want to?' he said with a laugh.

It stung. She couldn't help it. 'I can't.'

'When you're feeling better—'

'I can't drive,' she said angrily. It had been a small fight with her father, certainly not one of their greatest, but it had hurt just as much. Somehow it had become a larger symbol of all the things she wasn't allowed to do as a princess-in-waiting. But more than that, it had signified the true end to her freedom.

'I suppose you don't need to know how to drive,' Theo said as he pulled out of the hospital car park.

'No. I suppose I don't,' she replied bitterly, and almost growled when she saw Theo suppress a laugh. 'It's not funny.'

'I'm not laughing at you, Princess. It's just that you're cute when…when you're angry.'

'I'm not cute either,' and even she couldn't help but let loose a small laugh at the ridiculousness of her own sulk. This. This was what she had missed most about him. The ease. The ease and friendship that had turned into distrust and resentment the moment they had met again in Paris. 'Where are we going?' she asked to turn the wayward direction of her thoughts.

'Home. *My* home.'

Theo directed the car with the same ease with which he had directed the boat. He had always loved travel, movement, something that appeased the restlessness he'd always seemed to feel back in Greece. The freedom he felt at being in charge of his own destiny, especially having spent years at the whim of the elements and the vineyard. He couldn't imagine not being able to control that, and wondered whether that was what had made Sofia so bitter. Not being able to choose when and where and how she wanted to go.

He frowned as he remembered the thread of a conversation from the night in Monaco.

*'I have no choice in this whatsoever.'*

Casting an eye over to where Sofia slept, he felt unease stir in his chest. He hadn't given her a choice. Not really, no matter what he had said to her. Every single moment of that night in Paris, and then Monaco, had been carefully orchestrated to ensure Sofia's ultimate humiliation. But now? Was that still what he wanted?

He changed lanes and came off the motorway as they began to make their way through the Peloponnese countryside, travelling along the southern part almost to the border with Messinia.

Cypress and olive trees skirted the mountains in the distance, scarred with jagged lines of white stone and brown scrub, and through the open window the scent of home filled the Jeep. Large stretches of mottled green land were occasionally interrupted by red-roofed towns and he welcomed the sight of them. Arcadia might not be the typical tourist destination popular with travellers from across the world, as Athens and the islands were, but that just made it even more precious to him.

It had been hard hit in recent years, especially with so many of the younger generation leaving for America, or other parts of Europe, but its people were surviving, hard work and determination making the most of this place that could be made. He was pleased that his vineyard had grown to such an extent that he now employed almost half of the nearby town. The estate he and his mother had dreamed of building one day was now able to offer luxurious stays in the vineyard, wedding packages and tours, and the seven-course wine-tasting menu at the Michelin-starred restaurant enticed guests from all over the world.

He pulled off into the road that led towards the gated estate, slowing until the electronic security system at the side entrance recognised the car's plate, just as Sofia stirred from her sleep.

The gates opened and he guided the car down the long drive, the smooth turns allowing him to observe Sofia's eyes growing wide as she took in the large, sweeping vineyard to the left.

'This is…magnificent,' she sighed and he couldn't help the swell of pride he felt deep in his chest.

'This is only a quarter of the vineyard. There is more to the back of the estate.'

'Where is…?' She trailed off as they rounded the last bend and the building before them rose up to greet them. 'Oh.'

He took in the sight of it as if with her eyes—eyes that had never before seen the estate. The large central building was almost monastic in design, built from reclaimed grey stone, and had sweeping archways that his mother had loved from the first sight of it. It provided the entrance as well as the large dining restaurant and access to the front half of the wine cellars below, the area that was available for guest tours.

The more modern annex off to the left provided views both front and back from large windows on three floors for each of the guest suites, all of the twenty rooms lavishly designed with en suite bathrooms big enough to house the first home he and his mother had shared on the land. One that was still tucked away at the back of the large property.

'Theo, this is incredible,' Sofia said as he pulled up to the staff car park to the side of the building. He could tell from the number of vehicles in the guest parking area that they were at low capacity. He cast his mind over the appointments and remembered that the estate was winding down before a wedding booking in just two days' time.

She was out of the car before he was.

He watched her spin in a slow circle, taking in the view of the estate. 'Do you want to freshen up? There's—'

'No!' She turned, laughing. 'I want to *see*. I've been in bed for twelve hours or more, sleeping in the car for the last three, and now I want to move. Please? Show me?'

And he wondered when he'd ever really been able to deny her anything.

'I would love nothing more. But I intend to do it in something other than a pair of scrubs,' he said, pulling at the scratchy material of the blue top. 'It will still be there after a shower and a change of clothes. I promise.'

Sofia had been surprised by the sheer magnificence of Theo's vineyard. Oh, she'd known that he had made money from his business, clearly enough to gain entry to the society of the masquerade ball in Paris. As she cast her mind back she remembered his taunt about his billionaire status and couldn't help but marvel at what he'd achieved.

The marble flooring in the entrance to the main building was beautiful and shot with veins of dark green and black. She had watched, fascinated, as Theo had nodded to his employees on Reception, paused to ask after the father of one of the young girls manning the desk. It gave Sofia time to explore the room. She marvelled at the wooden bench that stretched the entire length of the room. On top were squares of slate, wedging wine bottles in between, with handwritten names and descriptions in italicised chalk. Beneath were large oak barrels that added a touch of authenticity as well as artistic integrity to the main hall.

When she turned she found Theo watching her, as if waiting for some kind of censure or disapproval. She sent him a reassuring smile, and he whisked her away to the private wing.

He had deposited her and her bag retrieved from the boat in a room most definitely fit for a princess. The large canopied bed had been an indulgence she had never personally given into, but loved the moment she set her eyes on it. Rustic luxury. She was surrounded by it.

The bathroom was something completely other. One entire wall was lined in antique mirrors, in front of which was a free-standing cast-iron bath. To the left was a large window that looked out on to a stretch of vineyard behind the property. She hung back slightly, wondering if she would be seen, but realised that from this height and distance only the birds would be able to spy her.

In the corner was a glass-fronted shower, large enough for two people...in her mind, two people that looked very much like her and Theo. A blush rose to her cheeks as her wayward imagination ran wild...a heady mixture of memory and fantasy, desire and need aching within her. When they had come together after the engagement party, anger and resentment had dominated despite her aching desperation to feel him. She wondered if that would be so now? If perhaps to make love to Theo would be different...

She turned the shower on and stripped off the clothes that clung to her aching body. She had said that she wanted to see the vineyard but knew that Theo had been right. She allowed the hot jets of water to ease the aches from the last few hours, gently washing her hair, careful of reawakening the dull ache from the fall into the sea. Scrubbing away the remnants of the salt water, she felt fresh, new and oddly happy.

Happy. She considered it. When had she last felt it? A small part of her was so sad that she couldn't remember when it had been. She padded into the bedroom wrapped in a towel and searched through the bag of clothes that had been packed for her by her assistant back in Iondorra.

Her fingers brushed something lacy, and with something like horror and fascination she produced a silk negligee fit for a honeymoon. Doubting very much that Theo had requested such a thing, she realised that her assistant had only packed what Sofia might have wanted for a last-minute getaway with her fiancé.

Because he *was* her fiancé. No matter how or why it had happened, it was the case. And she would be marrying him. But what would that marriage look like now? The start of their engagement had been all anger and vengeance, but somehow over the last few days that had changed, and it had morphed into something that she hardly dared to hope for.

Placing the negligee on the bed, she dug into the bag and produced a pair of tan high-waisted linen palazzo pants and a cream silk vest. With her hair still wet, she wound it into a knot and secured it high on her head.

She buckled a pair of brown leather low-wedge sandals at her ankles and, snagging the sunglasses on her way out, left her room and returned to the reception area, safe in the knowledge that Theo would find her there when he was ready.

When Theo found her, Sofia was leaning against the large domed archway, her slender hips shown to perfection by the trousers encasing her narrow waist, one ankle crossed over the leg bearing her weight, and the wind blowing the loosely tucked-in silk top. It was such a sight it gave him pause. Pause for what he was about to do, because he knew that he couldn't continue on his path of revenge without first finding out what had happened to cause the fracture of her arm and damage done to her ribs. Without finally getting to the truth of her. The fierce streak of protectiveness that leapt to life in his chest at the mere thought of it shocked him with its intensity.

As if she sensed his presence, she turned, her face cast in a shaft of soft sunlight peering through the shadows of the cool reception, and her smile caught him low in his chest. He stalked towards her, fighting with his desire to haul her into his arms and kiss her. Kiss her in a way he hadn't since he was seventeen. Kiss her in the way he should have that night in Iondorra.

Shame filled him as he thought of how they had come together that night. As if they were combatants on a battlefield, rather than lovers on a bed of silk sheets and roses. As he reached her, she turned her face towards him as if waiting for that same kiss. But instead of doing what he so desperately wanted to do, of taking what he so desperately needed, he offered his arm and escorted her away from the reception and away from his wayward thoughts.

Theo was thankful that she made easy small talk as they walked towards the rows of vines that made up the vineyard. Questions of what types of grape, how long they took to grow, when he had first known that he wanted to develop wine… All things he had answered a million times and knew by heart. And, if she noticed that he was distracted, she was restrained enough not to mention it.

Finally, as they drew to the furthest point from the estate, he turned to her.

'What is it?' Sofia asked. 'You've had something on your mind for a while. Ask.'

As if it were that simple. As if she would not deny him anything.

'At the hospital, I asked Lyssandros to run every possible test he could think of. The thought…the possibility that you were hurt—'

'I'm fine, Theo. Truly. Look,' she said, shaking her head from side to side in a way that made him wince, even without the possibility of concussion. She laughed. The sound should have soothed him, but it didn't.

'Lyssandros is a very professional man, but he also has a huge heart. He was concerned by… He saw there were fractures, from a previous injury. Did someone hurt you?' he asked, his voice drawn and gravelly to his own ears. Watching her closely, he saw the way she paled, the way her cheeks lost their rosy glow, her eyes filled with shadows and she made to turn away. Before she could, his hand snuck out and gently grasped her chin, guiding it back to him, snaring her gaze with his.

'Please. Don't hide from me in this. I need to know.'

She pulled a breath into her lungs, but it seemed to get caught there, the slight stutter in her breathing enough to tell him that he really did need to know. As if unable to bear the weight of his gaze, she cut her eyes to the ground.

'Sofia, whatever it is…whoever it was… If it was your husband—'

'No!' she cried, cutting him off mid-sentence. 'No,' she said again, more gently, more softly. 'Antoine never raised a hand to me. Ever.' He watched her pause and take another deep breath. 'My father isn't well.'

It was not what he'd expected her to say, but he silenced his inner thoughts and allowed her to continue.

'He hasn't been for…some time. I…we, the palace, have been sworn to secrecy, for fear of it destabilising the future of Iondorra.'

'What is wrong with him?'

'He was diagnosed with early onset dementia.'

She started to move away from him then and in the space between them his suspicions began to grow, like roots from somewhere deep within him, reaching towards the light, towards the truth.

'When?'

'When what?'

'Don't play games with me, Sofia—when was he diagnosed?'

'Just before I was taken out of boarding school.'

A curse fell from his lips as he stared to rearrange the past to fit with what she was now telling him.

'The night that I was supposed to meet you, he and my mother came. At first, I thought they'd found out somehow. About you, about the pranks… But it was worse than that. They explained what the diagnosis meant, that in time he would begin to lose more and more of his memory, of himself. I couldn't see it. This man, this powerful, loving, larger-than-life ruler of an entire country…it wasn't possible. Or at least that is what I thought at the time.

'He was only fifty. There should have been years before I needed to assume the royal responsibilities I was so ready to reject. But there was no one else. I was going to have to wear the crown, I was going to have to learn to be the ruler of Iondorra, and I couldn't do that to you.'

'*To* me, or with me?' he demanded.

'Neither,' she said, shaking her head helplessly. 'We were children, Theo. You…you had your whole life ahead of you, to do what you wanted to do, to be who you wanted to be. And who you are now is incredible,' she said, her eyes large and bright in her eyes.

Theo shook his head against her words, against the thought that she had been right. All this time he'd blamed her, hated her…

'Why didn't you tell me this?' he demanded, pain and anger making his words harsh on the soft summer breeze.

'I couldn't. Don't you see? No one could know of my father's diagnosis. The risk to the country, to its finances and its people…it was just too great. So I was taken back to Iondorra, and spent the next few years cramming in as much of the knowledge of a would-be ruler in the shortest amount of time possible.

'It's not like in the movies, where a simple makeover is enough. My wayward recklessness needed to be ironed out of me at every turn. It took years learning the rules, etiquette, languages, diplomacy needed to ensure the success of the throne. All the while keeping this secret. One that ate away at me each day.

'Could you imagine what the world's press would do with a sniff of hereditary early-onset dementia in the Iondorran royal family? They are tough enough on debauchery, let alone something as devastating as a genetic disease.'

'You have been tested.' It was a statement rather than a question.

'Yes. I don't have it. The gene. Not that it means I

won't develop the same condition, but the chances are significantly less.'

'So the injuries you sustained…'

She looked up at him then, her eyes matching the blue depths of the sky, large enough for him to see the sorrow, the pain and the frustration.

'My father had a bad turn. He…we'd been managing his condition fairly well up until that point. But that night, he was…not the man I knew. He had been restless and demanded to see me. He wanted to know how I was managing a negotiation with the Hungarian consulate, but… that had been months before. The negotiation done and dusted. Only…he didn't seem to remember that. He became frustrated and angry, furious even. I tried to calm him, but he saw it somehow as an attack, and he…he was just defending himself,' she tried to explain. 'The horror in his eyes, the moment he realised what he'd done…the guilt, shame…all of it was—' she paused as if searching for the right words '—so awful.'

Theo tried to shake his thoughts into clarity, as if they were flakes within a snow globe, hoping that they'd settle into some kind of sense. But no matter how they ebbed and flowed, all he could think of was that he believed her. That he could see the pain and hardship she'd been through. But, worse than that, he'd begun to feel as if his anger and hatred towards her for what happened to him and his mother was masking something else. He felt as if he'd been hit by an avalanche of guilt and it was covering everything.

A huge, fat, tear-shaped raindrop thudded on the ground beside his feet. Then another, and another. In just seconds, the heavens had opened as if they were crying for them, for him, for a pain he couldn't yet express.

Sofia looked up at him, seemingly heedless of the

rain pouring down on her, and reached her hand to his hard jaw.

'I'm so sorry. I'm so, so sorry,' she said, her voice barely a whisper amongst the pounding of the rain on the earth beneath them.

And in that instant, he honestly didn't want to hear anything more. No words, no explanations, no apologies. He reached for her as his lips seized her with the same ferocity as that of the storm, drew her towards him as if she were the breath he needed to exist.

His tongue delved between soft, sweet lips and it wasn't enough. He wanted it all. Desire drenched him as surely as the rain as he felt her body mould against his own, the firm jut of her breasts against his chest, and he pulled her even closer, his thumb tracing down her slender neck to her ribcage, snagging on her hip and anchoring her to him.

She gave him everything he demanded, gave herself completely over to him, until she began to tremble, and in turn he finally felt the stinging cold of the summer storm. He broke the kiss, glancing towards the main building, which was too far away. He grasped her hand.

'Come with me,' he said, asked, possibly even pleaded in that moment, as he took them towards the summer house nestled on the boundary of the vineyard.

# CHAPTER NINE

SOFIA COULDN'T STOP SHAKING, even as she took a second step and a third into the small beautiful wooden summer house. She knew it wasn't just because of the rain. She had never told anyone about her father. No one outside her mother, or her father's carers. She had put her trust in Theo. And it had been terrifying, but she wouldn't take it back. Not for a second.

She had seen him war with the truth of her words, with what it had meant for them all those years ago, and possibly even what it meant for them now. But she didn't want to think about her father, or Iondorra. No. Now she wanted to lose herself, or find herself, she couldn't say.

She turned to see Theo standing in the glass-fronted doorway, the fierce sky pouring rain down on the vineyard, casting everything else in dull grey, but Theo in full, bright glory. He looked like an avenging angel, dark hair even blacker than the night, his clothes drenched and clinging to the dips and hollows of his body as if he were a thing to be worshipped.

As he stalked towards her she fought the instinct to step back. She wouldn't hide from this any more, hide from her desire, she was now focused on him completely, the one man, the *only* man she'd ever wanted. The only man who had seen her for who she truly was, before duty had moulded her into something new. Something other.

They reached for each other at the same time, colliding in need and passion and want. She felt the beat of her heart leap as his lips crashed against hers, as his hands cradled her head, angling her in a position that felt as much like surrender as it did defiance. He thrust his tongue into her mouth, filling her, consuming her, and she needed it. It was too much. She felt like laughing, like crying, as if she simply didn't know which way was up or down any more, all she knew was him.

Her hands flew to his shoulders, large, solid, bigger than the breadth of her hands. Her nails dug into the thin, wet material covering his body and she wanted to feel skin, needed to. Her hands went to the buttons of his shirt, but the tremors shaking her body made her actions too slow.

He released his hold on her, and she swayed from the loss, the support, the anchor of his body. She watched as he tore apart his shirt, buttons flying and scattering on the wooden floor, marvelling at the smooth planes of his chest, the soft whorls of damp hair clinging to a deeply tanned torso. As he reached for her she gazed, fascinated by the cords of muscles rippling from the movement, and reached out a hand tentatively. She wanted to touch, needed to, but...

He swept up her hand in his and placed it on his chest, on his heart, and looked at her with such intensity she could hardly bear the weight of it. She felt the beat of his heart, powerful, strong and fast, raging in time with her own. His skin was hot beneath her cool palms and she shuddered, wanting to feel that heat wrapped around her, fill her, warm the places of her that had been left cold the moment she left him standing at the boarding school all those years ago.

It was then that she knew what it felt like to be in the eye of the storm—the moment of shocking quiet stillness while chaos raged around them. The moment that life as she knew it would change. She knew that he was giving her this. This moment to walk away. To stop. But she couldn't, wouldn't.

She reached for him then, raising to her tiptoes to reach that proud, utterly sensual mouth of his, desperate to feel it against her own. Her hands explored his rain-slicked skin, delighting in the feel of his strength, his power. His hands cupped her backside and he lifted her off her feet, her legs wrapping round his lean waist as if they'd always been meant to be there.

He backed up and sat them down on the large summer lounger, her knees anchoring against his hips, as he pulled at her silk top, freeing it from the waistband of her trousers, pulling it over her head and tossing it aside, snagging on the pins that held her hair in place and pulling it free as her long blonde hair hung down in thick, wet ropes about her shoulders. He stopped then and stared.

'You are so beautiful,' he said, placing open-mouthed kisses along her neck as she shivered under the feel of his tongue on her skin. His hands cupped her breasts, his thumbs brushing her nipples, stiff with pleasure, and Sofia's head fell back, relishing the feel of him, of what he was doing to her body, as he honoured her with his touch.

She gasped when he took her nipple into his mouth and sucked, teasing her with his tongue, his arm around her waist holding her in place against the onslaught of desire that threatened to overwhelm her.

Unconsciously she rocked against his lap, the hard ridge of his arousal at her core making her slick with need as much as the groan that fell from Theo's lips.

'You're killing me here,' he said, the words half huffed out on a laugh.

He pulled back, looking at her, his gaze taking its fill of her. He reached behind her, and began to unbuckle her sandals, first one, then the other. He took her foot in one hand and firmly pressed the entire length of the arch of each foot, sending delight and pleasure through her. He caressed her ankles beneath the wet linen of her trousers, encased her calf in powerful, calloused hands, rough against smooth, sensations overwhelming her. She moaned out loud and he cursed, wrapping one strong arm around her as he twisted them in an embrace and turned her back to the seat.

Her fingers fought against his to undo the button of her trousers, and, once done, he peeled them from her, slowly, languorously as if enjoying the unveiling as much as anything else. She couldn't find the words to describe him. He was glorious. Shirtless, his chest was magnificent, and she watched with the same delight as he kicked off his shoes and removed his trousers without taking his eyes from hers once. She almost shook her head against the impossibility of seeing him standing there naked, proud, and every inch her fantasy. She began to tremble again, not with cold, not from the elements, but from the sheer virility that was Theo, the magnetism, just him.

Theo stood naked before the most beautiful woman he'd ever seen. There she was, laid out before him like the last meal he'd ever taste, and he hovered on the brink of something indefinable, as if he didn't know where to start.

He wrapped a hand around her ankle and gently pulled

her so that she almost lay flat. He lifted her foot, pressed kisses against the delicate arch, the inside of her ankle, he made his way slowly, languorously along her calf, spreading her slightly to allow the space for his own body, as he trailed open-mouthed kisses over her thigh and upwards to the hollow at her hip. Her body quivered beneath his lips, and he dusted the gentle swell of her stomach with his tongue. He kissed over her ribcage, and bit back a smile as she twisted and bucked as if as overwrought by the pleasure they built between them as he was. He kissed between her perfect breasts as he moulded them with his hands, each kiss driving him closer to the brink of need and desperation. This wasn't the angry coupling from the other night, this was honour, and respect, and desire building pathways to his heart that he'd never imagined.

He wanted to give her the greatest pleasure, as if he could make up for the ills he had thought her guilty of, the ills he had almost wreaked upon her. Because he realised now that he could not go through with his plan… he could no longer leave her at the altar humiliated and abandoned. Because beneath the ache and sting of what he had felt for Sofia was something deeper, darker and something he did not yet want to face.

She reached for him, as if pulling him back to the present, pulling him back to her, and he was more than willing to take the comfort she offered, even as he realised that it should have been the other way round. After what she had told him, it should be him soothing her hurts.

Leaning on his forearm, he looked down at her, the damp golden ropes of her hair framing her face, the exquisite perfection of it, and the way her head cocked to one side elongated her neck made him yearn to devour her there, the pulse point, the connection to life, the flutter there speaking of her need for him.

Wide, round, azure-blue eyes stared up at him in complete trust, and part of him wanted to shy away from that gaze, from the hope and innocence within it. Instead he followed the trail of his hands with his eyes as his fingers traced the outline of her ribcage, the pad of his thumb dipping into the hollow at her hip, his hand delving beneath her, curving around her backside to pull her against him, their centres flush, their cores both throbbing with need, and he released her only to sweep his hand low across the gentle swell of her abdomen and between her legs to find the place that drove her wild with ecstasy.

His thumb caressed and played with her clitoris, the sounds of her need rising higher than the pounding of the rain against the wooden roof of the gazebo, ringing vibrations over his skin through to his very soul. This time he would not tease her, keeping her at the brink of an orgasm. No, he would drench her in as much pleasure as she could take, and then more.

He thrust into her with his fingers, feeling the walls of her body clench around them, again and again, all the while his body aching with need, an ache he felt he deserved to bear even though it was Sofia that cried out, Sofia's body that trembled beneath him, incomprehensible words begging and pleading falling from her perfect lips. He wanted to kiss them, to consume them with his own mouth, but he couldn't, wouldn't, stop watching how beautiful she was when she came apart in his arms.

It wasn't enough, not nearly enough. Sofia's body, still vibrating with the power of the orgasm Theo had pulled from her very soul, still wanted more. It wanted him and wouldn't be denied. Her hands reached for him, drawing him down upon her, and finally, as if they were puzzle pieces fitting together, she felt some kind of completion as he placed the tip of himself at her core, and as he thrust into her deeply she felt stripped bare, vulnerable and powerful at the same time, as if she had stolen something from him to bolster her own sense of self.

The thickness of him filled her completely, the smooth hardness within her she was afraid she was already addicted to. He reached beneath her, bringing their bodies to a place where he could drive into her with more power, more delicious friction, just more... And she gasped, the air almost lodging in her throat, her heart as they became joined at the deepest, closest part of themselves. Was this what she had turned away from all those years ago? This impossible to describe sense of rightness, sense of wholeness? It was the last thought she had as he drove her closer and closer to a second orgasm—and with no need for silence or discretion, with no need for secrecy she cried out her release into his mouth as his lips came down on hers with the same desperation, the same craving that she could no longer resist.

Walking back through the vineyards as the sun hung low in the sky, slashes of pink against the cornflower-blue creating a stunning sight, Sofia wondered at the warmth and safety she felt as Theo wound his arm around her waist, holding her to his side. Their clothes still damp from the rain storm that had caught them by surprise, she almost welcomed the rough feeling, knowing what pleasures it had led to. She knew that they would have to return to Iondorra tomorrow for the charity gala, which—even though only a week before their wedding—she wouldn't have cancelled for the world. Her role as patron for Gardes des Enfants d'Iondorra—a charity that supported child carers—had given her the first glimpse she'd had that her royal status could be a positive thing—

could help and support something both wider and yet smaller and more immediate than anything her 'duties' could effect.

But for the first time she was torn. Torn between her duty and wanting to stay here in this magical bubble where the outside world didn't exist and where she and Theo were finally feeling as one, feeling right, as if this was how it should have been all along.

She laughed out loud, then, when she felt the gentle vibrations at her side from the phone in Theo's pocket—both at the feeling, and the contradiction of her thoughts of it just being the two of them cut off from the rest of the world. But when Theo joined in her breath caught—she had forgotten what he had looked like when he smiled, when they laughed together, and the sight was...incredible, full of hope for the future and the pull of nostalgia from the past.

*'Nai?'* he said, still laughing as he answered the phone.

Trying not to feel a little stab of hurt when he pulled away from her to speak into his phone, she forced herself to tune out the conversation and turned her mind to tomorrow...to the future. With him? Married to Theo Tersi? After all that had happened to them years ago, and since?

Unconsciously she had walked forward, tracing her steps back towards the stunning hotel hidden amongst the rows and rows of grapevines that stretched as far as she could see. The little narrow lanes created between them were barely enough for one person to step along.

She felt Theo behind her, the heat of him, the awareness...

'That was my mother,' he announced, disconnecting the phone.

'Oh?' She'd hoped her word sounded nonchalant rather than...what, worried? Intrigued? How much did his mother know about what had happened between them? What on earth must she think of her?

'She has invited us for dinner this evening. If that's okay?'

Sofia pulled every one of her concerns beneath the well-worn mask she used almost daily for her royal duties. 'Of course that's okay. I would love to meet her,' she said genuinely, all the while hoping that Theo's mother didn't hate her quite as much as she hated herself for what she had done to Theo all those years ago.

Theo had never, ever introduced his mother to anyone he had been intimately involved with. He knew that she refused to read the articles written about him in the last two years, and only now did he realise how ashamed he felt of them. Ten years ago, he had intended to bring Sofia to his mother and...what? It was only now that he was beginning to realise that what Sofia had said on the boat was true. That what they had shared at school had been the stuff of fantasies and impossible dreams. Had she perhaps not been a princess it might have been different, but even then, Theo wasn't quite sure.

He almost laughed, bitterly, at the thinly fabricated future they had concocted in their minds. Even had she not been a princess, even with the scholarships, the reality was that he would have had to take one, maybe two jobs to pay for living expenses. He would have struggled just as much as he had in reality, but with her by his side. He would have spent hours, days away from her, and possibly in the end either resented that he wouldn't have been able to provide the life he had wanted for her, or, worse, her. And she? Would have been ruined by the hard life he would have taken them to. And he couldn't shake this feeling that perhaps what had happened was how it had been meant to be. That the very reason he'd been able to achieve such impossible success was the drive and determination that had fuelled him all these years. These thoughts struck a cruel blow as they reached the door to the small house on the border of his land.

He'd tried so many times to entice his mother to a grander home, an easier home perhaps on one floor, with cleaners, and staff even, but she had refused, loving the little home that they had first shared when he'd initially bought this land.

Before he could even raise his hand to the door, it swung open and he was instantly enveloped by his mother's small frame and a stream of adoring, loving Greek spoken so quickly, even he only picked up on half the words. Within seconds both he and Sofia were being practically dragged over the threshold, straight into the small kitchen full of smells that instantly made his mouth water, and heart lurch with memories of the past.

He looked at Sofia standing in his mother's kitchen—a smile one of her biggest and brightest as she stood there in a pretty summer's dress. She had told him, every inch the royal, that she refused to meet his mother in wet clothes, and they had returned to the rooms in the hotel to shower and change before coming here. But now—with no trace of any etiquette, no royal greeting on his mother's behalf, simply welcomed through the door and into the kitchen, Sofia seemed happier than she had in all the days he'd spent with her.

Aggeliki was tactile, even for a Greek mother, and he marvelled at how Sofia—usually protected by a dozen bodyguards from anything even close to physical contact—was taking all the touching and hugging. His mother was asking her about how she liked the vineyard, and he was about to translate, when Sofia, along with a surprising amount of gesturing, managed to explain that she liked it very much. In Greek. When had she learned Greek? he wondered. She was doing fairly well, but every now and then had to defer to him for the translation of a few words, and after he'd warned his mother to slow down they seemed to be able to understand much of what was said between them. Their evening became a strange mix of Greek, English and the occasional French, when even English wouldn't do.

They sat outside at a wooden table beneath a pergola almost buckling under the weight of the stunning bougainvillea they had planted when they had first bought the land. Aggeliki had lit citronella candles the moment she had seen Sofia's pale skin, knowing that the mosquitos would love nothing more than to feast on the perfect blood in her veins, and the lemony scent hung in the warm night air as they feasted on the numerous dishes Theo's mother had produced.

He watched his mother and Sofia, heads bent together almost conspiratorially, and realised that he could not go through with his plan for revenge. He had told Aggeliki that he was to be married, but had refused to sink so low in his mother's expectations as to admit the truth behind his actions. He couldn't help but feel a sense of rightness as he watched the two women together, forging a relationship in the way he'd once imagined ten years ago.

He hadn't missed the way that Sofia had been nervous about meeting his mother, but hadn't managed to reassure her that she didn't have to worry, that he'd never revealed the source of his shame. Because he'd been so consumed by the way the blame he'd laid at her feet—which had once been on such on solid ground—was now shifting.

Sofia sat back in her chair, more full of food than she

could ever remember being in her entire life. She had tried to help Theo's mother take the plates away, but she had shooed her with hand gestures, firmly keeping her in the seat, and Sofia had reluctantly stifled her manners.

For just a moment it was her and Theo, his brooding gaze on her, glimmering in the darkness—the thin shadows cast by the little citronella candles enough to create warmth but not quite illumination. Not that she needed it. She knew every millimetre of his face, his features etched in her heart for ever ten years before—she'd only had to let herself remember them. For one moment, barely the space of a heartbeat, there was peace between them. Peace and something she'd dare not put a name to. Because if she lost it again, she didn't think she'd survive.

Aggeliki returned to the table with even more food, this time the scent of sweetness hitting Sofia hard and making her mouth water.

She laughed, 'What is all this?'

'This is dessert!' Theo's mother proudly claimed as she put down the tray covered with enough sweet treats to feed an army. She also noticed on the tray a small plate with a number of pills and frowned as she watched Aggeliki take them with a mouthful of water in between each one. She raised a brow at Theo, who had yet to take his eyes from his mother, now swallowing down the last one, but Aggeliki must have caught the look.

'It's okay,' she said, rubbing warmth into Sofia's cold hand. 'It's nothing. I am fine,' she said with smiling reassurance, but it did nothing to ease the concern building in Sofia's chest.

'My mother…she had a heart attack and was treated and is now—as she says—better than ever.' Sofia didn't call him on the brief pause that spoke of his own concern, instead focusing on what she needed to know.

'When?'

Theo shrugged and shook his head. But she wouldn't let it go that easily.

'When did it happen?' she asked, purposefully gentling her tone.

'Five years ago,' he said, refusing to meet her gaze.

Something cold and hard twisted in her chest and ached for him, for his mother, for her own selfish actions. From what he had told her earlier in the vineyard, he'd barely won his first vintner's award. He may have had some success at that point, and she didn't know much about the Greek healthcare system, but knew enough. Enough that meant it would have nearly crippled them financially, especially with a fledgling business underway, not to mention the hard work and struggle that it must have taken to be torn between a sick parent and full-time duty. Yes. She knew enough about that to know what it must have cost him.

She searched her mind for the words that would explain how she felt, how truly sorry she was, but they wouldn't come. They didn't have to. Finally Theo met her gaze and she knew that what he saw in her eyes was enough. He nodded, as if he'd understood, all the while his mother explaining the different types of dessert she wanted Sofia to try. And, as full as she was, Sofia would take a bit of each and every one of them.

This time, when it came to clearing the table, she ignored Aggeliki and helped the woman back into the small kitchen with the empty plates and coffee cups from the end of their meal. She liked this small room, how homely it felt, how easy it was just to prepare a meal and eat—rather than the impersonal feeling of a meal served to her each and every night, alone in a dining room big enough to seat twenty. Usually she brought her

laptop, immersed herself in work to avoid the stark realisation that she was alone, that her mother and father
had retreated to another estate far away from the palace.
There was no laughter, as there had been this night, no
gentle teasing or recounting of family stories, or praise
of Theo's successes...and it hurt in a way she had never
allowed herself to feel before.

As she glanced around the beautiful little kitchen, her
eyes caught on an old black and white photo of Aggeliki
and a man standing beside each other, with easy smiles
and laughter in their eyes.

'Oh,' she gasped, moving towards it. 'This is such a
beautiful picture of you, Aggeliki. Is this Theo's father?'

It was as if the temperature in the room had dropped.

'No. It is Nikos. We don't speak of my father. Ever.'

The words were in English, and even though she didn't
think Aggeliki had translated them in her mind, Theo's
reaction couldn't have been more clear. Especially when
he retrieved his phone and left the kitchen.

She felt Aggeliki rub her arm softly and smile.

'It wasn't you,' she said in Greek. 'He doesn't...' She
shook her head sadly, as if trying to find the words. 'He
never got over it. The way his father left. I tried...to give
him everything, to be everything for him. But,' she said
with a shrug of her shoulder, 'he is a man. A man needs
a father. For a while in Switzerland...' Sofia didn't need
Aggeliki to fill in the gap—clearly her boss, the man
who had paid for Theo's education, had been a father
figure to him. 'But look at him now,' she said, calling
Sofia back to the present, to look at him through the window. 'And look at what you both have. It is a joy to me,
Sofia. *Efcharistó.*'

For the first time since they had arrived, Sofia began
to wish that she hadn't come. That she hadn't seen the

pain and the struggle that Theo had been through since he had been expelled from the boarding school. Because finally Theo had got his wish. She was learning about the consequences of her actions.

# CHAPTER TEN

SOFIA LEANED BACK in the plush cream leather seats of
Theo's private jet, hating the way that her stomach dipped
and swayed with the plane. The single air stewardess
made her way down the short aisle on very long legs and
retrieved the empty glasses and plates from the table between her and Theo.

'*Efcharistó,*' she said, forcing a smile she didn't feel
for the woman.

'You didn't tell me you could speak Greek,' he said,
the curve of his lips a rueful smile.

'You didn't tell me that your mother had had a heart attack,' she replied, shocking them both. She hadn't meant
to say the words. Hadn't meant to bring up the subject
she had hardly forgotten for a moment from the night before. Hadn't meant for the smile on his lips to die away.

'No. I didn't.'

Several times, Sofia tried to let loose the words that
clogged her throat and failed. But she couldn't leave it at
that. She had to know.

'Is that…was that one of the consequences you felt I
needed to learn?'

He studied her, half-lidded eyes masking a whole host
of emotions she desperately wanted to see the truth of.

'It was not your fault.'

'That is not what I asked.'

'I don't hold you responsible for what happened to my mother, Sofia.'

'But *did* you?'

The silence that fell between them was enough of an answer that she thought he would not speak of it again. Instead, she turned to look out of the small round window as the sprawling emerald-green stretches of Iondorran land came into view. Her country. Her home. The decisions she'd made to protect them now illuminated under the cost of her actions.

'Neither of us has had it easy, Sofia. The decisions we felt forced to make, each for other people. But this?' he said, the gesture between them drawing her gaze back to his. 'You and me? Our marriage? This is a decision that we make now, for ourselves,' he said. And she wondered at the vehemence in his tone, wondered who he might have been trying to convince…her or himself. 'It is one that I want very much,' he added, and his words soothed some of the ache that had taken up residence in her heart as he reached for her hand and drew the cool skin against the warmth of his palm.

She felt the rough calluses on his skin, marvelled at the texture as they spoke more of the hard work Theo had done than he admitted to. She knew that the fact he no longer resented her for the past should be enough, but despite the admittance she could feel a hurt emanating from him. A deeper, harder one than before.

'Do you remember my first prank? Do you remember what caused it?'

'I didn't think you needed a cause, Sofia, I thought you enjoyed playing Puck.'

'You thought me *"shrewd and knavish"*?'

'I thought you many things back then, Sofia. But yes,

your first prank—on Benjamin Reneux, I remember. It was the first time that I saw you. Holding back tears of laughter as he howled in horror when he opened the door to his locker to find everything covered in honey—his blazer, his books, his homework. You looked at me, and all I could see was you. You shone, in the dim corridor beside the Great Hall.'

Sofia nodded. 'It was not the first time I had seen you though.' She smiled, a sad smile. 'I had seen how the others treated you. How *Benjamin* treated you. The names he called you, the way even the teachers expected you to cause trouble, to be the first to throw a punch—'

'Well, I usually was the first to throw a punch...'

'No. You always threw the *second* one. I watched. I saw.'

Theo looked away as if no longer wanting to take this trip down memory lane. Unconsciously he rubbed his chest, seemingly trying to soothe an age-old ache.

'I hated it. The way they behaved towards you.'

'It was hardly less than what I had already experienced at the hands of my cousins, or...'

'Or the people who should have cared for you most.'

'Sofia, I don't want—'

'Did you ever look for your father?'

This time her name was growled on his lips like a warning.

'Do you know why he left?'

'He left because he was weak, because he was a coward who ran away from his responsibilities.'

'You were not just a responsibility.'

'What do you want me to say? That it hurt to know that my father never wanted me? That he ruined my mother and her happiness? That I swore never to be like him, only to grow into a young man who caused her more pain?'

'Is that what you think? That you caused your mother pain? That is not—'

'You know nothing of this. And I will not speak of it again.'

The gala was being held at La Sereine, a Michelin-starred hotel sitting on the edge of Lac du Peridot. As Theo leaned against the balcony looking out at the stunning sight, he tried with all his might to focus on the two large mountains in the distance meeting just at the horizon of the stunning lake, a vista of every shade of green stretching out before it. Further upstream, he'd been told, was a small town nestled around the top of a giant waterfall, feeding the river that wound its way through Iondorra to Callier.

But despite all this glory, all he could see, all he could hear were the faces and taunts of his past. He'd been shocked by Sofia's revelation—that the pranks he had so loved about her once, and then vehemently hated, had been started in retaliation against the behaviour he had received. That, all the while he'd thought to be the one who'd noticed her first, she had been there, watching him without his knowledge, and had seen him without being seen.

Somehow he felt both stunned and cheated. Cheated as if suddenly Sofia was reframing everything he thought he knew.

*'Did you ever look for your father? Do you know why he left?'*

He hadn't been able to answer her. Because yes, he did know why his father had left. His cousins had enjoyed taunting him with it. Older by several years, they had relished and recounted with venomous glee the story of the words he had hurled at his mother.

The story that his father had run from his mother, from the village, the same night he had been born. That he had refused to be weighed down by a child. His cousins had called him *bástardos*—bastard—for almost his entire childhood. And every time his mother had been shunned, every time his mother had been tutted at, or stared at, in the village, he knew he was the cause of it. And then later, when he had been expelled, Theo had felt as if it was happening all over again. That he had thrust shame upon his loving mother who had tried so desperately to compensate for the absence of his father, for the lack of security in their lives. So he had done everything he could, since then, to make sure that she would never feel shame or want again.

A knock sounded against the door to the suites he'd been given within the hotel, pulling him from his thoughts. A knock that sounded more like the nail on a lid that he was banging down against the memories of his father, of his childhood.

He had just walked back inside from the balcony, when he let out a bark of surprised laughter, put down the glass of whisky and greeted his friend in a warm hug.

'Sebastian! What are you doing here, my friend?' he asked.

Sebastian's grin matched his own as he explained that Sofia had arranged for him and his sister, Maria, to be in attendance for this evening's gala and for them to stay in Iondorra with Theo until the wedding. Theo poured them both drinks and, before settling down into the luxurious sofa, Theo couldn't resist one more hug. He had needed this. Had Sofia known he would? Was that why she had gathered up his closest friend and brought Seb to him?

'What is this? You getting soft on me? All this talk of romance—'

Theo laughed again, shoving at Seb before sitting down.

'Do not fear. My tastes have never run in your direction.'

'Fear? I am perfectly happy with my masculinity to appreciate another's attraction to me, no matter who it comes from. I just happen to prefer the female form.'

Theo quirked an eyebrow. 'Anyone in particular?'

'God, no. There is only one thing that would ever tempt me into the state of holy matrimony.'

'Money?'

'Amnesia.'

'I'm sure there are many women out there who would willingly oblige a good bludgeoning to ensure such a thing.'

'True. Perhaps I should start wearing a helmet.'

'A bicycle helmet?'

'Well, I was thinking something more dramatic like a knight's armour, but I suppose your suggestion would do just as well and be a hell of a lot easier to get my hands on. How have you been?' Sebastian demanded, an assessing gaze raking over Theo's features. 'You look... different.'

Theo shook off the question with a shake of his head. Sebastian was almost as close to him as his own mother, but he was not ready to open the can of worms that he'd been brooding on. Though he knew he could do with his friend's counsel. 'Honestly? I'm not so sure. Things are... different to what I had thought them to be. Sofia had her own reasons for doing what she did that night, and I... I think I understand them now.' And as he spoke the words he realised the truth of them. Theo refused to betray her confidence, even to Sebastian. But he did understand her choices, did believe her when she had said that she was sorry, and fully believed that she really did understand the consequences of her actions. And he couldn't shake the feeling that perhaps it was those very choices that had brought them to this point. This moment, where he finally had everything he'd ever wanted within his grasp.

But throughout it all was this rising sense of guilt. Guilt at what he would have done to her. Guilt for having preached all this time about the consequences of actions, when he had given little thought to anything of the consequences of his revenge. A guilt that was at once so familiar and terrible that it threatened to overwhelm him. But he could change his path. He could avoid those consequences. He *would*. This time, he could only hope that he would be good enough.

'I am going to marry her,' he said with a finality that did little to ease the feelings in his chest.

'Really?' Sebastian asked, shocked. 'I thought you might change your mind, but I didn't think you would actually get married.'

Theo shrugged off the weight on his shoulders, and Sebastian could have been forgiven for thinking that it was in response to his question.

'But I suppose it is still good business,' Sebastian said into the quiet room.

'That it may be, but no. It's more than that. It's... All these years I have thought her cold and calculating, but that's not the truth of her.'

'You love her?' Sebastian queried.

Did he? He might have been able to forgive the transgressions he thought she'd been guilty of, but love? Was he even capable of such a thing? When he thought of how he'd felt, seeing her struck by the boat's boom, when he'd paced the hospital hallways, devastated by the mere thought of her hurt, when he'd seen her share the laughter with his mother only the night before...the way it had eased a years-long ache in his chest... When he'd finally seen Sofia and how she had grown into a woman far greater than he had ever imagined possible...his lips curved into a smile, and something almost impossible to contain bloomed in his chest.

It was a strange thing, filling him from the inside out, covering and swelling to fit the empty places of his heart... Wondrous was the only word he could use to describe how it felt. And if there were edges of darkness, of a deeper hurt, of a twisted guilt in his chest, he pushed them aside with the same ruthlessness that had driven him to Sofia's doorstep.

'Yes. I do.'

'That is a wonderful thing, my friend,' Seb replied genuinely. 'Now, though, you just have to break it to my sister,' he said. 'For I believe she had pinned her hopes on the fact that you were going to abandon your princess at the altar.'

La Sereine was one of Sofia's most favourite places in Iondorra—and she had often wanted to come with Antoine, but they had never managed to find the time. She knew that being here with Theo should make her feel guilty, but she couldn't manage it. She hoped, believed, that Antoine would understand. They might not have shared everything, but they had understood each other and the pressures of duty.

Though could Sofia still claim that this wedding, this marriage, was solely for duty? She expected to feel unease as she questioned herself, but instead, she felt the thrum of excitement, of...happiness. Theo had said that he chose to do this, that he wanted it. And she was desperate to take him at his word, because somehow in the last few weeks she had begun to fall deeply for the pas-

sionate man who had woken her from a slumber of duty
and grief. Her heart ached for the man she knew still hurt
deep within himself. The man who had yet to resolve the
real hurt that beat in his heart.

But since that night in Paris he had coaxed out some
inner sense of herself—the one she had left behind
with Theo that night at the boarding school—and she
felt strange and new, and mysteriously whole. She felt
strong…in her love for him. Because wasn't that what
had really changed? That finally after all these years she
had allowed herself to feel that love for him? The love
that had always been there, waiting for a chance to escape, to be given to him?

With only a week before the wedding, Sofia didn't
think she had enough time to undo the pain of the past,
but after the wedding? Would they not have a lifetime
together? For her to show him how much he meant to
her, and just what he had done for her. Was it enough,
perhaps, for her to do the same for him?

A knock at the door to her suite pulled Sofia's gaze
from the lake and mountains beyond.

'Enter,' she commanded, her voice soft in expectation
of what was about to happen. A small woman with dark
hair pushed in a clothing rack with three heavy garment
bags hanging from the rail.

'Your Highness,' said Alexa—her dress designer—the
address slightly unfamiliar to Sofia after just a few days
away from Iondorra and the formal etiquette required by
her status. 'From our conversation on the phone, and the
description of what you require, I have brought the original design along with some alteration options, but also
two other suggestions in case they become preferable.'

'Thank you, Alexa, and thank you again for making
the trip out here.'

Alexa smiled. 'It is my pleasure, Your Highness. Lac du Peridot is always a welcome sight, and La Sereine is just as beautiful as I've always heard.' Sofia couldn't help but smile at the older woman's enthusiasm. 'Now, let's see what we're dealing with.'

Sofia untied the silk robe and slipped the sleeves from her shoulders to reveal the bruise that was still quite evident from where the yacht's boom had caught her. Alexa might not have winced, but Sofia didn't miss the concern in her eyes. Alexa had been dressing and designing for her ever since she left the boarding school. She tutted as she circled Sofia with an assessing gaze. Hmmed and humphed a few times, before nodding to herself.

'You are okay?'

Sofia nodded quickly, feeling like the little seventeen-year-old Alexa had first met before her debut ball. Unaccountably she was blinking back tears and struggled to find the cause of them. She felt as if she were in a sea of emotions, her love for Theo, her hopes for the future, her ache for the past. She wanted to look beautiful on her wedding day, and the thought that had begun to wind around her heart, the possibility that the Widow Princess had finally found her Prince Charming…was one she wanted to hold on to so desperately.

'I have just the thing,' Alexa said, and Sofia lost herself in the bustling actions of the last-minute alterations to the dress she had always wanted to wear…for him.

The gala was going well. Sofia had delivered the opening speech and the event had moved on to the auction part of the evening. Theo had been with her as she had met with a few of the child ambassadors for the charity—and she couldn't help but smile at his surprise at how well she knew them. This had been her first charity, and would always have a special place in her heart. As an adult, she'd struggled with the secrecy and care around her father, so she simply couldn't imagine how much worse it was for children.

He had barely left her side all evening. And it had been both wonderful and terrible. She hadn't realised just how alone she had felt without companionship, without someone by her side since Antoine had died. Her parents had retreated to their estate, and she felt as if she had been alone for so long. But having Theo beside her made her feel stronger, more capable. It made the weight of the responsibility on her shoulders so much lighter to bear.

The thought of having him beside her in the future made her feel more capable of the things she wanted to do for Iondorra. And for the first time, perhaps ever, she began to relish the idea of the changes, could feel the power and energy there, to do even the larger things she wanted to accomplish. Now she began to hope that they might actually weather the storm that would hit once her father's diagnosis was made public.

She cast a glance around the hotel's grand ballroom, but couldn't see where Theo was. But his absence failed to dim the thrill and excitement that had filled her when trying on the beautiful wedding dress, and suddenly the hopes for her future were almost too much for her to bear.

She looked around the room, once again, for a glimpse of the man she loved with all of her heart. She wanted to tell him. An urgency she couldn't explain began to wind within her chest. As if something, time perhaps, was running away from her.

Finally she caught sight of him on the veranda, speaking to a young woman with long dark hair that she recognised as Maria Rohan de Luen—Sebastian's young sister. They appeared to be arguing, which confused her, drawing her to the couple. The sliding floor-to-ceiling French windows were slightly open, the gauzy white curtains shifting in the breeze, doing very little to disguise their words.

'But you can't!' The hurt in Maria's voice slashed him. Theo truly hadn't realised the extent of her feelings.

'Maria, please.'

'No. You said...you said that you weren't going to go through with it. You said that you were doing it to teach her a lesson! She hurt you and you were going to leave her at the altar! You can't marry her, Theo!'

He searched his mind for explanations, something that would lessen the pain, but he didn't know what to say.

'Maria—'

His words were cut off the moment Maria's whole demeanour changed. Shocked and wide-eyed, she was no longer looking at him, but over his shoulder...and every single hair on his body lifted as if touched by the same electric lightning bolt that had struck Maria still.

Horror filled him before he'd even turned and he barely registered Maria's flight from the veranda wrapping around the ground floor of the hotel.

Sofia.

He'd never seen her look the way she did in that moment. All the lies and mistruths he'd imagined he'd seen in her features were nothing compared to the raw pain and shock vibrating from her now.

'What did she mean?'

'Sofia—'

'Is it true?' she demanded, her voice breaking over the words.

Sofia saw the moment that fear and panic truly entered him. It froze him as if he thought that should he move, should he speak, it would set into motion a chain of events he could not take back.

Finally he moved, his long legs pacing wide steps across the wooden veranda, each one feeling as if it took him further and further away from her, even as it closed the distance between them. She'd hoped, in some far corner of her heart, that Maria had lied, had misunderstood somehow. But she knew that hope was futile.

'Yes,' he said simply. And her whole world came crashing down. 'When I first met you again in Paris that night, I had a plan. I thought that I was being merciful, offering you a silent, unknown chance to apologise and release yourself of a path that would lead to your eventual humiliation. When you didn't, when you refused, I had the photographer find us in the garden—I even chose which photo he should use. And yes, when I forced your hand to agree to our engagement I knew that I wouldn't go through with the marriage. That on the day of our wedding you would be at the church filled with hundreds of guests and filmed by thousands…and I would leave you waiting as you once left me waiting.'

His voice had gained a power, a guttural tone that suggested he was almost trying to convince himself that he'd been right. That he'd been justified. Hearing the words on his lips sliced away the soft layers of her heart, until the knife struck stone.

Because that was what Sofia needed most now. A heart of stone. Because she *loved* this man. This man who would have hurt her, yes, but even worse hurt her country. The humiliation wouldn't have been hers alone to bear. It would have been theirs. And that devastated her. The one thing she had been raised and trained to do, to put her country first, and she had nearly failed even before the crown came to rest on her head.

'But I had changed my mind, Sofia. I didn't know... I didn't know about your father, about why you were forced to leave that day, about any of it. I didn't understand.'

Desperate pain filled her completely. Pain and anger, an anger that felt almost uncontainable. 'It wasn't for you to understand, Theo!' She wanted to lash out, to howl her hurt, but she couldn't. She wouldn't. Not here, with hundreds of people behind them. She had been ruthlessly trained to bear the weight of the crown and she would not betray them now by giving Theo the humiliation he had once so desperately wanted. 'But it *is* for me to protect my country and people from those who would do it harm, even those I love. *Especially* those I love. For years I have done so for my father. And now I'll do it for you.'

'But you don't have to. Sofia, I want to marry you. I want to be standing at the top of the aisle you walk down in five days' time. Sofia, I—'

'I think you've done enough, don't you? You will have what you wanted. I will break the engagement. My humiliation will still happen for you. It will just not quite be as public as you wished.'

Theo let loose a growl. 'That is not what I want. This doesn't have to happen.'

'You think I can trust you, after this?'

'Why not? I trusted you after you...' His bitter words trailed off.

'So you still have not forgiven me. Not really.'

'I *have*,' he growled again. 'But you're leaving me, again. Just like...'

'Him,' she said, completing his sentence. Speaking of the one man that Theo refused to name. 'Is that what this is really about? Your father, not me?' She didn't wait for an answer. 'Until you forgive, Theo, you can't truly love me. Not really.'

'How on earth am I supposed to forgive him? I don't even know where he is!' he shouted.

'Not him. *You*. All this time, this unworthiness...it's you, you can't forgive, not me or him. And I can't make up for that, I can't *be* that for you.'

'Don't you dare turn this back on me. I'm here, telling you that I love you and that I'm yours.'

'You were never mine, and you're still not,' she said, her voice barely even a whisper.

'And you're still afraid!' he accused.

'What?'

'Still afraid of letting yourself be loved for you and not *what* you are. So tell me. Who is it that really feels unworthy here? Why is it that you're so eager to fall at this first hurdle?'

'Hurdle? You're calling your plan to leave me at the altar a hurdle? The fact that you consider even doing that means you have no respect or regard for my people, my country! They *are* me and you would have left us all.'

'But I'm not! I'm not leaving you. You're the one who is walking away and if you don't see that then you're lying to yourself.'

She didn't want to hear it. Couldn't. Because deep within her heart, she knew that there was some semblance of truth to his words. But she had to. She had to leave him. Her country had to come first. Hadn't that been drilled into her as a child? As a young woman? By her parents, her father? There was no other choice here.

'I have to return to the party—'

'Let them wait!' he yelled, his voice so loud she felt it echo within her body. 'I'm trying to tell you that I love you.'

'And *I'm* trying to tell you that it doesn't matter.'

She turned to leave, but Theo blocked her path.

He crowded her, his shoulders, his body a barrier that wouldn't be breached. She pulled herself up short before she crashed into him, but he caught her elbow and stopped her fall.

'I love you, Sofia,' he said, the only notice he gave her before drawing her to him, flush against his body, and kissing her with more passion and pain than she was capable of bearing. The moment his lips met hers, the fury and anger driving him, driving her, softened, and his tongue swept into her mouth as if it had a right to be there, as if it belonged to her and not him, just like his heart. Everything in her roared for release, desperate to escape and join him in this passion play. Her heart soared as much as it fell, as she realised that this would be the last time she could kiss him, hold him, show him all the huge, complex, amazing but terrible things she felt in that instant.

Her hands flew to his head, fingers riffling through his hair, pulling him to her, as the tears escaped her eyes and rolled down her cheeks. The salty-sweet taste of them mingling with their kiss was the last thing she remembered, before pulling away from him and fleeing.

# CHAPTER ELEVEN

SOFIA HADN'T STOPPED crying for two days. She hadn't left her room in Iondorra's palace, she hadn't met with the council to help create the statement that would stop the wedding in three days' time, and even her sleep was broken by huge sobs that racked her body and tears that fell down her cheeks.

From the moment she had left Theo in the hotel by the lake it had felt as if her world had shattered, and somewhere deep down she knew that she deserved it. There were things she needed to do, but her mind couldn't hold on to them. It was as if her thoughts were being filtered, all else dropping away, to leave only grief and sorrow. If she had expected numbness, a deep, quiet agony to blanket over her heart, it had not happened.

Instead she felt raw, the constant dull ache of her broken heart her only companion.

*'I'm trying to tell you that I love you... You're the one who is walking away...you're lying to yourself.'*

Theo's words punctuated each breath, each thought. Because he was right. Once again, she had his heart. He loved her and she was walking away—only this time, she really was aware of what that meant. He had proclaimed to want to teach her the consequences of her actions... and now? She fully understood them.

She had been so sure in herself, so sure that she was right, putting her country first before a man who would have ruined it. Who preached consequences and gave no thought to the ones his own actions would have caused.

But beneath the words that ran around her head on a loop were the ones she didn't want to inspect. Didn't want to listen to, or believe. The ones that proclaimed her to be afraid of being loved for who she was and not *what* she was. As if the two things could be separated so easily.

This morning she had had marginally more success than the day before. She had made it to the bathroom and forced herself into the shower. Standing before the large mirror, she wiped away the steam and condensation from the cool, slick surface and stared at herself.

Her eyes, red-rimmed from the crying and a startling blue, stared back in accusation. *Coward.*

Sofia shook her head against her inner voice. No, she mentally replied. Broken-hearted.

She reached for the thick towelling robe and cinched it tight around her waist. All she wanted to do was go back to bed and pretend that the world didn't exist. She could have another day, surely. Because ten years ago, she hadn't been allowed even a minute, leaving the school and being thrust immediately into hours of lessons, measured, poked and prodded into the right dresses, as she kissed goodbye that moment out of time she'd had with Theo, kissed goodbye the young woman who had found fun and enjoyment and...love.

And four years ago, when Antoine had died, the world's press had documented her tearless grief—the loss of a man so precious to her... And for a moment she hated Theo. Hated him for showing her the truth of her relationship with Antoine—her friendship. Yes, she had loved him, but his loss had not had this devastating effect on her and somehow it made her feel as if she were betraying both men all over again.

Re-entering the suite of her rooms, she stifled a cry of shock with the back of her hand when she saw her mother standing beside the large window, looking out at the view. Shock turned into fear with lightning speed.

'Father, is he—?'

'He is fine, Sofia. He is not the one I'm worried about right now.'

Sofia's emotions seesawed, and guilt stirred in her breast. Was she so starved of love that her mother's concern—the simple fact that Sofia was being put first—made something shift in her heart? Guilt, hurt and love all mixed together in the headiest of potions, and for the first time that Sofia could remember in years she ran to her mother's arms and cried.

After what felt like hours, her mother released her and led her to the window seat.

'What are you doing here?'

'One of the staff was concerned when you refused to eat anything yesterday.'

Sofia wanted to hide, wanted to stay wrapped in her mother's arms, but knew that she could not. Slowly, haltingly, the words tumbled out. Of what had happened to Theo since she had left that night, of how he had orchestrated their engagement, but her words grew stronger as Sofia told her mother of how they had talked of the past, of the secrets she had entrusted to him, of the love she felt for him, and finally what had happened the night of the gala.

Her mother was quiet for a long while.

'Did you... Is it that you thought you couldn't have both?'

'After I left the boarding school, everything became about doing what was right for Iondorra and…'

'You didn't feel that you could have something for yourself?'

'I didn't know *how* to have both,' Sofia replied helplessly. 'It had, has, always been him. And I couldn't do that to him. I couldn't do what…'

'What was done to you.'

Sofia could hear the hurt in her mother's voice, the sheen of tears in the older woman's eyes almost too much to bear. She knew her words would hurt her mother. Knew that her mother would understand in an instant, that they had moved away from talking of Theo, and towards herself.

'Oh, my love,' her mother said, shaking her head. 'I'm so sorry that you felt that way. I… *We*…' Her words were interrupted by the shaking of her mother's head as she struggled to find the words that Sofia half feared. 'We never wanted you to feel that way. We love you dearly. And I am truly sorry that you ever felt as if you had no choice about your role.'

'I had to change so much about who I was, Mama. So much. But being with Theo again reminded me of who I once had been. And I missed that. I missed who I was.'

'And he helps you find that person you once were?'

'But it doesn't matter,' Sofia said, shrugging helplessly. 'His actions would have hurt Iondorra.'

'But they didn't, my love. And I am so happy that he brought something of you back to you. Because I have seen that smile…the one I thought lost ten years ago. I have seen what you are with him, the night of your engagement, and what you could be, in my heart's greatest hope.'

Her mother drew her into her arms again and this time

Sofia let go. Let go her fears, her resentments, the part of her she thought lost, found and lost again.

'Sofia, the crown, the country, it is important. But it is not worth the sacrifice of your heart. Theo,' she sighed, a small smile curving at the corner of her mouth, 'is clearly a man who made certain choices, and although that was his plan, did you believe him when he said he no longer wanted to abandon you? Did you believe the love he said to feel for you?'

'I don't know if I can trust him, Mama.'

'Trust him with what?'

Sofia frowned, unsure of what her mother was getting at. Seeing her daughter's confusion, she pressed on. 'Trust him not to make mistakes? Sweetheart, we all make mistakes, all the time. Just look at me and your father. Do you trust him to love you and be there for you? Do you trust him with your heart?'

'But how can I trust him with Iondorra?'

'Oh, Sofia. My one wish for you is not that you have someone who puts the country first, but who puts *you* first.'

For so long, everything had been about Iondorra. Leaving school, her first marriage, even the way she had planned her second marriage. The thought that it was even possible for someone to put her first, for her to allow that… Horror and hope mixed within the chambers of her heart, rushing out through her veins and around her body, setting it on fire with adrenaline.

Could she do such a thing? Could she really give herself over to that sense of trust…of love?

For two hours after her mother had left, with promises to return more often, to make more time for the two of them, Sofia stared at her phone.

Her heart knew what she wanted to do, and Sofia waited for her mind to catch up.

She dialled his number, her heart fluttering wildly, and was almost thankful when it went to the answering machine.

'Theo, I... There is so much we need to say to each other. But more importantly, I want you to know that I love you. I really do. And if you do love me, if you can forgive me the way we parted, then I will see you at the church in three days' time. Because I want nothing more than to become your wife. I want nothing more than to stand by your side for the world to see. I want nothing more than to show the world how much I love you and want to spend the rest of my life telling you that, each and every day. If you don't come, then I understand and will not hold it against you. I will issue a statement that takes full responsibility for the end of our engagement. But no matter what, please, please know that I love you.'

Theo sat on the stairs of his mother's decking, looking out at his vineyards from the veranda. He fished the phone out from his trouser pocket and threw it behind him, and leant his elbows on his thighs. It had been two days since he'd returned to Greece from Iondorra and he hadn't slept a wink. The early morning rays from the sun heated the rain-soaked earth, covering the ground in an unworldly mist, swirling in the still morning air.

For two days he had thought of little else than Sofia, of what she had said to him, of how she had accused him of being unable and unwilling to forgive, not her, not his father, but himself. The guilt that had settled about him that night had been slowly revealed as the layers of hurt and shock from their argument had dissipated. It was as if Sofia's words had picked at an invisible thread, wound

tight around his heart—as if she had tugged on it, showing him proof that it existed, that it had bound his young
heart and the muscle had grown around that binding…
And he could no longer ignore it.

He had tried to lose himself in estate business, but
that had failed and finally his feet had brought him to
his mother's door. And although she woke early, five
o'clock in the morning was perhaps a little much to be
banging on her door and seeking…what? Answers? Advice? Forgiveness?

The smell of coffee hit his nose long before he detected
the sound of his mother moving about in the house, and
before he could get up from the wooden decking, his
mother opened the door and wordlessly handed him a cup
of the strong, fresh Greek coffee that he loved so much.

She went to sit beside him on the steps, and he rose in
protest but she shooed him back down.

'I am not so old that I cannot sit on the steps with my
son and look at the amazing things he has done. I do it
even when you're not here, Theo. It is my favourite place
in the world.'

Theo felt a heaviness within him. The weight of all
the unanswered questions, of the guilt and anger and
pain, resting on top of his already tightly bound heart…
he thought he might actually break under the weight of it.

'I did something unforgivable, *mitéra*,' he said.

His mother humphed. 'There is very little in this world
that is unforgivable, *yié mou*.'

He swept a hand over his face, scrubbing away the
exhaustion and doubts and all the things that worked
to stop his words in his throat, and opened his heart to
his mother.

'I had this plan. This…act of revenge I wanted to
take against Sofia for leaving me all those years ago.

I blamed her for…everything. And all this time, it was me. I thought it was her fault, what happened to me at school, the expulsion, having to come back here… But those decisions and choices were mine—yet I would have humiliated her in front of the world.'

For a moment, his mother seemed to consider his words.

'But you did not.'

'Yet I would have.'

She smiled at him in the way only a mother could. 'But you did *not*.'

'The outcome will be the same. The cancelled wedding will ruin her.'

Aggeliki rocked her head from side to side as if to say maybe, maybe not, and he knew that there was only one thing to make her realise the truth of what he was feeling.

'I would have left her, just like my father left you.'

Aggeliki sighed and blew the deep breath over her coffee before sipping at the thick dark liquid. 'Theo, your father…he… I have not really spoken of him, because you never seemed to want to, or be ready to, hear of him. He was—' she let loose a little laugh '—charming—a little like his son. Very handsome—a lot like his son. But insincere and careless—*nothing* like his son.'

'Do you regret it?' *Do you regret me?*

'*Agápi mou,* no. I gave him my heart, and he gave me you. And I would do the same again and again, because you are my joy. He may have been my sadness, but *you*? You are my happiness and more precious to me than anything in the world.'

'If I hadn't been expelled I could have gone to university, and we wouldn't have had to struggle, we wouldn't have nearly lost everything when you became ill, we could have…'

'Could, would, should? Theo, you seem to think that it all would have been so easy for you had you not loved Sofia back then. But look at what you have now. Look at what you've achieved. It is impossible to say what might have happened if you had not been expelled, but it is undoubtable what *did* happen, and what you have now.'

'But we wouldn't have had to come back here. You wouldn't have had to feel beholden to your family, the cruelty and prejudice you experienced... And then with the vineyard... The hours, days, weeks, *years* of hard work—'

'I wouldn't change a thing. Life is not meant to be easy, Theo. Easy is...nothing,' she said, throwing her hands up as if throwing around air. 'Meaningless. It is the hard work that makes it all the more precious and wondrous. It is the difficult times, the sacrifices that make the joy all the more valuable, the *love*. And every sacrifice you *think* I've made? I would do it again and again, because I love you.'

'But Sofia is right. I would have brought humiliation not just to her but her country.'

'But you did not,' his mother repeated with much more emphasis than before.

'All this time, all I have thought about is myself, the vengeance I wanted, the debt *I* felt *she* owed.'

'Theo, from what I saw of Sofia, of the truly brave and powerful woman I met, she carries that burden herself. And will always carry that burden. But it is for *her* to do. You? You are the only one who can help her. The Sofia that you fell in love with ten years ago, and the Sofia that is the woman she has become. Yes, she may have to think of her country first...but you? You get to think of her first.'

He felt his mother's words deep within his chest. He

felt her acceptance of his sins, his mistakes, ease some of the guilt in his heart. Soothe the way towards his own forgiveness for himself. Not for his attempt at revenge, but something deeper. But was it enough?

Theo stood and rolled his shoulders, flexing the ache from his muscles before placing a kiss on his mother's cheek.

'I need some time to think.'

Aggeliki nodded in response.

'Maybe I'll go and see Sebastian for a few days, but I'll be back. Soon, I promise. I love you,' he said, placing one last kiss on Aggeliki's forehead before walking back to the estate through the miles of vineyards between the two buildings.

Within minutes he was too far from his mother's house to hear his phone vibrate with an incoming call, and within hours the phone's battery had died, long before Theo returned to retrieve Sofia's voicemail.

*What on earth had she been thinking?*

As Sofia stood tucked behind the door at the back of a church packed full of nearly eight hundred of the world's leading figures, she couldn't stop the tremors that had taken over her body. Was this how Theo had felt that night ten years ago? Hopeful that she would arrive and fearful that she wouldn't?

She cast a quick glance to where her assistant was peering through a small sliver of space in the doorway, watching for Theo's arrival at the wedding that Sofia had never cancelled. The scared look in the young woman's eyes enough to tell her that Theo was still not there.

She had sent her father back to sit with her mother, after kind, coherent words of love had eased an age-old ache, but not this fresh one. And this time she had not batted her father's words away, but really listened, taken them to her heart and held them to her as if something astounding and precious.

She tried to take a breath, but the tightly corseted white satin dress just didn't expand enough to allow for it. Her hold on the exquisite garland of flowers, peonies and thistles, had become looser and looser as time had worn on, and they now hung from her listless arms at her side. The smile she had worn with determination hours before was rapidly losing its brilliance as Sofia now became convinced that he wasn't coming.

The ache in her heart was devastating, but she refused to cower beneath the pain. If this was his decision, then she would bear it. Her country would bear her mistakes too. But they would survive. This wedding, this marriage, it had been for her. The one thing she had selfishly wanted all those years ago, and again now. But she knew that no matter what the future held, all she needed to do was put one foot in front of the other. And if that was down an aisle to tell her guests that the wedding was off, then she would do so.

She couldn't blame Theo. She understood the pain she had caused, and the hurt he felt not only from her actions, but also from his father's. Forgiveness was already there, in her heart, because she understood him, and loved him. Even if she never got to utter the words to him in person.

She gave a final nod to her assistant, who disappeared to instruct the organist not to play the wedding march as she opened the door and began to make her way down the aisle.

The unsettled and deeply curious guests all turned to watch her as she took her first step, her second and a third. Already aware that something was off, in the silence, Sofia's heart sounded in her ears like a drum.

She willed away the tears that threatened to fall. She did not want to share them with these people. She would hold them to her in the darkest of nights, but not let them fall here, beneath the streams of sunlight falling through the stained-glass windows.

As she reached the top of the aisle where the priest stood, but the groom did not, she turned. Her mother's sad smile, encouraging and understanding, was full of love and that was all Sofia needed.

She took a breath, ready with the words she had prepared just in case...

The sound of the large wooden door being pulled open with a force that screeched across its hinges cut through the silence and there, cast in shadow amongst the brilliant rays of sunshine, was Theo Tersi.

The open promise of love shining bright in his eyes was what she'd longed to see and a sob of joy escaped her, the smile no longer forced, but came to her lips without hesitation. He took proud, deep and quick steps towards her, perhaps a little unceremoniously, closing the gap between them in moments, pulling her close and into a passionate kiss full of love and joy, much to the twittering giggles from the church's many guests.

'I'm sorry I'm late,' he said in between delicate presses of his lips to hers.

'I thought you might not come.'

'I will *always* come for you.' He whispered the vow into her ear and her heart.

Theo pulled her close to him, her heart beating against his, through the layers of clothing and skin. Only then did he allow himself to breathe. He had returned to his mother's house only the day before, and listened to the message Sofia had left on his voicemail and left almost immediately, breaking every speed-limit law in two countries to get to his future bride.

The wild beating of his heart, caused from his desperate run to the church, showed no signs of slowing. And he knew that nothing would prevent it other than the words of love he longed to hear from Sofia in person.

For the second time that day the church's doors were thrown open and Sebastian launched himself through the doors, to find the entire church staring at him. With a half laugh, half gasp, he bent double, his hands on his knees, dragging in giant lungful's of air into his chest, causing even more laughter amongst the guests than the kiss Theo had shared with Sofia.

'We would have been here sooner, but it seems there is a no-fly zone over the church and we had to leave the helicopter about a mile away.'

'*Two* miles,' groaned Sebastian as he came to join them at the top of the aisle.

As the priest called for silence and calm, drew the guests to their role of witnesses to the marriage between Sofia and Theo, neither the bride nor groom paid heed to the ceremony, lost to each other and the love that shimmered between them. But before the priest began the vows, Sofia interrupted him.

'I have my own vows,' she whispered to the priest. 'If that is okay?' He gestured for her to continue.

Sofia took Theo's hand in hers.

'Theo, when we first met, you didn't know my title, you didn't know me as a princess, you simply knew me. You loved that person and gave her a happiness, joy and love that she had never known before. I lost a little of myself when I—' she nodded, holding back the tears '—when I left you that day ten years ago. A piece that I never thought I would get back. But in the last few weeks you uncovered that lost part of me, you showed me that I could be and have both parts of the life I so desperately wanted. And that piece was you. You were the first man I ever loved, and will be the last and only man I want by my side, whatever comes next. I want to share my joys, my heartaches and my future with you, every day.

'There are promises that I could make, some that I could struggle to keep, but the only important one is that, although I might be Queen one day, and although I will wear the crown and must think of my country first…it is our love that I will *put* first, because *that* is what gives me the strength to be Queen, to be me to the best of my ability. My love for you. My heart has, and always will be, yours.'

And as she spoke the words of her heart, Theo felt a rightness settle about his shoulders. And for the first time in so many years he finally felt whole, just as she had described.

'Sofia, you know better than most how hard the past ten years have been for me. I used to wish it had been another way. An easier way. But a very wise woman recently told me that nothing in life that is meaningful is easy. And now I wouldn't take each and every one of those hard days back for the world. Because they led me to you.

'I don't have fancy words to describe my love for you. I have only the truth in my heart, that lets me know that you are, and always have been, the only woman I would give everything for. The hard days and the good. Because you have always seen me, the truth of me, and loved me in spite of my flaws, in spite of my actions and in spite of the consequences. And I promise you here today, with *eight hundred* witnesses—' Theo paused, letting the gentle laughter of the congregation flow over the outpouring of love he felt for Sofia in his heart, before he continued '—I promise to love you, to hold you to me when things are not easy, to hold you to me when you need strength and when I do, and to hold you when we need nothing more than each other. Because you are my strength, my love and my heart.'

The truth of his words settled into the tears that pressed against his eyelids, and barely had the words left the priest's mouth declaring that he could finally, *finally*, kiss his wife, he poured his heart and soul into the kiss that would seal their marriage.

That evening, Sofia and Theo danced their first dance as man and wife to 'At Last' in front of the guests gathered for the evening's reception. The words of the song wound around their hearts as the cheers and joy of the entire room welled up around them. That night they made love, so heartfelt and poignant it felt like a dream, and it was the night they conceived their first child. Through the years to come, there would be tears of joy at the birth of their daughter, and later their son. There would be sleepless nights as Iondorra weathered the difficult revelation of Sofia's father's dementia, but there were early nights when as a family they came together to share their love. There would be tears of grief and sadness as their parents passed, but throughout it all they held each other close, whispering words of love and comfort that settled the beating of their hearts each and every single day they would share together.

\* \* \* \* \*

# FROM DOCTOR TO PRINCESS?

**ANNIE CLAYDON**

# CHAPTER ONE

THE LEATHER CAR seat creaked slightly as Crown Prince Hugo DeLeon shifted, trying to find a more comfortable position. There wasn't one. He'd only been out of the hospital for twenty-four hours, and the pain in his left shoulder was normal. It would subside in a day or so, and he knew that impatience wasn't going to make him heal any faster.

All the same, he *was* impatient. And if his father thought that he was helping Hugo to get back to normal, then he wasn't.

There wasn't a great deal of choice in the matter, though. The King of Montarino was accustomed to being obeyed, and when he had visited his only son in the discreet private ward of the hospital, he'd made it clear that he was taking no arguments. He'd smiled at Hugo, in much the same way as any father would, and told him that his duty to his country was clear and very simple. He had to get better.

In order to make sure that his son's recovery went smoothly, the King had recruited a doctor who would stay with him at all times over the next month or so. Hugo had still been drowsy from the anaesthetic and his back hurt from having lain still while the pacemaker had been inserted into his chest, but he had got the message. His father didn't trust Hugo to look after himself, and so he was appointing a minder to do it.

He hadn't told Hugo much about this minder, other than

that she was a woman, eminently qualified, and that she was due to fly out from London today. The last detail was another smart move on his father's part, because Hugo knew most of the doctors in the small principality of Montarino, particularly those who were well qualified in cardiology. He might well have been able to wriggle out of the arrangement with any one of them, but this woman was an unknown quantity.

He wondered briefly whether she'd come equipped with tranquillisers and physical restraints. And, more to the point, whether she'd been briefed about the requirement for discretion. Hugo assumed that she had, because discretion was one of the codes that his family lived by, and his father never let anyone forget it.

'That'll be her...' His bodyguard sat in the front seat of the car, and had the advantage of an unobscured view. Hugo squinted through the tinted windows, and saw the chauffeur walking across the forecourt towards the airport's short-stay car park. Beside him was a young woman with mid-brown hair and a supple sway to her walk, which made the short hairs at the back of Hugo's neck prickle slightly.

Probably another one of his father's carefully reasoned choices. Hugo had to admit that he wasn't known for saying no to beautiful women, but unusually the King had misjudged the situation this time. A career woman, particularly a doctor, wasn't someone that he could contemplate giving any part of his heart to.

'She doesn't look too formidable.' Ted spoke in English, turning slightly in his seat to display the hint of a smile.

'I wouldn't bank on looks. She's managed to keep hold of her suitcase, and I imagine that Jean-Pierre did everything he could to wrestle it away from her.' Hugo turned the corners of his mouth down. The first thing his father's chauffeur would have done was to try to relieve their guest of her luggage and wheel her suitcase for her.

'I must be getting slow, I missed that.' Ted had done nothing of the sort; he just hadn't seen fit to mention it. In the five years that he'd been with Hugo, since his retirement from the British police force, the two men had learned to read each other's thoughts and trust what they saw. It had been Ted who had happened to mention that he'd heard that the doctor was being picked up from the airport this morning, and Hugo had made the expected decision to go with the car to greet her. Sizing her up before anyone else at the palace got the chance to speak with her couldn't be a bad thing.

Ted got out of the car, walking to the rear passenger door and opening it. For all the world as if he were according Hugo the respect his position required, rather than helping him with the weight of the door. Hugo climbed out of the car, ignoring the tingle of pain that reached from his chest down his left arm.

Now that she was closer, Dr Penelope Maitland didn't seem as formidable as her old-fashioned name might lead one to suppose. She was all curves and movement, looking almost girlish in a tan jacket over a cream summer dress, creased from travelling. Her light brown hair glinted in the sunshine, and bare, tanned legs gave her the fresh, outdoorsy look of someone going on holiday.

Maybe the gorgeous Dr Penelope was a rare mistake on his father's part. This woman looked as if she was more likely to spend her time here enjoying the pleasures of Montarino, not nagging him about his health. When her honey-coloured gaze met his, there was a spark of recognition and she smiled. A carefree kind of smile that sent tingles down his spine and allowed Hugo to believe that she didn't have it in her to make his life difficult.

Then she stopped in front of him, letting go of her suitcase long enough for Jean-Pierre to grab it and wheel it around to the boot of the car. 'I'm Dr Maitland. I'm told that I shouldn't curtsey.'

Her voice was like honey but her tone was like steel. Clearly Dr Penelope wasn't going to be quite as much of a walkover as her appearance suggested.

'Thank you. I'd prefer it if you didn't.' Hugo held out his right hand, glad that the pacemaker was on the left side of his chest, and didn't hamper the movement of his right arm. Her grip was as firm as her tone. 'Welcome to Montarino. I'm Hugo DeLeon.'

'Yes, I know.' She shot him a questioning look, and Hugo wondered whether she was going to rebuke him for coming to meet her. He mumbled the usual invitation to call him Hugo, wondering if he'd get to call her Penelope. The name seemed suddenly as if it would taste sweet on his lips.

'Please call me Nell…'

Hugo smiled his acquiescence. *Nell* sounded soft and sweet too, even if it was a little shorter.

'You must be tired from your journey. We should be going…' Hugo's discreet gesture to Jean-Pierre prompted him to get into the car.

She raised one eyebrow. 'Yes, we should be going. I'm surprised to see you out and about so soon.'

Her words had an edge to them. If anyone should be feeling tired she clearly expected that it should be him, and Hugo had to admit that he was surprised at the effort involved in making a simple car journey.

'I'm grateful for the fresh air.'

At the moment, the fresh air was making his head spin. Hugo stood back from the open door of the car and she hesitated and then got in, sliding quickly across the back seat before Hugo could even think about closing the car door and walking around to get in on the other side.

All the same, he welcomed the move. On this side, the seat belt wouldn't need to rest painfully on his left shoulder. Hugo got into the car, and Ted closed the door before he could reach for it.

'Have you been to Montarino before?' Hugo had years of practice with small talk.

'No.' Nell shook her head, regarding him thoughtfully.

'It's very small, only eight miles across, but very beautiful. We have one city, half a mountain and, although we have no coastline, there are some beautiful lakes.'

'That's nice. I'll have to come back sometime when I'm not working. I probably won't have much time to see them this time around.' Her mouth was set in a firm line, and Hugo's heart sank. Clearly there was no hope of deflecting the redoubtable Dr Penelope from her intended purpose.

Four days ago, Nell Maitland had ridden home on the night bus, after the farewell party that her colleagues at the hospital had thrown for her. It had been the ultimate failure, after months of trying to work things out with the cardiac unit's new head of the department, and save the job that she loved so much. And now…

She was riding in a chauffeur-driven car, sitting next to a prince. It was an object lesson in how dramatically things could change in so little time.

'I gather you have a strong tradition of attracting the best musicians.' She smiled in response to Hugo DeLeon's indication of the Montarino Opera House, and the car obligingly slowed to allow her a more detailed look.

'We like to think that we can hold our own with the rest of Europe when it comes to our appreciation of the arts. You *do* know a little about Montarino, then?'

Anyone could use the Internet. Although Nell had to admit that the photographs didn't do the grand building justice. Its sweeping, modern lines, rising from the tree-lined plaza that surrounded it, would have made it a land-mark in the greatest of cities.

'Only as much as I could read in the last couple of days. In between packing.' Nell wondered whether he'd mind that she hadn't even known where Montarino was before she'd taken this job. It had just been a name, teth-ered somewhere at the back of her mind, along with a lot of other places that she knew nothing about.

Hugo nodded, smiling. 'That's one of the best things about living here. Most people have few preconceptions, and so we have the chance to attempt to surprise our visi-tors.'

And it seemed that Hugo DeLeon was giving it his best shot. Nell had been told that he was a doctor as well as a prince, and that her advice would be a matter of reinforc-ing a message that he was already well aware of. In other words, he reckoned that the physical limits that applied to ordinary people weren't for the likes of a prince, and he needed to be kept in check.

Nell had no idea in which direction they were supposed to be going, but she was aware that the car seemed to be taking a circuitous route past a number of notable build-ings, all of which Hugo was intent on pointing out. If he thought that was going to deflect her from her purpose, he was wrong.

'I'm looking forward to seeing the palace.' She smiled brightly, wondering whether he'd take the hint.

'We're nearly there now.' Hugo raised his voice a little. 'Jean-Pierre…'

The driver nodded, turning smoothly onto a wide, straight boulevard and putting his foot on the gas. It seemed that everyone here responded to Hugo's every word, which was the first challenge attached to this new appointment.

The ambassador, who had interviewed her at the embassy in London, had said little but implied a lot. He'd got her medical qualifications and the fact that she spoke French tolerably well out of the way in the first five minutes. Then he'd turned the conversation around to her patient.

'Hugo DeLeon, Crown Prince of Montarino, can be...' The ambassador had paused slightly before coming to a conclusion about how to describe it. 'He can be self-willed.'

Nell had read *arrogant* into his words and had smiled politely. She had experience of dealing with all kinds of patients, and self-willed wasn't a problem. Neither was arrogant.

What the ambassador hadn't warned her about was his smile. It was polite, appropriate, and yet it seemed to hold real warmth. His high cheekbones lent a touch of class, and his shock of dark blonde hair, no doubt artfully arranged to make it appear slightly tousled, added a boyish note. Green eyes gave a hint that Hugo DeLeon was capable of some pretty serious mischief. Nell would have to watch out for those eyes.

But however handsome he was, however his smile made her stomach quiver, Nell had a job to do. Her fingers tightened on the strap of her handbag, which lay comfortingly across her knees. A man had gotten between her and her job before, and no one, not even this handsome prince, was going to do it again.

White knuckles. Hugo was used to looking for the little signs that told him what people were really thinking, and he'd noticed that Nell was clutching her handbag on her lap like some kind of defensive weapon. Despite the firm tone and the clear hints that he shouldn't have come to the airport, there was a chink in her armour. One that he may well need to find and exploit if it turned out that the restrictions she placed on him got in the way of his current plans.

They'd driven through the grounds of the palace and the car stopped at the ceremonial entrance to allow them to get out. She gave the high, pillared archways a glance and then turned to him as the car moved smoothly away.

'My luggage…'

'Jean-Pierre will arrange for it to be taken up to your apartment.' A sudden flare of panic had shown in Nell's eyes, and Hugo almost felt sorry for her. But keeping her a little off-balance, a little over-awed was exactly what he wanted.

'Right. Thank you.'

'Perhaps I can show you around.' The palace was big enough and grand enough to disorientate her even further.

'I think that's best left for some other time.' She was as sweet-smelling and soft as a summer's day, but there was no getting over the determination behind it all. 'This… apartment. I was told that it would be next door to yours.'

'Yes, it is.' If Hugo had had any say in the matter, he'd have put her on the other side of the building, but he hadn't. His father didn't often step into his life, but when he did, he did it thoroughly.

'With a connecting door?'

So someone had told her about that, too. Or maybe she'd asked. Hugo had rather hoped that he could just keep the connecting door closed and that it would never occur to anyone to open it.

'Yes, that's right. It's generally kept locked…' Finding the key was an easy enough matter on the rare occasions that he brought a girlfriend with him to stay at the palace for a few days, but he was sure he could just as easily lose it.

'I imagine someone has the key. Being a doctor yourself, you'll understand the need to have access to your patient.'

'And I'm sure *you'll* understand where your duties begin

and end.' Since the pleasantries didn't seem to be working all that well, it was obviously time to make things clear.

'The ambassador outlined them, yes.' She pressed her lips together and Hugo imagined that the British Ambassador had deployed all of the expected diplomacy in the matter. 'The King's letter of appointment, on the other hand, was a little less circumspect.'

Great. So his father had decided that he needed to weigh in on that as well. And even if the tiny quiver at the side of Nell's mouth told Hugo that she was feeling over-awed and nervous, her cool gaze indicated that she wasn't going to let that stop her from doing her job.

'Perhaps we should talk, over some tea.' Since deflection wasn't working, maybe negotiation would. The next step would be outright battle, and Hugo would prefer to avoid that.

'Yes. I think that would be a very good idea.'

# CHAPTER TWO

HUGO HAD OPENED the door that concealed the lift, and when she'd seen the old-fashioned gates, she'd slipped in front of him, heaving them to one side. Part of him was grateful, but a greater part decreed that as a gentleman, and her host, he should have been quicker in insisting he open the gates himself. When he motioned her ahead of him into the lift, she hovered annoyingly next to the gates, giving him no opportunity to open them when they reached the third floor.

He showed her to her apartment, leaving her alone to freshen up. That would give him at least three quarters of an hour to rest before he had to submit to another onslaught from her.

Hugo sank gratefully into the chair in his private sitting room and closed his eyes. This morning he had woken feeling invigorated, and it had only been the pain in his shoulder that had reminded him he was unable to move mountains. Wide awake, his body feeling the immediate benefit of a heart that was now paced and doing its job properly, he'd jumped at the chance of getting out of the constriction of four walls, but it had worn him out. His own advice to pacemaker patients—that they might start to feel better almost immediately but must rest and get over the operation first—would be given with a lot more certainty in the future.

Fifteen minutes later, a quiet knock sounded on the main door to the apartment and he shouted to whoever it was to come in, keeping his eyes closed. If someone was here to make the tea or fuss over him, then he'd rather they waited until he was strong enough to smilingly refuse their help.

'How are you feeling?' Nell's voice made his eyes snap open.

'Fine. Thank you.' Hugo's eye's darted to the clock above the mantelpiece. Surely he hadn't been asleep…

Apparently not. She was pink-cheeked, as if she'd just got out of the shower, and Nell had changed out of her travelling clothes and into a slim pair of dark blue trousers with a white shirt, open at the neck and buttoned at the cuffs. She looked businesslike and entirely delicious.

He shifted, wishing that the ache in his left shoulder would go away, and Nell stepped forward. Without any warning at all, she caught up one of the cushions from the sofa and bent over him.

Her scent was… It was just soap. The soap that was placed in all the guest bathrooms at the palace. But Nell made it smell intoxicating. The brush of her hair, one soft curl against his cheek, almost paralysed him.

'Is that a little better?' She'd placed the cushion carefully under his left arm so that it supported his shoulder.

'Yes. A lot better, thank you.'

Nell nodded, looking around the room as if she'd mislaid something. 'Does your apartment have a kitchen? Or do you have to send out for tea?'

'The kitchen's through there.' The desire to stay where he was battled with a strong disinclination to have her make tea for him. Hugo shifted, ready for the effort of standing up, and she reached forward, her hand on his right shoulder.

'I didn't go to all the trouble of arranging cushions for

you to spoil it all by making the tea. Stay there.' Her voice was kindly but firm. It occurred to Hugo that if he didn't feel so tired he might have delighted in having Nell be kind and firm with him all afternoon, and then he reminded himself that business and pleasure was a very bad mix.

He heard her clattering around in the kitchen and closed his eyes. Listening to Nell was almost as good as watching her, because he could still see her in his mind's eye. That was another thing that was going to have to stop.

Nell found a set of mugs in the kitchen cupboard. It was a surprise, since she'd expected that a prince would drink only out of bone china, but a good one. She'd been up very early this morning and could definitely do with a decent-sized cup of tea.

She looked in the cupboard for biscuits and found a packet of chocolate digestives. Things were definitely looking up. Next to them was a packet of painkillers, wrapped around with a piece of paper with a typed chart, each dose ticked off neatly. Hugo had taken this morning's tablets but was past due for the lunchtime ones.

He was clearly overdoing things. And her letter of appointment had spelled out exactly what she was supposed to do in response to that likely eventuality. She had to make sure that he took the rest he needed.

She put the tea things on a tray and walked quietly into the sitting room. Large and filled with light, the furniture was stylish but comfortable, allowing the baroque fireplace and the gilded mirror above it to take precedence. Hugo seemed to be dozing, but when she put the tray down, moving a small side table next to his chair, he opened his eyes.

'This is…quite unnecessary.' He seemed quite devoted to the idea that there was nothing wrong with him.

'And these?' She raised an eyebrow, putting a glass of

water and his tablets down next to him. 'Pain's generally the body's way of hinting that you should slow down a bit.'

'I thought I'd take them when I got back.' He seemed to be watching her every move as he downed the tablets in one, then took some sips of water. 'Please. Sit down. We really must talk.'

It was almost a relief. It seemed that Hugo wanted to make their relationship clear as much as she did, and it was a grey area that Nell was feeling increasingly uncomfortable with. She put his tea on the table next to him and sat down on the sofa, reaching for her cup.

'The first thing I need to say is that your job here is strictly confidential.' Nell took a breath to protest that she knew all about doctor-patient confidentiality and he silenced her with a flash of his green eyes. 'More so than usual. I don't want anyone to know what your role is here or that I'm your patient.'

Nell felt her heart beat a little faster. 'Is there a reason for that?'

'Yes, there is. A very good reason.'

'I'd like to know what that reason is, please.' She injected as much firmness into her voice as she could.

Hugo smiled suddenly. If he was unused to anyone questioning his decisions, it didn't seem to bother him all that much. 'I imagine you've done your homework and that you know I've been working very hard in the last few years to raise awareness about heart disease and promote early treatment.'

'I know that you're the patron of a charity that has done a lot of work in the field...' How much work Hugo had personally done hadn't been made clear in the article she'd read.

For a moment, it seemed that finally she'd managed to offend him. And then he smiled. 'I'm a doctor and it's my mission. You have a mission?'

'Yes. I suppose I do.'

'Then you'll understand the compelling nature of it. Weakness on my part can only undermine the message I'm trying to give.'

Nell swallowed hard, trying to clear the rapidly growing lump in her throat. 'Or…it might be seen as a strength. That you understand…'

'My job is to make things happen. And I'll freely admit that I'm a prime example of someone who hasn't followed the most basic advice and sought help at the first signs of any problem with my heart. Which is inexcusable, since I have a very clear understanding of what those signs are.'

So he couldn't allow himself this. In Hugo's mind, his illness gave him feet of clay. Nell might disagree, but it was his decision.

'What you choose to share about your own medical issues is entirely up to you. Of course, I'll say nothing.'

He nodded. 'Thank you. I see from your CV that you've taken an interest in the psychological aspects of recovery from heart disease.'

Something about his tone gave Nell the impression that this irritated him. 'Yes, that's right. I did a module on the psychology of recovery at medical school, and when I decided to specialise in cardiac medicine, it seemed very relevant. I co-authored a study on patients' post-operative experiences, in partnership with doctors from five other hospitals.'

'I'd be interested in reading it.' He turned the corners of his mouth down, and Nell felt her muscles in her stomach twist. Maybe he'd decided that questioning whether he needed a doctor wasn't enough, and that he'd take a leaf from her ex-boss's book and undermine her by questioning her professional ability.

She stared at him, wordlessly, and Hugo smiled suddenly. 'I'd be interested to know which category of patient I fall into.'

That charm again. That smile, which seemed calculated to make Nell's head spin and throw her off guard. 'Psychology isn't a matter of putting people into boxes, it's a way of understanding what's there. I'm sure you know that already.'

Perhaps she should mention that understanding exactly why Hugo was so desperate to pretend that there was nothing wrong with him would be a good start in getting him on the road to recovery. Or maybe she should wait until Hugo was ready to voice that idea for himself, even if scraping through the layers of charm and getting him to admit to anything seemed likely to be a long process.

'Yes, I do. And please forgive me if my welcome has fallen short of expectations. Your presence here wasn't my choice, it's my father who thinks I need a minder.'

Nell swallowed down the temptation to take the bait. 'I'm a doctor. If my duty of care to you, as my patient, makes me seem like a minder then...' She shrugged.

Hugo leaned forward, the cushion at his side slipping to the floor. 'Why don't you go ahead and say it? I can take it.'

If he thought that she couldn't look into his green eyes and say exactly what she meant, he was going to find out differently. Nell met his gaze and felt shivers run down her spine. Okay, so it was difficult to do. But not impossible.

'If you think that I'm here to be your minder, then that says a lot more about your approach to this than it does mine.'

'I suppose it does. But I want to make one thing clear. Duty to my father and professional courtesy to you require that I listen to your advice. But I have specific goals, in connection with a project at the hospital, that need to be met over the next six weeks. I won't allow anything to get in the way of that.'

'Even at the cost of your own health?'

'I can handle it.'

The battle lines had been drawn, and in the heat of his gaze it felt almost exhilarating. Then Nell came to her senses.

In the last three weeks, Hugo had faced a crisis. If that appeared to have had no effect on him, then maybe that just meant he was more adept at covering his emotions than most. He was hurting and unable to trust his own body any more, and if his reaction to that was stubborn failure to face facts, it was her job to get him to a place where he felt strong enough to admit how he felt.

His smouldering green eyes were suddenly too much for her to bear, and she looked away. 'Compromising on the way you get there doesn't necessarily mean you have to abandon your goals. Let me help you.'

He thought for a moment. 'What kind of compromise did you have in mind?'

Nell took a deep breath. This might be the first of many hurdles, but she'd made a start. 'I don't know yet. I'll need to examine you first and hear exactly what your commitments are. Then we can talk about it.'

'All right.' He smiled suddenly, as if he'd just remembered that he ought to do so. 'I'll make an effort to be a model patient.'

Somehow Nell doubted that. 'I appreciate the thought. But you've a long way to go before you qualify for the title of my most awkward patient.'

This time Hugo *really* smiled. 'Shame. I'll have to try harder.'

'Yes, you will.' Nell rose from her seat, picking the cushion up from the floor and putting it back in place, behind his shoulder. 'You can plan your strategy while I go and get my medical bag.'

Maybe his father knew him better than Hugo had

thought. His doctor at the hospital had been highly qualified, deferential, and had treated the whole thing as if it were an afternoon at a health spa. Nell was something different. Honest, no-nonsense and quite capable of cutting him down to size when he tried all the usual diversionary tactics.

*Dr Penelope.* He didn't dare call her that, she'd told him she preferred *Nell*. Which was charming in its own way but didn't seem to sum her up quite so well. Fierce, beautiful and unstoppable.

It was a little easier to think when she was out of the room. A little easier to remind himself of the flat in London, right at the top of a tenement block, where the lift sometimes worked and sometimes didn't.

A little pang of regret for times that had seemed altogether simpler. The sofa that had creaked slightly under the weight of two people too tired to move and yet happy to just be together. The awful green bedspread that Anna had chosen, and which hadn't matched the curtains but which Hugo had liked because she had. It had been the one time in Hugo's life when duty hadn't weighed heavy on his shoulders. All he'd needed to do was work hard at medical school and love the woman who shared his life.

He'd brought Anna back to Montarino, two newly minted doctors, full of so many possibilities and dreams. The ring on her finger had been replaced by something more befitting a princess, but Anna had always preferred the old one, which Hugo had saved for out of his allowance. It wasn't until she'd left that Hugo had stopped to think that maybe she had been unhappy at the palace.

And that had been his doing. Anna had trained to be a doctor, not a princess. She had fitted the bill well enough, but it hadn't been her mission in life. Hugo had been too intent on pursuing his own mission to see that until it had been too late and Anna had been packing her bags, a ticket back to London with her name on it lying on the bed.

*'If you'd just looked, Hugo, you would have seen that this isn't enough for me. I have a career, too.'*

There had been nothing that he could say because he had known in his heart that Anna was right. He'd let her go, and had watched from afar as she'd risen to the top of her chosen field, like a cork held underwater for too long and bouncing to the surface of a fast-flowing stream. One that had taken her away from him, and had never brought her back again.

Since then, Hugo had confined himself to women whose career aspirations were limited to being a princess. And if he hadn't found anyone who truly understood him yet, then one of these days his duty would outweigh the yearning for love and he'd marry regardless. It had never made its way to the top of his to-do list, though, and it could wait.

The sound of a chair being pushed across the carpet towards his broke his reverie. It seemed that the doctor was ready for him now.

'Would you unbutton your shirt for me, please?' Nell sat down opposite him, briskly reaching into a small nylon bag to retrieve a stethoscope.

Suddenly he felt slightly dizzy. At the hospital, he'd submitted to one examination after the other, distancing himself from the doctors and nurses who quietly did their jobs while he thought about something else. But Nell was different. She challenged him, demanding that he take notice of what was happening to him.

'My notes are…somewhere…' He looked around, trying to remember where he'd left the envelope.

'I have them. They were emailed through to me yesterday. I'd like to check on how you are now.'

Whether he'd managed to throw any spanners in the works. Her meaning shone clear in her light brown eyes, almost amber in the sunshine that streamed through the high windows.

He looked away from her gaze. Hugo had no qualms about his body, he knew that it was as good as the next man's and that he didn't have to think twice before he allowed anyone to see it. But things were different now. The new, unhealed scar felt like overwhelming evidence of his greatest weakness.

Nell sat motionless opposite him, clearly willing to wait him out if need be. He reached for the buttons of his shirt, his fingers suddenly clumsy.

Hugo was finding this hard. Nell pretended not to notice, twisting at the earpieces of her stethoscope as if she'd just found something wrong with them. The very fact that he seemed about to baulk at the idea of a simple examination told her that Hugo wasn't as confident about his recovery as he liked to make out.

That was okay. Nell would have been more comfortable if she could maintain a degree of professional detachment too, but that wasn't going to work. The main thing at the moment was to maintain their tenuous connection, because if that was lost then so was their way forward.

'What about official engagements?' She'd pretty much exhausted all the things that might be wrong with her stethoscope, and perhaps talking would put him at ease.

'My father's beaten you to it. He's taken care of all my official engagements for the next month. There are various members of the family stepping in.'

'I'll have to be quicker off the mark next time,' Nell commented lightly, trying not to notice that he was slipping his shirt off, revealing tanned skin and a mouth-wateringly impressive pair of shoulders. She concentrated on the dressing on Hugo's chest, peeling it back carefully.

'There's still the hospital project.' He shot her a grin

and Nell felt her hands shake slightly. Being this close to
Hugo added a whole new catalogue of ways in which he
made her feel uneasy. The scent of his skin. The way she
wanted to touch him…

'What does that involve?' Nell did her best to forget
about everything else and concentrate on the surgical incision on Hugo's chest.

'We're building a new wing at the hospital. It's going to
be a specialist cardiac centre, with outpatient services, a
family resource department and a unit for long-stay pae-
diatric patients.'

'That sounds like a very worthwhile project.'

'Yes, it is. And there's no alternative but for me to be
out there, raising money for it.'

'There's always an alternative…' Nell murmured the
words, clipping the stethoscope into her ears and pressing
the diaphragm to his chest.

'The work's already started and we've run into some
unforeseen problems. There's an underground chamber
that needs to be investigated and made safe. With men
and equipment already on-site, every day of delay costs
money, even without the cost of the new works. If we don't
raise that money, we can't afford to complete the project.'

'And you're the only one who can do it?'

'No, but I have the contacts to raise what we need in the
time frame we need it. We're looking for large donations.'

Nell frowned. There might be a grain of truth in Hugo's assertion that he was indispensable and couldn't take
a break, although she still wasn't ruling out the possibility that pig-headedness and ego were also factors. 'I don't
know much about these things but…couldn't your father
help out with a loan?'

'I'm sure he would have made a donation, and I would
have, too. But the Constitution of Montarino forbids it.'

'Really? You can't give money to charity?' Nell's eyebrows shot up.

'We can and we do, but it's very strictly regulated. The royal family is only allowed to donate five percent of the total cost of a public endeavour, and that ceiling has almost been reached already. You can blame my great-great-grandfather for that—he tried to buy up key parts of the country's infrastructure in an attempt to maintain his influence, and so the legislation was rushed through. For all the right reasons, in my opinion, but at the moment it's an inconvenience.'

'But it's okay if you *raise* the money?'

'Yes. History and politics always make things a great deal more complicated.'

As a doctor, this wasn't complicated at all. But Nell could feel herself being dragged into a world of blurred lines. Hugo's charm, the way her fingers tingled when she touched his skin. That was one line she couldn't cross.

'So you have to rest but you can't. We'll have to be creative...'

Hugo chuckled. 'I'm beginning to like the way you think.'

'Don't start liking it too much. If your health's at risk, I'm going to do everything I can to stop you.'

'Noted. Does that mean I can do everything I can to stop you from stopping me?'

'If that means you're going to get enough rest, and make sure you don't compromise your recovery, then feel free.' This war of words was fast becoming a little too intimate. A little too much like the delicious push and pull of meeting someone who could become a *very* good friend.

But it worked. Hugo nodded, his hand drifting to his chest. 'So what's the verdict, then?'

'Everything looks fine. You can see for yourself.'

He shook his head, and Nell realised that she hadn't

seen him look down at his chest once. 'I'll take your word for it. So…the day after tomorrow…'

'What's happening then?'

'It's a lunchtime fundraiser. I get to sit comfortably in the sun and make a two-minute speech. Actually, you could come along if you like.'

'There are spare tickets?'

'I'm your ticket.'

Nell gulped down the realisation that she'd be there as his plus-one. What mattered was that she'd be there, which meant that Hugo would have a doctor, and hopefully a re-straining influence, on hand.

'Okay. Let's see how you are tomorrow and make the decision then.' Twenty-four hours and a night's sleep might just be enough time to get her head straight.

'Fair enough.' His green eyes seemed to see right through her. And it was worrying that when he turned his gaze onto her, his lips twitched into a smile.

# CHAPTER THREE

NELL HAD SPENT as much of the afternoon as she could un-
packing. Laying things into neat piles and hanging dresses
in the large wardrobe. Smoothing the already immaculate
covers of the great bed, which would have dominated a
smaller room but here was simply in proportion. It had
been an exercise in restoring order, pushing back the chaos
that seemed to follow Hugo like the scent of expensive
aftershave.

He seemed intent on playing the host, inviting her for
dinner in his apartment. Over a beautifully cooked and
presented meal, Hugo talked about the charity that seemed
so close to his heart. How they'd raised awareness about
heart disease and increased the number of people who had
regular 'healthy heart' checks. How they wanted to move
forward and provide a centre of excellence, which would
cater to both inpatients and outpatients, for all the people
of Montarino.

It was a dazzling vision. And yet here, at the centre of
it all, was a man who felt the need to risk his own health.

She returned to her apartment tired but unable to sleep.
A long bath didn't help, and neither did reading a book.
Nell scarcely registered the words in front of her, because
Hugo seemed to fill her mind, chasing everything else
away. He'd said that he would be going straight to bed
after she left, but when she went out into the darkness of

the hallway she could still see a sliver of light escaping
under the connecting door to his apartment.

She could hear Hugo's voice, distant and muffled behind the heavy door. Either he was talking to himself or
there was someone there.

Someone there. There were pauses, as if he was waiting
for an answer and as Nell pressed her ear to the door she
thought she heard another voice, this one too low and quiet
for her to be even sure whether it was a woman or a man.

Whoever it was, they shouldn't be there. It was midnight, and Hugo should be asleep by now. Nell's hand trembled as she took hold of the door handle. Walking into his
apartment and telling him to go to bed might be one step
too far.

But they'd had an agreement. He'd promised. And Nell
had believed him. The feeling of empty disappointment
in him spurred her on.

'Hugo…' She opened the door an inch, and heard the
soft sound of classical music, coming from the room beyond. 'Are you still up?'

Silence. Then the door handle was pulled out of her grip
as Hugo swung the door open, standing in the doorway
and blocking her view of the sitting room.

'This isn't the time, Nell.' He spoke quietly, as if he
didn't want the person behind him in the room to hear.

He obviously wanted some privacy and the thought
struck Nell that his companion might be a woman. She
felt her cheeks flush red. The last thing she wanted to do
was come face-to-face with a girlfriend, who for some
reason Hugo hadn't seen fit to mention.

'I'm…sorry, but we had a deal, Hugo.'

'I'm aware of that. Something came up.'

'That's not good enough…' Nell stopped herself from
telling him that he should be in bed. In the circumstances,

that might be a catalyst for even more exertion on his part. She felt her ears begin to burn at the thought.

'It's not what you're thinking, Nell.'

'Really? What do you think I'm thinking?' If she really was that transparent then things had just gone from very bad to much worse.

'What I'd be thinking. But on this occasion, we'd both be wrong.' He stood back from the doorway, allowing her to see into the room. Two seats were drawn up to a games table, which had been set up by the fireplace, and an elderly man sat in one of them. He wore immaculately pressed pyjamas and held himself erect in his seat. When he turned towards Nell, his milky blue eyes seemed not quite to focus on her.

'Jacob, we have a visitor. This is Nell.'

'A pleasure, miss.' The man spoke quietly, in heavily accented English. Despite his neat appearance, there was something vulnerable about him.

'It's a pleasure to meet you, Jacob.' Nell went to advance into the room, but Hugo stepped back into her path.

'Nell can't stay…' He threw the words over his shoulder, turning painfully to Nell and motioning to her to comply. She didn't move.

Hugo took a step forward, and she took a step back, instinctively avoiding touching him. He pulled the door half shut behind them.

'Jacob is…fragile.' He was whispering, but Nell could hear both urgency and fatigue in his voice.

'I can see that. But you need your sleep.' Whispering back seemed rather too conspiratorial for Nell's liking but having Jacob hear what was going on didn't seem like a good idea.

'I'll take him back to his apartment as soon as I can.'

'No, Hugo. You said we'd take things as they came and that you'd accept my help. Let's give that a trial run now, shall we?' Hugo hesitated and she glared at him. 'I'm not going to walk in there and order him out.'

Silently he walked back through the doorway, and Nell followed him. Jacob turned to Hugo, a fond smile on his face. 'Hugo, my boy… What's going on?'

'Nothing. It's all right, Jacob. I've asked Nell to join us.'

'Very good.' Jacob seemed to approve of the plan, gesturing towards the draughts, which lay on the chequerboard tabletop. 'You play, miss?'

'Not very well.' Nell smiled at him.

'Jacob taught me to play thirty years ago.' Hugo went to pull up a chair for Nell and thought better of it, allowing her to move it across to the table. 'I used to sneak downstairs when my parents were out in the evening, and we'd play draughts and drink hot chocolate.'

'Hot chocolate!' Jacob's eyes lit up suddenly, and he gestured towards the pot that lay on the coffee table, along with two gold-rimmed cups and saucers. 'I remember now. Would you like some, miss?'

Maybe that would bring the evening to a close. 'Thank you. I'll get another cup, shall I?'

Nell glanced at Hugo, and he nodded, resuming his seat opposite Jacob. His smile barely concealed his fatigue and he was moving as if he was in pain. The sooner they could end, this the better.

As Nell walked to the kitchen, she heard the two men talking quietly in French behind her.

'Who is she, Hugo?'

'She's a doctor, and her name's Nell.'

Hugo repeated the words, no hint in his tone that this wasn't the first time he'd told Jacob.

'A doctor? What does she want?' Jacob's voice took on an air of perplexed worry.

'She's here for me. Not you, my friend.' Hugo's tone was smooth, reassuring.

'Where's she going?'

'Just to get another cup. We're having hot chocolate.'

'Ah, yes. Hot chocolate and draughts…'

Jacob's memory had become fragmented by time. Some things were still clear in his mind, but he was groping in the dark, trying to make sense of others. It was common in patients who had dementia, and it was clear that Hugo was trying to reassure Jacob by re-creating the sights and sounds of things he did remember. The sound the counters made on the draughts board. The taste of hot chocolate. But that was all coming with a cost to him.

She fetched the cup and re-joined the two men, wondering whether Hugo knew that she'd heard and understood their conversation. Smiling, she poured the hot chocolate and sat down. Jacob moved one of his pieces and Hugo chuckled quietly.

'You have me…' He made the only move possible, and Jacob responded by taking four of his counters in one go.

'Another game?' The old man still seemed wide awake, and Nell wondered how long this was going to go on before he tired and they could take him back to wherever he'd come from.

Hugo nodded, and Nell shot him a frown. He couldn't do this all night, but it appeared that he was perfectly capable of trying if it kept Jacob happy.

'Will you teach me, please? I know how to play, but I don't know the tactics.'

'Of course, *mademoiselle*.' Perhaps Jacob had forgotten her name again, but he remembered how to play draughts, and that was the way that Nell could keep him occupied while Hugo rested.

Hugo stood, giving Nell his seat, and retreated to the sofa. As she and Jacob set out the pieces, ready to play, he seemed to be dozing.

At least Hugo was relaxing, now. As they played, Jacob

became animated, suggesting better moves to Nell, slipping from French into English and then back again, sometimes in the course of one sentence. Finally he began to tire.

'Hugo's tired. He's ready to go to bed now.' Nell nodded towards Hugo. If Jacob had known him since he was a boy, then he would also remember taking care of him, and some part of that relationship would still exist somewhere in his head.

'Is it time?' Jacob glanced around the room and then at his own attire. 'It must be. I'm wearing my pyjamas.'

That posed a second problem. Nell had no idea who Jacob was or where he'd come from. But Jacob turned, calling softly to Hugo.

'Wake up, lad. Time to go to bed.'

Instantly, Hugo's eyes were open and he roused himself. Jacob clearly came first, however tired he was. 'Let's go.'

Nell was perfect. Hugo had been prepared to exert his authority and order her out of his apartment, but she'd realised Jacob's situation very quickly and had played along. More than that, she'd taken charge, allowing Hugo to relax and get comfortable. Despite all his efforts to conceal it, he had to admit that he was very tired.

He led the way through the quiet corridors of the palace, Nell and Jacob arm in arm behind him. As he ushered them through one of the back doors and across the small courtyard towards the neat row of cottages used by palace employees, he wondered whether she'd be quite as gentle and understanding when Jacob was no longer within earshot.

It took Celeste a while to answer the door, and when she did so she was bleary-eyed, pulling on her dressing gown. Looking after Jacob was becoming a twenty-four-hour-a-day task for her, and she'd clearly been fast asleep when Hugo had texted her to say that Jacob was with him.

He waved away her apologies and said goodnight, hearing Nell's voice behind him echoing the sentiment.

The door closed and he turned to Nell, watching as the smile slipped from her face. That capable, no-nonsense expression didn't fail to send a tingle down his spine, even if he was far too tired to make the best of whatever conflict was brewing.

'So, Jacob wanders at night?' She walked next to him back across the courtyard.

'Yes. I'd appreciate it if you didn't say anything about it.'

He couldn't see the flash of her eyes in the darkness, but imagined it there. 'This place is full of secrets, isn't it? How long do you think you can cover this up?'

'I don't need very long. Before I went into hospital, I was talking to Celeste about getting a carer for him at night so that she could get some sleep. I contacted her after I was taken ill and she said that things were okay and she was managing on her own.' He turned the corners of his mouth down. Clearly things hadn't been okay, and Celeste had just not wanted him to worry.

'Celeste's his daughter?'

'Yes. Jacob came to work here at the palace when he was sixteen, it's the only home he knows. My father's always said that he and Celeste have a place here for as long as they want.'

'So why all the secrecy?' Nell frowned, clearly bothered by it.

'When he heard that Jacob had been wandering at night, my father went to see Celeste and mentioned to her that a nursing home might be the right place for Jacob, and offered to pay the bills. Celeste took that as a royal command...'

'But he was really just trying to help.' Nell gave Hugo's father the benefit of the doubt. Maybe Hugo should, too.

'I'm sure he was. But Celeste doesn't think it's the right thing for Jacob and neither do I. Like I said, this is his only home and he'd be even more disorientated than he is now in a new place.'

'Okay. Let me get this clear.' Nell stopped suddenly in the middle of the courtyard, and Hugo felt the hairs on the back of his neck stand up. They were in full view of the palace, and he didn't take anonymity for granted the way that Nell obviously did. He saw a light flip on, and then back off again. Probably nothing.

'Your father thinks that the best place for Jacob is a nursing home, and you think it's best for him to stay here.' Hugo dragged his attention back to what Nell was saying. 'So instead of talking to him about it, you're going to get a night carer in, see if that works and then tell your father about it.'

When she put it like that it didn't sound the best way of doing things. But then Nell didn't know his father. 'Yes. That's essentially it.'

She held up her hands in a gesture of resignation. 'Okay. You have an agency in mind, where you can get this carer?'

'Yes…' Hugo had wondered how he was going to break the news to her that tomorrow he'd be busy making those arrangements.

'Right. Give the details to me. I can do an assessment of Jacob and talk to Celeste about what she thinks is best in the morning, and we'll get things moving. If we can get someone in for tomorrow night, then Celeste can get some sleep and think better about her long-term options.'

Her tone brooked no argument, which was generally like a red rag to a bull where Hugo was concerned. But Nell was right. And although he'd only known Nell for a matter of hours, he trusted her. She'd take good care of his old friend.

'Thank you. I'd appreciate that.' He started to walk towards the back door of the palace, where they'd be out of sight of anyone who happened to be traversing one of the rear corridors.

'That, of course, is dependent on your not taking advantage of my being busy elsewhere to do something you shouldn't.' Nell caught up with him.

'Of course.' He opened the door for her and she walked through.

'I'd feel happier if you said it.'

He could see her face now, shining in the dim light of the corridor. A little humour mixed with the kind of determined compassion that he reckoned must make her a very good doctor.

'My mother's intending to cheer me up over lunch tomorrow. You can hand her the keys to the ball and chain if you want.' Nell raised her eyebrows and he sighed. 'If you'd be good enough to see Jacob in the morning, you have my word of honour that I'll rest.'

A stab of guilt accompanied the thought that he'd been a little hard on Nell. For the last two weeks, he'd gritted his teeth and submitted as gracefully as he could to the authority of his doctors and nurses and the limitations his own labouring heart had put on him. Yesterday morning, when he'd arrived back at the palace, he'd resolved to leave all that behind. He had to get back to normal as quickly as possible if he was to achieve the goals he'd set himself.

None of that had anything to do with Nell, though. She had a job to do, and when she smiled at him, everything else seemed to retreat back into obscurity.

'Thank you.' She gave him a *now we're getting somewhere* smile. Maybe they were.

# CHAPTER FOUR

HUGO LOOKED RESTED and relaxed. Like someone who had spent yesterday in his apartment doing nothing in particular while Nell assessed Jacob and made all the arrangements for a carer to come and help Celeste. Which was just as Nell wanted things to be.

But today was sure to bring new challenges. Hugo had wished her a good morning, and Nell had responded by picking up his car keys and giving him a lecture about staying within his limits. Ted, his bodyguard, had flashed her a quiet smile and got into the front passenger seat of Hugo's car, while she fiddled with the driver's seat, pulling it forward.

'Remember to drive on the left.' Hugo's quiet voice had sounded from the back of the car, and she'd ignored him, slipping off her high sandals and starting the car.

Ted directed her through the morning traffic to a large house, set back from the road and gleaming white in the sunshine. She'd followed the ushers' signals and parked the car between two others, which would have cost her the approximate value of her own flat had she been careless enough to scratch them.

'You look very nice.' Hugo bent towards her as they walked together to the circle of awnings laid out behind the house.

'Thank you.' On the basis that she couldn't compete

with anyone here, Nell had decided on a plain dress with
no jewellery. That seemed to fit well enough with Hugo's
approach, a grey suit with a white open-necked shirt. No
signet rings, no diamond tie pins. He really didn't need
that kind of thing, he was striking enough already, tall
and tanned, with an easy manner that marked him out
as someone who would always be acceptable in any social setting.

She was introduced to their hosts, and Hugo kissed the
lady of the house on both cheeks. A drink appeared magically in her hand, and Hugo shook his head when he was
offered one, obviously feeling that the juggling of drinks
and handshakes would be too much for him to accomplish
while taking care not to compromise his recent surgery.

'Prince Hugo!' A middle-aged woman marched up to
him, and Hugo responded to her greeting with a hug. His
face and body showed no signs of the pain that it would
have caused him, but Nell knew that his left shoulder must
be pulling at the movement. Then someone brushed against
his left side, and this time he jumped imperceptibly.

This was no good. Nell carefully slipped in between
Hugo and the people on his left side, curling her fingers
around his left elbow. She knew exactly which angle his
arm would be the most comfortable at, and she made a
show of seeming to hang on to his arm, while making sure
that it stayed immobile.

A nod, and a smile in her direction. And then, just for
her, a mouthed *Thank you*.

'Nell's here from London. A friend of the family.'

The woman who was with him smiled. 'What do you
do?'

'She's in between jobs.' Hugo had obviously decided to
speak for her, in case she got their story wrong. 'Taking a
well-earned holiday.'

'I'm particularly interested in the work of Hugo's char-

ity.' Nell decided that taking Hugo's arm could be forgiven, under the circumstances. Acting like a glove puppet
couldn't.

'Ah...' The woman nodded. 'Well, he's risen to the occasion yet again. Are you going to make a bid for him in
the charity auction? So generous of His Highness to donate a trip with him on the royal yacht as one of the lots!'

Nell gave her brightest smile. 'He didn't tell me that
there was going to be an auction after lunch until yesterday
evening. It would be rude of me not to put in a bid for him.'

The woman laughed, and Hugo smiled graciously. Nell
gritted her teeth.

A seemingly endless amount of small talk was cut short
by their hostess, and everyone found their places at the
tables. Champagne was served, and Nell leaned towards
Hugo.

'What happens if the amount I have to bid for you goes
over the limit you can donate to the project?' She hadn't
thought that would be possible last night, but now she
wasn't so sure.

'You over-estimate my desirability.'

'Not really. These women all look as if they can spend
a large amount on just a whim.'

'I'm suitably crushed.' He put his hand to his heart,
not looking even slightly crushed. 'Remember this was
your idea.'

'Were there any other options?'

'There's always another option. But your solution was
the best.'

'So you weren't looking forward to entertaining some
lucky girl on the royal yacht for the weekend?'

'What makes you think it's going to be a woman? The
trip on the yacht is the point of it all—a family with children would enjoy it, too.'

Right. Nell would bet a pound to a penny that there

wouldn't be any men bidding for this particular lot. But telling him that would only add to the chorus of appreciation that surrounded him, and Hugo already seemed to be under the misapprehension that he could get away with almost anything.

'What's Montarino doing with a royal yacht, anyway? It's completely landlocked.' Nell hadn't thought to ask last night.

'It's moored in France. Montarino has an ancient treaty that allows us safe harbour there. Unfortunately the treaty doesn't mention bills for the marina, so we have to pay those.'

'So you were intending a three-hour drive to the coast, in addition to swimming and sailing and…whatever else you do on a royal yacht? You do know that you're not supposed to be driving for six weeks.' Last night this plan had seemed a matter of pretending to pay a nominal amount to get Hugo out of a fix. Now the stakes were looking a lot higher.

'I won't be doing any of that, though, will I? Not if you win the bidding.'

The look that she gave him made the large hole that this afternoon was going to make in his bank balance seem more than worth it. Hugo could have changed his contribution to this afternoon's auction to something that demanded a little less activity on his part, but the programmes were all printed, and somehow the idea of having Nell stake her claim on him publicly had made him lose touch with the more sensible options.

Lunch was eaten, and a frisson of excitement ran around the tables when the auctioneer climbed up onto his podium. Nell's hand moved to her bidding card.

'You're sure there's no limit?' She smiled suddenly and

the sunlight playing on the ornamental fountains, on each side of the group of tables, dimmed in comparison.

'I trust you.'

'That might just be your first mistake…'

She was enjoying this. It occurred to Hugo that Nell might be about to teach him a lesson, and the idea didn't fill him with as much dismay as it should have done.

Premier tickets for a football match, courtesy of Montarino's one and only football team. Seats for a hotly anticipated rock concert. Some silver jewellery, from an up-and-coming new designer, who had cannily decided that it would do her no harm to have her work seen by the guests here today, was snapped up after a bidding war.

'That's a beautiful piece. It'll really suit her.' Nell was completely caught up in the proceedings, leaning over to murmur the words in his ear as she watched the winner talking excitedly to her husband.

'Would you like one? I can have another made…' The abstract curves of the silver necklace would actually suit Nell far better than they would Monique LaTour.

'Don't you dare!' She turned to him, a look of reprimand on her face. 'For what she's just paid, she deserves to have something unique.'

Hugo thought about telling her that Jacques LaTour was a multimillionaire and that Monique had enough jewellery to fill a wardrobe. But he doubted the information would make any difference to Nell, and anyway her attention was back on the auctioneer's podium now.

'Now, a special treat, ladies and gentlemen. Hosted by His Royal Highness Crown Prince Hugo DeLeon, a weekend trip on Montarino's royal yacht.' A gratifying buzz of excitement ran around the tables. Hugo smiled in acknowledgement, and then glanced at Nell. Her champagne flute was in her hand, and she'd just downed the whole glass in one.

\* \* \*

Ted would have to drive back, or they could call for the chauffeur. Nell was sure that something could be arranged, and she needed something to calm her nerves. Bubbles hit the back of her throat and she almost choked.

This was it. She was about to spend an unknown sum of Hugo's money just to have his company for the weekend and ensure he didn't over-exert himself, something she was being paid to do anyway. The doctor's common room would have had a field day with that, but suddenly she couldn't have cared less. This felt like an adventure, one that might wipe away all the slights that had hurt her so over the last year.

As soon as the bidding started, three women held their cards up. The auctioneer managed to come to a decision over who had bid first, and as his finger moved briskly to and fro the price began to rocket upwards.

Nell saw Hugo's head turn towards her, and caught a glimpse of his worried expression. Then she held up her card, waving it to attract the auctioneer's attention.

'Two thousand from the lady on the right…' Nell felt slightly giddy at the idea that she was spending this much money.

There were many more rounds of determined bidding and one by one her rivals shook their heads. When the auctioneer rapped his hammer, an unexpected burst of exhilaration made Nell catch her breath. A few people looked round at her as Hugo leaned towards her, smiling.

'I thought for a moment you were going to let me down. Do I detect an element of risk-taking in your approach?'

Let him think that. If this was an exercise in each keeping the other off-balance, it couldn't do any harm. Nell gave him a smile and reached for her glass, which had been refilled at some point during the bidding. Clearly one of the attentive waiters had thought she might need it.

Hugo's lot was the highlight of the afternoon. There were a couple more, to round things off, and then the ring of a silver spoon against a crystal glass called for quiet as their hostess got to her feet. She thanked everyone for being there, and introduced Hugo.

He got to his feet, smiling, and Nell saw more than one person smile back. Taking a sheet of paper from his pocket, Hugo scanned it and then tore it in two.

'Ladies and gentlemen, I had a speech prepared, but I find that there's little more I can do to add to this afternoon.'

Nell took a sip of her champagne. This sounded pretty much par for the course. This afternoon was all about delighting in smoke and mirrors, not getting to grips with the serious issues.

'First, I'd like to thank Yvette, our hostess today...' He paused as a round of applause ran around the tables, and Yvette nodded a smiling acknowledgement. 'Second, I'd like to thank you all for your generosity.'

He paused. Five seconds' silence, which was enough to catch everyone's attention. Hugo's timing was impressive.

'You all deserve to know what that generosity means. Under your placemats, you'll find a leaflet...' He held up a glossy trifold, and Nell looked under her place mat and found one just like it. 'We're not in the business of bricks and mortar, or of reputation, although we're rightly proud of Montarino Hospital's record of excellence. We deal in people.'

Hugo's gaze dropped suddenly to the trifold in his hand. Almost against her own will, Nell opened her own copy of the leaflet, seeking out the photograph inside that he seemed to be studying. A little girl in a pink dress, cuddling a battered teddy bear. She was smiling, reaching for someone or something behind the camera.

'I'll let these photographs tell you how much your kindness means. Thank you, ladies and gentlemen.'

Hugo sat down abruptly, seeming to be almost overcome by emotion. Applause ran around the tables, followed by a buzz of conversation, which seemed to be centred around the leaflets in everyone's hands.

It was a great speech. Short and to the point, and tugging nicely at the heartstrings. Nell had noticed that he'd put the paper he'd torn in half safely back into his pocket. She wondered vaguely if there had ever been anything written on it.

It didn't matter. If Nell had seen the reality of heart disease, and knew that it wasn't all smiles and teddy bears, that wasn't what today was about. She'd lost count of the amount of money that had been raised, and it seemed the auction was just the tip of the iceberg.

A middle-aged man in a silk suit had approached their table, and Hugo had turned in his seat to talk to him. He pressed a folded cheque into Hugo's hand.

'Thank you, Henri. We'll use this well.'

The woman standing next to Henri spoke. 'Next time, I insist on being the hostess, Your Highness.'

Hugo hesitated. 'You're too kind, Justine. Think about it…'

'No, I don't need to think about it. I've thought about things for too long and it's about time I did something.'

'I'll have Nathalie contact you, then. She'll talk through all the options with you.'

'I think I have an idea that will be perfect.' Justine brushed off any other options with a wave of her hand.

Henri smiled suddenly. 'We must be going. It seems that my wife has a plan that needs my attention.'

'You shouldn't work so hard, Hugo…' Justine frowned suddenly at Hugo and caught Nell's eye, reverting to English. 'Take him away, my dear. He is neglecting his responsibilities to you.'

Nell smiled, not knowing quite what to say, and Hugo bade the couple goodbye. When he turned, his face was suddenly ashen and drawn. This was the first time that Nell had seen Hugo betray any weakness, and he was obviously tired.

Nell leaned towards him, speaking quietly. 'We're going. Now.' She injected as little room for argument into her tone as possible.

'I think you're right… Yvette will wrap things up.'

Nell glanced across at their hostess and saw that she too was accepting cheques, tucking them into a small designer clutch bag that lay on the table in front of her, which seemed to contain little else.

'I'll…go and make our excuses…' Maybe something would spring to mind on the way over to Yvette's table.

'That's all right. I said we might have to leave a little early.' Hugo reached for an auction programme, taking a pen from his pocket and scribbling something on it, then beckoning to one of the waiters. The note was carried to Yvette, who read it and smiled over at them.

Whatever he'd written, it seemed that their hostess was now happy to allow them to leave with as little fuss as possible. Nell bit back the thought that they should never have been here in the first place. Perhaps this would serve as a lesson to Hugo, and he'd respect his own limitations a little better from now on.

He swayed a little as he stood, wincing in pain. Nell hung on to his right arm, supporting him as well as she could and ignoring the glances and smiles from the people who crossed their path on the way back into the house. If they wanted to jump to the conclusion that there was something between her and Hugo, then let them. She imagined that she was just the latest in a very long list, which had the virtue of rendering her unremarkable.

Ted appeared out of nowhere, and Nell breathed a sigh of relief. 'Would you be able to bring the car round, please, Ted?'

'Yes, Doctor.' Ted flashed her a conspiratorial smile and hurried away.

Hugo almost stumbled at the bottom of the steps at the front of the house, and when she put her arm around him to steady him, Nell found herself almost in an embrace.

'I'm sorry.' He made to pull away, but Nell held him tight.

'That's all right. We'll just get home, shall we?' She could see his car now, moving towards them, Ted at the wheel.

He nodded, and she felt his arm curl around her shoulders. 'Yes. Thank you.'

# CHAPTER FIVE

HUGO HADN'T QUITE been feeling fine, but he had at least been in charge of himself. And then suddenly he'd hit a wall. The one that he told his own patients about and reassured them wouldn't be there for ever.

If Nell hadn't been there, he wasn't sure how he would have managed. But she had, and he'd felt her next to him, holding on tight as he'd walked what had seemed like a marathon to get to the car. Somehow, her scent had strengthened him and stopped him from just sitting down right where he was and not getting back up again.

Ted had helped him back up to his apartment and Nell had fussed around, taking off his shoes and jacket and loosening the collar of his shirt, then making him lie down on the bed. He'd protested and she'd ignored him, and then suddenly a wave of fatigue had pulled him into sleep.

When he woke, the room was in semi-darkness. He could make Nell out, sitting by the window, reading in the last rays of the sun.

'Do you want me to say it?' When he spoke, it felt as if his mouth was full of cotton wool.

She looked up from her book. 'You can if it makes you feel any better.'

It did. Hugo pulled the bedspread down from his chest, sitting up slowly. 'I overdid it today. I felt okay and I was sure I could manage it but…I couldn't.'

She smiled and suddenly overdoing things and proving Nell right didn't seem such a bad thing after all.

'You know, of course, that this happens. After the shock of being taken ill and then going through a surgical procedure.'

'Yes. Primitive instincts. We fight to survive, and then, when the danger's passed…'

She nodded quietly. 'And now you have to come to terms with it all.'

'What if I don't want to?' The words escaped Hugo's lips before he had a chance to stop them.

Nell shrugged. 'That's just too bad. You can command it to go away all you like, but it's not going to listen.'

Maybe. But if he couldn't rule his own feelings, then he could return the favour and not listen to them. Not let anyone know his weakness.

He swung his legs slowly from the bed. They seemed strong again. All he'd needed had been to sleep for a while.

'You're getting up?' Nell was looking around the room as if she was trying to figure something out.

'I feel much better now. What are you looking for?'

'Your wardrobe.'

'Through there.' Hugo nodded towards the door to one side of the bed, and Nell got to her feet. It seemed she'd decided to lay out a change of clothes for him. The idea that she might stay and help him into them didn't seem quite as deflating as it had when the nurses at the hospital had done it.

'Oh…' She'd opened the door and put her head inside the dressing room. 'Sure you have enough to wear here?'

'I go out a lot.' Hugo chuckled. 'Casual is on the left, at the end.'

She disappeared inside the dressing room, and Hugo heard her opening drawers and closing them again. Then

Nell reappeared, with a dark polo shirt and a pair of pale chinos over her arm. 'Will this do?'

'That's great, thanks.'

'Bathroom?'

'Through there.' Hugo indicated another door, staying put. He wondered how far Nell intended to go with this.

She disappeared into the bathroom and he heard the sound of water running. Then she popped her head around the doorway. 'I'll take a look at your chest and then leave you to it.'

Hugo heaved himself from the bed and walked into the bathroom. She'd moved the shower chair in front of the basin, and motioned him to sit down.

'How do you really feel?' She bent down, unbuttoning his shirt.

He wanted to say that he felt fine. Hugo *meant* to say that he felt fine, but in her quiet, fragrant presence he couldn't.

'As if I've been hit by a truck.'

Hugo closed his eyes, feeling her slip his shirt from his shoulders and carefully threading it off his left arm. Coming to terms with the piece of cutting-edge technology that was now implanted in his chest was the easy part. It was the thought that he was somehow flawed that he just couldn't shake.

More flawed. He hadn't been perfect to start with.

He felt her carefully remove the dressing over the surgical incision. It was hard not to shiver at the touch of Nell's cool fingers.

'It's looking good. A little bruising, still, but there's no infection and it's starting to heal. It's a nice job.'

*Nice job.* She'd said that before and he'd wanted to turn his back on her and tell her that he didn't need that doctor-to-doctor reassurance. If he'd still had a gaping wound on his chest, a scar that would never heal, it might reflect the way he felt a little better.

'Take a look.'

Hugo had purposely *not* removed the dressings to see what was underneath. But it seemed that parts of his body answered to her and not him, and his eyes flipped open. The first thing he saw was her face, composed in a reassuring smile, and even though he knew that smile was probably something she wore for all her patients it did its job. He smiled back.

'What do you think?' She stepped out of the way, and Hugo found his gaze on the mirror above the basin.

'It's...' Hugo tried for a shrug, and felt his left shoulder pull. 'You're right. It's a neat job.'

She nodded and turned to the basin, leaving him alone for a moment with his own reflection. Hugo didn't like the way it made him feel and he concentrated on watching Nell instead.

Her hands were gentle but capable as they dipped a flannel into the basin, twisting it to wring out the excess water. In his experience, that was only a short step away from tender. She laid the flannel over his shoulder, her entire concentration on what she was doing. It felt warm and comforting.

'That feels good. Thank you.'

She nodded, removing the flannel and dipping it back into the water. Wiping it across his skin, careful not to allow any drops of water near the wound. He'd seen this so many times before at the hospital, and had always felt that this was one thing that no amount of technology or learning could replace. When the nurses washed a patient, there was a tenderness about it that spoke of the kind of care that only human beings could give one another.

And now he felt it. The warm touch of water against his skin calmed Hugo, and the suspicion that everything would be all right floated into his consciousness, with all the reassurance of a forgotten friend.

She leaned towards him, rubbing the flannel across his back. Stopping to rinse and then repeat, her movements slow and thoughtful, like those of a craftsman plying his trade. Hugo closed his eyes, not ready to let go of this feeling just yet.

She finished with the flannel and gently patted his skin dry with a towel. Then he felt her fingers on the top of his left arm, gently massaging. He knew what Nell was doing. He wasn't supposed to lift his left arm above shoulder level for six weeks, and it was common to get a frozen shoulder during that time. It was just straightforward care, but it felt like so much more.

'Would you like help to shave?' He opened his eyes and saw that Nell was now opening one of the sterile dressings from the box that lay on top of the bathroom cabinet.

It had been a while since he'd let a woman shave him, and then it had been purely for pleasure. Anna had done it, but since then he hadn't let a woman get to know him that well. Hugo regarded the shaving cream on the shelf above the mirror and decided against it.

'Thanks, but I'll go with the designer stubble.'

Nell gave him a half smile. 'It suits you.'

It was the one thing she'd said that betrayed some kind of emotion locked behind the caring, and it sent tingles down Hugo's spine. Nell checked that the new dressing over his wound was firmly anchored, and then turned abruptly, leaving him alone in the bathroom.

If it worked, then it worked. Society lunches and bidding for a weekend in the presence of a prince wasn't a strategy that Nell had been called on to adopt before, and neither was washing a patient. But talking to someone, learning what made them tick and suggesting ways of coping was.

And if the sudden closeness with Hugo had left her wanting to just touch his skin, simply for the pleasure of feeling it under her fingertips, then that could be ignored in the face of a greater good. Her job here was not really to look after him in a medical sense but to get behind his suave, charming exterior, and find out what drove him so relentlessly that he was willing to risk his health for it.

Nell rang down to the palace kitchen, wondering if anyone was there at this time in the evening, and found that not only was the phone answered immediately but there was a choice of menu. She ordered a salad, on the basis that it was probably the least trouble to make.

Apart from raiding the fridge, of course. Nell had suspected that the top-of-the-range fridge in Hugo's kitchen was pretty much for show, and when she'd opened it, she'd found a selection of juices and other drinks. Nothing that involved any culinary activity other than pouring. She could have made him a milkshake, but that was about all, and a decent meal would help him recover.

The formal dining room in his apartment seemed a little too much like keeping up appearances, when that was exactly what she was trying to encourage Hugo not to do. A small table on a sheltered balcony was better, and she opened the French doors at the far end of the kitchen and arranged two chairs beside it. It would have made an excellent place to cook and enjoy food, and it was a pity that Hugo's gleaming kitchen didn't look as if it saw too many serious attempts at cooking. Nell wondered what he would say if she expressed the intention of baking a cake, and smiled to herself. Maybe she'd try it, just to see the look of bewilderment on his face.

Their meal arrived, and Nell directed the young man who carried a tray loaded with two plates and various sauces and condiments through to the balcony. He looked a little put out that she'd laid the table herself, and adjusted the position of the knives and forks carefully.

She called Hugo, and he appeared from the bedroom, looking relaxed and rested. When Nell had chosen his clothes, she been considering comfort, and hadn't spared a thought for how well they might fit or how her eye was drawn along the hard lines of his body. Chest. Left arm. It was permissible to allow her gaze to linger there, on the grounds that she was checking up on him. The strong curve of his shoulder, the golden skin of his arm, which dimpled over bone and muscle, were both visual pleasures that Nell could pretend not to have seen.

'Thank you. This is nice.' Hugo pulled one of the seats away from the table, waiting until Nell sat down before he took his own place. Even now, he couldn't quite let go and let her look after him.

'I just made a call down to the kitchen. Is someone always there?'

'No, not always. My parents are hosting a dinner party tonight.' He smiled at her, and in the muted lights that shone around the perimeter of the patio his face seemed stronger. More angular and far more determined, if that was even possible.

'So calling down for a midnight snack is usually out of the question.' Nell picked up her fork, stabbing at her food.

'Yes.' He grinned. 'If I want a midnight snack, I usually have to walk all the way down there and make it myself. Life at the palace can be unexpectedly hard at times.'

Nell couldn't help smiling in response to the quiet joke. Hugo knew exactly how lucky he was. Maybe not exactly, he probably hadn't ever battled his way around the supermarket on a Saturday morning, but he understood that he was privileged.

'If we'd been at my place, this might have been cornflakes. With chocolate milk if you were lucky.'

'You think I haven't done that?' Hugo looked slightly hurt. 'I trained as a doctor, too. You're not the only one who's eaten cornflakes with chocolate milk at three in the morning then fallen asleep on the sofa.'

Probably a nicely upholstered sofa, and not too much like the lumpy one that had been in Nell's shared digs, when she had been training. She wondered if Hugo's memories of medical school were quite as good as hers were.

'Where did you stay in London?' Holland Park, perhaps. Somewhere near the embassy.

'Shepherd's Bush. We had a flat over a pizza place for a while, and it always smelled of cooked cheese. Then we moved to Tottenham. That was a great flat, in a high-rise. You could see right across London.'

Perhaps his experience had been a little more like Nell's than she'd thought. 'It must have been a bit of a culture shock for you.'

He laid down his fork. 'People are people. That's what every doctor learns, isn't it?' He said the words as if he was explaining a simple concept that Nell had somehow failed to understand.

'Yes, of course. But some people find things easier than others.' Waiting lists. Doctors who had enough time to see to the physical needs of their patients but not always the opportunity to talk for as long as was needed... The list could go on.

'You met Justine and Henri earlier today. What did you think, that they were a couple of privileged people who like a nice lunch?'

'They...' Yes, that was exactly what Nell had thought. 'They were very generous.'

'Yes, they always are. They lost their son to heart disease when he was only two years old. Justine became very depressed and it was years before she would even talk about him. Holding a lunch event is a massive step for her.

It's not all about the money. Yvette lost her father to heart disease when she was fifteen.'

Nell felt herself flush. 'I'm sorry. I did think less of what they were doing because they're rich, and that was wrong of me.'

Hugo shook his head. 'You're not entirely wrong. A lot of the people who were at the lunch today were there because they wanted to be seen in the right places. But many of them have a real and personal commitment to what we're trying to do.'

'The little girl in the leaflet. She's really a heart patient?' Nell had had her doubts, wondering if the leaflet was principally an exercise in PR. It was important now, to know whether she'd been wrong.

'Yes, she is. One of my patients, in fact. She had her ninth operation a few days ago. She wanted to help me build her new clinic.'

Nell laughed. '*Her* new clinic.'

'Yes, it's hers. She might let a few other patients in if she likes them. No boys. And she wants it to be completely pink, like a giant marshmallow.' He was smiling now.

'Sounds like my kind of hospital.'

'So what *are* you doing here?' He asked the question quietly. 'You don't strike me as the kind of person whose ambitions lie in the direction of keeping errant princes in check.'

Hugo had a way of dropping the charm and cutting right to the chase. It was uncomfortable. 'I'm…in between jobs at the moment.'

'I saw your curriculum vitae. Someone with your talents isn't usually in between jobs unless she wants to be.'

He'd seen what the employment agency hadn't, and there was no explaining it away with clichés. Nell wanted to tell him the whole truth, but that probably wouldn't be all that wise.

'My last job was challenging, both professionally and personally. I want to spend six months looking around for another that will…'

'Just be challenging professionally?'

Nell caught her breath. How did he know so much about human nature, when he seemed so protected from it? 'Something like that.'

'So you thought that one patient might be a bit of a holiday.' He was taking her apart, piece by piece, and Nell felt powerless to stop him. 'But I imagine you're someone who gets a little bored on holiday.'

She could feel her cheeks heating up. She wasn't going to give Hugo the satisfaction of admitting that he was absolutely right. He held her gaze for a moment longer, and then leaned slowly back in his chair. Maybe he'd already seen what he wanted to see, and her reply was unnecessary.

'Then maybe I should consider diversionary tactics. To keep you from feeling that you're wasting your time here.'

He reached for the bottle of water on the table, and Nell took it from him. 'How can I be wasting my time when there are bottles to be opened?'

If he could hide his innermost feelings under a layer of charm, then so could she.

# CHAPTER SIX

THE SUMMONS HAD arrived first thing the following morning, and Nell had followed the messenger to the King's study. Despite the early hour, he was already working at his desk. He had offered her a cup of coffee and then pushed the morning paper towards her.

The King hadn't expressed the horror that Nell had felt when she'd looked at the pictures on the front page. It was just one of those things, an innocent action could be misinterpreted under the glare of scrutiny that the royal family were subjected to. But he had taken issue with a number of other things.

Nell had felt her heart close. Unable to look at him, she'd given no reason as to why she and Hugo had been seen at the back entrance to the palace at one in the morning. How could she? She'd promised to keep silent about the business with Jacob and Celeste until Hugo had had a chance to approach his father.

The King moved on to why exactly she'd been seen bidding for Hugo's company at the auction yesterday. This time Nell did have an answer, even if it wasn't a very good one.

'It was my idea. I thought that…well, it's too much for him to be hosting a weekend like that so soon after the operation. And Hugo wouldn't back out.'

'And you didn't consider how it might look?' The King's

tone wasn't unkind, but it was very firm. He tapped the paper with one finger. 'My real concern though, is that it's clear to me that this photograph does not show an embrace, as the papers seem to believe, it shows Hugo leaning on you. Your one responsibility was to ensure that he didn't take on too much, and damage his health.'

Nell nodded her assent, her hands clasped tightly in her lap. How could she object to the King's request that she submit a written account of Hugo's activities and medical condition every day, when she had already failed so spectacularly? And how could she complain when he hinted that unless things changed, he would be finding another doctor for Hugo.

She was trembling by the time the King dismissed her. Hurrying back to her apartment, Nell blinked back the tears. They were her own business, fit only to be seen by the four walls of her sumptuous bedroom.

Nell sat down on the bed, gulping for breath. She was just being stupid. The King had every right to ask questions, and if he'd been unfair, it was because he didn't know about Jacob's visit to Hugo's apartment, and Nell hadn't enlightened him. This *wasn't* a re-run of all that had happened in her last job.

All the same, it had a similar sting to it. Nell had rejected Martin's advances, and he'd taken advantage of his position as her boss to deliver payback. She'd come to dread seeing him on the ward, because there had always been some barb or put-down. And she'd learned to sit in silence when he'd called her to his office, because replying to his catalogue of her faults and flaws had only made things worse. She'd thought his anger might subside over time, but if there was one thing that Martin knew how to do, it was hang on to a grudge.

This wasn't the same. In some ways it was worse, though. The King had been painstakingly correct, and in his own way he'd been almost kind, but his concerns were justified. She couldn't put his criticism down to spite, the way she'd been able to with Martin. And she'd hardly looked back when she'd left the hospital, but leaving Hugo…already he was quite a different proposition.

There was nothing else for it. She had to get the crying over and done with, pull herself together, and do better.

She was expecting the knock on the connecting door between their apartments. Hugo would have finished his breakfast, and would be ready for another battle of wills over whether he was well enough to do whatever he pleased. Nell had dried her tears and was ready for him.

She opened the door, trying not to look at him, just in case he happened to be smiling. Hugo's smile was his most effective weapon.

'You did too much yesterday. You need to rest today.'

He raised one eyebrow. 'All right. Now that you've got that off your chest, would you like to join me for coffee?'

Maybe she could have waited a little longer than two seconds to say it. 'Yes. Thank you.'

'You've had breakfast?' He moved away from the door, leaving Nell to follow him into his sitting room.

'No, I…' Saying that she felt sick with apprehension wasn't the best way of appearing strong. 'Coffee's fine.'

'Right.' The tray was standing ready on the table, and he filled two cups, watching silently as Nell added milk to hers. 'What's the matter?'

'Nothing.' She smiled breezily at him, and he frowned.

'So I'm going to have to make a guess, am I?'

Nell puffed out a breath. Maybe she should tell him, he'd probably hear about it anyway. And perhaps Hugo would respect his father's wishes better than he did her advice.

'The King called me to see him this morning. He's not happy.'

'He isn't happy about a lot of things. Ignore him.'

'I can't ignore him. Apart from the fact that he happens to be the King, he's also my employer.'

'I'm Crown Prince, don't I get a say?' Hugo grinned, and Nell ignored the temptation to forgive him anything and everything.

'This isn't a game, Hugo. If you want to bait your father then go right ahead and do it, but don't put your own health at risk just because you won't admit that he's right.' Nell pressed her lips together. She could have put that more tactfully, but right now she wasn't in the mood to do so.

He was suddenly solemn, his gaze searching her face. Nell felt herself redden, the tears that she'd only just managed to control pricking at the corners of her eyes.

'What did my father say to you?'

'He heard about you being up so late the other night. There was nothing I could say to him in response, without telling him about Jacob.'

'So you took the blame yourself.' His frown grew deeper.

'What else could I do? He heard about my bidding at the auction as well. And there are photographs of me supporting you to the car in this morning's papers.'

'He can't hold you responsible for that.' Hugo pressed his lips together, obviously aware of the conclusion that the papers had drawn.

'He doesn't. But he holds me responsible for the fact that you're doing too much. He says that things have to change and that from now on I have to submit a daily report to him.'

'Nell, I'm sorry. I'll make it right.' His jaw hardened into a determined line.

'No, you won't. You can't. But if you're reckoning on carrying on like this, then tell me now, because I'd rather leave than be fired.'

'No one's going to fire you, Nell.'

She shook her head silently. Hugo didn't understand, he'd never been squeezed out of a job or bullied by a boss. He was the golden boy, who everyone wanted.

Even Nell wanted him. Despite all her exasperation, she'd started to enjoy their battles, almost to look forward to them. And in doing so, she'd forgotten the reason why she was here.

'There's a meeting arranged for this afternoon at my charity's offices. It's only going to be for an hour, the construction company is going to update us on how things are going. If I asked everyone to come here instead, I'd find it less taxing.'

Hugo's tone was almost contrite. When Nell looked up at him, there was a trace of concern on his face.

This was a start. 'That sounds like a good idea, Hugo.'

Shame was something that Hugo usually tried to avoid. If he worked hard, and met the standards that he set, he generally found that he could live with himself. But now he felt thoroughly ashamed.

Being ill had made him crazy. It had stripped away the feeling that he was in charge of his life, and he was struggling to find the man he'd once thought himself to be. But in trying to pretend that it hadn't happened, he'd hurt Nell, and that was unforgiveable.

He knew exactly where his parents would be during the week, they were creatures of habit. As he expected, he found them sitting at the twin desks, placed back to back to allow murmured conversation and smiles while they completed their correspondence for the day.

'Mother…' He smiled, and his mother rose for a hug, made awkward by his lame shoulder.

'Hugo, darling. How do you feel today?'

'Much better, thank you.' Hugo's relationship with his

mother was an effortless synergy of respect for her position and warmth. The one with his father involved rather more effort. 'I'd like to speak with Father.'

His mother sat firmly back down, waving her hand towards his father, who had looked up from the papers in front of him. Her smile told Hugo that she knew exactly what all this was about, and she wasn't going to give either of them the chance to argue in private.

'Go ahead, darling. He's right here, in case you didn't notice.'

Right. Hugo turned to his father, and found himself locked in the familiar combative stare that was their usual greeting to each other. He sat down, knowing that it probably wouldn't defuse the situation. Pacing up and down wasn't going to help much if he wanted to imply that he was taking things easy.

'It's not Nell's fault, Father.'

His father turned the corners of his mouth down. 'I'm inclined to agree with you. It is, however, Dr Maitland's responsibility to make sure that you rest.'

'And she's doing that.'

'I disagree, Hugo.'

The silence between them wasn't broken by his mother's voice. Usually her intervention avoided conflict between father and son, neatly suggesting a solution that everyone could live with. But this time there was just a silence.

'My behaviour isn't her fault. Nell's a good doctor, and…she's exactly what I need at the moment. In the future, I'll follow her instructions.' This was a climb-down of gargantuan proportions. But Hugo had seen humiliation and rejection in Nell's face this morning, and they haunted him.

'So things are going to change, are they?'

'They will. Don't punish her in order to get to me.'

His father leaned back in his chair. 'You've seen the papers this morning?'

'It'll blow over. How many other young women have been photographed in my company in the last year?'

'Goodness only knows. I don't know where you get the time,' his mother interjected suddenly, and both men turned on her, frowning. 'It's just an observation, darling. It would make things a great deal easier if you decided that your health wasn't such a secret.'

'I want it to remain private.'

That was one of the few things that Hugo and his father had agreed on lately, even if it was for different reasons. His father had always drawn a line between his family's personal lives and their public duties, and that had allowed Hugo to grow up outside the glare of publicity. For Hugo, it was more a matter of not wanting to be seen as irrevocably flawed.

King Ferdinand nodded. 'You know I have no argument with you there, Hugo. But you have a duty…'

Hugo nodded impatiently. 'I know what my duty is. To be strong enough to serve the people.'

His father nodded. 'I assume from your presence that Dr Maitland *wants* to stay.'

'I have no idea. But *she* gets that choice.' Hugo felt his heart quicken and he ignored it. He would have to stop gauging everything by the beat of his own heart.

'There's only one person who can make sure that Dr Maitland keeps her job. That's you, Hugo.'

Hugo got to his feet, making an effort to swallow his anger as he turned to his mother. He bade her goodbye, omitting the same gesture towards his father, before turning and walking out of the room.

Hugo had been oddly compliant all day. It was as if he'd suddenly come to his senses, or at least decided that it was more politic to appear to have done so. He'd spent the morning reading through the reports from the construction company, and the meeting was a short one. Nell had been able to relax a little and take an interest in the plans for the clinic. She could see why the project excited Hugo, and why he was willing to give up almost anything to see it come to fruition.

'What did Celeste say?' Nell had gone to speak to Celeste alone, while he stayed in his apartment.

'She said that last night, when the carer was with them, she got the first good night's sleep she's had in months.'

Hugo nodded. 'That's something. It's working, then?'

'It's early days. But, yes, I think it'll work very well.'

'Good. I'll speak to my father...'

'Not yet, Hugo. I... I've already taken the blame for the other night, and I'm still in one piece. Let's wait a week and make sure that the arrangement's working for Celeste first. Then you can speak to him.'

'He should know now. That you weren't to blame for that either.'

*Either?* 'You've already spoken to him, haven't you?'

'Yes. I told him that yesterday was entirely my fault and that it wouldn't happen again.'

The sudden feeling of warmth in Nell's chest caught her by surprise. Nell didn't dare wonder if she was really that important to Hugo, that he'd comply with his father's wishes for her sake.

'You didn't need to do that... But thank you.'

'My pleasure. There are always plenty of other options when it comes to defying my father. You'd be surprised at the scope his position affords.'

He was making light of it, but the look in his eyes said something different. That she could trust him and he'd be there for her.

The sound of the bell, at the front door of the apartment

broke the silence. It couldn't have come at a more inopportune time, and Nell willed him to ignore it, but he didn't, rising from his seat. Maybe he was glad of the interruption.

She heard voices in the hallway, and jumped to her feet when Queen Margaux entered the room. She was more casually dressed than in the pictures Nell had seen on the Internet, wearing a pair of tan trousers and a matching shirt, but she was still immaculate.

'I'm glad to see that you're here, resting, Hugo.' Queen Margaux bestowed a smile on Nell that seemed to indicate she thought Nell had something to do with that. 'Penelope. I'm very glad to meet you.'

'She prefers Nell, Mother. Nell, meet my mother.'

Nell wondered whether she should curtsey, and remembered she didn't know how. Queen Margaux held her hand out and gave Nell's a surprisingly firm shake.

'I'm very glad to meet you, Your Majesty.' Nell hoped that was something close to the right form of address.

'Margaux, please.' The Queen dropped a slim file that she was carrying onto the table and sat down.

'Would you like some tea…?' Hugo's mother was obviously here to speak to him, and it was a good means of escape. It might be rude not to address the Queen by name, as she'd instructed, but Nell couldn't quite bring herself to call her Margaux.

'Thank you, but no. I've come to speak with both you and Hugo.'

'What about? If you're here to try and talk some sense into me, Nell already has that covered.'

Margaux flashed another smile at Nell. 'Then I won't go to the trouble. Anyway, this is far more pressing. I think you should both read this.'

She slipped two sheets of paper from the folder, holding them out. Hugo took them both and started to read.

'What is it?' Nell reached across, and he threw the papers down on the coffee table.

'It's rubbish. Outrageous… You don't need to see it.'

'If it's rubbish then it can't do any harm to look.' She picked up one of the sheets.

'You have to understand, Nell, that the papers will pay for stories, and people will make things up. It gives them a misplaced sense of importance.'

'All right. Let me read it, will you?' How bad could it be? Nell turned her attention to the paper and started to read. She immediately recognised the name involved. Three sentences in, she realised that it was worse than she could have possibly imagined.

'This is a request for comment.' Queen Margaux's voice broke through her horror. 'It's from one of the more responsible papers, and if I speak to the editor I can refute the claims and at least delay publication. If they can't get any corroboration then it'll stop it completely. But if the man making these claims goes somewhere else, that might not be so easy.'

'Is…there any indication he might?' Nell felt her cheeks redden at the thought.

'I had my secretary examine his social media pages, and it seems he's already shared the story that was in the paper this morning and made a few comments. Nothing of any substance, they're more of the *I know something you don't* variety, but it shows an intention. But you know this man, Nell, he's your ex-boss. What do you think?'

'I don't think he's going to give up.' Nell shook her head miserably. The one thing that neither Hugo nor Queen Margaux had asked yet was whether the allegations were true. It didn't appear that Hugo was going to, and his mother was clearly taking his lead.

She took a deep breath. 'I want to say…that it's not true. I didn't make any passes at my former boss, he was the one who propositioned me. And I'd never offer sexual favours in return for covering up my mistakes. The previous Head of Department knew me well, I worked for him for three years, ask him—'

'Don't, Nell.' Hugo interrupted her. 'You shouldn't have to defend yourself.'

'I want to. It's the truth.'

Queen Margaux turned to Nell, laying her hand on hers. 'I didn't doubt it, Nell. But thank you for clarifying things. This is a situation where we must be clear and direct in all of our dealings.'

'Yes, we can be clear and direct in completely refuting these allegations.' Hugo's brow was still dark.

'Of course, Hugo. But if you'd read the whole piece, you'd see that there's a reference at the end to a romantic entanglement between the two of *you*. If Nell's real relationship with you were known, then it might well defuse the situation.'

Nell shook her head. 'I'm sorry but…no. I'm Hugo's doctor, and it's my responsibility to make sure that if he wants to keep the details of his medical condition private, that's what happens. I can't allow it.'

'Nell, that's up to me.'

If Hugo was about to make an abrupt about-turn on the question of his own privacy, Nell wasn't. 'You've already expressed your wishes, Hugo, and while I don't altogether agree with them, it's my duty to uphold them. I won't have it.'

'But—'

'There's always the Royal Agreement,' Queen Margaux cut her son short.

'That doesn't apply here, Mother.'

'It might. Since the papers seem already to be jumping to conclusions…' Queen Margaux reached for the folder, taking off her reading glasses. 'I'll leave you both to consider the options. But in the meantime, Nell, I want you to understand that you have my full support in this. We will do whatever it takes.'

Nell stammered her thanks, and Hugo rose to see his mother out. While they were gone, Nell concentrated on keeping breathing. Because it appeared that was about the only thing that Martin could never take away from her.

# CHAPTER SEVEN

'I HAVE TO EXPLAIN.' Hugo had returned to the sitting room and was regarding her silently.

'No, you don't. I don't make a habit of explaining what the papers say about me...' He broke off, seeing the tears that ran down Nell's cheeks.

'I do...really.'

Hugo came to sit next to her on the sofa. 'If you *want* to tell me something about this, then I'll listen. All you *need* to say is that you want this stopped.'

'It's good of you to say that. I want to tell you.'

'Okay.' He was sitting close, but still not touching her. The temptation to ask for Hugo's comfort was almost too much to bear, but Nell couldn't do that. Not until he knew all the facts, and he believed her.

'When I was a student, Martin was a visiting lecturer. He was brilliant, he has a very fine mind.'

'Okay. I'll take your word for that.' Hugo didn't look very convinced.

'I went to speak to him after the lecture and he asked me for coffee. One thing led to another...' She glanced at Hugo and he nodded. 'I was dazzled. He was older than me, of course, and very handsome. He knew about loads of things that I didn't. Introduced me to a lot of new experiences.'

She expected Hugo to nod and understand. Instead,

he rolled his eyes. 'I've seen that type. No feeling of self-worth, so he has to pick on someone in a subordinate position to impress.'

His words chipped away at the dream. The feeling that Martin had been all-knowing and that it was she who'd done the wrong thing. She *had* done the wrong thing, and maybe Hugo would think a little differently when she told him.

'He was based in Newcastle, and he came down to London every couple of weeks. I saw him then and I used to count the days...' Nell shook her head at her own stupidity. 'It went on for six months and then he told me that he was married. He said it didn't matter, that he and his wife had some kind of understanding, but I broke it off immediately.'

Nell looked into Hugo's face, wondering if he could understand. 'I thought he loved me. And even though I loved him, I couldn't do it.'

'Sounds as if you were the one who was the adult in that relationship.'

He thought so? Nell had always considered herself as the silly little girl, blinded by love. Slowly Martin was developing feet of clay.

'I don't know about that. But I stuck to it, even though he contacted me a few times afterwards. Finally he left me alone, and I reckoned that it was just a life lesson and I should chalk it up to experience. I graduated, and got a job at the hospital and things were going well. Then the head of department retired, and...' Nell felt herself start to shake. That feeling, that she couldn't escape and that her mistakes would always come back to bite her, had turned out to be about the only true thing in this whole business.

'And when the new head of department showed up, it was him?' Hugo was filling in the gaps now. 'Any reasonable man would have spoken to you privately, admitted that he'd acted very badly and hoped that you might find the goodness of heart to draw a line under the whole business. I'm guessing he didn't do that.'

Nell shook her head, finding herself smiling grimly. 'No, he didn't. There were a couple of weeks of extreme awkwardness, and then I couldn't bear it any longer. I spoke to him and apologised...'

'*You* apologised?'

'It seemed reasonable. I had been one very willing half of the affair.'

Hugo let out a short, sharp breath. 'Are you saying it was all your fault?'

'No, I...' In truth, after the last six months, Nell had been reduced to not knowing what was and wasn't her fault.

'We talked a bit and I thought we'd come to an understanding, but the following day he said he wanted to talk a bit more and could he meet me for coffee that evening.'

Nell still didn't understand how she could have been so stupid. But when she looked at Hugo, there was no sign of reproach in his face. Perhaps he was just waiting to hear everything before he made a final decision on that.

'I went, and he started telling me about how his marriage had broken up because his wife had found out about our affair. I don't know if that was true, but I was horrified. Then he said that the least I could do was give things another try. I said I didn't think that was a good idea and he offered to take me home. He walked me to my door and then he told me he knew I wanted it really and pushed me inside. Somehow I fought him off...' The words had tumbled out, and Nell was suddenly breathless with shame.

'I hope you hurt him.'

'I... Actually, I had a copy of *Welman's Clinical Procedures* in my bag. I managed to get free of him and hit him with it.'

Hugo grinned suddenly. 'Good girl. The full edition, I hope.'

'Stop it, it was the abbreviated edition. It still hurt him, though. He made some comment about my obviously not being in the mood tonight and left.' She was shaking. Not so much as she had that night, but she still couldn't stop.

'Did you report him?'

'No, I…' Nell shrugged miserably. 'I was the one who asked him in. And it wasn't as if we'd just met, we had a history.'

'No means no. Nothing trumps that.'

It seemed so simple when he said it like that. Hugo's sense of honour made it simple. She wished that he'd reach out to her, but knew that he wouldn't. As far as Hugo was concerned, one touch now would make him as bad as Martin and she wished she could find a way to tell him that wasn't true.

She had to finish the story. Get this over with as quickly as possible. If she could do it without breaking down, that would be a bonus. Nell squeezed her hands together in her lap, feeling her nails dig deep.

'He…tried it on a few times after that. I rejected him and started to make sure we were never alone together. Then one day he called me into his office, and went through a very comprehensive list of all the things I was doing wrong. All from a clinical point of view, there was nothing personal.'

'Payback time?'

'Yes. That went on for a few months, and I started to wonder whether there really was something wrong with the way I did my job. Then he blocked my promotion.'

'On what grounds?'

'He said I was an excellent doctor but that realising my full potential meant staying in my current post a little while longer.' If Martin had criticised her performance, Nell could have fought it. But this had been impossible.

Hugo thought for a moment. 'He's done this before.'

'What? What makes you say that?'

'He always put you in a position where you felt you were in the wrong, he was married, then his divorce was because of his relationship with you. And he was always in a position of power, your teacher, and then your boss. I'm not saying he engineered all that, but he exploited it. He's an abuser, and he probably didn't just do it to you.'

'But…' Nell had thought she was alone. The idea that Martin might have done this to other women was horrific, but it did make her feel as if it wasn't so much her fault. 'Maybe you're right.'

Hugo got to his feet, starting to pace. 'We're going to stop him, Nell. My mother will refute the allegations and we'll release the details of my operation. That'll keep the papers busy for a while, and in the meantime we'll find a way to shut him up permanently.'

'No, Hugo. I know that's not what you want, and this is *my* battle. You shouldn't be dragged into it…' The heat in her heart, at the idea that Hugo was prepared to defend her, was burning too hot and threatened to consume her. He couldn't be allowed to do this.

'It's what works.' Hugo had obviously made his mind up about this.

'No, it won't work. Martin will just find another way to make these allegations…' If Hugo was so determined to make this sacrifice, Nell needed to find a different approach.

'If he does, then we're in a good place to refute them.' A grim smile quirked his lips. 'You underestimate the power of good contacts.'

'It's not about having power, Hugo, it's about what's right and wrong.'

He shook his head slowly. 'It's about picking a side, Nell. Allow me to pick mine.'

She stared at him. Hugo was on her side. The thought that he would protect her washed every objection she had to the idea away for a moment. He took full advantage of that moment, turning and walking out of the apartment.

It was done. Hugo had spent an hour with his mother and the palace press advisor, and a call had been made to the managing editor who had contacted them for comment. The promise of a press release within the next twenty-four hours had oiled the wheels, and Martin Jarman's story was suddenly dead in the water.

'I'm proud of you.' His mother had stopped him as he'd gone to leave, murmuring the words.

'It's a matter of principle.' Hugo had been telling himself that. He was doing this for everyone caught in this kind of situation, and not just for Nell. Not because he wanted to hold her close and keep her safe.

'Yes, it is. Anyone in your position has a duty to defend someone who...' His mother paused. 'You are quite sure that Nell is innocent of these allegations, aren't you?'

'Of course I am. I'm perfectly capable of noticing when a woman is trying to seduce me. Nell's a good doctor, and she acts appropriately.' His thoughts might touch on the delights of the inappropriate from time to time, but that was his business.

His mother nodded. 'Your judgement is always sound, Hugo. And whatever you say, I'm still proud of you.'

That was something. Hugo reflected that he wasn't all that proud of himself at the moment. The idea of having his most humiliating secret blazoned across the front pages of the papers was something he was trying not to think about. While he was still obviously recovering, people might look at him with sympathy. But sooner or later, they'd come around to seeing him as a hypocrite. How could he advocate for a heart clinic when he—a doctor no less—hadn't seen the signs of his own heart issues?

That was just something he'd have to put up with. Maybe Nell was right. Maybe an admission that he'd made the mistakes that he was urging others not to make would emphasise his human side. But right now Hugo's human side was cowering somewhere in a corner, and it felt far more comfortable to pretend that there was nothing wrong with him.

He walked back to his apartment, pondering the question. Things had to change—there would be no more battles of will with Nell, no more creative solutions. Even though the alternative sounded dull in the extreme, their relationship from now on would be entirely professional. If he were blameless, that would give Nell the opportunity to prove herself blameless, too.

Nell had waited for Hugo in his apartment. She'd made a cup of coffee, leaving it untouched while it had gone cold, and then emptied and washed the cup. Then she'd retreated to her own apartment, leaving the connecting door wide open, and switched the television on, hoping it might drown out the clamour of her own thoughts.

This was wrong. She'd been unable to say conclusively that she was entirely blameless in the business with Martin, but Hugo was different. No part of this was his fault, and yet in defending her he was the one who would feel humiliated.

Nell thought for a long time. When he came back, she'd put a stop to all this.

She heard the front door of his apartment close quietly, and hurried to the connecting door, stopping short at the threshold. When Hugo walked into the sitting room and saw her, he smiled.

Nell imagined that this was the smile he reserved for the most formal of occasions, devoid of any emotion other than the one he wanted to project. 'It's done, Nell. I'm going to…get some rest now.'

Normally she would have applauded the sentiment. Now, keeping Hugo awake until he'd told her exactly what had been done, and how it could be unravelled, seemed far more important.

'What's done?'

'Our press officer has stopped the story. We've promised a press release on another matter during the next twenty-four hours.'

Things had moved faster than Nell had thought they might. But it still wasn't irrevocable. 'We can undo it then. I can find another way.'

He paused for a moment, just long enough for Nell to wonder whether he was reconsidering. But he was just choosing his words. 'As I said, Nell, this is my battle too, and you don't have to find another way.'

This was too much. Standing, yards away from each other, trading appropriate conversation. They should be past this by now, but somehow Martin had inveigled his way in between them, and Hugo no longer felt comfortable with the relationship they'd started to build.

It was obvious that Hugo wasn't going to ask her into the apartment, but she couldn't say what she wanted to say from the doorway. Nell took the initiative, walking over to the sofa and sitting down.

'What did your mother mean by the Royal Agreement?' Hugo had dismissed the idea quickly, but maybe this was an alternative.

He shook his head. 'It doesn't apply here. When my parents were first married, they were keen to bring up their family without the constant press attention that my father had when he was young. They made an agreement with the press, and until I was eighteen, the only news stories published about me were official press releases from the palace.'

Nell frowned. That didn't seem to apply, but Queen Margaux had obviously thought it did. 'There's something you're not telling me.'

'My mother showed a great deal of foresight in negotiating certain extensions to that protection. My grandmother was allowed privacy during her final illness. And an engaged couple can expect the same privacy.'

*An engaged couple?*

What was the Queen thinking? Nell swallowed down her own objections to the plan, because it was something, anything, that would provide an alternative to what Hugo was planning to do now.

'So your mother's suggesting that…if we got engaged then there would be no difficulty in stopping this and other stories about us.'

'Yes, that's exactly what she's suggesting. But I won't put you through that…'

'You make it sound as if you're committing me to the palace dungeons. It's not as bad as that, is it?'

The flicker of a smile crossed his face. 'No. Not quite.'

'Well, can't we consider it? I don't have to actually marry you, do I?'

'No, you don't. We'd have to make a show of being together for a few months, but after that we'd break the engagement off quietly… But look, Nell, your career is at stake here. There's no point in saving it, only to have it ruined by being engaged to me.'

He had a point. Leaving her job and getting engaged to a prince might not look great on her CV, but it wouldn't be as disastrous as having Martin's story in the papers, and it wouldn't hurt Hugo as much as his current plan would.

'I don't have to spend all my time just pretending to be

engaged, do I? I could do some work with your charity, if
that's okay with you.' He shook his head and Nell puffed
out a breath. 'This isn't doing my ego any good, Hugo. Is
it that bad to have to pretend you're engaged to me?'

He laughed suddenly, all his reserve dissolving in his
smile. 'I'd be very honoured to be engaged to you. Even
if I was just pretending.'

'Then stop this nonsense about having to release the
private details about your surgery. It's not necessary, we
can find another way.'

Nell had started to boss him around again and his resolve
to keep her at a distance had melted. But at least she didn't
seem so beaten and dejected as she had when she'd recounted how she'd been treated by her last boss.

He'd begged her not to go through with this, and had
told her that it was no sacrifice to allow his own medical
details to be released to the papers instead, but she'd seen
straight through him. So he'd called his mother, hoping
that she might regret her mention of the Agreement, and
talk some sense into Nell.

Fat chance. His mother had made a comment to the effect that she wished he'd make up his mind, and had gone
on to embrace the idea. She appeared at the door of his
apartment within minutes, and it seemed that she saw eye
to eye with Nell over this compromise solution.

The details were worked out over a glass of wine. Nell
insisted on giving up her employment, which seemed only
sensible to Hugo. He insisted on her being involved with
his work for the clinic as much as possible, so she'd at
least have something to show on her CV later on. Even if
that hadn't worked out so well with his real engagement
to Anna, it seemed that it could at least be accomplished
in the context of a fake engagement.

'This will work well, Hugo. You're obviously already

good friends.' His mother's habit of not leaving before she'd
made some private comment about the situation could be
trying, even if it did usually elicit her real thoughts.

'We're…' Hugo shrugged. '*Good friends* doesn't happen in the space of four days.' Even if it did feel as if he'd
known Nell for much, much longer than that.

'You want to protect her. She wants to protect you.' His
mother turned on her heel, leaving Hugo to think about
the implications of her statement.

He was too tired to think about anything very much.
Nell cleared away the glasses, and thankfully skipped any
examination of the healing incision on his chest. Perhaps
she knew that the intimacy would be too much for him to
bear tonight, when he was fighting to remain detached,
now that they were alone.

He slept deeply, not remembering his dreams. In the
morning, a package sent from his mother set the seal on
the agreement that had been made last night, which was
itself the stuff of crazy dreams.

He tore open the package and, looking inside, found a
short handwritten note from his mother.

*Treat her with the greatest respect, Hugo.*

Right. He didn't need to be told. He reached into the
envelope again, finding a bundle of tissue paper wrap-
pings and another note. He looked at both briefly, before
putting them in his pocket.

# CHAPTER EIGHT

NELL HEARD THE knock on the connecting door between their apartments, just as she was putting the last of her clothes into her suitcase. When she answered it, Hugo was looking rested, which was a great deal more than she felt.

'You've had breakfast?' He grinned at her and she felt her stomach lurch. That would have been entirely appropriate if the engagement they were planning wasn't all a fabrication.

'No, I've been packing my bags. I was going to get that done first.' They'd agreed last night that it would be best for them both to leave the palace. Hugo's house in the country had no staff and was small enough that Ted and his team could maintain close security.

'Would you like to join me, then?'

She nodded. 'Yes. That would be nice, thank you. Just toast...'

An awkward silence accompanied the arrival of the tray from the kitchen, and Hugo motioned towards the balcony table, indicating that the tray should be set down there. Nell sat down, reaching for the coffee and pouring it.

'You still want to go through with it?' He didn't need to say what.

'Yes, I do. I'm even more sure this morning.'

He nodded, taking a tissue paper package from his pocket, undoing it and laying four rings in a line on the

table. 'These are my mother's. She'd like you to have something nice to wear.'

In Nell's book, *something nice* didn't necessarily have
to cost as much as the average house. 'They're real?'

'Yes, of course they are.'

'I can't wear any of these, Hugo, they must be worth…
I can't even think how much they might be worth. Can't
I wear a fake?'

He shook his head. 'No fakes, Nell, please. This engagement may not be real, but I want to say to you now
that my promise to protect you is. I believe that you want
to protect me, too.'

It wasn't the proposal that every girl dreamed of. But
suddenly Nell felt that there was something real about this.
Hugo was a better man than she'd thought he was, not just
a spoiled prince who could destroy her if he wanted, the
way that Martin had tried to.

'I will protect you, Hugo. I promise you that.'

He nodded. 'Then I'd like it if you would choose whichever ring you like the best.'

That sounded like something she could put her heart
into. She looked at the rings, not daring to touch any of
them. One had a massive ruby at the centre, and it looked
far too opulent. The other three were all large diamonds.

'That one…' She pointed awkwardly to a diamond sol-
itaire that flashed blue-white in the morning sunshine.

'That's a very good choice. It's the best stone.'

Nell went to protest that the only thing she'd seen was
that it was the smallest stone, and he silenced her with a
laugh. Picking up the ring, he held it out towards her. 'Will
you wear it now?'

'The announcement hasn't gone out yet. I shouldn't
wear it until tomorrow, should I?'

'We've made a promise. I'd like it if you would wear

the ring now, because that's what it is to us. You can wear it on your right hand until tomorrow.'

Still he wouldn't touch her. It was as if this new arrangement had blotted out any possibility of an innocent touch, and anything physical was now laden with some kind of meaning. Nell reached out, putting her hand in his.

'Then…would it be appropriate for you to put it on for me, please?'

'I think that would be entirely appropriate.' His voice sounded inappropriately husky, and Nell avoided his gaze. Looking into his eyes wasn't necessary.

She felt him slip the ring onto her finger, twisting it a quarter turn to get it past the knuckle. 'It looks nice.'

*Nice* was a bit of an understatement. It looked amazing, and far too good for Nell.

'It's beautiful. I'll take care of it and return it to your mother in good condition.'

He wrapped the remaining three rings in the crumpled tissue paper, and then put them back into his pocket, withdrawing a piece of folded notepaper. He handed it to Nell and got to his feet. 'I'll leave you to read that.'

Nell read the note. Queen Margaux would be most grateful if she could accept whichever ring she and Hugo chose, as a gift. It would be a symbol of gratitude and of enduring friendship between them.

Nell put the letter down on the table. It was too generous, and she'd have to ask Hugo if there was some way she could express her gratitude to his mother, whilst refusing the gift. She had the feeling that wearing it after the arrangement was over wasn't going to be a particularly comfortable option.

But while she had it on her finger, she'd do her best for Hugo. She'd take care of him, and help him raise the money he needed for the clinic. That was a promise.

* * *

Hugo was aware that this arrangement had to be treated with the utmost delicacy. He must show how much he valued Nell as a friend. Slipping into anything more would be horribly easy, and something that he had promised himself he wouldn't do.

All the same, their departure from the palace seemed like the start of something new and exciting. With the top of his convertible rolled back, and Nell at the wheel, it felt as if he was making an escape with a beautiful woman at his side. Who knew what might happen when they were finally alone, away from the bustle of the palace?

Ted's voice from the back seat jerked him back into reality. 'Left-hand side...'

Nell obligingly swerved to the left of the palace driveway, and came to a halt, waiting for the palace guard to open the gates.

'Thanks. I nearly forgot.'

She waved to the guard, the ring flashing bright on her finger. Then she turned out of the gates into the anonymity of the busy city on a warm summer's morning.

Their destination was only half an hour's drive away, which was about as far as anyone could go from the capital of Montarino and still remain within its borders. There was no suburban sprawl, just a sudden change from houses to open countryside. And the countryside in Montarino *was* beautiful.

Hugo directed Nell through rolling hills and around the edge of a wide, blue lake. Another mile and they reached a high wall, built of weathered bricks, driving the length of it until they reached an archway, protected by a heavy wooden gate.

The gate swung open and Ted got out of the car, speaking briefly to the man who had opened it. He waved the car through, and Nell drew up outside the house. It was small by the standards of the palace, built in stone and shaded by trees. A small garden at the side was overlooked by arches, the weathered stone now housing state-of-the-art single sheets of glass.

'It's lovely. This has been in your family for a long time?'

Hugo quirked his lips downwards, shaking his head. 'No. I bought this place with my doctor's salary. Since I have almost everything else provided for me, it seemed like a good idea to have my own bolthole.'

Nell wondered what it must be like to have to take your own independence that seriously. She took it for granted that everything she had was the product of her own work, but Hugo seemed to need to make a distinction between what he'd been given and what he'd earned.

Inside, the house was light, airy and simple. None of the folderols of the palace, just plain furniture in neutral colours, exposed wooden beams and a utilitarian kitchen. Upstairs, there were three bedrooms, one of which was clearly Hugo's. He directed her towards a second, which commanded stunning views of the hills stretching off into the distance.

'I suppose I'll have to keep away from the windows when the news breaks.' Nell wasn't exactly sure what to expect.

'Not really. Because of the Agreement, the paparazzi won't be able to sell any pictures they take, so it's not worth their time. And Ted's team will make sure that no one disturbs us here.'

'You usually have this much security?' Nell had counted four men outside.

'No, it's usually just Ted, and he generally doesn't have all that much to do. He stays in the guest house at the back.'

Nell walked over to the window, looking out. Beyond

the garden, and shielded by trees, was a small cottage, nestling against the perimeter wall.

'It all sounds reassuringly normal.'

'Not quite. But we try to make it so.' Hugo was watching her speculatively. 'There is one thing I want to ask you.'

'What's that?'

'Nadine, the little girl in the brochure, wearing a pink dress. I told you she'd had an operation recently...'

'Yes, I remember.'

'Dr Bertrand, the head of department, is the only one there who knows that I've been ill—everyone else thinks I'm taking a leave of absence for fundraising. He told me that he'd have me removed by security if I went in to see Nadine earlier than seven days after my own operation.'

Nell grinned. 'He sounds like a good man...'

'He's a very good man. You'd like him.'

'And since this is the seventh day, you'd like to go and see Nadine.'

'It would be best to go today. After the news of our engagement breaks, my turning up on the ward might cause a bit of a stir.'

'Where is the hospital?'

'On this side of the city, so it'll only take twenty minutes to get there. I'm feeling better every day, and I'd really like to see Nadine.'

If this was normal, then it was a new normal that Nell hadn't experienced before. Hugo asking her whether or not he could do something. 'It sounds like a lovely idea. May I come along? I'd like to see the hospital.'

Hugo smiled. As time went on that smile was surfacing more and more, and it convinced Nell that everything was going to be all right. 'I was hoping you might. You'll have to drive.'

# CHAPTER NINE

No one seemed to notice Hugo's presence as they walked through the reception area at the hospital. He exchanged smiles with the receptionist at the main desk, who waved him through in much the same way as she probably would have done with anyone else she knew. Here, Hugo appeared to shed the mantle of royalty.

He led her through a maze of corridors, mysterious box in hand, and a high-speed lift took them to the seventh floor. Hugo punched a code into a keypad at the entrance to one of the wards and the doors opened automatically, allowing them through.

This might just be Hugo's greatest test. Fooling a group of luncheon diners that there was nothing wrong with him was one thing. Fooling a senior nurse was quite another, and just such a person had looked up from her conversation at the nurses' station and was heading straight towards them.

'Hugo. This is unexpected.' The woman spoke in French.

'I've come to see Nadine. This is Dr Nell Maitland, she's a cardiac specialist from London. Nell, this is Senior Nurse Adele LeFevre.'

Adele smiled, holding out her hand to Nell and switching to English. 'I'm pleased to meet you. I hope you see much that you like here.'

'I have already. This is a beautiful hospital.'

'Thank you. We are proud of it. When the new cardiac unit is built, we will be even more proud.' Adele's English was almost perfect, like that of so many of the people of Montarino. And she was keeping hold of Nell's hand, staring at her.

'I called Dr Bertrand to let him know we were coming. Is he free?' Clearly Hugo didn't expect everyone here to drop what they were doing as soon as he arrived.

'He is finishing his rounds.' Adele barely seemed to glance at Hugo. 'Ten minutes.'

'Very well. May I show Nell around, and then go to see Nadine?' He had the grace to ask that as well.

'Of course.' Adele flashed Nell a smile and turned back towards the nurses' station.

They walked through the cardiac unit, and Hugo showed her the light-filled wards, exchanging greetings with some of the nurses as they went. There were treatment rooms and a small sitting room with a dining room to one side for ambulatory patients. Everything was gleaming and state of the art, but Nell could see that the unit was working at its full capacity, with no empty beds in any of the wards.

'Why is everyone staring at me?' Nell whispered to Hugo as he punched a number code into a keypad next to the door at the far end of the ward.

'This is the first time I've ever brought a friend here.' He turned to her, looking a little sheepish.

So this was a first taste of the interest that would be shown in her, then, after the press release went out. Nell had anticipated something of the kind, but she hadn't expected to feel so exposed, as if she wanted to cling to Hugo for shelter.

'I suppose…if they're staring at me, then at least they're not looking at you. A lot less chance of anyone noticing that you're still recovering from an operation.'

'There is that.' He leaned closer, his arm moving protectively around her but not touching her. 'There's still time to change your mind. The press release won't go out for another couple of hours.'

Maybe this was why he'd wanted her here with him. To give her one last chance to back out of the engagement.

'I'm not changing my mind, Hugo. I've got the ring now.' She'd be wearing it on her left hand and not her right tomorrow. But today it meant the same as it would tomorrow, a symbol of their agreement to protect each other.

'Thank you for wearing it…' He reached out, as if to take her hand, and Nell heard a stifled giggle coming from somewhere behind them. Two young nurses were at the other end of the corridor, staring at them. Adele bore down on them, shooing them back to work, and then shot a smile in Nell's direction.

Hugo ushered her through the door and one look told Nell that this was the children's ward. There was a riot of colour on the walls of the reception area and an open door revealed a play area, where young patients were being supervised by play leaders in bright tunics.

Hugo led Nell into a small ward, nodding a greeting to the nurse. Nell recognised the little girl who lay in one of the beds, as well as the teddy bear at her side.

'Hey, Nadine.' He dangled his fingers over the safety rail on the side of the bed, tapping the back of her hand, and she opened her eyes.

'Uncle Hugo.'

'I told you I'd come. I brought you something.' He opened the box he was carrying and drew out a beautiful silk flower, dangling it over the rail so that Nadine could see it.

'Thank you, Uncle Hugo.'

Nadine smiled, but didn't reach for the flower. Nell saw concern in Hugo's eyes and she knew what he was about to do next.

'Speak to Dr Bertrand,' she whispered in his ear and he ignored her.

'How do you feel, sweetie?' He reached forward to brush her forehead with his fingertips.

'I'm all right, Uncle Hugo.'

Hugo went to reach for the notes at the end of the bed, and Nell bowed to the inevitable and fetched them for him. 'I'm just reading about you.' He smiled at Nadine and she gave him a smile back.

He studied the notes carefully, and then checked the monitors by Nadine's bedside. From what Nell could see, everything was completely normal, and Nadine was just a little drowsy.

Hugo wasn't giving up, though. He reached for the sheet covering Nadine's body, pulling it back slightly to reveal her shoulders and a large plaster over the right side of her chest.

'No, Hugo. You are not to examine that child. You're on sick leave.' He'd probably survive, but goodness only knew what kind of medical liability issues it might raise.

'There's clearly something the matter with her.' He reached for a pair of surgical gloves from the dispenser on the wall, wincing slightly.

'Then we'll call for a doctor.' Nell beckoned to the nurse, asking her in French to fetch someone.

'I'm a doctor. Nadine is my patient.' She could hear the pain in Hugo's hushed voice, and Nell wondered what she'd do in his shoes.

'All right. Out of the way, I'll do it.' She grabbed the surgical gloves, pulling the heavy ring from her finger and putting it into his hand. Nell wasn't entirely sure what kind of liability issues that might also raise, but at least she was officially fit and well. And the thought that Hugo knew Nadine, and his instinct told him there was something wrong, was nagging at her.

'Thank you.' His green eyes flashed with warmth, and he turned to Nadine. 'Sweetie, this is Dr Nell. She's my friend.'

He stepped back but Nell could feel his eyes on her as she carefully moved the sheet that covered Nadine's chest further down. Everything seemed fine. The dressings were clean and there was no blockage that Nell could see in the surgical drain. When she gently touched Nadine's skin, it was cool.

All the same, she took the thermometer from the cabinet by the bed, inserting it carefully into Nadine's ear. The little girl was watching her solemnly. Nell looked at both her hands, and even her feet, for some sign that something might be wrong.

'I don't know, Hugo. I can't find anything.'

'Okay. We should try Claude.' He nodded towards a teddy bear propped up at the side of the bed.

Nell picked up the teddy bear. 'Hey, Nadine. Is Claude all right?' She spoke slowly, in French.

Nadine shook her head.

'No? Will you tell me what's wrong with him? I'd really like to make him better.'

'He has a pain.'

It was too much for Hugo. He moved in close and Nell shooed him back, out of the way. She leaned over the bed, holding Claude where Nadine could reach him. 'Where does Claude have a pain, Nadine?'

'There.' Nadine traced her finger over Claude's chest. Out of the corner of her eye, Nell could see Hugo flipping through Nadine's notes again.

'She's been having pain relief regularly. Not as much as she might, and my guess is that she's been telling everyone that it doesn't hurt. Nadine will do that.'

'Don't the nurses know?'

'They should. But the nurse who usually looks after her

is on holiday at the moment. I was supposed to be here.' Nell heard Hugo's voice crack suddenly.

There was no answer to that, other than to remind Hugo that he'd been under orders to stay away. Nell smiled at Nadine. 'Uncle Hugo's going to find someone to make Claude better.'

'Thank you, Dr Nell.' Nadine spoke slowly, her eyelids drooping. Nell arranged the sheet carefully back over her and stripped off her gloves. When she turned to follow Hugo, she found that he was already gone.

She caught up with him, deep in conversation with another doctor, an older man. This must be Dr Bertrand. Nell wondered whether Hugo was admitting that they'd carried out a brief examination of Nadine, and guessed he probably wasn't. Dr Bertrand was nodding, and he turned to walk quickly back to the ward with Hugo.

It was all worked out in the space of a couple of minutes. Dr Bertrand examined Nadine, listened to what she had to say about how Claude was feeling and spoke to one of the nurses, who hurried away.

Dr Bertrand gestured to Hugo, motioning him out of the ward. He clearly had more to discuss, but Hugo seemed reluctant to leave Nadine.

'I'll sit with her.' Nell plumped herself down on the chair next to Nadine's bed, holding her hand over the guard rail and feeling the little girl squeeze her fingers. Hugo shot her a smile, and followed Dr Bertrand out of the ward.

By the time Dr Bertrand returned, a nurse had given Nadine the extra medication, and she seemed a little happier, declaring that Claude felt better now. He spoke briefly to Nadine and then pulled up a chair next to Nell.

'I gather that you too are a doctor.' Dr Bertrand spoke in studied, careful English.

'Yes, that's right. I'm sorry, I know that this is highly irregular…'

Dr Bertrand smiled. 'I have known Hugo for some years. His talent for being highly irregular, when circumstances require, is what helps make him one of my best doctors. This little one is feeling better now, and I have made sure that this will not happen again. Her nurse says that she was not in pain twenty minutes ago, on her last half-hourly check.'

'We just came at the wrong time, then.'

'No, it was quite the right time. If we can spare Nadine ten minutes of discomfort, then we are grateful. I have told Hugo that I cannot have him working while he is certified as sick.'

'How did he take that?'

'He has apologised and the matter is closed.' Dr Bertrand regarded Nell thoughtfully. 'He has many responsibilities, and is under a great deal of pressure. More than most men would be able to deal with.'

'Do you have any advice for me, Dr Bertrand?' Nell wanted to hear what this kindly, perceptive man had to say.

He leaned forward, as if he was about to impart some gem of wisdom. 'No. I do not.'

Nell had to think for a moment before she got the point. 'We all have to find our own way?'

'If anyone can, Hugo will.'

'Thank you.' Nell got to her feet, shaking his hand. 'May Hugo come to say goodbye to Nadine? He'll be no more than five minutes, I promise.'

'You will give him five, and he will take ten. And that is quite all right.' Dr Bertrand smiled at her.

One of the nurses directed Nell to Hugo's office and she found him sitting behind the desk, staring out of the window. She sat down and waited for him to say something.

'You don't need to tell me. I know I was wrong.' He didn't look at her.

'Yes, you were. For all the right reasons, though.'

'I know that Nadine's well cared for…' He swung his chair around to face her, and Nell saw that his face was full of anguish.

'But you can't help feeling that this is all your fault. For not being here.'

'I know it doesn't make much sense.'

'What happened, Hugo? When you were taken ill?'

'You know what happened. It's all in my notes.'

'I want to hear it from you.'

He frowned. 'You're psychoanalysing me?'

'No, I'm off duty, on account of an impending engagement.'

'Same as me, then. On account of not following my own advice.'

'So what happened?'

Hugo sighed. 'I knew my heart rate was lower than it should have been. And when I was in bed at night, I could…feel an irregular beat. I thought it might just be stress or overwork.'

'But it wasn't.'

'No. Surprisingly enough, despite being not only a doctor but also a prince, I couldn't just snap my fingers and tell myself to get better.' His voice was laden with heavy irony.

'And then you collapsed,' Nell prompted him for the next part of the story.

'Yes. Pretty much as detailed in my notes.' He shot her an exasperated look. 'Apparently my heart started beating again of its own accord, but when I was monitored overnight in the hospital, they found that it was beating too slowly and actually stopped every now and then.'

'How long for?'

'You know that, Nell. Up to three minutes. Which was almost enough to kill me if it wasn't corrected.'

'So they inserted a pacemaker. Which will help you live a completely normal life.'

'I don't *feel* normal, Nell.' He shook his head. 'It seems I'm not that good at coming to terms with my own flaws.'

'A pacemaker isn't a flaw, it's what makes you well.' So many pacemaker patients connected their device with the illness that had made it necessary. It was an obvious piece of logic, but it didn't help much when it came to accepting that their heart now needed a little help in order to function properly.

'I don't *feel* well. My shoulder aches still, I run into a brick wall whenever I try to do more than take life at a snail's pace... I can't even be at work, Nell. You see my desk? They've cleared it and given my cases to other doctors.'

'So you got sick. And you need a bit of time to get better. You're not superhuman and you're not perfect. Welcome to the world, Hugo. It's a place where pink marshmallow hospitals get built for little girls because only an imperfect world has the imagination to create that.'

Nell stopped, a little breathless. She wondered whether she might be accused of bullying a sick man, in a hospital of all places. You could probably get struck off for that kind of thing.

'You're sure about that?' He was looking at her solemnly.

'Yes, I'm sure. We're going to get the money you need.' Somehow, somewhere Nell had found a commitment to that.

He felt in his pocket, bringing out the ring. With everything else that had been going on, Nell had forgotten about it, and she was glad he hadn't lost it. She held her right hand out and he slipped it onto her finger.

'I feel... Sometimes I can't help listening to my heart, just to see if it's still beating. I'm not sure it's even possible, but I'd swear I feel the pacemaker kick in at times. It's as if my body isn't quite my own any more.'

He'd found a place where he could voice how he felt. There was still a journey ahead, but he'd found the starting point. 'That must be really hard for you. But in time, I promise you'll forget you even have it.'

Hugo nodded, slowly. 'I'm being an idiot, aren't I?'

'Yes, since you mention it.' Nell looked at her watch. 'You have five minutes to say goodbye to Nadine. Then you're coming with me.'

# CHAPTER TEN

HUGO LAY ON his bed, staring at the ceiling. He had slept a little after their return from the hospital and then lain awake, thinking mostly about how Nell was both magnificent and unstoppable when she was angry.

He could hear her clattering around in the kitchen downstairs. Hugo got up, walking slowly into the en suite bathroom to splash his face with water. The scar on his chest was still there, but the stitches would be out soon. It seemed somehow to be fading already.

'I think I might cook this evening.' He made sure that he spoke while he was still a good twenty feet away from her so as not to make her jump. All the same, she did jump, turning around and flushing a little when she saw him.

'You can cook?' She smiled suddenly.

'Of course I can cook. I know how to deal with all the appliances in this house. Even the vacuum cleaner.'

'Well you're not dealing with that for a while, vacuuming requires too much reaching. Although it's something I'd really like to see as soon as you're well enough.'

Hugo chuckled. Everything was going to be just fine. 'I *can* cook, though. You can help if you like, and get things out of the cupboards.'

'What were you thinking of cooking?'

'I do a mean lasagne. I asked Ted to get the ingredients when he went shopping this morning.'

'Okay. I do a pretty mean lasagne myself, so let's see what yours is like.' She grinned as she threw down the challenge. 'Perhaps Ted can give us his opinion.'

'I'll give him a call when dinner's ready.' Hugo opened a drawer and took out an apron. A number of people had said he was a good cook, but no one had ever accused him of being a tidy one.

Nell walked across the kitchen, taking the apron from his hand and unfolding it. Then she reached up, putting it over his head.

'Thanks.' Hugo wasn't sure he could reach behind him to tie the apron, and he wondered whether Nell would do that for him as well. And whether she'd do it the way a fiancée would, reaching around from the front, or whether she'd prefer to do it from the back, the way a doctor might.

She reached around from the front. Somehow she managed to do it while hardly touching him, but she was so close that Hugo caught his breath.

'I was thinking...' She'd tied the bow in the apron strings but she didn't step back.

'What were you thinking?' he encouraged as she tailed off.

'That... Well, if I were called upon to kiss you, in light of our announcement...'

If she felt able to do that Hugo wouldn't object in the slightest. 'You're not going to be called upon to do anything you don't want to, just for the sake of appearances. We'll just do the same as we've been doing up till now.' He wasn't in the habit of pawing women in public anyway, and the thought that Nell might not welcome it made it a complete no-no.

'So no kissing?' It was extremely gratifying that Nell looked almost disappointed. Hugo supposed that a woman might close her eyes and kiss someone while overlooking their other physical flaws.

'I'd be extremely happy if you kissed me. And extremely unhappy if you felt in any way pressured to do so.'

'I don't.' There was a mischievous glint in her eyes, which made Hugo's heart beat faster. 'I just wouldn't like to do it for the first time in front of a crowd of people.'

Before Hugo could think of a suitable reply, she'd raised herself up on her toes, planting a soft kiss on the corner of his mouth. For a moment, she stared up at him and then lowered her gaze shyly.

He wanted so badly for her to do that again. It had been just a moment and it hadn't felt real, but it still felt special. 'May I…put my arm around you?' Hugo decided that asking first would be the best course of action.

'Yes. I'd like that.'

He put his right arm gently around her waist, resisting the temptation to pull her hard against his aching body. Then Nell reached up suddenly, putting her left arm around his right shoulder, her fingertips touching the back of his neck.

It was delicious. If she'd thrown all her clothes off it could hardly be any more arousing than this. He felt himself trembling at her touch, all the more powerful because she was touching so little of him.

He saw her pupils dilate suddenly, and that small reaction almost made him choke with desire. Nell kissed him again, this time on the centre of his mouth, lingering just long enough for him to return the kiss.

Neither of them needed to say anything. Nell had to know how much he liked this. And it was very clear that she was enjoying it, too. Too far gone to even worry about whether she might feel his arousal if she got any closer, he tightened his arm around her waist.

She melted against him, as if it were the most natural thing in the world. Chemistry wasn't going to be a problem. Not kissing her again was…

It happened again, almost of its own accord. One moment their lips were tantalisingly close and the next Hugo was kissing her, and Nell was kissing him back. Soft and slow, as if to imply that perhaps there was control over it.

He thought he felt her lose control, her fingers tightening suddenly into a fist against his chest. Her heart beat against his and… That sudden feeling, as if the pacemaker had just kicked in to accommodate the screaming urge to take this as far as it would go, and then further. It reminded him that he couldn't. Not yet, and very probably not ever.

Hugo drew back slowly, planting a last kiss on her waiting lips. 'This is a role I'm not going to have any trouble with at all.' This was special, even if it did promise nothing.

'Me neither. I think we're good with that part of it.' She gave him a luminous smile as Hugo released her from their embrace, and turned back to the kitchen counter. 'Now. How about something a little more practical? Let's see if you really *can* cook.'

It was as if Hugo had swept her up and they'd danced together through the last ten days. Nell had reorganised his diary, and although Hugo had put up a few token objections, they'd always come to an agreement. Even the round of golf was made easier for him by giving up his own opportunity to play in favour of teaching his new fiancée.

She'd stayed close to him in public, the obvious implication that they were in love disguising the fact that she kept to his left, always protecting his arm and shoulder. When she leaned across to whisper in his ear, the words she breathed were questions about how he felt, and his smiling answer was often accompanied by the brush of a kiss.

Hugo's manners were impeccable, always making sure she was seated before he was, his hand guiding her when she was faced with a crush of people and didn't quite know which way to turn. And they managed to waltz through seemingly difficult obstacles. When a particularly heavy door blocked their path, and Nell stepped forward to heave it open, a smile flickered on Hugo's face. He bowed to her, catching her hand up to kiss it, and Nell made a mock curtsey. It seemed like the relaxed playfulness of new lovers, and not a concerned doctor making sure that Hugo came to no harm.

The ring on her finger still felt odd, but Nell was getting used to it. She was getting used to always being watched. And she was beginning to understand how Hugo felt. Living his life, all the highs and lows of it, at the centre of everyone's attention must be hard.

And now there would be another test. A private dinner at the palace, attended by the royal family of Montarino and visiting French and German ambassadors. It was an important occasion, and Hugo was expected to be there, which meant that Nell was expected to be with him.

The morning dawned fresh and clear, and they were on the road as soon as Nell had gulped down a cup of coffee.

'I'm a bit worried about this dress…' Nell frowned as she drove out of the gates of the house.

'It's no big deal. My mother's got it in hand.'

'That's what I'm worried about.' The thought of being closeted with the Queen and a personal stylist from the largest store in Montarino, who would be bringing a selection of suitable gowns for the evening, was frankly terrifying.

'They'll help you pick something nice. And my mother will have the jewellery to go with it, she's got something to go with everything.'

'I'm going to feel foolish, Hugo. I'm not used to wearing a lot of jewellery.'

'Fine. No big jewellery. Just tell them.' He grinned. 'Anything else you don't want?'

'No sequins. And no frills. Definitely no bows.'

'Sounds good to me. I doubt my mother will have frills or bows in mind either, she generally goes for a more classic look. You might have to mention your aversion to sequins, though. What about colour?'

Nell sighed. Hugo didn't sound as if he was taking this as seriously as she was. 'No pink. And definitely no yellow.'

'Right, then. You've practically picked your dress already.' He stretched his long legs into the footwell, obviously ready to move on and enjoy the drive.

Driving *did* calm Nell a little, but as soon as she reached the palace car park, her fears returned. Hugo seemed intent on hustling her through the corridors to his parents' apartment as quickly as possible.

The apartment was larger than his, and more lavish. His mother greeted them both with a kiss, and Hugo followed them through to her dressing room, sprawling onto one of the cream silk upholstered chairs.

'Hugo, darling. You have something to do…' Queen Margaux fixed him with a determined glare.

'Nothing that I can think of.'

'I'm sure you might think a little harder, then.' The Queen took the words out of Nell's mouth, and Hugo ignored her.

A rail-thin, elegant woman appeared, a couple of assistants behind her wheeling a rack full of dresses. In any normal circumstances, she looked as if she might have chased Nell away from the confection of silks and satins that were far beyond her purse, but she greeted Nell obsequiously.

An analysis followed of Nell's colouring and figure, both of which were apparently perfect. Nell shifted awkwardly from one foot to the other, and out of the corner of her eye she caught Hugo's grin.

'I think it all goes without saying, *Madame*, that my fiancée is perfect in every way.' He got to his feet, advancing towards the rail, and Queen Margaux shrugged, dropping into a seat to watch. Clearly the preferred course of action when Hugo was in one of these moods was to wait a while, to let it all blow over.

'Of course, Your Highness.' *Madame* smiled beatifically at Nell.

'Let's have a look at these…' He was shuffling through the dresses. 'No…no…no… What about this one, Nell?' He held up a dark blue dress and then shook his head. 'No, it's got a bow at the back.'

'Detachable, of course, Prince Hugo.'

'Oh. What do you think, Nell?' He turned to Nell, suddenly still. Somewhere, deep in his eyes, she saw that maybe this wasn't going to be as excruciating as she'd thought.

'It's…very nice.'

'Watered silk, Miss Maitland.' *Madame*'s voice held a tang of disapproval. Clearly *very nice* wasn't the right reaction.

'Hmm.' Hugo peered at the bow at the back of the dress and shrugged. 'Well, perhaps that can go on the "possible" pile.'

He looked around, obviously trying to decide where to put the dress, and *Madame* clicked her fingers. One of her assistants sprang to attention, wheeling an empty rail forward and taking the dress from Hugo.

'This one, Prince Hugo?' *Madame* tried to reassert herself, grabbing a fuchsia-pink sequined gown.

'My fiancée is a doctor, *Madame*, not the Christmas Fairy.'

'Hugo!' Queen Margaux had been watching quietly, but now murmured a reproach.

'Apologies, *Madame*. What do you think, Nell?'

'It's…not really my style.' Nell smiled apologetically at *Madame*, who pursed her lips. 'What about this one?'

'Very plain.' *Madame* took the dark green velvet dress from the rail. 'Of course, with Queen Margaux's emeralds, it would be most striking.' Nell's heart sank as *Madame* held the dress up against her.

Hugo shook his head. 'Better without. What is it you say, Mother, wear the dress and don't let the dress wear you?'

Queen Margaux stifled a laugh. 'Yes, exactly. When did you become so interested in women's couture, Hugo?'

'Nell's been teaching me all kinds of things,' he responded dryly, and his mother smiled. 'Let's put that with the "possibles" and leave the emeralds for later.'

They'd whittled the dresses down to four. Three blue and the green one, which *Madame* was obviously regretting putting on the rail to bring to the palace. Hugo was questioning *Madame* closely on the latest trends in menswear, which gave Nell a chance to slip away alone to put the first dress on. When she returned, *Madame* practically ran over to her, tugging unnecessarily at the bodice.

'Perfect…perfect.' She turned to Hugo as if Nell didn't exist, looking for his reaction.

'You like it, Nell?' Hugo's gaze found hers.

'It's…it looks beautiful.' Nell looked at her own reflection in the mirror. Was that really her? 'It's a little tight.'

'Form-fitting…' *Madame* murmured the words.

'I'd recommend breathing over form-fitting. Can you breathe, Nell? On a scale of one to ten.'

Nell grinned at him. 'About three and a half. Maybe only three if I'm sitting down.'

'Well, go and take it off quickly. Before I have to resuscitate you…'

\* \* \*

The dress was chosen. Hugo had somehow managed to infer that the diamond earrings and bracelet that his mother was lending to go with it were all *Madame*'s idea, and she'd left, trailing the scent of slightly mollified disapproval in her wake. Queen Margaux had asked Hugo whether he was going to interfere when the hairdresser arrived, and he'd shrugged. Nell had laughingly told him that she thought she could manage alone.

'It's a matter of knowing your power.' Since the choosing of the dress had been accomplished in record time, they were now free until three o'clock, and Hugo had taken Nell for a stroll in the palace gardens.

'I'm not sure I have any power, do I?' Nell looked up at Hugo. Caressed by the sun and relaxed in the warm breeze, he seemed the epitome of a handsome prince.

'Of course you do. You know, when you're a prince, people will tell you that you're the one in charge. And then they tie you up in knots over all of the things you can and can't do.'

'Like having to accept your own private doctor?' Nell knew now that Hugo's studied avoidance of her advice hadn't been just a game. He'd been fighting to express his own feelings over his surgery.

'Well…that worked out. And you were right, I did need to rest a little more. And I needed to be told that I'm not indestructible.'

'You needed to accept that for yourself. Not to be told.'

He chuckled. 'Yes. Big difference. And you don't need to be told which dress you like, so remember that next time.'

'There probably isn't going to be a next time.' Nell had to remind herself every day that this wasn't permanent. That she wasn't really Hugo's fiancée and that in a few months' time she'd be leaving.

'No. I suppose not.' Suddenly the space between them seemed to grow. Their leisurely pace was the same, but they were just taking the same path through the gardens, not walking together.

'Thank you for stepping in, though. I'm not sure what I would have ended up with if you hadn't been there.'

'My mother knows how to handle *Madame* and her entourage. It might have deteriorated into a squabble, though.'

'A squabble? Surely not!'

Hugo chuckled. 'They've known each other for years. *Madame* has access to all the best dresses, but she's not that flexible in her approach. There have been a few full and frank discussions.'

'I didn't realise...'

'That's what I mean about taking your own power. People like *Madame* love to tell you what to do, but if you stand up to them, they've got nothing.'

'And you take a lot of pleasure in standing up to them, don't you?'

He didn't answer. The complex politics, the unspoken expectations of the palace must be hard to live with. Being a doctor seemed suddenly a lot simpler.

'I've been thinking. About Martin...'

He raised an eyebrow. 'Yes? You do that a lot?'

'Not all that much.' The last ten days had been busy. And full of the kind of achievement and joy that didn't naturally bring Martin to mind. But that respite had served to consolidate Nell's thoughts.

'I'm glad to hear that.' There was a note of possessiveness in Hugo's tone.

'I checked his social media accounts. He's been very quiet recently.' Nell had wondered whether Hugo had had anything to do with that.

'The email that our legal team sent him might have had something to do with that.'

'So you *did* do something.'

'Nothing very much. They simply made contact and made a polite request that any future public statements be copied to them, as a courtesy.'

'But coming from an eminent law firm, with the backing of the palace… That sounds like a threat to me.'

'There were no threats. All bullies are cowards, don't you know that? If Jarman backs off because you have powerful friends, that's his business.'

'I was thinking maybe…that I might make him back off by myself. I'm considering lodging an official complaint with the hospital.'

Hugo nodded. 'If that's what you want. It won't be easy, though. Our lawyers can support you through the process.'

'I know, but I don't want that. I thought about what you said, about him probably acting that way towards other people. I'd been so bound up in my own problems that I thought I was alone, but if there *is* anyone else…'

'You want to support them.' He clearly approved of that wholeheartedly.

'Yes, I do. And I want him to know that I did it alone. That I have the power to fight back by myself.'

'Okay. Does that mean I'm not allowed to help?'

'As a friend?' That was a far more demanding proposition. One word and he could have the weight of highly placed contacts and a hotshot legal team crashing down on Martin's head. It would take a lot more input from him to support her through the process as her friend.

'Yes. Always.'

'If I wrote everything down, would you be able to look through it? Give me your opinion?'

His hand drifted to hers, and he tucked it into the crook

of his elbow, his thumb brushing against the ring on her finger.

'Yes, of course. Partners.'

'Thank you. I'd like that.' The ring meant one thing to everyone else who saw it and quite another to her and Hugo. That they couldn't love each other but they could be friends, who protected each other.

# CHAPTER ELEVEN

HUGO HAD LET her go, and Nell had set off for his parents' apartment with a hint of determination in her step. Whatever happened with her hair and make-up, he was pretty sure that Nell would have a say in it.

He took more time than usual dressing, his left arm still hampering him as he sorted through his wardrobe to find a waistcoat that was exactly the shade of the dress she'd chosen. He'd never done that before, not for any woman, but Nell… They were of the same mind. Beneath all their differences they were cut from the same cloth.

He heard her let herself back into his apartment and rose from his chair to meet her. A little thrill ran up his spine, tempered by a reminder to himself that he shouldn't expect too much.

And then, not expecting too much became irrelevant. He couldn't possibly have expected her to look this stunning. The slim-line green dress traced her curves, the hem high on her ankle. A slender row of diamonds at her wrist and neck and a pair of high-heeled, strappy shoes balanced the look perfectly.

'What do you think?' She was pressing her lips together, and Hugo realised that his over-awed silence had left Nell waiting a little too long.

'I think the dress is very nice.' He wanted to touch the soft folds of material, but instead he allowed his hand to trace the shape of her waist, just millimetres away from it. 'The diamonds are just right for it.'

She gave him a nervous smile and he permitted his fingers to follow the curve of her chin. Still not touching her. Somehow not touching was almost as sensual as feeling the softness of her skin. 'They'd be nothing without you, though. *You* are exquisite.'

'You think…it's all right?' She was smiling now.

'It's so much better than all right that…no, it's not just all right.'

Nell nodded, obviously pleased, walking over to where his jacket hung across the back of the chair. Picking it up, she helped him on with it, smoothing her hands across his shoulders.

'Will I do?' He smiled down at her.

'For an everyday, handsome prince? You'll definitely do.'

He made her feel good. Clinging to his arm had become a matter of each supporting the other now. Nell protected him from being bumped and jostled, and he protected her from the enquiring heads that turned to look her way.

Everything glittered, from the magnificent chandeliers high above their heads down to the jewels of the assembled company. The great and the good of Montarino, along with delegations from their neighbouring countries. Hugo passed effortlessly between them all, his arm always there for her, the place by his side always reserved for Nell.

The King and Queen led the way into the grand dining hall. Queen Margaux shone in a canary-yellow dress, which complemented her blonde hair, and King Ferdinand was upright and gracious beside her. Everyone was seated, and Nell looked around nervously, feeling Hugo's fingers brush hers under the snowy tablecloth. She looked into his smile and nodded an answer to his unspoken question. As long as she waited and followed his lead in picking the right one from the array of silver knives and forks in front of her, she'd be fine.

Hugo had taken charge of the conversation at their part of the table, asking questions and including everyone. Soon their group was animated and laughing and even Nell began to relax. Underneath the fine clothes and the magnificent surroundings, they were just people getting to know each other.

'Would you like a break?' As they rose from the table, Hugo bent towards her, murmuring in her ear.

'Can we...? Don't you have to stay with your guests?'

'My parents have it covered. Just for ten minutes, so that you can stop having to keep smiling.'

That would actually be nice. Nell's jaw was beginning to ache a little. She followed Hugo as he slipped through the open French doors and out onto the stone-flagged terrace. A number of people seemed to have had the same idea, and Hugo led her out of the circle of light cast by lanterns that were positioned around the terrace, down the steps and into the garden.

'You're *sure* we won't be missed?'

He chuckled. 'This is Montarino, not England. Protocol practically demands that a newly engaged couple disappear for at least ten minutes during the course of the evening.' Hugo walked slowly along the paved path, which was flanked by a sculpted hedge.

'Ten minutes. Not much time, then?' She grinned up at him.

'Something else you need to learn about Montarino. We know how to make very good use of just ten minutes.'

Suddenly ten minutes seemed like ten hours. Out here in the warm evening breeze, the lights and noise of the house were beginning to recede behind them. Nell shivered at the thought.

'Cold?'

'No, it's nice to be out here. It was beginning to get very hot inside.'

Their leisurely pace grew more leisurely, until they were standing together. She had to touch him. Nell ran her fingers down the lapel of his jacket and felt Hugo's hand resting lightly on her waist.

'So…while everyone thinks we've escaped to do what every engaged couple does…' Hugo chuckled.

'We could read the paper?'

'We could. Or play a game of cards.'

'Not enough time.' Nell reached up to touch his face. There was only one thing she really wanted to do right now. And since tonight was all about their public personas, an engaged couple who were naturally very much in love, maybe that one thing was permissible.

'No. You're right.' His gaze never left her face as he raised her hand to his mouth, kissing her fingers.

They could have stopped there. But Nell didn't want to, and she knew that Hugo didn't either. Ten minutes.

His lips were almost touching hers. This wouldn't be the formal kiss, planted on her cheek or hand, to delight the people around them. This was just for her.

Hugo's arm tightened suddenly around her waist and she felt his body tighten against hers. 'Who's there?'

There was a rustle in the bushes behind her. Hugo pulled her away, facing the hurried whispers coming from the darkness. And then a shape detached itself from the deepest of the shadows, followed by another.

'Who's there?' Hugo asked again, his tone demanding an answer.

'The necklace…' A low voice, full of menace, spoke in French and Hugo pushed Nell behind him. Not a good idea, even if he had been in full health. Nell kicked off her shoes, ready to run, clinging to Hugo's arm.

'All right.' He held one hand out in a gesture that was clearly intended to calm the situation.

'Quickly!' The man spoke again, taking another step forward. He was holding something in his hand, and Nell wondered whether he was armed.

This must have been so easy. Any one of the women here was wearing jewellery that would fetch a high price. The men had only to get through high railings at the perimeter of the palace, conceal themselves in the garden and then wait.

'Nell. Give me the necklace.'

'What?' Queen Margaux's diamond necklace. She'd promised herself to take good care of it. But if giving it up was unthinkable, the alternative was even worse.

She fumbled with the catch at the back of her neck, but it was too firmly secured for her trembling fingers. And she'd hesitated for a moment too long. The man lunged towards her as if to tear the necklace from her throat, and she felt Hugo's body pushing her back and taking the brunt of the impact.

'No…Hugo!' He was stumbling to one side and Nell cried out in terror. 'I'll give it to you.' She pulled frantically at the necklace, trying to get it off.

But it was too late for that. She felt a gloved hand close around her wrist, trying to get at her bracelet, and then she was free again as Hugo let out a great roar, tackling her assailant. The man lashed out at Hugo, and she saw a spark. In the silence, broken only by the sound of the wind in the trees, the clicking sound seemed to last for a very long time, even if it was just a few seconds. Then Hugo screamed in pain, dropping to the ground like a stone.

'Hugo!' There was no possibility of just giving the men what they wanted and letting them go now. Nell yelled for help at the top of her voice, hoping that if the assembled

company in the palace didn't hear her, there would be a
security patrol in the grounds that did.

The men were running now, and Nell dropped to her
knees beside Hugo. He was still groaning and gasping for
air, and she grabbed his arm, feeling for his pulse.

'Uh…' He tried to speak, but couldn't. All Nell could
do was to hold him, as if that might absorb some of his
pain into her own body and spare him.

'I know. He had a stun gun. They're gone now.' Nell
knew that a jolt from a stun gun could disable the strongest man. It dealt excruciating pain, rather than injury, but
a recent operation and a pacemaker complicated things.

Hugo knew that as well as she did. 'You're okay, Hugo.
I can feel your pulse.'

His body relaxed a little, but there was still fear in his
eyes. 'You're…sure?' His voice sounded thick and strange,
and his free hand drifted to his chest.

'I'm sure. I feel it beating, Hugo. Strong and steady.'
Fast. But who could blame it for that?

A noise behind her made her jump and Nell looked
round to see three men from the palace security team.
People were running down the steps of the terrace and
Nell could see the King at their head, no longer the stiff
monarch but a man of action like his son.

'I'm a doctor. Stand back, he's all right.' She waved
the security men back, and they formed a triangle around
them, keeping watch. Nell clung to Hugo, trying to comfort him, as he rolled painfully onto his back, his head in
her lap.

'Hugo!' The King practically skidded to a halt, bending
down, his questioning gaze meeting Nell's.

'He's been hit by a stun gun. It's very painful but it'll
pass. The jolt from a stun gun shouldn't affect a pacemaker.' Her words were for Hugo, as much as they were for
the King. It must have been terrifying, feeling only pain,

his body out of control. Knowing that the pacemaker was there in his chest and wondering whether his heart had already stopped beating.

The King knelt down, suddenly just another father. 'You hear that, son?'

Somehow Hugo managed a smile. 'Never contradict a lady…'

'No. That's right.' King Ferdinand flashed a tight smile at Nell and reached for his son. Hugo took his hand, gripping it tight.

The King had asked one of the men who came running towards them to tell the Queen that Hugo was all right and then his attention was for Hugo alone. He hardly seemed to notice the security guard who had approached and was standing at a respectful distance, waiting to be acknowledged.

Nell caught the guard's attention, keeping her fingers on Hugo's pulse. Now wasn't the time to interrupt the King. 'You have something to report?'

'We've apprehended the two men, and called the police.'

'Thank you for acting so quickly. I'll tell the King. Do you have the stun gun?'

'Yes, ma'am.'

'Would you find out the make and model for me, please?' Obtaining the information would stop the guard from hovering here, and finding out exactly what Hugo had been hit with couldn't do any harm.

'Yes, ma'am.' The guard turned and hurried away.

Maybe she'd overstepped her authority, but there was no trace of reproof in the King's face when he looked up at her.

'Thank you, Nell. Should we move him, now?'

'I'd like to take Hugo to hospital. It's just a precaution, but I want a pacing check done, and he should be monitored for a little while. Just to be on the safe side.' Scar

tissue hadn't had a chance to form around the newly implanted leads yet, and they might have been dislodged
by the scuffle or the sudden convulsions of Hugo's body.

'I think that's wise.' The King nodded, looking down at
Hugo. 'What do you say, Hugo? Still in no mood to contradict the lady…?'

'No mood at all.' Nell had been sure that Hugo would
protest, but he just nodded. This had frightened him even
more than she'd thought. 'You should go back to our
guests, Father.'

For a moment the King seemed torn. Then he shook
his head.

'He'll be all right. And I'll keep you and the Queen informed.' It seemed wrong to break the new bond that had
surfaced between father and son in the heat of this emer-
gency, but Nell was beginning to understand that duty was
a hard taskmaster.

'Every step of the way?' The King's voice was cracked
with emotion.

'Yes, I promise.'

The King bent over his son. 'You know we'll be there,
Hugo. Your mother and I…'

'Yes. Just give me a bit of space.' Hugo's words were
clearly a fond joke, and his father laughed quietly.

'Perhaps you'll help me get him up on his feet and we
can walk him over to the car.' Before now, Nell would
never have asked the King to do such a thing. But he
seemed to need this, and Hugo clearly did, too. It had taken
a stun gun and a lot of pain before the two men had been
able to bury their differences, but maybe it was worth it.

# CHAPTER TWELVE

ALTHOUGH THE JOURNEY to the hospital was a short one, the car was starting and stopping in the evening traffic. Ted had been fetched from the palace kitchen and arrived stony-faced, clearly annoyed with himself that he'd done what had been expected of him and relied on the security measures at the palace to keep Hugo safe for the evening. He sat in the front seat of the car, next to the chauffeur.

'I feel fine now. There's no need for the hospital. Ted...?' Hugo appealed to the back of Ted's head from the back seat of the car, where he sat with Nell.

'You know what I think.' Ted didn't turn around, and Hugo looked across at Nell in a silent appeal.

'We're going to the hospital.' Nell glared at him. If he thought that she was an easier touch than Ted, he had another think coming.

'Yes, ma'am.' Hugo settled back into his seat. 'Only I'll prove you wrong when I get there.'

'That's exactly what I expect you to do. And it's never wrong to be on the safe side.'

She heard Ted chuckle from the front of the car, and Hugo rolled his eyes.

By the time they arrived at the hospital, the cardiac surgeon who had implanted Hugo's pacemaker had been roused from his bed. Nell quickly told him what had happened and he nodded in agreement with her assessment.

She left him alone with Hugo for a moment, and found Ted brooding outside the door.

'He's okay, Ted.'

'I know. But *I* should have been there. A stun gun hurts like the blazes.'

If Ted had been on duty, she and Hugo would have found a way to evade him. The sweet promise of those moments with Hugo, alone in the darkness, made Nell shiver. 'You can't be with him all the time. You were off duty.'

Ted knew that she was trying to make him feel better, and flashed her a wry smile. 'He knows what to do if there's an incident. He should stay back and shout for help.'

'He was protecting me.' Nell had been feeling just as guilty as Ted obviously was.

'Understandable.' The creases in Ted's forehead relaxed slightly. 'Maybe I'm getting a bit too old for this.'

Nell laid her hand on his arm. 'He trusts you, Ted. And Hugo needs people he can trust right now. I don't think age has anything to do with the fact that you can't be in two places at once.'

'Maybe...' Ted didn't look convinced, but at least he was thinking about it.

'Why don't you go and get a cup of tea? I'm sure there'll be somewhere...'

Ted nodded. 'The café on the ground floor is open all night. Would you like me to get you something?'

'No, I'll stay here and talk to his doctor. I'll call you when we've finished and you can see him.'

'All right.' Ted went to turn, and then stopped. 'Thanks.'

Hugo was lying in bed, a heart monitor by his side. His smile was back in full force, as his coping mechanisms kicked in.

'Don't you think this is a bit over the top? People get hit with stun guns all the time, and they get up and walk away.' He'd waited to come up with his objections until the door had closed quietly behind the cardiac surgeon.

'Yes, they do. But they're generally people in good health who haven't just had surgery. Give it a rest, Hugo.'

'I *am* in good health. Reasonable health, anyway. I'll feel better when I can get back into the gym.'

Nell rolled her eyes. 'Don't give me that, Hugo. This might be just a precaution but it's one that I believe is warranted, and your cardiac surgeon agrees with me.'

'I know what the risks are as well as you do...'

He broke off suddenly, seeing the tears that were filling Nell's eyes. This time she'd made no effort to hide them from him. Why should she? Nothing else seemed to get through to him.

'I'm sorry, Nell. I know you must have been really frightened tonight.'

'Yes, I was. And the bit that frightened me the most was hearing you scream and seeing you hit the ground.' She grabbed his hand, holding on to it tight.

He twisted his mouth down in a show of embarrassment. 'I heard that everyone cries like a baby when they're hit with a stun gun. I know why now...'

'Stop it, Hugo! Stop trying to make out that you weren't afraid. And don't pretend that your first thought wasn't that your heart had stopped, or that you needed your father and he was there for you.'

'Please... Don't cry.' His voice was suddenly husky.

'Well, someone's got to. Ted's maintaining a stiff upper lip, while wrestling with the idea that he should have been there. Your father was really cut up about letting you leave without him, but he had to put on a brave face for his guests. He really cares...'

'Yes, I know. I do too, we just... Sometimes we lose sight of that.' Suddenly he reached for her, shifting a little in the bed.

'Come here. Please… I need you, Nell.'

There wasn't a great deal of room on the bed but there was enough. Nell slipped off her shoes, lowering the bed a little and then climbing carefully up beside him. What the hell, if anyone found them like this, they were supposed to be engaged, weren't they?

He put his arm around her shoulders, holding her close. 'I couldn't protect you, Nell. I'm sorry.'

'I couldn't protect you either. And I'm sorry about that.' She nestled against him. Suddenly everything seemed all right.

They lay together for long minutes. No more words needed, just the silence and the feel of her heart beating. His, too. Finally Nell felt Hugo move, and when she looked up at him he brushed a kiss against her forehead.

'Much as I love having you here, you should go.'

'You're sending me away?' Perhaps Hugo felt he'd admitted a bit too much, and he wanted some time on his own to reconstruct his armoured exoskeleton.

'I can't sleep with you next to me. And you're going to need some sleep, too…'

'Me? I'm all right.'

Hugo chuckled. 'Don't you start. I'm all right enough for both of us. But I need you to do something for me.'

'What?' Right now, she just wanted to stay here and hold him. Or if that would keep him awake, she'd go and have a cup of tea with Ted and then creep back after Hugo fell asleep and sit in the chair next to his bed.

'If I'm going to be here for the next twenty-four hours, I need someone to fill in for me at the meeting tomorrow afternoon. I thought you might do it.'

'Me? But I can't!'

'Why not? You know all the issues, and I think that the clinic means as much to you as it does to me.'

'Yes, it does. But it's *you* they want to see. We can put it off…'

'That's not going to be so easy, the arrangements have already been made. And you'll be speaking directly for me.' He moved his left arm stiffly, catching her hand, his thumb moving across the ring on her finger. 'That gives you the right.'

'That's just a pretence, Hugo.'

'You want the same things I do. I trust you to speak for me. That's not a pretence.'

'Is it what you really want?'

'Yes, it is. Isn't it what you'd want?'

In his place, she'd do exactly the same. She'd want Hugo out there, working for the thing that was most important to her, instead of cooling his heels, drinking tea at the hospital. Even if the prospect of going to the meeting alone was terrifying, Hugo seemed to think that she could do it.

'Okay. I'll stay a little longer…'

'No, you'll go now and get some sleep. Ted will take you to the meeting, and he'll point you in the right direction, who to greet first and so on. You'll knock them dead.'

'You really think so?'

'Yes, I do. Go. Although if you could get me a phone first, I want to call my father.'

'I'll find Ted, you can use his.'

'Thanks.'

Nell climbed off the bed, pulling her dress straight. It seemed to have survived the evening tolerably well, which was a tribute to its quality. She fussed with it, aware that she was putting off the moment of leaving.

'I'll…call you. In the morning.' She picked up her clutch bag, checking unnecessarily that the diamond necklace and bracelet, which she'd finally managed to take off in the car on the way to hospital, were still safely inside.

'Wait…' Hugo was grinning now. 'You were thinking

of leaving without kissing me goodbye? Just on the cheek, I don't want the monitor to register anything that gives my doctor pause for thought.'

Nell laughed, bending over him. 'First you tell me how you really feel.'

'Dreadful. I ache in muscles I never knew I had.'

'Good. You'll be well cared for here, and I'll be back tomorrow, after the meeting. Think you can be awake for me?'

'I'll do my very best.' Hugo pulled her down for a kiss that set Nell's heart thumping. Goodness only knew what was going on with the monitor, and she didn't dare look. 'Go. Before I decide I'm feeling a lot better now and I need another one of those…'

Having Nell walk away had been more difficult than he'd thought. Hugo kept it together until Ted had come and then gone again, and then there was nothing to prevent his thoughts from ranging wherever they wanted to go. However much he craved having her with him now, this was what he wanted her to do. He wanted Nell to walk out of that meeting tomorrow feeling the exhilaration of having taken it by storm. She'd been bullied and made to feel ashamed for much too long.

Maybe if he'd done the same with Anna, given her some way of taking her own career forward while she was with him, then things might have been different. But he doubted it. Anna had told him that she lived in his shadow even when he wasn't there, and that she couldn't handle it. Things were working with Nell because, despite what everyone thought, they weren't in love. He should remember that, just in case he felt any temptation to fall in love with her.

It wouldn't be all that hard. She was beautiful and brave, and when she was there he forgot all about whether or not his heart would keep beating. He knew that it would, just so he'd be able to spend another moment with her. But if he fell in love, things would change. However hard he tried, Nell's career would have to take second place to the duties that he'd been born to.

His limbs felt heavy, and he could hardly keep his eyes open. Hugo realised that the tablet he'd taken from the nurse, not even thinking to question what it was, was probably a sleeping pill. As he drifted into sleep, he wondered briefly what it might be like to fall asleep with Nell at his side.

Nell had called him before going into the lunch meeting, her nerves jangling in the cadence of her voice. When she called him again, a little more than two hours later, she sounded quite different.

'I did the presentation, just the way you did last time. They really liked it, Hugo.'

'I'm sure they did.' Hugo leaned back against the pillows, smiling.

'They're going to help us.'

Hugo grinned. 'It didn't occur to me for one moment that they wouldn't.'

'Well, it occurred to me. I thought they might chase me away and say that they'd come to hear you, and I just wasn't good enough.'

'When are you going to realise that you're always good enough, Nell?'

There was a pause, and Hugo imagined Nell frowning, the way she did whenever he complimented her.

'I'm not sure how you can say "always" good enough. There are a lot of things you haven't seen me do yet. But I was good enough today.'

That was something. If large oaks could grow from little acorns, then one of these days Nell was going to stand up and command the attention she deserved. Until then, Hugo would just keep pushing, one inch at a time.

'Did your parents come to see you?'

'My father did. Mother obviously decided that it was safe to allow us in the same room unsupervised.'

'And was it?'

'We disagreed on a few things. Patched it up again. We're good.' Better than they had been for a very long time. Hugo wondered whether Nell knew that it was her influence that had made that possible.

'Are you getting out this afternoon?'

'Yes. I've been pronounced none the worse for wear and I can go as soon as you can collect me.'

Nell laughed, the sound of pure happiness reaching him despite the less-than-perfect phone connection.

'That's great. We're on our way now.'

She almost danced into his room a little later. Nell was wearing a red summer jacket over a red-and-white printed dress, and Hugo began to wish that he'd been with her at the luncheon. But then she would have sat quietly beside him, supporting him but hardly speaking up for herself. She could do so much more than that.

'Are you ready? Before we go, I have someone who'd like to see you.'

Hugo just wanted to go down to the car and get home. But then Nell ducked outside the doorway, appearing again with a wheelchair.

'Uncle Hugo!' Nadine beamed at him.

'Nadine. What are you doing here?'

'I came to see you, silly.' Nadine wrinkled her nose at him and he laughed.

'That's very kind of you. Who told you that I was here?'

'Dr Nell. She said you were ill but you're better now.'

'Yes, that's right.' Nell pulled up a chair and Hugo sat

down, facing the wheelchair and leaning forward towards Nadine.

'Are you *all* better?'

'Yes, every bit of me. And what about you? You look much better than when I saw you last.'

Nadine nodded. 'Mama and Papa are taking me home soon.'

'That's good news.' Hugo flipped his gaze up towards Nell, and she nodded, smiling. Clearly she'd taken a moment to find out how Nadine was, and the little girl was recovering well.

'Were you lonely?' Nadine looked around the room that Hugo had occupied. He supposed that the exaggerated quiet of the private wing of the hospital must seem a little lonely to her.

'Yes, I was a bit lonely. But I was only here for one day.'

Nadine nodded, tugging at the teddy bear that was squashed down beside her in the wheelchair. A little tattered now, Claude had accompanied Nadine through most of her stays at the hospital. When she stretched out her hands, offering him to Hugo, he felt his eyes fill with tears.

'Are we going to see how Claude is?' How many times had he pressed his stethoscope to Claude's chest to dispel a little girl's fears? He knew something about those fears now, the unspoken shadows that defied everything he'd learned as a doctor.

'How *you* are.' Nadine was growing up. She knew that Claude was just a way of talking about her own difficulties, and she was offering him to Hugo in the hope that he might speak for him, too. Hugo's hand automatically reached for the stethoscope that wasn't in his pocket, and decided instead to just press his ear to Claude's chest.

'I hear it…' He nodded, hearing only the pounding of his own heart. 'That's very good…'

'Perfect.' Nadine echoed the word he usually said when

he listened to Claude's heart. It had been on the tip of Hugo's tongue but somehow he'd been unable to say it in connection with himself. Hugo nodded, giving Claude a hug and then passing him back to Nadine.

'It's time to go back now, Nadine.' Nell spoke in her careful, studied French, but the warmth of her smile was unmistakable. 'Your mother will be here to see you.'

Hugo couldn't let her go yet. This little girl who had been through so much but had still found it in her to offer him the comfort of a teddy bear. 'Would you like me to come with you?'

Nadine nodded, and Nell flashed him a querying glance. Hugo realised that his jeans and casual shirt weren't his usual attire for the hospital, but that didn't seem to matter right now. He got to his feet, releasing the brakes on the wheelchair.

Hugo had breezed past the nurses, smiling as he went but not stopping to receive his printed discharge papers. Nell had collected them for him, and followed him through the building to the children's section of the cardiac unit. A couple of the staff obviously noticed that he was dressed particularly casually today and might have wondered, but Hugo didn't seem to care and neither did any of the children in the ward. Nadine was settled comfortably back into her bed, and Hugo spent time talking and playing with her and all the other children.

He seemed to light up when he was around them. After an hour, it still didn't seem that Hugo was about to leave and Nell stepped in, dragging him away. He'd had enough for one day and there was no question about whether Hugo would be back soon, despite the fact that he was still on leave of absence from the hospital and had so very recently been one of its patients.

'They've been through so much. I feel like a complete

fraud.' He murmured the words as he got into the back seat of the car, next to Nell.

'You need to stay strong, Hugo. Who's going to champion them if you don't?' This afternoon had brought exactly what she and Hugo were doing into sharp perspective. If the endless meeting and lunches had seemed less important than being on the wards, it would make a huge difference to both the patients and the doctors and nurses who worked here.

He laughed suddenly, taking her hand, even though no one was looking. 'And who's going to champion *me* if you don't?'

'I expect you'll find someone.' Every time he got too close, she instinctively drew back. Then kicked herself for it, because being close to Hugo was the best thing that she could imagine.

The car slowed a little and Hugo nudged her. On the pavement a couple of women were waving at them, and Hugo waved back.

'Wave…' he murmured to Nell.

'They're not interested in me.'

'No?' He turned to her in disbelief. 'Try waving and see what happens.'

Ted had obligingly bought the car almost to a halt. Nell leaned across and waved at the women, feeling rather stupid, but they reacted by waving even more enthusiastically. A small boy standing next to them on the pavement started to jump up and down, catching their excitement.

Hugo caught her hand up, pressing it to his lips, and the women laughed, nudging each other. Ted waited a few more seconds and then applied his foot to the accelerator.

'That's nice of them.' Nell watched through the back window as the car moved away.

Hugo nodded. If only the women knew that this was

all a sham. Nell sat back in her seat, suddenly feeling dispirited.

'By the way, I've postponed my meeting for tomorrow. We can fit it in next week.' Perhaps he felt the same. Hugo seemed keen to change the subject.

'Are you sure you're feeling all right?'

'I feel fine. But another day's rest couldn't hurt.'

Nell had assumed that as soon as Hugo got out of hospital he'd be as unstoppable as the last time. 'Have you got something up your sleeve, Hugo? You're not going to tell me you're going paragliding or something?'

'No. Seems you've got me under control…'

Nell snorted with laughter. 'Right. That's never going to happen, Hugo.'

# CHAPTER THIRTEEN

HUGO HAD TO admit that these few days' rest had done him good. He felt stronger, less fearful, and less of a slave to the imagined beat of his heart.

But now it was time to get back to work, and Nell accompanied him to a presentation to the board of directors in the most prestigious of the few high-rise offices in Montarino. It was one of their most important meetings so far, and Nell seemed to dwindle into the background, hanging on to his arm and supporting him. It wasn't until he'd got up to speak that the idea in Hugo's head became a reality.

He thanked everyone for being there, and reiterated the importance of the project that they were being asked to help sponsor. Then he introduced Nell, and sat down.

She kicked him so hard under the table that he jumped. But she got to her feet, smiling. She made a charming apology for any shortcomings in her French, making a joke about having to learn so that she knew what her fiancé was up to. Everyone laughed, and then the lights went down and the first of the images from Hugo's laptop appeared, projected onto the wall. She then proceeded to make a presentation of such vigour and freshness that even Hugo felt he would have given anything that she asked of him.

She waited until they were in the car again before she turned on him. Hugo shifted his feet away from her, just in case she decided to kick him again.

'What are you doing, Hugo?'

'I'm doing the best I can for the clinic. You had them eating out of your hand.'

'You!' She pointed at him accusingly. 'They wanted you, not me.'

'Maybe they went in wanting me. Unless I'm very much mistaken, by the time you'd finished with them, they'd forgotten about tax deductions and publicity, and they wanted a clinic.'

'You might have told me first.'

'Yes, you made that plain. I'm sorry, I was improvising.'

'Well, don't do it again, Hugo. Next time you *tell* me what you're about to do.'

The pink of her cheeks, Nell's passion, and her unerring sense of how to capture hearts. He'd do anything not to see that subsumed into the quiet, submissive woman who had walked next to him into the building.

'All right. So that means you'll do the next presentation?'

'This is *your* project, Hugo. You're the boss.'

He didn't want to be the boss, in Nell's eyes. He wasn't someone whose opinion of her might drag her down and make her feel any less than she was. But on the other hand, being the boss did give him the opportunity to build her up, and he decided to let go of the question of who was supposed to be telling who to do what.

'So I'm making a decision. You do it better than I can.' He leaned forward, hoping for some support. 'Don't you think so, Ted?'

Ted was keeping his eye on the road and didn't turn. 'I didn't catch that...'

Right. Ted was keeping out of it. Wise move, probably. But if Hugo was venturing where angels feared to tread, he wasn't going to back down now. It meant far too much to him.

'So you'll do the presentation tomorrow?'

Nell was trying to glare at him, but she couldn't quite conceal her pleasure. 'I'll think about it.'

Hugo closed his eyes, trying to conceal *his* pleasure. Things were going in the right direction.

'Ted… Ted, look…'

'I see it.' The car slowed suddenly, and Hugo opened his eyes. For a moment he remembered the pain from the stun gun, and almost threw his arm protectively across Nell before he realised that they weren't under any threat.

At the side of the road, a car had veered off the road, breaking through a fence that bounded a field. Another car, which had stopped at the side of the road, was crushed at the front right-hand side and a young man was climbing slowly out of it.

Almost before Ted had brought the car to a halt, Nell had the door on her side open and was climbing out. Wobbling a little on her high heels, she ran over to the man, calling to him and then changing direction, making for the car that was in the ditch.

'We're going to need the first aid kit, Ted.' Hugo climbed out of the car, knowing that Ted would follow him with the medical kit they carried in the boot. He ran over to where Nell was sliding precariously down a grassy slope towards the stricken car.

This time, he supported her. Reaching out with his right hand, he grabbed her elbow to stop her from falling as they both hurried towards the car. As they approached, Hugo could hear the sound of a baby crying.

Nell carefully pulled the driver's door of the car open. A woman was sitting inside, trapped by the crushed dashboard and steering column. Mercifully, it seemed that she was just unconscious.

'I'll take her.' Hugo knelt down on the grass, reaching in with his good arm to find a pulse. 'You get the baby out.'

'Right.' Nell opened the back door of the car, reaching in towards the baby carrier in the back seat. It was still firmly strapped in, and that seemed to have saved the child from any injury if the noise it was making was anything to go by. But the angle of the car made it awkward to get to.

She crawled inside without a moment's hesitation. Hugo felt a flash of regret, wanting to be the one to go inside the car but knowing that Nell was the better choice right now. He bit back his feelings, turning quickly to the woman in the front seat.

Behind him, he could hear Ted calling for an ambulance and a fire and rescue truck. Then another voice came to his ears.

'Is she all right?'

The man from the other car was standing right behind him, blood beginning to trickle down the side of his face. Ted ended his call and stepped forward, ushering him away. He would check him over for any signs of serious injury, and with the information that Hugo had now, he had to concentrate on the woman. He could see blood beginning to pool under the seat but couldn't see where it was coming from. She was pinned down by the infrastructure of the car, and even if she hadn't been, Hugo was loath to her until the ambulance arrived with the proper equipment.

The woman was breathing but still unconscious. Carefully he pushed his fingers between the seat and her legs, but there was no blood there. The bleeding must have been further down, and he couldn't see her lower legs. Quickly checking her chest and stomach, Hugo turned his attention to craning inside, cursing quietly as he felt his left shoulder pull. There was no time to think about that right now.

* * *

Nell climbed inside the car, sliding across to where the baby was secured on the back seat. Fumbling with the nylon mesh straps, she found that one of them had become caught when the front passenger seat had been forced back a few inches in the crash.

But it seemed that the baby was unhurt. Quickly she crawled backwards out of the car, opening the medical kit that Ted had brought and searching for a scalpel. It registered at the back of her mind that as car medical kits went, this one was particularly well-stocked and it looked as if Hugo might need it. The woman in the front seat of the car still wasn't moving.

She climbed back inside the car, cutting the straps around the car seat with the scalpel and carefully pulling the car seat free. Laying it down on the grass, she examined the baby for any signs of injury.

'Okay?' Ted's voice behind her sounded as if he was fighting with a lump in his throat.

'Yes, I can't see any injuries at all.' The baby was still screaming, tears squeezing their way down its crumpled little face, and Nell tried vainly to comfort it. 'How's the driver of the other car?'

'Okay. Cut on his head. Someone else has stopped and they're sitting with him.'

'Right. Let me know if things change. Can you…um… do anything…?' She gestured towards the carrier. If the baby and the other driver were all right, she should help Hugo.

'Yep.' Ted leaned over the car seat, his thick fingers suddenly tender as he smoothed the child's head then brushed his finger against the palm of its hand. It opened its eyes, still grizzling fitfully.

'Great. Nice one.' Nell assumed the manoeuvre wasn't in any royal bodyguard's manual, so it must be in the one that came with being a father of three girls. Ted nodded, picking up the seat and carrying it over to their car.

'How is she?' Hugo was bending down awkwardly, trying to see into the footwell of the car.

'Airways are clear, and I can see no signs of internal bleeding. She's injured somewhere, though, and I think it's her lower legs.'

'Let me see.' Nell pressed her lips together. Implying that he couldn't do his job was a bitter pill for Hugo to swallow, but right now their feelings didn't matter. They had to make the right decisions for the woman in the car.

Hugo stepped back immediately. 'Can you see anything?'

'No, not from this side. I'll see if I can get to her from the passenger seat.' Nell straightened up and started to walk around the car. Hugo couldn't do this. He was bigger than she was, and although his shoulder was improving, it still hampered his movement.

'Be careful…' He shot her an admonishing glance and Nell nodded.

It was a struggle to get the passenger door open, but she managed it. Climbing inside, she bent down, trying to see through the twisted metal.

'I can see her legs. She's pinned but…yes, I can see where the blood's coming from.' Nell stretched out, gripping the woman's leg just below the knee, and the blood that was coming from a large gash on her lower leg began to ooze slower.

'Can you reach the wound?'

'Just about. Pass me some dressings, would you? I think I can pack a temporary dressing around it, just to stop the bleeding a bit, until they get her out.'

Hugo leaned in to pass the dressings to her. 'Give me the ring. If you get it caught on something…'

'Yes. Thanks.' Nell had seen de-gloved fingers, where

rings had been caught in machinery, during her stint in A & E, when she'd been training. She pulled the bulky ring off and put it into Hugo's hand. 'How's she doing?'

'Vital signs seem steady.'

Nell wriggled forward, leaning down to apply the dressings to the woman's wound. It was awkward work in the confined space, and she ended up half on the seat and half lying in the footwell. As she finished, she saw the woman's foot twitch.

'She's moving, Hugo. Might be coming round…' Hugo would need to try and keep her still, and that wasn't going to be easy.

'Okay. I've got her.'

Nell heard the woman moan, and what sounded like an attempt at words. Hugo's arm across her legs was keeping her relatively still, and he was talking to her, replying to her incoherent cries.

'Your baby's safe and well. I'm a doctor and we'll have you out of here soon. Try to stay still for me.'

The woman's leg moved a little and she screamed in pain. Hugo quieted her and Nell heard the sound of weeping.

'All right, sweetheart. Hold on to me.'

A siren, which cut off abruptly, heralded the arrival of the ambulance. Then voices, telling Hugo to move back, which changed their tone considerably when he turned around and the ambulance crew recognised him. He updated them on the woman's condition and asked what analgesics they carried with them. After some conversation he turned back to Nell.

'I'm giving her a shot of morphine. Are you all right down there?'

'Yep.' Nell's back was twisted uncomfortably and her arm was beginning to ache. But she didn't dare move in case the dressings were dislodged and the woman started bleeding again.

After what seemed like an age, but was probably only a few minutes, Nell heard another siren. She heard Hugo talking to someone and squeezed her eyes closed, concentrating on holding the dressings in place and ignoring the ache in her back. Hugo would take care of things. He would deal with it, and the woman would be brought safely out of the car.

'Okay… Nell, are you still with us?'

'Yep.'

'Good job. They've decided to take the roof of the car off.'

'Right.' Nell had expected that. It made it easier and safer to move someone who might have a spinal injury. And the Jaws of Life should make short work of the car's structure and allow the rescuers to peel the car roof off.

'It looks as if once that's done, they'll be able to free her legs easily. Shouldn't take too long.'

'Good. That'll be good.'

'Tuck your legs in a bit. They'll be using a shield to protect you both from the broken glass.'

Nell moved her legs, tucking them under her as well as she could manage, without letting go of the dressings.

'That's great. Hang on in there, honey.'

Nell felt the car move slightly as it was propped and steadied. Then the sound of the mechanised cutters and the breaking of glass. She concentrated on the woman's leg. It looked as if it needed attention soon.

*Hang on in there, honey.*

Hugo was always kind and encouraging towards his patients. And perhaps he was, even now, keeping up appearances—she was supposed to be his fiancée. But there was a note in his voice that no one could counterfeit.

The words were just for her, no one else. She repeated

them over and over in her head as she felt the rough brush of a gloved hand against her ankle, moving her leg a little in the constricted space and sending showers of pins and needles down it.

Sunlight filtered down into the footwell as the rescuers peeled the roof off. Then Hugo leaned into the car, his gloved hand over hers, taking over the pressure that she was keeping on the wound.

'Got to stop meeting like this.' His grin and the murmured words were for her too, despite the quiet, concentrated work going on around them.

'Have you got it?' Nell slipped her hand out from under his, and he nodded, his gaze flipping up to somewhere above and behind her.

'Okay, someone's going to help you out now.'

Someone gripped her waist firmly, pulling her backwards. Her leg muscles began to cramp painfully and she grimaced, trying not to cry out as she was hauled out of the car.

'Ça va?' A tall fireman was looking down at her as she sat on the grass, rubbing her leg.

'Oui.' Nell pulled her rumpled skirt down. Not all that demure for a wannabe princess, but as a member of the team who'd just spent the last fifteen minutes in an awkward, half upside-down pose, flashing a little leg could be forgiven. She wondered briefly which one the fireman saw her as.

The latter, clearly. He turned away, leaving her to it, and got on with his job. Nell watched as Hugo and the paramedics quickly ascertained the woman's condition a little better, and Hugo gave the signal for the fire and rescue team to remove the twisted metal that was holding her legs down.

As soon as Nell could stand, she hobbled out of their way and sat back down on the grass, watching. It was a quiet, professional operation, everyone updating everyone else on what was happening, the woman in the car the centre of their attention. The paramedics backed off, leaving Hugo with the woman, as the fire and rescue team made the last, careful removal of pieces from the car. Then they closed in again, carefully lifting the woman from the car and securing her onto a stretcher.

Hugo was still directing operations, speaking briefly to Ted, who climbed into the ambulance with the baby, still in its car seat. Hugo followed him, obviously intent on a last examination of the woman and her child, to make sure that they were ready for the journey to the hospital. Nell sat alone and unnoticed, watching the fire and rescue team pack up their equipment.

Then Hugo climbed down from the back of the ambulance and the driver shut the doors. He walked across the grass towards her and sat down stiffly.

'How is she?' Nell looked up at him, knowing that the answer would be written on his face.

'Her legs are broken and she's lost a lot of blood. No sign of spinal injury, and although she's drifting in and out of consciousness, which is a worry, I don't see any head trauma either. They'll do a CAT scan...' He lapsed into silence, realising perhaps that his face had already told Nell what she wanted to know. There was every reason to be optimistic.

'Good. And you're okay?'

'Yes. I knew there was a reason for the last couple of days' rest.' He chuckled, and then saw Nell's hand, still absent-mindedly rubbing her leg. 'Cramp?'

'Yes. It just aches a bit now. Ted's going with them?'

Hugo grinned. 'He's going to see that the baby's all right and handed over to its family.'

'Good.' Nell chuckled. 'Think he'll give it up that easily?'

'They might have a bit of a struggle on their hands. He's bonding fast.'

They sat together in silence as the ambulance drew away, followed by the fire and rescue truck. The other driver was standing by a police car that had arrived at the scene and was parked a couple of hundred yards along the carriageway, and the people who had stopped had got back into their cars and resumed their journeys.

It was suddenly quiet. In between the swoosh of passing vehicles, Nell could hear birds singing and the sun was warm on her face. If it hadn't been for her own crumpled dress and the spots of blood on the rolled-up sleeves of Hugo's white shirt, it would have been a fine day for a walk in the countryside.

'Have you seen my shoes?' A thought struck her.

'Ted put them in the car.' Hugo turned his face up to the sun, as if he were thinking the very same thing. It was the quiet after a storm, in which they both began to move from the urgency of a wrecked car by the roadside back into the other reality of their everyday lives.

Or back into Hugo's reality. However much he tried to involve her, it seemed as if he was just giving her something to do, making her feel as if she wasn't just an accessory on his arm. But in truth, that's what she was. This was Hugo's country, and his mission, and Nell was just helping him out for a while. She'd be back in London, reading about him in the newspapers, before very long.

'Why so glum?' Nell turned to find that he was looking steadily at her.

'Nothing. I was just hoping that the woman will be all right.' She got to her feet, flexing the still-sore muscles in her leg, watching as Hugo stood. He was holding his left arm loosely by his side, not moving it but seeming to have suffered no ill effects from his exertions.

He opened the back door of his car, motioning her inside, and Nell stood her ground. 'If you think you're going to drive…'

'No, I don't think that.' He reached into his pocket, drawing out the car keys and put them into her hand. 'Just get into the back for a moment.'

Nell got in, shifting over to let him follow her. He closed the door and then turned, reaching for her ankle and propping her leg up onto his lap. 'Looks as if your leg's still sore, which gives me a marvellous opportunity to return the favour you've been doing me.'

The look in his eyes wasn't anything like Nell hoped that her demeanour was when she massaged his shoulder. But his face was the model of propriety. She sat still, feeling his fingers on the back of her leg, just above the knee.

'Ah!' For a moment, all she could think about was his touch. And the way that the sore muscle at the back of her leg was reacting and then relaxing as his fingers pressed a little harder. 'That's it. A bit higher?'

It sounded a little bit like sex, and felt a lot like it, too. Rather than stare into his eyes, the way that she wanted to, she squeezed them shut.

'Right there?' Even his voice sounded like the honey-smooth tones of a lover.

'Yes, you've got it. That's much better.'

Her leg felt a great deal better. The rest of her body was beginning to ache for the same touch. Very slow, and as sure as the careful progress of his fingers on her leg. Closing her eyes hadn't been such a good idea after all, she could practically see Hugo making love to her behind her eyelids.

'Thanks. That's fine now.' When she opened her eyes, she thought that she saw the hint of a smile on his face. The dark echoes of what she'd been imagining in his green eyes.

'Wouldn't want your foot to slip off the clutch…' His fingers kept massaging.

'This is an automatic.'

'Ah, yes. Silly me.' Hugo let her go and Nell pushed her skirt back down to her knees. Feeling in his pocket, he brought out the ring. 'Don't forget this.'

Nell smiled, holding out her hand. Whenever she took the ring off, he always put it back on her finger again. She liked that, even if it was only temporary and didn't mean what everyone thought it did.

He leaned towards her, as if he were about to kiss her. But something attracted his attention and Nell turned to see one of the policemen strolling towards the car. Hugo grinned at her, getting out of the car and walking towards the man.

He seemed to have a sixth sense about that. Hugo was always on guard, aware of who was around him and what they were doing. Nell supposed that came from living his life in the spotlight, never being able to walk down the street alone and unnoticed. It was why he guarded his secrets so carefully. He had to know that something was private.

He exchanged a few words with the policeman and Nell climbed into the driver's seat of the car, pulling the seat forward. In the rear-view mirror, she could see him walking back towards her. Relaxed, stains on the knees of his trousers from having bent down beside the injured woman, but still handsome. Still so perfect that Nell could hardly bear it.

She started the car, waiting for him to get in beside her. It was time to get back on the road.

# CHAPTER FOURTEEN

HUGO COULD FEEL his strength returning. The bruises were long gone, and the red gash on his chest had knitted well. It would heal into a fine white line, as barely noticeable as the slight change in the contour of the skin above the pacemaker. It was there but rapidly becoming hidden.

He needed Nell less and less each day. He could make his way through a press of people now, without wanting to shy away from them and protect his shoulder. He'd be able to drive in another few weeks, and the exercises that he did every morning, to prevent his shoulder from freezing, could become a little more strenuous.

Nell had thrown herself into raising money for the clinic, and they'd decided that, working apart, they could cover twice as much ground as working together. Hugo missed having her with him, but he knew she enjoyed it, and as time passed, her confidence seemed to be growing.

The best part of the day was always the morning. Dressed in a T-shirt and sweatpants, her hair scrunched on the top of her head, and without a scrap of make-up, Nell was the most beautiful woman he'd ever seen. They'd have breakfast together, discussing their respective commitments for the day. Then he'd put a suit and tie on, and Nell would put on a dress and her engagement ring, and they were ready for the day, their public faces firmly in place.

'So…how would you like a day off?' Hugo had been

thinking of broaching the subject for a while and had decided that there wasn't much to lose by doing so. The worst that could possibly happen was that she could say no.

'A day off?' She was sitting in the sun, the breakfast things in front of her on the patio table. One leg was curled up beneath her, and there was a smudge of marmalade on her thumb. Hugo tried not to look as she licked it off.

'Yes. Remember I still owe you a trip on the royal yacht.'

'That was just for show, Hugo.'

'It doesn't mean we can't go. Take a weekend off, we've both earned it.'

'Isn't there…? Don't you want to spend the time somewhere else?'

Nowhere in the world that he could think of. 'We're supposed to be engaged. I wouldn't dream of spending a weekend anywhere other than with you. And I paid enough for the pleasure of your company.'

Hugo winced. He hadn't meant that quite the way it had sounded and from the look on Nell's face, the joke had fallen flat. It had been a long time since he'd been this tongue-tied when asking a girl out.

'We're not really engaged, remember,' she said quietly.

'I can still enjoy spending time with you, can't I?'

'You don't have to say that here. No one's listening.' There was an edge to Nell's voice now that cut away at Hugo's heart. Suddenly the morning sun seemed harsh and altogether too bright to sit here for any longer.

'Of course. I'm sorry.' He stood up, reaching for his diary, which lay with hers on the table. 'I have an early start this morning. I'll see you this evening.'

She hadn't needed to say it, not like that at least. Nell sat on the patio, wondering whether Hugo would forgive her, and when she heard the front door open and then close, it seemed that he hadn't. She ran to the front window and saw him, immaculate in his suit and tie, getting into the car, while Ted waited at the wheel.

A weekend with Hugo. Sun and the sea, a chance to relax. It had sounded too wonderful to be true.

And in Nell's experience, that usually meant that it was. Beneath all the excitement and glamour, beneath the very real relationship that was growing between them, Hugo was still a prince. He could buy whatever he wanted, and even though there was no contract of employment between them any more, he was as much in control of her future as Martin had been. And she'd allowed that.

She had to get ready. She was due to speak to a women's club at noon, a talk that was designed both to educate them about the signs of heart disease and ask them to spread the word about the plans for the clinic. That was what she was here for, a shared goal and an agreement, which protected his secrets and her reputation. She needed to remember that whenever it started feeling too much that her rightful place was on his arm.

'Nell, I'm so sorry.' Hugo marched into the sitting room, clearly gripped by the urgency of being on a mission. Nell jumped. She hadn't heard him come in.

'You took the words right out of my mouth.' The magazine lying open on her lap had gone unread, while she'd mentally rehearsed her apology.

'I…' He looked suddenly perplexed. Clearly he'd been rehearsing too, and his speech wasn't going entirely to plan. 'You have nothing to apologise for. And since I do, I'm going to break the ladies-first rule.'

'Okay.' When Hugo was in one of these moods, there was no stopping him. Nell had learned to just go with the flow.

He took a breath, as if reorienting himself back on his

trajectory. 'I'm really sorry about this morning. It was just a joke and...all I meant was that money pales into insignificance in the face of the pleasure I'd take in spending a weekend away with you. You owe me nothing, and there's no obligation on your part to join me.'

'I know. It's all right, Hugo, I never thought that was the case. I was just being a bit over-sensitive.'

'No, you weren't. I know you have good reason not to mix business with pleasure, and any implication that I—'

'Please stop, Hugo. Let's just say we're okay, shall we?'

He nodded, bringing out a glossy paper carrier bag from behind his briefcase. 'I was going to bring you flowers but decided on this instead.'

What was this? The carrier bag looked as if it had come from an exclusive store somewhere, and when Hugo handed it to her, Nell saw an embellished cardboard box inside. Too big for jewellery and too heavy for underwear. But in this situation, they'd be gifts that an unsubtle man would bring, and Hugo was never that.

She took the lid off the box and smiled. Perfect. 'Chocolate! Thank you, Hugo.'

He grinned, finally taking his jacket off and sitting down. Nell proffered the box. 'Would you like one?'

'You first.'

The chocolate was delicious, with a centre of dark brandy truffle. 'Mmm...these are gorgeous. You should try one.'

'Thanks... One can't hurt, right?'

'No. One can't hurt.' Even though he had no problem with cholesterol, Hugo's diet was strictly balanced and healthy. Perhaps too much so. Nell had never seen him eat sweets or sugary foods, even as a treat.

Hugo loosened his tie, leaning back on the sofa, taking a moment to appreciate the forbidden chocolate. 'That's good.'

They were friends again. Clearly Hugo didn't care about receiving any apology from Nell, but she cared about giving it.

'Hugo, I'm sorry, too. I didn't mean to infer that you were being in any way insincere. This is just…a difficult situation. I don't know quite how to act sometimes.'

'You're doing just fine. You should never apologise to me, because it's my weakness that's put you into a difficult situation.'

That assumption, again, that he was somehow flawed. Hugo seemed to take it for granted, as if it were beyond argument, and a given thing.

'You're weak because you have a pacemaker? Is that what you say to all your pacemaker patients, that they'll never be the same again?'

'No, of course not…' He broke off, as if the incongruity had only just occurred to him.

'Then why say it to yourself? You know it's not true. Why keep it such a secret?'

He shook his head. 'I don't know, Nell. I feel…different somehow. Less than what I was.'

'But you don't mind relying on a watch to tell you the time. You don't mind relying on your phone to keep you in touch.'

'That's not the same thing. I'm not relying on either of them to keep my heart beating, that's a bit more important.'

'Yes, it's a great deal more important. But what happens if the pacemaker fails? Your heartbeat will probably slow up, but it's not going to stop completely. Most of the time, your heart's beating just fine on its own, the pacemaker only activates when your level of activity increases and you need a little extra help. So the worst that can happen is that you have to stop and sit down. You *know* all this, Hugo.'

'Yes, I do. I…' He looked at her suddenly. 'You're pushing me, aren't you?'

'Yes, I'm pushing you. Because what you know up here…' Nell reached forward, tapping his forehead lightly with her finger '…isn't what you actually feel inside, is it?'

He shrugged. 'No. But I can't change that.'

'You could look at the reasons. Why you blatantly disregard everything your head is telling you.'

'Is this your usual psychology chat?' He narrowed his eyes, and Nell could see that he was only half joking.

'No. This one's just for you.'

Nell had a habit of asking all the questions that Hugo didn't want to answer. He supposed that on some level, he must have known that she'd get around to this sooner or later. Perhaps on some level he'd wanted her to.

'I can't fall short, Nell. I've been given a great deal in life, and it's my duty to repay it.'

'What makes you think you aren't?'

'You've seen the kids at the hospital.' He knew that Nell would understand that.

'Yes, I have. And I know you're doing your best for them. We can't do any more than our best.'

'And my best may not be good enough.' Hugo's greatest fear was right there, on his lips. As if somehow Nell had managed to entrance it, and coax it from its hiding place.

'It's all we have. And we're allowed to take some time out and have a life, to have holidays and take some time off when we're sick.' Nell frowned, and Hugo braced himself for whatever was to follow. He knew that look.

'I can't believe that you don't have someone to come home to at night. That you're so sure you won't that you can commit yourself to a fake engagement for the next few months.'

Hugo had got used to coming home to Nell at night, and it was almost a shock to be reminded that it wasn't real. But he'd made that decision a long time ago.

'That's not as easy as you think, Nell.'

'It's never as easy as anyone thinks. I know that.'

Suddenly he wanted to explain. It was the first time that he'd felt that someone might understand, as a friend.

'I did have someone once. I was going to get married. Anna and I met at medical school in London, and we lived together for a couple of years. I told her that I wanted to come back to Montarino and she wanted to come with me, but when we got here...'

Nell nodded him on.

'I had a new job and got caught up in that and the round of engagements that the palace had planned for me. I was happy to be home and...I didn't look closely enough at what was going on within our relationship. I didn't see that Anna was feeling trapped on the sidelines.'

'She didn't have a job?'

'Everyone expected that she was going to be a royal bride. She was offered a lot of roles as patron of various medical facilities, which would take effect after our marriage, but she didn't want her success to come through me. Anna was worth a great deal more than that, and leaving me and going back to London was the best decision she ever made. She has a fulfilling career now, and a husband who doesn't take up so much space that she can't breathe.'

'It seems a bit unfair to give yourself all the blame.'

'I knew what my life was going to be like, I should have seen that it wouldn't be enough for Anna to live through me. I could have followed her back to London but I didn't, because I felt it was my duty to give whatever I could back to Montarino. That's what I have now, and I feel I'm failing.'

'You're not failing, Hugo. You're just recovering from an operation.'

Hugo looked for the understanding he craved, and found it in her eyes. Suddenly it was too much to bear and he got to his feet. 'Is that our chat done, then? I'll go and make dinner…'

'No, it's not done. I'm not finished with you yet.' She called the words after him, but there was humour in Nell's tone. Maybe she knew that the burden of his duty was feeling a little heavy at the moment.

'What are you going to do?' He chuckled, turning on the tap to wash his hands. 'Find me someone who doesn't mind trailing around after me and playing princess?'

'Are there women like that?' Nell professed just the right amount of surprise, before turning her attention to the box of chocolates. He wanted to walk back into the sitting room and hug her, but right now it was probably better to keep his distance.

'Plenty of them.'

'That sounds a bit boring.'

And that was it, in a nutshell. A career woman, someone like Nell, would always want their own life, free of the constraints of his life. Women who wanted him just because he was a prince generally weren't that interesting after the first couple of dates.

It was a catch-22 situation that held him in limbo. There was no way out that Hugo could see, and he suspected that Nell couldn't either. If she could, she would have mentioned it.

The invitation to spend a weekend on the royal yacht had been given again, and this time Nell had accepted it straight away. If his admission that he felt no woman would want the life he offered her was horribly sad, it also neatly let Nell off the hook. There were no expectations from him, and she could match that by allowing no expectations to infiltrate her own thinking.

They set off early. As they crossed the border into France, the sun came out and Hugo retracted the roof of his convertible. A warm breeze and a handsome prince beside her.

As they approached the motorway, Nell took over the driving, and Hugo lounged in the front seat of the car, enjoying the journey. Dressed in a pair of shorts and a sweatshirt, his short hair ruffled in the breeze, he seemed to finally be getting it into his head that they were on holiday.

It was almost midday when they reached the small, bustling French port where the yacht was moored. Hugo took his place at the wheel again, negotiating the narrow streets of the old town, before driving along the quayside and into the marina.

He drew up alongside a young man in pristine white shorts, with the name of Montarino's royal yacht sewn across the sleeve of his white shirt. He stepped forward, opening the passenger door of the car before Nell could reach for the handle.

Hugo gave him an affable grin. 'Thank you, Louis. How are you?'

'Well, Your Highness. It's good to see you.'

Hugo got out of the car, taking a draught of sea air into his lungs, as if it felt easier to breathe here. 'It's very good to be back. How are your studies going?'

'I've just been sitting my exams. They went well, I think.'

Hugo nodded, tossing the car keys to Louis. 'Let me know when you get your results.'

'Will do, Your Highness.' Louis got into the car, driving it towards the car park, leaving Nell and Hugo standing on the quayside.

'Which one is it?' Nell surveyed the boats moored around the marina. Smaller yachts were tied up against the piers, which extended out into the water, and larger ones were anchored further out.

'That one.' Hugo pointed towards one of the yachts.

It wasn't the largest of the boats there, but it seemed the most elegant, glistening white, and bobbing gracefully on an azure sea.

'It's beautiful. How do we get to it?'

He grinned. 'This way.'

Another man in the same uniform as Louis's helped her down into a motor launch. She looked around for her luggage, but it didn't seem that they were going to be waiting for that. As soon as Hugo was on board, the engine was started and they began to speed way from the land.

'This is wonderful.' Hugo's arm was slung across the back of the seat and she had to move a little closer to him, so that he could hear her over the noise of the engine. 'I already feel spoiled.'

'That's exactly how you're meant to feel.' Hugo's lips brushed against her ear.

She was helped up a set of steps onto the deck of the yacht, Hugo following. Waiting for her was a man who bore the word 'Captain' on the sleeve of his shirt.

'Welcome, Dr Maitland.' He stepped forward, holding out his hand. 'I'm Captain Masson.'

'Thank you.' Nell shook his hand, looking around her. The yacht looked just as white and gleaming close up as it had from the land. 'This is a beautiful vessel.'

'Thank you, ma'am.' Captain Masson beamed at her. 'Where would you like to go?'

Nell turned to Hugo and he shrugged. 'Your call. We can dock somewhere for a little shopping. Or if you prefer swimming there are some nice places to stop off.'

Nell thought for a moment. It seemed a little bit of a waste to spend time shopping and swimming when she could enjoy being here on the yacht. 'The sea. I'd like to go…somewhere on the sea if that's all right?'

'A short trip along the coast perhaps, ma'am?'

'Yes, I'd like that.' Nell glanced at Hugo, wondering if that was what he'd had in mind.

'That's an excellent idea. Thank you, Captain Masson.' Hugo smiled.

'Very well. We'll be on our way very soon, we just have to wait for your luggage. In the meantime, drinks have been laid out on the main deck.'

The captain gestured to his right, and Nell took a couple of uncertain steps in that direction. She felt Hugo take her arm and followed his lead, walking towards a short flight of stairs that led up onto a deck, shaded by awnings and dappled by the sun.

'It's…very formal here.'

Hugo nodded. 'This is the royal yacht, my parents bring important visitors here. The crew don't call the captain by his first name, and neither should I. When we're at sea, his word is law, and it's his responsibility to keep us in one piece if we run into a squall.'

'Are we going to run into a squall?' Nell looked up into the blue, cloudless sky.

'I very much doubt it. Captain Masson will have already looked at the weather forecasts all along the coast, and he'll be counting on giving us a smooth ride. It's just a principle.'

He led her onto the main deck, where a table was set out, with champagne on ice and canapés. Nell ignored the seats arranged around the deck in both the sun and the shade, preferring to lean against the wooden-topped rails to watch as the motor launch sped back towards the land and then returned with Louis and their luggage.

As the muted sound of the engines reached her, and the yacht began to move slowly, Hugo joined her, leaning with his back against the rail. 'What do you think?'

'This is wonderful, Hugo. A real treat, thank you.'

# CHAPTER FIFTEEN

HUGO WAS HAPPY. Nell was happy, and shining with excitement as he showed her around the yacht. She expressed surprise at the size of her cabin, insisting on looking through each of the portholes to ascertain whether there was a different view from any of them. She explored all the decks, leaning over the rails to see as much as she could.

When the expected message came from Captain Masson, inviting her to the bridge, she ran after Louis's retreating back, seemingly determined to deliver her acceptance of the invitation herself.

He watched as she asked questions about all the instruments and examined the navigation charts that were brought out for her to see. When she was accorded the singular honour of being allowed to take the helm for a while, Captain Masson talked her through making a small corrective manoeuvre, rather than simply letting her hold the wheel, and Hugo saw the helmsman smile. If they weren't careful, the crew would be renaming the yacht after her.

'I hope I didn't take up too much of Captain Masson's time.' The yacht lurched suddenly and she almost stumbled down the steps from the bridge. Hugo caught her arm to steady her.

'All right?' She'd stopped, clutching the handrail, one hand on her chest.

'Yes…yes, I'm all right. I felt a little bit queasy just

then. It's passed now.' She squinted out towards the horizon. 'Are the waves getting bigger?'

'A little, yes. You'll get used to the motion of the ship soon, but if you feel sick we've got a full stock of medication to choose from.'

'No, thanks. I'm fine now. I think my sea legs are kicking in.'

Hugo nodded, watching her down the remainder of the steps. It was probably best to take her mind off the idea of being sick, and mention to Captain Masson that a smooth ride would be appreciated.

'The captain doesn't let just anyone take the helm, you know.' He took her arm, strolling towards the main deck so that they could sit in the afternoon sun.

Nell's cheeks regained their colour suddenly. 'He's very kind. And it's all so interesting. I wonder if he'd let me watch when we stop for the evening and put the anchor down. I'd keep out of the way.'

'I'd be very surprised if he hasn't already got that in mind.' Nell didn't seem to care much for the prestige of being here, but she loved the yacht and wanted to know everything about it. Captain Masson and his crew had seen that, and Hugo reckoned that the dropping of the anchor would be carried out under Nell's command.

And that was the difference. The one that meant that Nell was beyond his reach. She didn't care to spend her days off in the usual leisure pursuits, she wanted to know how things worked. He'd seen her out in the garden at his house, questioning the gardener about how the mix of planting gave year-round colour and helping him weed. She threw herself into her work with the same gusto. Her life had purpose, a life that should never be squashed by his.

But for today and tomorrow, he had her here with him. That had to be enough, because it was all he dared take from Nell.

* * *

At dusk, they came to anchor outside a coastal town, and Nell watched the lights begin to come on, growing brighter as the sky became darker. Then stars appeared in a sky that looked as if it were putting on a show just for her.

Dinner was in the open air on the main deck. Candles on the table, protected from the warm breeze by glass shades. And Hugo, looking far more handsome than he had any right to, in a white open-necked shirt.

'Tonight's a night for dancing.' They'd had their after-dinner coffee, and all that Nell could think was that he was right. Tonight *was* a night for dancing.

She rose, smiling, wondering where the music would come from. Hugo took her in his arms, humming the snatches of a tune and moving her to its slow rhythm.

Perfect. On a perfect night like this, it seemed quite natural that he should kiss her. When he did, it felt as if she were melting into him. As if together they could be at one with the stars and the breeze and just be, without needing to think about the consequences.

'I wish...' They were still moving, dancing together as they kissed.

'What do you wish? If it's anything that I can grant, it's yours.' He whispered the words, leaving a kiss behind them.

'I wish that there was nothing to stop us.'

He knew what she meant. Every line of his body hinted that this could so easily be a seduction, if they'd only let it.

'Is there anything? What happens at sea might be persuaded to stay at sea.'

'We're not exactly at sea.' Nell clung to the last vestiges of her sanity. Even if stars were dancing in the sky, the lights of land were closer than that.

'We're not on dry land either. We might be able to see them, but they can't see us.'

It was tempting. *Very* tempting. Surely she and Hugo could leave everything behind, just for one night?

'I can't leave myself behind. I brought my baggage with me, and you brought yours.'

'You're right. As always.' He kissed her again, warm and unhurried, as if to show that being right didn't mean that she could escape his tenderness.

'Thank you for a wonderful day, Hugo. And a wonderful evening…' The thought that this wonderful evening might so easily become a wonderful night was tearing at her resolve. Nell broke free of his arms. She had to go now, while she still could.

What…*what*…had he been thinking? Hugo put his head around the galley door to thank the chef for his efforts tonight, and walked to his cabin.

It had seemed so natural. Taking her in his arms, letting the breeze take them with it, away from the land and into a place where only desire mattered. But Nell was always the more sensible of the two of them. He should heed her judgement, and remember that there was no possibility that they could make a future together, however tantalising tonight might be. He sat down on the bed, slowly unbuttoning his shirt.

And there was another thing. Hugo rose, walking into the en suite bathroom, pulling his shirt to one side, as if seeing the scar could finally convince him. However many times Nell told him he wasn't, he still felt flawed. And Nell deserved only the best.

A knock sounded, and he dragged his gaze away from the mirror, closing his shirt before he opened the cabin door. Hugo froze.

'You'll keep me standing here?' Nell smiled up at him. Her hair was still gathered up around her head, stray curls escaping around her face. Her eyes were as bright as the moonlight, as if she'd brought a little of it below deck with her.

'No! Come in.' He stood back from the door and she walked into his cabin. For a moment, all he could think was that her feet were bare, and that she walked as if she were floating on air.

Hugo closed the door behind her and leaned against it, as if somehow that might stop this dream from escaping.

'I came to ask you if you'd like to come to my cabin. We could…see the sunrise tomorrow.'

He reached out and touched the sleeve of the ivory-coloured wrap that covered her body. Even that seemed unbearably erotic, since it was clear that she had little else on.

'I would love to come to your cabin. Although I can take or leave the sunrise.'

She nodded. 'Me, too.'

Suddenly she was in his arms, and Hugo found his strength again. He kissed her, tracing his fingers across the soft, silky fabric of her wrap. It was so thin that he could feel her response, the heat of her skin and the sudden tightening of the muscles of her back. He could do this. He could make her cry out for him.

Wordlessly, he wrapped his arm around her and opened the door, looking out to make sure that no one was in the corridor outside then hurrying her forward to her own cabin door. When they were inside, she turned, twisting the lock. The sharp snap seemed to echo through his senses.

'I'm at your mercy now.' Hugo could feel that his own body was ready for hers, and if it let him down, then he knew she'd be kind. Nell was always kind.

'And I'm at yours…' She began to undo the knot in the sash at her waist, leaving the last twist in place, as an obvious invitation for him to finish the job. Hugo stepped forward, taking her in his arms and pulling the sash open.

It seemed unlikely that Nell could be prey to the same

madness that he was, but he felt it. Her whole body was
trembling, moving against his. When he pulled the wrap
from her shoulders, finding a narrow lace strap underneath, she let out a little gasp and he heard the same need
as he felt.

Moonlight slanted across the bed. He wanted so badly
to be a part of that moonlight, making love to her in its
cool gleam. No sooner had the thought occurred to him
than he felt Nell's hand, bunched in his shirt, pulling him
towards the bed.

His heartbeat seemed to ramp up, leaving him almost
breathless. Suddenly she was still.

'It's okay, Hugo.' She laid her hand on his chest. 'It's
not going to let you down.'

It was Nell who wouldn't let him down. Always knowing, always understanding. He kissed her, feeling the
thump of his heart against hers. And suddenly it didn't
feel like a precursor of doom. It felt good.

'Your heart and mine, Nell. Beating together.'

'That means we're both alive.' She smiled up at him.

'I feel more alive than I have for a long time…'

Hugo sat down on the bed, spreading his legs and pulling her close, kissing the wide strip of flesh between the
open fronts of her robe. He felt her hands on his shoulders,
and heard her cry out when he ran his tongue lightly across
her stomach. He could see now that the robe had concealed
ivory lace underwear, and he felt another jolt of longing.
More time, more pleasure involved in taking that off.

She sank down onto his knee, and he held her close,
kissing her and gently working her free of the wrap. It slid
down, draping around his leg.

'You are so beautiful, Nell.' He heard his own voice,
thick with desire.

'You are, too. I want you to make love to me, Hugo.'

She was working on the last few buttons of his shirt, pulling it from his shoulders.

A stab of self-doubt cut through the desire. It was impossible that she couldn't have felt it, he was hers already in as many ways as he could think of. She ran her fingers lightly over the scar on his chest, and he shivered.

'It'll be okay.' She laid her hand on the side of his face, kissing him on the lips. 'Believe me, Hugo.'

Suddenly he did. He let her pull his shirt off, and as she ran her fingers across his chest, he gave himself up to her caresses.

They were both so aroused already that even the smallest gesture seemed to provoke a reaction. When Hugo brushed his fingers across the lace that covered her breasts, Nell felt a sharp tug of desire. When she laid her hand on his belt buckle, she felt him tremble, as if just the thought, just the implication of an action, was as potent as the deed itself.

Undressing each other slowly was an expression of a shared need, which demanded that they take each moment and make it last. The leisurely rocking motion of the yacht seemed to follow their pace, as unstoppable as the movement of the ocean.

And Hugo was all hers. No more fears, no looking over his shoulder. He took pleasure just as wholeheartedly as he gave it, smiling up at her when she found herself on top of him, astride his hips.

'Doesn't anyone ever call you Penelope?'

'No.' On his lips, her given name seemed to sparkle. 'You like it?'

'Yes, I do.'

'I like hearing you say it.' This was something that she could share, just with him.

He chuckled, pulling her down for a kiss. 'Penelope.' He said it again, gasping it when she lowered her body onto his, taking him inside her. When he gripped her hips, pushing her further towards her own climax, he may have said it. By that time, Nell was a little beyond thought. But he did say it again as she clung to him, turning her over to explore every angle of their lovemaking.

He was her heart. Even that thought didn't seem out of place tonight, because there *was* no tomorrow.

'I loved the lace...' They were sprawled together on the bed, whispering the quiet minutes of the night away. 'Is that what you usually wear?'

Nell grinned. She'd hoped he *would* like it. 'It's my body armour.'

'Really? Can't say it worked too well in that regard.' Hugo kissed the top of her head.

'I noticed. But a good friend always used to say that if you're feeling a little under-confident, nice underwear helps.'

'You've been feeling under-confident?'

'I'm not as used to standing up in front of a lot of people as you are. Or having people notice me on the street, or seeing my face on the front pages of the paper.'

He laughed quietly. 'Okay. So you were wearing lace when you first met me?'

'No, if you remember I was fresh off the plane. I was dressed for comfort.'

'So when we talked, that first time at the palace?'

'Yes.'

He sighed. 'At the luncheon? When you bid for me?'

'Of course. What part of that day did you think wasn't a challenge?'

'If I'd known...' His hand went to his forehead, as if he'd just realised an irrefutable truth. 'Actually, if I'd known I wouldn't have been able to get a word out. Probably best that I didn't.'

'I don't imagine you as ever being lost for words, Hugo.'

He rolled over, covering her body with his. Kissing her, with more than a hint of the desire that had filled them both tonight. 'Maybe you should consider the idea. You leave me speechless.'

Hugo felt whole. Wholly happy, more than wholly satisfied, and...just whole. He hadn't felt that way since he'd first felt the signs that his heart might not be working as well as it should. Nell had somehow seen something different in him, and had never shown any doubt about his ability to recover and lead the life that Hugo had thought he'd lost.

That had been his mistake. He'd wanted to put his illness and his operation behind him so badly that he'd tried to rush it. Hugo saw a lot of things differently now. And one thing that he saw with complete certainty was that tonight wasn't going to be enough.

Nell was sleeping now and Hugo fought the temptation to watch her sleep. If he wanted to keep everything that he'd found, he needed to be strong.

Opening her eyes came with a sudden burst of nausea. The whole cabin seemed to be pitching and rolling, taking her stomach with it. Nell closed her eyes, and then opened them again quickly when the feeling that she might be about to die washed over her.

She wasn't about to die. She was just going to be— No. Not now. Please, not now...

Her stomach wasn't listening. Hand over her mouth, Nell rolled off the bed, half staggering and half crawling to the bathroom. The door banged shut behind her, and the whole world lurched.

'Nell...?'

She heard Hugo's voice, but even that couldn't stop her from being sick. Trembling, she called back to him.

'I'm okay. Go away…' Naked and being sick in the bathroom wasn't the best way to wake a lover. The lock on the bathroom door seemed about a mile away and rocking dangerously.

And he ignored her, dammit. She felt him wrap a towelling robe around her trembling shoulders.

'All right. Try to relax.'

How could she? Humiliation wasn't conducive to relaxation. 'Go away!'

'Be quiet.' His voice was firm, and Nell reckoned that begging wasn't an option. Another bout of sickness chased any further thoughts away.

'I'm sorry. I'm so sorry…' She moaned the words, wishing that she could be somewhere else. Anywhere else.

'It's okay. You're just seasick.'

'Uh. Just…?'

'You'll feel better in a minute.'

No, she wouldn't. She felt so ill that she was almost glad that Hugo was there. In between wanting him to go away and somehow forgetting that this had ever happened.

'Is that everything?'

Maybe. Nell wasn't sure, but she felt cold now, instead of burning hot. Hugo seemed to think so because he was gently guiding her to her feet.

'Come…'

'No!' At least she'd made it to the bathroom. Now she was here, she wasn't taking any chances. Hugo reached for the large, well-stocked bathroom cabinet. It seemed that in addition to condoms, which she'd found in there earlier in the evening and made use of later, the cabinet was also prepared for seasickness. Hugo took out a cardboard dish and gave it to her, collecting a bottle of ginger tablets.

He walked her through to the cabin, sitting her down on the bed. She felt a little better. Just well enough for embarrassment to take a better hold around her heart.

'The sea's a little choppier now than it was earlier.'

'Yeah? Thought it was just me.' Nell groaned as another wave of nausea took hold, but this time, she managed to quell it.

'No, it's unusually rough for this harbour. Try looking at the coastline, that might help orientate you a bit.'

Nell looked at the lights, still shining around the bay. They seemed a long way away at the moment, and enticingly still. 'Can't we...dock or something?'

'I'm afraid not. There's nowhere *to* dock.'

'Oh-h-h...!' Nowhere to run. Nowhere to hide. This was turning into a nightmare.

He supported her gently through to his cabin, saying that it was further back and so the roll of the ship would be less. If it was, Nell couldn't feel it. He let her sip water, sitting with her as she looked through the porthole, trying to tell her brain which way they were moving before her stomach reacted to it. Gave her ginger tablets to chew, but they just made her sick again.

'Drugs, Hugo...'

'Yes. I think so, too. Do you have any allergies?'

'No... I need the drugs...' Surely he wasn't going to make her go through the preliminary questions. But he did, and Nell responded automatically to his calm, gentle tone, trying to distance herself from what was happening.

He was good at this. Even the injection was accomplished with the minimum of indignity.

'That's going to work pretty quickly now.'

'Yeah... Quickly...' Thinking was suddenly like wading through treacle. All Nell could feel was Hugo's arms around her and the sudden feeling of drowsiness.

# CHAPTER SIXTEEN

SHE WOKE TO half light. A slight breeze was playing through the cabin, and the sun must be shining outside the closed curtains. Nell's first thought was that she didn't feel sick any more.

Her second thought was for Hugo. He was sitting quietly in the corner of the cabin, looking the way a lover should in the morning. Freshly showered, not yet shaved, wearing a pair of shorts and a polo shirt. She wondered if he had fresh coffee somewhere and decided her stomach wasn't quite up to that.

'I'm so embarrassed.'

He didn't even pretend to shrug it off. 'Want me to show you my scar? We can feel embarrassed together.'

In an odd way, it was the nicest thing he could have said. Saying it didn't matter would have been ridiculous. Sharing the way he felt was oddly comforting.

'Your pacemaker isn't as messy as being seasick.'

He shrugged. 'You have excellent aim, which must be entirely intuitive, since you clearly weren't up to thinking about it.'

Nell smiled. 'Glad to hear it.'

'Feeling better now?'

'Yes, much. If I'd known, I'd have taken something before I came on board.'

'I should have mentioned it. But then we doctors can be

trusted to look after our own health so well.' He quirked his lips down, to give the obvious lie to the statement.

'Don't we just.'

She almost wanted him to come back to bed. Actually, she *did* want him to, but she wasn't going to ask, not after last night. Maybe that wasn't such a bad thing. It made the transition, between lovers and friends, a little easier. Something that might be laughed about even, when the sting of embarrassment had lost its bite.

*We slept together, then I got seasick and he had to give me an injection. Yes, right there...*

'Can you face something to eat? Toast, maybe?'

That sounded like a good idea. Something to get her back on her feet and put this behind her.

'I'd love some.' Nell was still wearing the robe that Hugo had wrapped her in last night. She pulled back the bedcovers, finding that standing up was hardly even a challenge.

'Stay here. I'll go and get a tray.' He rose, stopping to curl his arm around her shoulder to give her a hug. Hugo was clearly pretty good at this morning-after *we're still friends, aren't we?* thing. She felt him kiss the top of her head, and then he turned and walked out of the cabin.

By lunchtime, Nell felt well enough to eat some more, and then take another trip to the bridge, so that Captain Masson could demonstrate the complexities of getting back into the marina without hitting anything. She said her good-byes, and the motor launch took them back to land, where Hugo's car was waiting for them.

Something had happened last night. Something outside the obvious.

It wasn't just the amazing sex, or the look in Hugo's green eyes when he'd given himself up to her. He'd met her embarrassment with his own shame, and somehow that had created an understanding. Acceptance in the face of what each of them was most afraid to show.

They could be friends now. They *must* be friends, because anything less would be a tragedy. As they walked towards the front door of his house, and Hugo turned the key in the lock, this seemed like a new beginning. One that would see them both succeed in the dream that Nell had so recently begun to share. The clinic.

They left their bags in the hall for later, and walked through to the kitchen. Hugo opened the fridge and took a can of ginger beer out, and Nell laughed.

'No, thanks. I think I can manage without it. Would you like a cup of tea?'

'Love one.' He was suddenly still. The man who had moved through today with the ease of a practised diplomat was suddenly unsure of himself.

'Nell…?'

'Yes?'

'Last night. I…'

She could handle this. Nell took the can from his hand, putting it down on the countertop. He looked at it for a moment and then his gaze moved to her face.

'I had the very best night. And then the very worst. I'm glad you were there for the best part, and sorry you had to be for the worst.'

'I'm not sorry…' he started.

She laid her hand lightly on his chest, and he fell silent. 'I'm very grateful you were there to look after me. That's the advantage of sleeping with a doctor. And, like you say, what happens at sea stays at sea. We have a clinic to build.'

He nodded. 'And you don't feel you can work with me and sleep with me? I can understand that, if that's what you're saying.'

At some point, she'd become a different person from

the one who had been taken in by Martin, and then bullied by him. Nell wasn't quite sure when that had happened.

'I'm think I'm still working that one out.'

'Then…are you somewhere that might allow a bit of flexibility? On the working together and sleeping together thing?'

It was as if someone had opened a door, letting sunlight into the room. All the knowledge of chemical reactions in the brain didn't make it any less a work of magic.

'What kind of flexibility?' The sudden desire to be wooed flared in her chest, making Nell's heart beat a little faster.

That smile of his was a very good opening salvo. The way he stepped a little closer, not quite touching her, made Nell's head begin to reel.

'I want to touch you again. I know I can't keep you for ever, but it doesn't make it any the less sweet that you're here now.'

Nell reached up, brushing her fingertips against his cheek. 'I want to touch you, too.'

He reached for her, pulling her close. When he kissed her, she could feel all the tension buzzing between them. Last night hadn't even begun to sate it; instead, it had only made it grow.

'Upstairs.' He whispered the word, but it still held all the promise of a command.

'Yes. Upstairs.'

It was odd. Before they'd been sleeping together, no one had doubted their devotion to one another. The papers had used the official photographs taken to celebrate their engagement and painted a rosy picture of a couple who were completely in love. But now…

Hugo was laughing on the phone with his mother as he walked her from the car to the front door. He walked into the kitchen, pulling a carton of juice from the fridge, and Nell fetched two glasses.

'Yes, I'll give her your love… Love you, too.' Hugo had seemed more openly affectionate with his mother in the last few weeks, and he'd even taken to chatting with his father on the phone.

'What was that all about?' Nell picked up her glass, taking a sip from it.

'Apparently we're cooling off.'

'Really?' Nell raised her eyebrows. She hadn't noticed anything of the sort. The last two weeks had been all heat.

'My mother was talking to a friend of hers who was at the gala we went to at the weekend. She said that I hardly looked at you all evening.'

Nell grinned. 'Perhaps we'd had an argument.'

'Perhaps. Maybe I was just looking the other way, trying not to imagine what you were wearing under that dress.'

'Oh. So you can do that, can you? Look the other way and get your imagination under control.'

'No, not really.' He took a step towards her, laying his hand on her waist. 'What are you wearing under this dress?'

'What if I said long johns?'

He laughed, taking the near-empty glass from her hand and putting it on the kitchen counter. Nell backed away from him and he followed, closing in on her.

'Long johns would be fine. Just as long as you're in them.' He wound his arms around her waist, pulling her against him, his body suddenly taut.

'Ah. What about something in stout cotton? Plenty of buttons and safety pins.'

'Wonderful. They'd take a bit more concentration to get off. I might just faint from anticipation while I do it, and then you can revive me.'

Nell laughed. Hugo loved the act of undressing her.

Made an art of it, as if he were slowly unwrapping something precious. She loved it, too. It was one of the ways he made her feel special.

'I've been wanting you all day…' Every time she touched Hugo, she wanted him. That was probably why she studiously avoided touching him in public.

'I'm glad to hear that. You want me now?' His hand slipped beneath her jacket, moving towards her breast. Nell began to tremble and she felt his lips curve into a smile against hers. 'You *do* want me. I can feel it.'

'Come and find out how much…'

Nell couldn't remember being any happier than she was now. Hugo was becoming stronger and the scar on his chest was fading. It felt as if maybe the scars in Nell's heart might be finally fading, too.

They reached their fundraising target, and celebrated it with champagne in bed. All that mattered in these early days of their heady romance was that every moment spent alone was spent in each other's arms.

They sat on the patio, eating breakfast, and Nell tore open the thick envelope, drawing out the heavily embossed paper. Hugo was watching quietly. He knew it must be a letter from the legal team he'd persuaded Nell to use in her complaint against Martin.

'What do they say?' He gave her time to read, hope kindling in his eyes when he saw her smile.

'Four other women have come forward and said that Martin made persistent and unwelcome advances towards them. Apparently one of them had the presence of mind to record him on her mobile phone.' She grinned at him. 'He used exactly the same phrases as I wrote in my complaint.'

Hugo chuckled. 'Open and shut case, then.'

'I think so. The hospital have suspended him, and there may be criminal charges in connection with one of the complaints.' She slid the letter across the table so that Hugo could read it all. 'Thank you.'

He shook his head, laughing. 'You did it all. I just… watched and admired.'

'Well, thank you for watching and admiring. You do it so well.'

They finished breakfast and drove to the hospital. Hugo had a planning meeting to attend, and Nell had decided to spend the time in the ward, helping the children's play specialist.

'It'll be great when we have more space.' The young red-headed woman grinned at Nell.

'Did Dr Bertrand tell you? We have the money now, and the work can go ahead again. There should be some progress during the next few weeks.'

'Yes, he did. We'll be able to watch it go up. I'll take pictures for you every day, so you can see what's happening.'

It was a nice thought, but Nell wondered why Louise thought she wouldn't be able to take pictures for herself. 'Thanks. I won't be here every day, so it would be good to have those.'

'You won't be here at all, will you? What about the celebrations?'

'I forgot about those,' she hedged. Maybe this was something that Hugo hadn't told her about?

'Well, once you've been, you won't forget them for next year. Montarino's royal anniversary fortnight is a bit special, there's always lots to do. I expect you'll be really busy.' Louise's voice rang with anticipation.

'Mmm. Well, yes. It would be great if you could take some photos. While I'm busy.' Nell turned her attention to the little boy who had just been wheeled into the play-room by one of the nurses, gathering up some bricks and putting them on the table in front of him.

* * *

'Montarino's royal anniversary fortnight.' Nell couldn't help keeping the sharpness from her voice. Over the course of the day, she'd made discreet enquiries about it, as well as looking it up on the Internet. Apparently the whole royal family took part, and there were concerts, exhibitions and other events over a full two weeks. Why hadn't Hugo told her about it?

A small voice at the back of her head told her why. But Nell was trying to ignore it.

'Ah. Yes.' Hugo put his car keys down on the table. 'I was going to mention that.'

His tone had a guilty ring to it. The small voice got louder.

'Okay. It's just that one of the play therapists at the hospital mentioned it. She says it's really good fun.'

'Yes, it is.'

'And that the whole royal family takes part?'

'Yes, we do. It's a tradition dating back hundreds of years. It's said there used to be a banquet that lasted two weeks, but we've skipped that bit now.'

'And it's in two weeks' time.' Nell was getting a very bad feeling now.

'Yes.' He paused, frowning. 'Nell, I think… Maybe we should give it a miss.'

'That's entirely up to you, Hugo. But shouldn't you be with your family?' Hugo seemed to be getting on so much better with his father these days. They still occasionally had their ups and downs, but Nell had encouraged Hugo to voice his affection and respect for his father. No doubt under similar pressure from his mother, Hugo's father had begun to voice similar feelings about his son.

'Well… I'll have to go to some of the events. Now that I'm back to full health, I should start taking on some of my royal duties again. I may have to stay at the palace for…a few nights. Maybe more.'

This wasn't like Hugo. He was usually so decisive. Nell knew for sure now that something was up. 'Hugo, just say it. What's going on? Don't you want me to go with you? You know I'll support you, in whatever you want to do.'

He sat down at the kitchen table, tracing his fingers across its surface. Then he seemed to come to a decision. 'I don't want you there.'

'Okay. Fine.' Nell swallowed the feeling that suddenly the world was turning in the wrong direction. It was making her feel a little sick.

'It's not that I don't want you with me. I just…' He shrugged, letting out a sigh. 'I don't want you involved with my official duties. These two weeks are always really busy and… I promised you that you'd never be just the woman on my arm. That you'd always have your own career.'

Nell didn't remember him promising her that. Maybe he'd just promised it to himself. 'I can see why you'd say that. But I don't mind. If you want me to be there, I'll happily support you. That's what we do for each other, isn't it?'

'Yes, it is. And my way of supporting you is to draw that line and stick to it. You…you've only been to one official function and that seemed…stressful for you.'

'Yes, it was stressful. You got hit with a stun gun.'

Hugo shrugged. 'I meant the bit before that. The dress and everything…'

'It was my first time, of course I was a bit stressed.' Nell frowned. 'This isn't about me, is it?'

'It's all about you, Nell. It's about my not taking you for granted, and giving you the room to have your own career.'

'It's about Anna.' His *real* fiancée. Nell felt a sudden stab of jealousy, knowing that the ring she wore was the symbol of an agreement, not of love.

'Anna's in my past. We've been finished, in every way, for a long time.'

'Yes, but what happened isn't finished. You can't let go of the idea that Montarino is your duty, and that you can't escape it. Or that your duty is incompatible with having a partner who has a career.'

'No, I can't. Because that's the truth of it, Nell. Believe me, I've tried and it doesn't work.' His voice was suddenly cold. Nell knew that she was pushing Hugo too far, into places that she'd resolved never to go with him. But if that could break them apart then maybe it should. Because it was an issue that they could only avoid for so long.

When had she started thinking about the long-term? Their engagement was one of convenience, and they'd agreed that three to six months would be enough. They'd decided to part after that.

But that was before they'd slept together. They'd promised that it would change nothing, yet it had changed everything. And suddenly Nell saw that while Hugo was kind and honourable, and Martin was neither, she would still always have to play the mistress with Hugo. His first loves were his work and his country, and he would never truly believe that there was room for her in that situation.

Nell deserved more than this. At the very minimum, she deserved his honesty. Hugo had almost deceived himself into thinking that it could work between them, but in truth he'd been careful to show her only one side of his life. Just as their engagement had sheltered her from the press, he had sheltered her from the realities of sharing her life with a prince.

Much as he wanted to, he couldn't do this to her. He couldn't take away her independence, and her career, and watch her fade and wilt in the bright light of his responsibilities.

'Nell, we agreed.' He didn't want to say it, but he had to.

'Yes, we agreed. A three-month engagement and then we go our separate ways.' As usual, she was ahead of him. The connection between them, which up till now had been a conduit for love, seemed now to be pushing them inexorably towards a parting.

'I'm fit and well now. And you're safe from the lies.' Was that really all there was to their relationship? A convenience? It had started out that way, and it seemed that it was going to end that way.

'So you'll go back to your life, and I'll go back to mine.'

'I think that's best for both of us.'

She turned away from him suddenly. As if she didn't want to even look at him any more. 'Fine. We'll do that, then.'

'Nell…' He hadn't wanted things to end like this. Maybe he should have thought about that when he'd first reached out to touch her. 'Nell, you can stay here for as long as you want. I'll go to my apartment at the palace…'

She faced him, her cheeks flushed red. Even now, if she had cried, Hugo could never have let her go, but she didn't. 'I'm not your employee, Hugo. You don't have to give me a notice period, I can leave whenever I like.'

Anger started to mount in his chest. If that was the way she wanted it. 'Fine. I'm going to the palace anyway.' He picked up his car keys and walked back outside to the car. Starting the engine, he pulled out of the driveway and onto the road.

# CHAPTER SEVENTEEN

HUGO BROODED ON the matter for two weeks. Then he got on a plane and flew to London.

Nell's flat was in a nice road, with trees on each side of it. As he got out of the taxi, he noticed that her front gate needed mending, and that the brass on the front door had been recently polished. It felt as if everything had suddenly shot into sharp focus.

A young woman answered the door and stared at him blankly.

'I'm looking for Nell. Nell Maitland.'

'Oh. She's not here any more. Sorry.' The woman made to shut the front door and Hugo wondered if he should put his foot against the frame. Probably not, it might scare her.

'Please...' The door opened again, and Hugo breathed a sigh of relief. 'Do you know of any way that I might contact her?'

'No, I'm sorry. We've been here for three months and we've just signed another lease. The agent said that she was going abroad again.'

'I don't suppose you know where?'

'No. She didn't go back to...' The woman clicked her fingers, trying to recall the name.

'Montarino.'

'That's right. The agent did say that she wasn't going back there.'

Okay. That was Montarino ticked off the list. It was a start. All Hugo had to contend with now was the rest of the world.

'Would you be able to give me the name of the agent, please? I'm trying to get in contact with her.'

The woman looked him up and down, seeming to come to the conclusion that it would be okay. 'It's Green's in the High Street. You know it?'

'No, I'm sorry, I don't. Which way is that?'

'End of the road, turn left. Walk down to the very end of that road and then turn right along the High Street. You can't miss it.' The woman shrugged. 'There's a big green sign.'

'Thank you.' Hugo smiled. It seemed as if this was going to be a long journey, but this was at least the first step.

The woman smiled suddenly. 'Good luck.'

'Thank you.' He was going to need it. He had to fly back to Montarino tonight, but he had time enough to speak to the estate agent and if Nell was still in London, he might be able to see her today.

This was Nell's third job in a few weeks. Maybe this one would be a keeper.

She'd told her employment agency that she'd take any job anywhere, as long as it wasn't in London and they would guarantee absolute discretion as regards her whereabouts. They'd taken her at her word. The first job had been a week or so as a supply doctor on nights in a busy Huddersfield A & E department. The second had taken her to Manchester for a few days, and the third had brought her to Northern Germany, where she was helping an overworked and understaffed clinic that had been set up to cater for refugees.

It might be classed as overkill, but you didn't just

walk away from Hugo. He had contacts everywhere. If he missed her one quarter as much as she missed him, he might try to get in contact. And if he did, she couldn't trust herself not to respond.

It was better not to give him that chance. Not face the dilemma of his having tried to find her, and not to feel the heartbreak if he hadn't. This way she could draw a line under their affair and find a way to start again. Let him start again, and have the life he deserved.

The clinic was hard work. Nell's German wasn't up to scratch yet, but it was improving every day, and her French and English were both useful. The families under her care tore at her heart, but it was work that was important. The director of the clinic had already asked whether she was available for another month, and she hoped that might be extended even further.

It was late, almost nine o'clock, when she finally packed up her things and grabbed her coat. Tomorrow was her one day off per week, and she might just spend that sleeping and eating, since she hadn't had a great deal of time for either in the last couple of days.

'I'll see you on Thursday.' She smiled at the receptionist, who nodded back. Pulling her coat around her against the first chill of winter, she walked outside, nodding to the security guard at the gate and making for her car, which was parked some way down the road.

He was under a lamppost, next to her car. Huddled in a thick jacket, pacing back and forth to keep warm. Hugo must have been waiting a while. Nell had one moment to escape, but then he saw her. She saw his face in the light of the lamp, and there was no running away now. He waited, suddenly still, as she walked towards him.

'Hugo.'

'Nell.' His voice was thick with emotion. It carried with it the long weeks of running and the inevitable search he must have made to find her. And suddenly that was all nothing. She wanted to fall into his arms and kiss him.

'It's cold.' There wasn't any point in asking him what he was doing here, that was obvious. And Hugo was shivering.

'Yes. They wouldn't let me into the clinic.'

'Security's pretty tight there. How long have you been waiting?'

'A couple of hours.'

Nell unlocked her car and opened the passenger door. 'Come and sit in the car.' If she switched the engine on, the heater might warm him a little.

'Would you mind coming to mine? I'm parked just around the corner.' He gave a hesitant smile. 'Heated seats.'

He'd found her. He'd come for her and had stood in the cold for hours, waiting for her. And despite everything, that unspoken connection between them was still as strong as it had ever been. This was like walking on the edge of a precipice in the darkness, but Nell couldn't stop herself. She took his arm, and Hugo started to walk.

'What's the clinic like?'

'It's tough. There are a lot of kids who are sick and have been through a lot. Adults, too. Any progress is hard won, but it's rewarding work.'

'Do you think you'll stay?'

If what he meant was would she forget about all this and come back with him to Montarino, the answer was no. Not to see their relationship crumble once more and feel that heartbreak all over again.

'Yes, I'm thinking about it.'

'Good. I'm glad you've found this.'

What did he want? To sit in the car and reminisce about old times? It didn't really matter, whatever it was, Nell knew she'd see it through to the end. He stopped beside his car and opened the passenger door. Nell got in.

He was cold, and the long wait had given all his fears the chance to settle heavily around his heart. But Hugo had found out what he wanted from life, and he wasn't going to give it up without a fight.

Nell's warmth hadn't changed. He still felt it, binding them together the way it always had. If her voice was tempered with sadness, it was the sadness that he felt in his own heart, too.

She pulled off her knitted hat, putting it in her lap with her gloves. She was staring at the steering wheel, as if that was safe middle ground. Not straight ahead, Nell was never that cold. Not at him, because he'd broken her heart. She didn't need to say it; he could see it in her eyes.

'Nell, I've thought about this a lot, and there are only four things that truly matter.'

She glanced at him, turning her gaze away quickly. 'Four?'

'Yes. That you follow your calling as a doctor. That I follow mine. That's two. The third, and most important, is that I love you.'

'But…you don't want me.'

'I've always wanted you, Nell. I sent you away because I thought I couldn't have you without you having to sacrifice number one. Now I know better.'

She turned suddenly, wide-eyed. 'And the fourth?'

'That's up to you. If *you* love *me*, then we can work everything else out.'

Her lip began to quiver. If she cried now he wouldn't be able to stop his own tears. Maybe that was just yet another proof of the connection that he felt with Nell.

'What about Montarino?'

Hope thumped almost painfully in his chest, and he ignored it. It was just his heart beating, and that was proof that he could live long enough to show Nell how much he loved her.

'There are people who will oversee the building of the clinic, just as well as I can. The royal calendar can do without me from time to time, my parents have it all pretty well tied down. Montarino doesn't need me, it was me who needed Montarino. I needed something to dedicate myself to.'

'And you don't now?' She frowned, shaking her head. 'Hugo, you love the place.'

'Yes, I love it. It'll always be my home. But you're the one and only love of my life, Nell. You're a lot more important to me.'

Her gaze searched his face. Then one tear dropped from her eye, tumbling down her cheek. 'You're the one and only love of my life, too.'

He reached for her, wishing that they were somewhere less cramped so he could hold her properly. But it didn't matter. Hugo knew what really mattered now, and that was being able to look into her eyes. Wipe away her tears and brush a kiss onto her lips.

'Where are you staying?' Finally she broke the warm silence that curled around them like a blanket.

'At the Grand.'

'That's right across town!'

'I booked it from the lamppost. There wasn't a great deal of choice.'

Nell chuckled. 'Okay, so we can drive across town and have room service, or it's ten minutes to mine. Fifteen if we stop for pizza on the way.'

'Pizza sounds great.'

Crown Prince Hugo Phillipe DeLeon, only son of the King of Montarino, had to carry the pizza up three flights of stairs because the lift was broken. He looked around her flat, which didn't take long, because there were only two rooms and a bathroom, and pronounced it delightful. He kept his coat on while the heating took the edge off the chill in the sitting room.

They ate pizza and drank coffee, and her small flat became the centre of the world. The one place where they could both be happy, because it was the place they were together. Curled up on the sofa together, talking about plans and dreams, futures and possibilities.

'That's what we'll do, then?' The sun was rising but Nell didn't feel tired any more.

'You're sure that's what you want?' Hugo leaned over, kissing her.

'I'm sure. You're sure you really *can* take a holiday for the next month? So that I won't let the clinic here down?'

'Positive. I'll be waiting here for you every evening with a smile on my face and a tasty meal in the oven.'

Nell snorted with laughter. 'You will not. If you're staying here, you can earn your keep. I'm sure the clinic will take you on, they could do with more doctors. And being a prince has its advantages.'

'They don't have to pay me?'

'Yeah, they don't really have the funds for that. You'll spread a little happiness, though.'

'That sounds great. Can't wait to start.' Hugo got to his feet, stretching his limbs, and walked over to the window, looking out at the glow on the horizon. 'Come with me.'

'Where are we going?'

'See that little park down there? It looks a nice place for an early morning stroll. We can watch the sunrise.'

They pulled on their coats, tiptoeing down the stairs so as not to wake any of the neighbours. Across the street and through the park gates, into a cold, fresh morning. Hugo seemed to know exactly where he wanted to go, and Nell followed him over to a small playground, sitting next to him on the swings.

He grinned, feeling in his coat pocket. Then he opened

a box, holding it out for her to see the ring inside, flashing bright in the new day. 'Nell, this is a symbol of love between the two of us. That you'll love me, and I'll love you. That we can make happen the things we both want.'

He'd said almost those same words before. This time it was real. Nell began to tremble with excitement, as he fell onto one knee in front of her. 'Will you marry me, Nell?'

'Yes, Hugo.' She leaned forward, kissing him. Holding on to him tightly, in case this was just a beautiful dream.

'This isn't a royal jewel. If you'd prefer one of those, there are plenty to choose from…'

'No. No, Hugo, this is much better. I want this one, please.' It wasn't some anonymous jewel. Hugo had chosen this just for her. It was exquisite, a gold band with square cut diamonds set all the way around it. Clearly expensive, but not so bulky that it would tear a pair of surgical gloves.

'You don't need to take this one off when you're at work.' Hugo had obviously been thinking exactly the same as she was.

'Hugo, thank you for coming for me. Thank you for believing in me. I'll never take it off.' Nell could feel tears streaming down her cheeks. He pulled at her glove, tugging it off, and she held out her hand.

'I'll be taking it off on our wedding day. Just for long enough to slip your wedding ring on.' He kissed her, sliding the ring onto her finger.

'Come home with me, Hugo. I have a three-quarter-sized bed, and I want to see how well you fit into it.'

'I'll fit. Particularly if I have you in my arms. Are you tired?'

'What? No, I'm not tired. Are you?'

'Not even slightly.' He got to his feet, wrapping his arm around her shoulders. Then Nell walked her prince back up to the tiny flat that now contained every dream she'd ever had.

# EPILOGUE

THEY'D STAYED ON at the clinic in Germany for two months, working for nothing so that other doctors could be recruited and paid. Hugo bade the little flat goodbye with more regret than he'd ever left anywhere before. It held the best memories of his life.

But there was more to come. Nell was a quiet force to be reckoned with, planning a wedding and a reception that didn't follow any royal protocol that Hugo had ever heard of. The idea was received with hardly a murmur from his father, and warm approval from his mother.

Everything went off without a hitch. Nell's father and his had become friends over a shared interest in gardening, and Hugo's mother had finally managed to persuade Nell's mother that her outfit was perfect for the occasion. They were married in the presence of close family and friends in a small private ceremony. Nell looked more beautiful than he could ever have imagined, wearing a knee-length fitted dress in cream silk, her only concession to royal splendour being a small diamond tiara, which held a shoulder-length veil in place.

There was nothing but love. When he recited his vows, and she said hers. When he slipped the ring onto her finger. But the moment that made Hugo proudest was the one when his new bride took his arm and he walked into the children's cardiac unit at the hospital. She sat with each of the children, letting them hold her bouquet and even taking off the tiara so that the little girls could try it on.

Then there was cake in the children's playroom, which for some reason that Hugo couldn't fathom had candles on it. It turned out that one of the children had a birthday today, and Nell duly helped her to blow out the candles, to cheers and clapping from the parents. The nurses supervised the cutting and distribution of the cake, while Nell managed to retrieve the tiara, finding a handkerchief to wipe the sticky finger marks off it.

'Oh, dear.' She held it up to the light, twisting it back and forth. 'It's got icing on it.'

'Probably the best use it's ever been put to.' Hugo grinned, sitting down next to her on one of the plastic chairs that lined the ward. 'I dare say my mother will know the best way to clean it.'

'I can't give it back to your mother like this. She's already been so good about delaying the start of the reception so that we could come here first.'

'I thought it was rather a good idea. Gives everyone a chance to put their feet up and loosen their ties.'

'Like you've loosened yours?' Nell gave him a mischievous look. 'What *will* people say?'

'They'll say I've married the most beautiful woman in the world. The most dedicated doctor and...' Hugo brushed a crushed petal from her dress '...the best person I know.'

'And I've married the most handsome prince in the world. Actually, I should widen the scope a bit. The most handsome *doctor* in the world.'

'I like that a lot better.' Hugo kissed her hand, and heard a camera shutter click. He turned and smiled, his arm around his new wife. A picture for the hospital scrapbook.

'I'm so proud of you, Hugo. Last week, a man told me how much your speech about having a pacemaker had meant to his wife. She said that if it was good enough for you, then it was good enough for her.'

'And I'm proud of you, too. Your project is going to make a big difference to a lot of people.'

He and Nell had decided that they would work together, but each concentrate on different special projects. Nell had already formed a partnership between the hospital in Montarino and the London hospital where she'd worked, to create a joint initiative to promote research and care for elderly patients with heart disease.

'I hope so. It's early days yet.'

'We have plenty of time. All our lives.'

Nell smiled at him. 'I'm so happy, Hugo. You're my one true love.'

'And you are mine.' Hugo kissed his wife, and a cheer went up around the room.

'Do it again!' a child's voice piped up from somewhere, and everyone laughed.

There was nothing else he could do but kiss Nell again.

\* \* \* \* \*

# FALLING FOR THE
# PRINCESS

## SANDRA HYATT

To Mum and Dad

# One

"You're going about this all wrong." The deep, low voice shattered the serenity of the bright fall morning.

*It sounded like...*

*But it couldn't be. Not here.*

Regardless of the impossibility, Rebecca Marconi's fingers tightened around the handle of her mug and she looked warily over her shoulder. The dark-haired man at the beachfront café's only other occupied table lowered his newspaper and raised his sunglasses.

Amusement glinted in Logan Buchanan's chocolate-colored eyes.

The last person she expected to see. The last person she *wanted* to see. Rebecca shook her head, disbelieving. "Where do I have to go to get away from you?"

"To the ends of the earth, Princess."

"I thought I had." She'd spent the past two weeks traveling across Europe and North America until, after a twelve-hour flight and a drive a third of that time, she'd ended up on a remote part of a remote peninsula in New Zealand. Here, along the whole sweep of beach before her, she could see fewer than half a dozen people.

Of all the cafés in all the towns in all the world... "How did you find me?"

Straight dark eyebrows lifted. "Please. Give me some credit. You haven't exactly been discreet."

Actually, she'd tried. She'd attended just two unavoidable gatherings of friends, one in New York, and one in San Francisco. She hadn't expected either of those gatherings to end up on celebrity gossip websites. Her friends weren't the type to court publicity. She couldn't, however, say the same for the friends of her friends. That was the trouble, you never really knew who else was at these things or what they truly wanted no matter how innocent and open they seemed. It was a lesson she ought to have learned before now. "Sophie's engagement party?"

"To name but one."

Here, finally, she'd been planning on laying low for a time while she figured out a way forward. A way that would work for both her and her father, the reigning monarch of the small European principality of San Philippe.

She wasn't well-known outside of Europe—outside of San Philippe even. Here, she'd counted on some privacy and anonymity. "I was going to go home." She left the *eventually* off of her sentence.

She'd turned down the two unexpected requests from Logan to meet with him in the week before she left home. She'd been busy, but she'd also seen no reason to meet with a man who'd made his views on royalty and the archaic ways of her country abundantly clear.

A man who also always managed to unsettle her, making her feel as though she didn't quite fit her own skin.

"I don't have that much time," he said.

"I have a news flash for you, Logan. This isn't about you. It's about me."

"It always is."

She met his steady gaze, kept her own unflinching. There were times when her training—to show no reaction—came in handy. "That was unkind. Even for you." She wouldn't let herself care what he thought.

He'd arrived in San Philippe a few months ago, introduced into society by her brother Rafe. And he'd been an immediate hit with both the men and the women. The women, for his looks and for the down-to-earth honesty and Chicago charm that was, admittedly, a refreshing change from the restrained niceties of royal circles; and the men, for his phenomenal business success and skill on the polo field that had helped their team to its last three wins.

For a time she, too, had been secretly captivated. There was something so different about him.

Rebecca turned back to her hot chocolate. That time had passed. She'd *made* it pass.

She felt a movement beside her and watched from the corner of her eye as he stood. If he left, even for a short while, she could head back to her bed-and-breakfast, collect her bags and leave. And this time she would be even more discreet. He wasn't the only thing she'd been trying to escape in San Philippe so it hadn't occurred to her that he'd follow her. But now that she knew...

Dashing her hopes, Logan set his espresso on her table, pulled out the chair beside her and lowered himself into it, seeming almost too big—too broad-shouldered and long-limbed for the ornate wrought-iron chair. As he stretched out his denim-clad legs his foot brushed against hers.

Rebecca tucked her feet beneath her chair and picked up her mug, cradling it with both hands as though it could provide some kind of shield. What would it be like to say what was on her mind, to meet his unspoken challenges head-on? To leave her feet where they were, touching his? To return that direct gaze, not backing down? She wouldn't—couldn't—know. Even here she was still who she was. A member of a royal family. And that position dictated her actions and words every waking minute.

Her thoughts and her dreams were another matter. Fortunately, nobody could see inside her head. Unfortunately, not even she could always control the direction of those thoughts and dreams.

For now, all she wanted was for Logan to leave her be. "I don't suppose asking you to go away is going to work?"

"No. But you could try ordering me to go away. Make it a royal command. I dare you." Challenge glinted in his eyes.

And wouldn't he just love that, the opportunity to laugh at someone trying to order him to do anything. "I know what you think of royalty and of me." His honesty hadn't been quite so refreshing when it was directed at her. She must have met other people who shared his thoughts on royalty—she just didn't know who they were because they hid their sentiments from her. She'd tried to be glad of Logan's honesty. But his openly voiced opinions had had her questioning herself, her role in her country, her future. "So, why have you followed me here?"

"I had business here. Meeting you is a happy coincidence, given your inability to see me in San Philippe."

"I'm sure you don't believe in coincidence any more

than I do. And I don't believe for a moment that you have business here."

"No? But coincidences happen all the time and I have interests all over the world."

"America and Europe, yes. But not here."

The light in his eyes changed. "I didn't realize you paid such attention to my activities."

"I don't." She felt as if she'd stepped into a verbal trap. "I listen when people talk, that's all. It would be rude not to."

"Of course." Amusement glimmered.

It was that easy for him to undermine her. A fact he seemed to be infuriatingly aware of. "Don't pretend to agree with me when you don't. The very least I've come to expect from you is honesty. Usually brutal."

"Now who's being unkind?"

"I'm sorry. Did I injure your delicate feelings?"

He threw back his head and laughed and she couldn't remember whether she'd ever heard that sound from him. She decided on not. Because surely she wouldn't have forgotten the rich warm depths that seemed so at odds with the self-serving businessman. The sound—and the mirth behind it—coaxed an involuntary smile in return. And for a moment their shared amusement created a tenuous bond that warmed her. Made her feel not quite so alone.

She quelled the smile. She had to. He'd see it as a weakness. And she'd once heard him attribute his success in business and in sport to discerning his opponents' weaknesses and exploiting them. "Just tell me what you want, Logan. I'll try to help."

He met and held her gaze. "I want you."

The three baldly spoken words hung in the air and any desire to smile evaporated. Rebecca swallowed. For just a moment she imagined the possible interpretations. No man had ever said those words to her and she would have much preferred not to have heard them from this man and in this particular circumstance. Would a man like him, raw and honest, ever want someone like her, whose existence was founded on birthright and image?

She ought not to care.

"What do you really want?" She tried for a look of royal disdain, but the only result was a broadening of his smile, effectively conveying just how little her so-called disdain meant to him.

"I've told you."

"That you want me? No. You might want what I can do for you. But you don't want me." She knew how things worked. She held political sway in San Philippe.

"And if I did want you?" He imbued the words with a hint of curiosity. Again, possible interpretations flickered in her imagination.

She had to end this now. The words, the low tone, the possibilities his question raised—and her resulting foolishness—almost hurt. "Stop wasting my time, Logan."

"Time you're clearly using so productively." He glanced at her hot chocolate and the cuisine magazine on the table beside it.

Contrary to what he thought, she didn't get to spend a lot of time doing nothing in particular. She treasured it when she did. Rebecca stood. "If you're not going to go away, then I will." Leaving the magazine and the drink she'd had only a few sips of, she walked back along the beach. She headed for the rocky promontory at the end of the bay, the Pacific Ocean on one side of her, a quiet strip of luxury housing on the other. And behind the houses a steep, forested hillside.

He took so long to catch up with her she'd almost allowed herself to believe it would be that easy. But his shadow, long from the setting sun, came into view, drawing level with hers. As he fell into step beside her, he handed her a take-out cup. "You hardly touched your drink."

"Thank you." What else could she say?

"Hot chocolate? I'd have thought you were more a cappuccino kind of girl."

"Coffee keeps me awake if I drink it at this time of day."

"You have trouble sleeping?"

She hadn't meant to give him anything so personal. "Logan, I'm hardly going to discuss my sleeping habits with you. In fact, I'm not going to discuss anything with you. So you may as well go."

"Order me to."

She had nothing to lose by trying. She took a deep breath. "I command you, in the name of my father, to go away."

Rebecca managed to get several paces ahead of him while he was doubled over with laughter, and she couldn't quite help her own smile at the futility of her attempt. She'd never actually tried issuing a royal command before. Now she knew why.

He jogged to catch up. "But your father, and what he wants you to do, is the reason I'm here."

Any desire to smile faded. She'd feared as much, ever since Logan's first request to meet with her. The timing, so soon after her father's announcement, had been too coincidental to be anything else. "I'm dealing with it. In my own way."

"Which is where we come back to what I said at the outset. You're going about this all wrong. But I have an idea that might help."

"I'm not going to ask. I have no desire to hear your thoughts on my private life." Though her private life—thanks to her father—was rapidly becoming even more public than usual. They walked past the gated entrance to her bed-and-breakfast, which was tucked up in the forested hillside. She didn't so much as look at the steep-roofed building and its inviting balcony. It was quiet and quaint and not at all the style of place she usually vacationed. But it had been cleared by security for her to stay at. One of her brothers had even stayed here a year ago. Logan wouldn't know that and it certainly wouldn't be where the high-flying businessman would expect to find her.

"You don't want my advice?" he asked, friendly and helpful.

"I'll bet the wolf sounded just like you when he told Little Red Riding Hood about the shortcut through the woods." She glanced at him. "And the smile was probably similar, too." That smile broadened. Red Riding Hood, naive and innocent, wouldn't have stood a chance against the tempting warmth so silkily offered.

They walked on, sun shining on their backs, the surf rolling in beside them—it could almost have been pleasant. The sort of quiet stroll along the beach she'd dreamed of. Except in her dreams there was a man at her side who wanted her, not something *from* her. Fifteen minutes later they reached the end of the bay. A track led into the forest, a weathered sign announced a steep twenty-minute walk to the lookout point. Rebecca started up the track and Logan followed. Despite the shade, sweat was trickling down her back and between her breasts by the time she reached the top. Below and beyond, the white-edged bay swept toward distant hills. She sat gratefully in the middle of the bench set a little back from the edge.

Logan, broad-shouldered and lean-hipped, stood at the railing, every bit as captivating as the official view. He looked as cool as though he'd been for a five-minute stroll, not slogged up the same hill she had. He stepped away from the railing then sat beside her, his long legs stretched out. Too close. She moved to the edge of the bench, sat straight, her legs tucked beneath her. "Nice view," he remarked.

"You didn't come for the scenery."

"No, but I can appreciate it while I'm here." At that he lifted his sunglasses and turned and looked at her. She knew he found her physically attractive, he'd told her as much almost the first time he met her, in the same breath that he'd told her he thought her role in her country was perfectly useless. That *she* was perfectly useless but that he supposed the perfection went some way to making up for the uselessness.

Until that moment she hadn't thought him unattractive, either. He was tall with a lean strength and a ready smile and eyes that saw everything. It was that all-seeing gaze with its hidden depths that had first intrigued her. But her opinion had changed in that instant and nothing he'd done or said at their subsequent, unavoidable but blessedly brief, meetings—at the consulate or through her brother—had done anything to make her revise it.

He knew what she thought of him.

But now he, and the mocking amusement in his eyes, and his blunt way with words, and his disapproval of everything that she was, was here. Teasing her senses. Teasing *her*.

Rebecca knew enough of him, and men of his ilk, to realize that her best, almost her only, course of action was to hear him out, to at least pretend to consider what he wanted to say. "All right. I give in. You have something to say, so say it. Clearly it's the only way I'm going to get rid of you."

"I'm almost disappointed. I expected more resistance, Princess."

"I'm not going to give you a fight, Logan, but I didn't say I had any intention of taking your advice."

"Of course not."

"So?"

"Dinner?"

She stared at him.

"I'll explain my strategy to you over dinner. I know a charming restaurant not far from here."

"Why not just tell me now?"

"Because it's an…unusual strategy, and if I tell you now you're going to try to walk away without properly thinking it through. And if we've only just started eating our mains, I have a better chance of you staying to hear me out."

There was the honesty she'd come to expect from him in their few brief encounters. She could almost appreciate it. "The stomach is the way to a man's heart, not a woman's."

"I don't want your heart…only your ears. And your time."

Of course. "And once you've told me your *strategy* you'll leave me be."

"If that's still what you want."

"You have a lot of faith in your persuasiveness."

"Yes."

"But you don't know me." And nothing he could say would sway her.

"I know you well enough." He stood. "I'll pick you up at seven."

"Name the restaurant, I'll meet you there." Not only did she not want him to know where she was staying, but she also didn't want to be dependent on him for transport. Once she'd heard his so-called strategy she'd leave. On her own.

Logan smiled that too-knowing smile of his. "As you

wish, Princess," he said with mock civility. He held out his hand and without thinking she put hers in his and let him help her to standing. The touch of his palm, calloused and strong, sent an alien thrill through her that warned her that this man was like no other.

Logan looked at the woman seated across the table from him. When he'd first seen her this afternoon he almost hadn't recognized her. Dressed for the beach in a slim-fitting yellow dress with a light cardigan, her blond hair loose about her shoulders, she'd looked younger and more relaxed than he'd seen her before. He'd known a moment's regret at being the one to bring wariness and suspicion to her gaze. Now her lush hair was tied back, and she wore a fiercely elegant black, long-sleeve dress. The only thing it had going for it was that it molded nicely to her curves. But her arms were currently folded across her chest. Even without the schoolmarm dress, it didn't take an expert to read her body language.

He needed her to relax, he needed her on his side. That challenge looked even more Herculean than gaining the foothold in Europe he currently sought for his company. It had been a long while since Logan had anticipated a challenge so keenly. "Another glass of sauvignon blanc, *ma chérie?*"

"I'm not anyone's *chérie,* Logan, least of all yours."

She was her prickly, defensive best. Which might go some way to explaining why she wasn't anyone's darling, a fact that would otherwise amaze him. He knew she had her fair share of suitors but, despite press speculation, none of the relationships had ever come to anything. "So that's a yes to the wine?" He began pouring.

She was way too uptight and way too suspicious. He was taking a gamble here and he needed her a little more open-minded. A little relaxed. Had she ever been even the least bit tipsy? Hard to imagine the always restrained and regal Ice Princess giggling, maybe getting expansive and effusive. An image flashed into his mind of her head tipped back, her pale throat exposed to him, inviting the touch of his lips.

"So what's this strategy of yours?"

Logan blinked away the image, let the prim, almost grim, reality replace it. "Not until the mains."

"We've finished the appetizers. The appetizers that weren't necessary."

"But the mains haven't arrived and a deal's a deal. So tell me," he said, hoping to distract her, and perhaps himself, "what exactly were you expecting to achieve in running away from San Philippe?"

Her gray eyes, almost colorless in the dim lighting, darted away from his. "I wasn't running away. I was taking a break. A well-deserved break," she said with a note of challenge in her voice.

He liked unsettling the ever cool princess. "Call it what it is. You were running away."

"I don't have to explain myself to you."

"I was just curious to know whether there was any truth to the rumor I heard." Her posture was already perfect but somehow she managed to sit a little straighter. Confirming what he already knew, that his information was correct. After all, he had it from the best of sources.

"You shouldn't listen to gossip."

"Sometimes it pays to have my ear to the ground. I never know when I might be able to turn a situation to my advantage."

A waiter set two plates of crayfish, the New Zealand equivalent of lobster, in front of them as the wine waiter brought a new bottle to accompany this course. Logan took a sip of the chardonnay as the young man waited for his approval. "Excellent." Though to be honest, he'd rather be drinking a beer.

After their glasses were filled, Logan raised his in a silent salute to her. She watched him steadily, regally, but beneath her cool gaze he glimpsed her uncertainty. The uncertainty of someone who didn't quite know where to turn.

He could help her with that.

He set his glass down. "Assuming the gossip I've heard is true—" he watched her expressive eyes "—you will soon be somebody's *chérie* even though you don't want to be. So, I'm suggesting you...be mine."

# Two

For a moment Rebecca's expression was comically blank and her pretty, royal mouth dropped open, her soft lips parting as she stared at him. Quickly, she closed her mouth and a frown wrinkled her brow. "Did you just say…? Did you suggest…?"

Logan nodded. "It's the perfect solution."

She pushed back her chair and stood. "I think I should go."

Surely that wasn't hurt clouding her eyes.

"Thank you for the meal."

Logan stood, too. He'd more or less expected that reaction, but she had the cool, serene act down to perfection and he'd wanted to ruffle those perfectly preened feathers of hers. So why did he now regret it? "Stay. Hear me out."

"I think I've heard enough."

She turned and he reached for her wrist, circling it

easily with his fingers, her skin cool beneath his touch. "Wait."

Maybe royalty really were different. Merely touching her sent a subtle charge through him. The same sensation he'd experienced up at the lookout point when she'd placed her hand in his.

She stilled and glanced at his hand but otherwise didn't acknowledge his touch, making no attempt to pull free. "Logan, we're both wasting our time here." She looked almost endearingly earnest as though she were trying to let him down gently. But her pulse beat surprisingly fast beneath his fingertips and a hint of color brushed her cheeks.

"Stay. What have you got to lose?"

She was silent a moment and he watched her searching for an answer. "An otherwise perfectly lovely evening?" she said tentatively.

He laughed lightly and held her gaze until finally her lips twitched and her gaze softened. "Stay." He released her wrist and tried not to think about wanting to coax a full smile from her. "The food's good, the setting beautiful." He gestured to the nearby ocean and she, too, looked out at the white, cresting waves, something wistful in her expression. "And otherwise I'll have to follow you. Because I only said I'd leave you be once you'd listened."

"I just don't think anything you're going to say is going to make sense."

"It'll make perfect sense once you hear it all. Just let me explain properly."

"You're not just making fun of me?"

"No." His denial was emphatic. And surprised. Her question revealed an insecurity he would never have guessed she had.

They faced off for long seconds and he could see her

hesitation, her desire to be away from him. But that desire was for more than a temporary reprieve. She wanted his absence to be permanent. Almost as much as she needed a solution to her current problem. If she wanted either of those things she needed to hear him out. And if he was to seal the deal that would secure his company's future in San Philippe he needed her to listen.

And to agree.

"I know you're used to getting your own way. But so am I. And I've had to fight far harder for it than you. I never give up." It was how he'd gotten, against everything thrown at him, to where he was now. "My way will be quicker."

Slowly, she sat. "Tell me," she said on a sigh. He could see her shutting herself off from him. Maybe that subtle withdrawal was how she got through the tedium of so many of her royal engagements.

She folded her arms across her chest. He was guessing she didn't realize how that movement subtly lifted her breasts, increasing the creamy swell at the otherwise demure neckline.

Logan brought his focus back to what he had to say. He didn't want to be noticing her breasts. He raised a forkful of crayfish to his lips, all the while keeping his gaze fixed on hers.

A flush stole up her cheeks and she looked down and picked up her fork. She was easier to disconcert than he'd expected. "Your father expects you to…wed, yes?"

She didn't say anything but she dipped her head once. Her younger brother had recently married—although he'd married the woman her father had intended for Rebecca's older brother. But her father had eventually been satisfied with the outcome. There had even been speculation that that was the match the reigning prince had intended all along. The only thing beyond speculation was the fact that he was unambiguously on record as stating he expected that soon all his children would be married.

And when Prince Henri expected something of his family, it happened.

Which meant that Rebecca and her oldest brother, Adam, were both to get married, and sooner rather than later. Off the record, her father had been even less subtle. He'd told friends that he wanted royal weddings for the morale and the economy of the country and the reputation of the royal family. And he was going to do what he needed to see that it happened.

Rebecca lifted a morsel of crayfish to her mouth. As she chewed she glanced at him in surprise. It really did taste sublime. She hadn't expected that. She took another bite and he realized that he'd stopped eating just to watch her savoring the flavors. "Admit it," he said, "I was right about the crayfish."

She sighed. "Yes."

And he knew that getting her agreement on even that small detail was important. It was a tried-and-true sales technique. Get the prospect to agree on something small—anything—and then build on that. For a time they both ate, but Logan could keep only part of his attention on his meal. The rest was on her.

She looked up, caught him watching her and set her fork down. "You were talking about my father?"

He almost regretted the switch in focus. "I believe he's even drawn up an unofficial list of suitable candidates." Rafe, Rebecca's brother, had shared that information with him one evening after a particularly close fought polo match. "And I'm on it."

"In last place," she pointed out.

"Hard to believe, I know. A few European aristocrats and assorted eager young politicians are ahead of me."

"The only difficult thing to believe is that you're on it at all. Although…I guess you could be there to make the others look good." Mischief glinted in her eyes.

Logan laughed. She sounded so sweet even as she tried to shoot him down in flames. Before tonight she'd been nothing but coolly reserved; he hadn't been on the receiving end of what was a surprisingly sharp wit. He could only assume she was unsettled by both him and her situation.

The entire thing with her father had come as a shock to him, but apparently they did things differently in San Philippe. Who was he to criticize? It was a country that would soon prove lucrative to his business interests and, more importantly, was pivotal to his plans for expanding into Europe, so hey, whatever worked for them.

"You don't want to get married?"

The glint vanished from her eyes. "Not at this point in time."

"But your father wants you to."

She inclined her head. He noted the deep plum color of her lipstick as her mouth tightened. And now, along with the image of her pale throat, another surfaced of her lips parting for him. It was only the challenge of the forbidden. All his life he'd been a rule-breaker. Living a life like hers—following *all* the rules—would destroy a part of him. He didn't know how she did it. And it wasn't his problem, either.

"You know, I think I can hear your teeth grinding."

Surprise flickered in her eyes and a reluctant smile tugged at her lips. The other thing he'd never be able to stand about the way she lived was the fact that clearly, so few people ever said what they genuinely thought to her. "Between my father and you I'm surprised I have any molars left."

She fought that hint of a smile away and looked at the slim gold watch encircling her wrist. "One more minute, Logan. That's all I'm giving you."

The thing they apparently had in common was that they both liked control. And she was fighting for it now.

It was time to stop playing games. Logan leaned forward. "You love your father, and you want to please him. You are, both literally and figuratively, his princess. Furthermore, he's not well." His failing health was another of the rumors Logan had heard. "He wants you to get married. But of all the things you *would* do for him, that's a little extreme. But the people of San Philippe want it, too, and they know he expects it. So, in short you have the pressure not only of your father's wishes, but of an entire nation watching you. You have to at least try to please him. Or be seen trying to please him."

Her gaze dipped to her watch.

"Apparently most of the candidates on your father's list, for reasons I can't begin to fathom, are practically salivating at the prospect of dating and then marrying you. I, on the other hand, don't want to get married. Least of all to someone like you."

"Flatterer." She lifted her wineglass so that it was a subtle barrier between them.

Had that been another flash of hurt? Surely not? She was the last person to care what someone like him thought. He paused. Maybe he wasn't going about this the best way. But usually being straight up worked for him, so he pressed on, watching her closely. "What I'm suggesting is that we be seen to have a relationship. We date for a time. I was thinking four intense weeks. One here, three back in San Philippe. I can fit that in before I have to be back in the States."

She took a sip of the wine.

"We'll be seen publicly together, with a few more private photos also making it into the media. It'll be clear to everyone that we're blissfully happy. In private, between our dates, we don't have to have anything to do with each other. At the end of the four weeks you'll be spotted with a diamond on the ring finger of your left hand."

"I'm supposed to fall in love with you in a matter of weeks?" Her frown deepened.

"Stranger things have happened. People see what they want to see. And if they want to see you in love, it won't be hard to imagine. Especially if you smile a little more. Don't forget nobody will know precisely when we began seeing one another. It could have been going on for some time already. Perhaps since I first saw you at the ambassador's gathering, surrounded by people but looking so remote and so alone. The night I asked for an introduction."

Her eyes widened in surprise. "You asked for that introduction?"

He nodded. He'd seen her and wanted to meet her. It had been that simple.

"And then two weeks after we get engaged," he continued, "the ring will suddenly no longer be on your finger. Our breakup will be amicable, but you'll be heartbroken." She lifted a hand to her mouth to stifle her sudden amusement. That was precisely the kind of smile he'd been thinking of for the media shots. He'd never seen her eyes dance with merriment the way they were now. It transformed her face, lifting the seriousness to reveal someone else entirely. Unfortunately, now was not when he wanted to see that reaction. "All of a sudden," he continued, "public sympathy will be back on your side and your father will see that pushing you into a relationship when you weren't ready was a mistake and that you'll need time to recover. It's got to buy you at least a year." And all of a sudden there was a glimmer of interest in those pretty gray eyes.

The interest turned just as quickly to cynicism. "What's in it for you?"

He met the suspicion in her gaze. "It'll be good for business. I'm in the process of buying out a subsidiary of leBlanc Industries. If I get it, it'll be the one that cracks Europe open for me. One of the unstated factors holding things up is that several members of the board of directors are deeply traditional and I'm seen as a newcomer with no history and not necessarily any future in the country. Dating the princess will be just what's needed to tip the scales in my favor."

"What happens when we break up?"

"We won't break up until after I have board approval and the necessary contracts are signed. All I need now is a nudge in the right direction at the right time, something to tip the scales. And if we're seen to still be friends afterward, I can manage the PR. Besides, people will take their lead from you. If you're not mad at me, no one else will have the right to be."

"So the charade would have to go on?"

"Periodically. Nothing taxing. I'll be over for business and polo anyway. All you'll have to do is smile and wave if we happen to be at the same event."

"And that's everything? That's your strategy?" She sounded far from convinced.

But that was okay because he was far from finished. "Simple but effective." People too often failed to see the strength in simplicity.

She glanced at her watch and stood. He stood, too, and

calmly endured her silent, perplexed scrutiny. Finally, she spoke. "Thank you for the meal and your honesty. It's been a truly…enlightening evening."

He sat back down and watched as she glided from the restaurant. The stillness of her head and the regal line of her back couldn't quite negate the feminine sway of her hips.

The sun peered over the horizon, spilling bright golden light onto the sea as Rebecca sat at the little linen-covered table on the balcony of the B & B. Yesterday, the chorus of birdsong and the view over the treetops and out to the ocean had captivated her. Today she was too distracted and too tired to properly appreciate the beauty. She'd had a dreadful night's sleep. For which she held Logan Buchanan and his outrageous suggestion totally responsible.

Until Logan's proposition, she'd thought—thanks to her father—that her mortification was complete.

Now Logan wanted to pretend to date her for no more reason than financial gain, expanding his systems design company into Europe. She'd have to be far more desperate than she was to consider a proposition like that.

As if she would try to deceive her father. As if anyone would believe she'd fall in love with someone like Logan, her opposite in so many ways, and in such a short space of time. Her cousin had dated his current wife for five years before getting engaged.

She wouldn't think about her brother Rafe's whirlwind romance with Lexie, his wife. The woman he'd fallen head over heels in love with. Nothing Rafe did was ever ordinary.

She knew better than to let Logan get under her skin, and yet he had. She gently slapped her hand on the table. Time to forget about him. It was over. He was gone.

Voices drifted from the room behind her. The lilting accent of Colleen, the proprietor, and someone quieter, a man whose deeper voice didn't carry so well.

Sensation tingled from her scalp and down her spine. Slowly, Rebecca turned her head. Logan lounged against the side of the open ranch slider. He wore jeans and a navy blue T-shirt and had yet to shave. He held two steaming mugs in his large hands. Dark glasses hid his eyes but a grin tugged at one side of his mouth. So male, so appealing, so...antagonizing. If only he wasn't Logan. Much as she wanted to, she didn't leap from her chair. Instead she turned back to the view. "What are you doing here?"

He strolled into her line of sight, placed a mug in front of her then hitched a hip onto the railing. "I'm staying here. It's so restful, don't you think?"

She frowned. "You followed me here last night."

"I think you'll find, Princess, that I booked in yesterday an hour or two before you."

"How did you know I was coming here?"

"This is you being stealthy?" He looked about them, shaking his head. "Put it this way, if you ever decide to take up a false identity or go on the run, get someone else to advise you."

Rebecca closed her eyes and counted silently. When she reached ten she opened them again. "Nobody, except palace security and possibly my father, if he's asked to stay briefed, knows I'm here. And I can't believe that either of them told you where I am."

"Rafe knows, too. He stayed here a year or so ago." Rafe, for reasons she couldn't fathom, was good friends with Logan. "I visited him while he was here and decided if I was ever back in the country..." He sipped his drink. "Colleen makes the best coffee. I remember that, too."

"What are you doing here—" she tapped the table "—now, annoying me?"

"I thought I'd see if you'd had time to consider my suggestion."

"It's like talking to a brick wall." Except brick walls didn't watch her with such casual nonchalance. A nonchalance that nevertheless concealed an unnerving intensity, and an implacable force of will. "I gave you my answer last night."

"You thanked me for your meal and left."

"I walked out on you." She spoke calmly, fighting a most unroyal urge to shout. Five minutes with this man and a lifetime of training went out the window.

"You needed time to think about it."

"I knew my answer by the time you'd finished your explanation."

"You can't possibly have thought it through properly. It's the perfect solution. I was sure you were smart enough to figure that out, even if it took you a few hours."

"Truly, you're astounding."

He grinned. "Why, thank you."

"It wasn't a compliment."

"Insults, compliments, it's all in the interpretation. Now, back to my suggestion."

"You can't for one minute think I'd choose to endure your company just—"

"*Endure* seems a harsh word. I thought we might even manage to have fun, particularly if we mainly do things that don't require us to talk to each other. We can attend things like the rowing regatta, where we'll sit side by side. You can occasionally lean over to whisper in my ear."

She tried to figure him out but had no idea whether he might actually be serious or was just trying to get a reaction from her. She'd seen him do that before, say deliberately provoking things guaranteed to garner a response.

She wasn't playing that game with him.

"You go right on deceiving yourself, Logan, but trust me when I say I choose my words carefully to express precisely what I mean. And spending any amount of time in your company, particularly if I was supposed to look like I was enjoying it, would be a supreme test."

"My apologies." He pulled out the chair beside her and sat down. "Go on."

He watched her closely, his dark eyes intent and looking anything but apologetic. She doubted he knew how. "I wouldn't choose to *endure* your company for any length of time in order to try to deceive my father that way." Rebecca wrapped her hands around her mug of—she glanced down at it—hot chocolate. Oh. "Thank you."

He ignored her thanks. "Your father has no qualms about trying to force you into marrying someone of his choosing."

"He'd never actually force me."

"No?"

"He might try to urge or maneuver me in certain directions."

"Sounds mighty similar to forcing."

In truth, the subtle pressures her father brought to bear did at times feel that way. But it wasn't a truth she'd admit to Logan. "No," she said lightly, "I'm used to him. I know how to deal with him. And with any other man who tries to force me, subtly or unsubtly—" she looked pointedly at Logan "—into doing things his way."

"By running away?"

She paused. "In this case, some time away from San Philippe seemed the best option. It gives us both time to think." Enough time, she was hoping, that her father would forget his schemes altogether.

"Curious."

"What's so curious about it?"

"It just doesn't seem to tally with that snippet on the internet this morning."

She shouldn't let him play her like this but she asked anyway. "What snippet?"

"He's holding an impromptu ball in your honor."

He was? There had been no talk of one before she'd left. Her father was fond of making unilateral decisions but when they concerned Rebecca he always consulted her. Almost always. Doubt gnawed at her. He just might feel strongly enough about this and would have been able to persuade himself that it was for her own good, that she'd enjoy it, just as she had the surprise parties he'd thrown for her as she was growing up. "That's no big deal," she said with a blitheness she didn't feel. "He held one for me when I turned eighteen." Eight years ago.

"Yes, but he wasn't specifically inviting San Philippe's and Europe's most eligible bachelors to that one. Was he? Marcia What's-her-name, the gossip columnist at the *San Philippe Times* is comparing it to the Cinderella story. Perhaps there's some poor bachelor out there as we speak, sitting in front of the fire amongst the cinders, polishing his half-brother's shoes and just waiting for a chance to go to the ball and win the heart of the fair princess. If only he had something to wear."

She almost smiled at the image he conjured. "Don't be ridiculous. I'm sure you're wrong. My father has said nothing about a ball to me. And inviting eligible bachelors would be far too crass." But still the doubt niggled at her. She *had* told her father she'd start at least considering potential suitors when she got back from this trip. She'd meant it to buy herself time, not for her father to go ahead and start organizing balls on her behalf.

"I suppose you're right." He pulled his phone from his pocket, scanned the screen for a few seconds and shook his head. "Marcia What's-her-name must have it all wrong. But it's right here in black and white. Actually, in color. Isn't technology marvelous."

"Show me."

"Surely you know better than to believe half of what you read in the press."

"Show me." She held out her hand.

He slid the device back into his pocket. "You'll only get upset. No doubt she'll print a retraction tomorrow."

But Rebecca knew that Marcia Roundel not only had excellent sources, but was also careful not to raise the ire of the royal family.

Colleen came out carrying two plates of breakfast and set them down on the small table.

"Thank you."

Rebecca hadn't ordered breakfast and certainly wouldn't have ordered the great stack of pancakes that had just been set before her. She opened her mouth to speak.

"This looks fabulous." Logan spoke before she could. And Colleen smiled so broadly at him and then Rebecca that she didn't have the heart to tell her she didn't want the breakfast. Usually she ate little more than a croissant or fruit and yogurt. But she could try a few mouthfuls.

"This is your doing, I take it?"

"She makes the best pancakes."

"Why is everything superlative with you? Last night's crayfish and wine were the best, her coffee's the best and now her pancakes are the best."

For a second his face clouded, the expression quickly

replaced by his usual self-assurance. "Try them and then disagree with me. I dare you."

"You have brothers, don't you? It's such a male thing, thinking if you dare someone to do something they couldn't possibly not accept the challenge. Rafe and Adam used to do it all the time."

"Three. I have three brothers. All younger than me. And daring them still works almost every time."

It was easy to imagine him in a houseful of competitive males. Rebecca looked at the stack of blueberry pancakes in front of her. "It won't be hard for you to be right this time—I've never eaten pancakes."

Logan gasped. "I knew you'd try to make me feel sorry for you. Poor little rich girl. Poor spoiled princess. But truly? No pancakes?"

"Crepes, yes. Pancakes, no."

"Crepes." He made a dismissive grunt as he pulled his chair around the table so that they sat practically shoulder-to-shoulder. He smelled good. Better even than the pancakes. Something fresh and masculine. Not meaning to, she watched the play of muscle in his arms as he reached for the jug of maple syrup. Closing large deft fingers around the small handle, he passed it to her. "You have to have maple syrup. And lots of it." For the first time since she'd seen him yesterday his focus was on something other than her. Rebecca made no move for the syrup.

He turned to look at her, his expression deadly serious. And then suddenly he smiled, a flash of white teeth, and it was like the sun coming out. Once again she pictured him as a boy with his three brothers, all of them intent on their breakfasts. She imagined laughter and arguments. Without thinking she smiled back at him.

The connection lasted no more than a second. They were

so close, both smiling, gazes locked. It was a fragment of perfection. Related to nothing, just its own small thing.

Something curious flashed in Logan's eyes, but then he blinked, the expression vanished and he leaned back in his seat, moved a little away from her. And she felt the loss. "I take my pancakes seriously."

"I picked up on that."

He turned his attention to his own breakfast. "Try them or not. It makes no difference to me." Suddenly defensive, as though in smiling at her he, too, had revealed a weakness, he shifted his chair and opened the paper Colleen had brought out with their meals. "There'll be others after me, you know, if you don't take up my offer," he said as he turned the front page.

Rebecca ignored him and tried a mouthful of syrup-drenched pancakes. They were every bit as good as she'd been led to believe. But she wasn't going to tell Logan that. He was far too sure of himself as it was. She ate almost the entire plateful before she gave up, defeated.

"What do you think?"

"They were fine."

He smiled. Not his earlier, almost boyish smile. This one knowing, unsettling and far too smug. "They were better than fine, but that's not what I was asking about."

"You can't mean your…suggestion?" What did she have to do or say to get through to him?

"That's exactly what I mean."

"Nothing you've said since last night has convinced me to change my mind."

He shook his head. "You haven't thought it through."

"Logan, you don't even like me." And she didn't care for him. He was too different, too unpredictable and unsettling.

"That's why it's the perfect solution."

She hadn't expected him to disagree with her, but still it hurt—just a little.

"You don't like me, I don't like you. If you were to try my idea with one of the other candidates on your father's list they'd undoubtedly take it wrong. They'd see it as an opportunity to get closer to you. Whereas our arrangement will be strictly regulated and strictly business."

He might have a point. But it wasn't enough.

"I have motives but they're not ulterior. And I have no feelings that can be hurt. Call me—" he stood and placed a business card on the table between them "—when you change your mind."

Rebecca didn't even have time for a royal putdown before he'd gone. Leaving a strange absence. But she didn't let herself breathe a sigh of relief until five minutes later when a solitary figure walking away from the B & B came into view on the beach, the long easy stride instantly recognizable.

Then, not touching his card, she left not only the table, but also the B & B.

And on her way out ordered herself to leave all thoughts of Logan Buchanan behind.

# Three

"Yes. I think it could be serious." Rebecca crossed the fingers of her free hand. "Dad, I'm losing the signal. I'll tell you more about it later." As the water taxi motored toward the mainland, Rebecca turned off her phone and dropped her head into her hands.

One day. For one day she'd thought she was back in control. Admittedly a day that she'd spent looking over her shoulder half expecting Logan Buchanan to stroll out from behind the nearest tree.

Because Logan had been right, and he'd known it. Her father was hosting a ball in her honor. Under various pretexts, eligible bachelors from all over Europe had been invited. He'd denied that that was what he was doing but the denial didn't hide the facts of the guest list. And every one of the men her father considered suitable husband material for her and suitable son-in-law material for himself was on that list.

She'd received mail this morning. Colleen, far too efficient, had couriered Logan's card to her with a note that she'd left it on the table. Rebecca had thrown it out then turned around and retrieved it from the trash after Eduardo had called her. The son of a prominent San Philippe senator, Eduardo wanted to escort her to the ballet when she returned home. She'd been out twice with Eduardo several years ago. It wasn't an experience she cared to repeat. She'd formulated a diplomatic, but resolute, refusal. But mere minutes after she declined Eduardo's offer her father had called with his "wonderful" news. He also told her to expect a call from Simon Delacourte, who wanted her to accompany him to the opening of his latest jewelry store in Venice. Rebecca could think of only one way out. She told her father she was seeing someone. And when he'd asked who, she'd said Logan.

So now she just had to tell Logan himself.

Slowly, she dialed the number on the card. It was a lousy choice but he was the lesser of two evils. "It's Rebecca," she said when he answered.

"Rebecca who?"

She hung up. He knew who she was. He had to. She stared at the phone. The lesser of two evils was still evil. A second, better, thought occurred to her. She could buy herself time by just pretending to her father that she was dating Logan. Her father didn't need to know that she wasn't really, and Logan didn't need to know at all.

The perfect solution.

Ten minutes later her phone rang. "Logan here."

"Logan who?"

He laughed. "Logan Buchanan, the man you're dating."

She watched the churning wake stretching behind the boat. "I'm not dating you."

"Funny, because I just had the strangest phone call from

your father. He wants to see me as soon as I'm back in San Philippe. Apparently there's a talk he likes to have with all men who want to date his daughter."

Rebecca groaned.

"The call came through just a minute or two after you hung up on me."

"Oh." She bit back the words she wanted to utter.

"Care to enlighten me, girlfriend?"

"Don't call me that."

"Sweet thing? Punkin? *Ma chérie?*"

She could always call her father back and tell him she'd broken up with Logan.

"Is that your teeth I can hear grinding?"

Rebecca unclenched her jaw. "I'm sorry, Logan. I've made a mistake."

"I knew you'd see the error of your ways."

"Not that mistake—decision," she corrected herself. "I made one this morning when I was speaking to my father. On the spur of the moment I told him that—"

"Where are you?"

"In Russell, in the Bay of Islands." Or she would be in a matter of minutes when the water taxi docked.

"Are you going to be there for the whole day?"

She hesitated. "Yes."

"Good. I'll be there in two hours. We need to have this conversation in person. Stay where you are. Read a magazine or a book or something. I'll call you when I get there."

"No. Don't—" But it was too late. He'd hung up.

She didn't have to stay. She could just phone him back. A text came through from Eduardo suggesting they get together to discuss a charity they both sat on the board of, the pretext transparent. She didn't leave and she didn't phone Logan back. Instead she wandered around Russell, trying to enjoy the anonymity as she waited.

Her broad-brimmed sun hat shaded her face as, two hours later, she stood on the main wharf watching yachts and launches and fishing boats coming and going in the harbor. A few feet away two boys dangled fishing lines into the water. Her phone rang. Already she recognized the number. "I'm on the wharf."

"I know." The voice sounded from both her phone and from behind her.

She stayed where she was, looking out over the water as Logan come to stand beside her, casting his shadow over hers. "So this relationship we're having...?" Was that smug amusement she heard in his tone?

"I told my father I was dating you in the hope he'd cancel the ball. Apparently it's too late for that. I didn't know he'd phone you."

An old-fashioned sailing ship with rigging and square sails slid through the water toward the wharf. Men scurried over the decks and up the rigging. The ship wasn't sleek and shiny like the other boats around but it had its own charm and beauty. If she focused hard enough on it she could almost forget about the man at her side.

"It doesn't work that way, Princess. Telling him that gets you what you want but there's nothing in it for me. Plus it's a stopgap measure. With no public appearances it'll only buy you a couple of weeks at best."

"You think I don't know that. I was desperate."

"Desperate times call for desperate measures."

"So it would seem." The sailing ship—*Shanghai,* according to the faded green lettering on its side—drew up to the wharf with a grace and precision she wouldn't have thought possible from such an old craft.

"It doesn't have to be a measure taken in desperation."

Logan's voice was low and thoughtful. "You know where you stand with me. After a lifetime of subtlety and underhanded political maneuvering I'll be an uncomplicated change. I also make you look good. We're an intriguing contrast. My rugged looks with your delicate—"

"I'm still going with desperation, pure and simple." She turned to face him. Rugged? Not exactly, but there was something elementally masculine about him. He was nothing like the few men she'd dated, who all had a far more polished veneer of sophistication. Logan was tanned with a lean muscular strength. He had a look about him that said he was a man who made his own way in the world.

"Suit yourself," he said easily. "Desperation works just as well for my purposes."

A man on the *Shanghai,* with arms like Popeye, threw a rope to a teenager on the wharf. The throw went wide and Logan reached for her as she stepped out of the way and came up against him. For just a second his arm tightened around her waist, his shoulder cushioned her head and her body pressed flush against his, her back to his chest. For a second, everything within her stilled. They stepped apart at the same time and turned to watch the teen secure the heavy rope around a bollard. Rebecca used the precious minute to regain her equilibrium after the unintentional intimacy. By that time more people had gathered around them. Touching a hand to her back, Logan guided her out of the small crowd.

Farther along they stopped and watched as out in the harbor a speedboat towed a parasailor. How would it feel soaring high and fast? Too perilous for her tastes and yet here she was contemplating doing something that in its own way was just as daunting.

"I have a list of occasions I need to be seen with you

at," he said, all business. "You're welcome to add more of your own. Within limits."

"Within limits?" Oh, how the balance of power had changed.

"Yes. I don't want you getting all demanding and expecting too much. I won't do the opera and I won't go shopping with you or make nice to your sycophantic friends."

Could she push him in the water? She might lack his strength but she'd have the element of surprise on her side. He could insult her all he liked but she wasn't having him insult her friends. "My friends aren't sycophantic."

"I'm pleased to hear it, for your sake. But I still don't want to have to make nice to them. One spoiled woman is enough."

"Spoiled?"

"Admit that much at least. You're a princess, how could it be otherwise?"

Who knew? Maybe he was right. But it didn't win him any points. "Do you even think this can work?"

"Of course it can," he said with the assurance that seemed inherent in him. Did he ever doubt himself?

"But we're so different."

"That's the beauty of it. Won't it be refreshing to be with someone different? There needn't be any pretense, except in public. And who you can be honest with in return. You can say what you actually think. Nothing will offend me. Nothing will go further than me. It won't damage political relations or cause a diplomatic uproar. Try it."

It was almost tempting. But she'd had a lifetime of keeping her thoughts hidden. And much as she might get some kind of pleasure from pointing out to Logan just how overbearing he was being, not to mention insulting, she wasn't going to do it. She couldn't.

He nudged her with his elbow. "Go on. You can do it. I'll bet you've got a long list of fancy words you'd like to call me. Tell me I'm insufferable and deplorable. You know you want to. I've never been called names by a princess."

"That's the difference between you and me. Good manners. Breeding, some might say."

He looked sharply at her, then guided her out of the way of a kid on bicycle heading straight for them. "What do you know about me?"

They strolled to the other side of the wharf. "I know you're a successful entrepreneur, your primary business is systems design but you have diversified business interests in many countries. But not, I think, New Zealand. And I know you're a friend of Rafe's—which, trust me, is not in itself a recommendation. I also know you think monarchy is an outdated and elitist concept. And that's everything. Apart from the fact that you think extremely highly of yourself. So all in all I know very little. Which is all the more reason to make what you're proposing and I seem to be considering ridiculous."

"You've gone past the stage of considering if you've told your father you're seeing me."

"But only just past it. I'm definitely still in the 'perhaps I've made a mistake and should back out' stage. Is there more I should know before I get any further into this?"

"You mean am I going to give you the reason or excuse you need not to do this? No. I'm certainly not the type of man you've dated before. My background's not great, very common, very poor, in fact, but there's nothing seriously unsavory in it. Nothing that will reflect badly on you."

"I'm pleased to hear it."

"So, let's get this show on the road. We need somewhere private where we can discuss the terms of our arrangement."

"Terms? There are going to be terms?"

"Of course. Think of it as setting out our mutual agreement."

"That's insane. We're only going to be pretend dating."

"But we both need to be clear on what we expect. Because it's not dating. I want all the parameters in place. It's for your own protection as well as mine."

A middle-aged woman on the wharf ahead of them nudged her partner and pointed at Rebecca. As her partner lifted a camera, Logan deftly turned Rebecca around.

He took her hand and walked her toward the land end of the wharf. "I thought you'd want people getting shots of us." She'd half expected to be ambushed by photographers the instant Logan had appeared at her side.

"I do. But not until you've said yes unequivocally. Not until you've admitted to yourself that this is what you need and want to do. After that there will undoubtedly be photos. Lots of them."

"So you're not going to just bully me into this by making it seem the only option?" Did he know he still held her hand? His larger, calloused fingers engulfed hers, his self-assurance evident in even his grip. He was clearly too used to taking control, and she would have to be vigilant about protecting her own interests. No one else was going to do it for her.

"It's not your only option but it is your best option. I've thought it through from both of our points of view. It has to be a win-win situation or it'll never work. But the sooner it starts the sooner it's over. Where are you staying?"

Rebecca sighed. He was right. Delaying beginning only delayed the end. Once they broke up she would be given space and privacy and most importantly time. "Friends have a place on one of the islands."

"George and Therese? I thought they were in South America."

Of course he knew them. Though Therese was one of Rebecca's best friends, George was one of Rafe's. And if Rafe knew them, then odds were that Logan did, too. "They are."

"I'll come out there with you now. A little privacy while we get this hammered out will be a good thing. I want our public appearances carefully planned."

"And no more than necessary."

"My thoughts exactly. See, we're on the same page already. We'll be able to make this work."

For the first time a flicker of hope replaced the desperation. Maybe they really could make it work.

One hour later, shaded by an enormous market umbrella, they sat on sun loungers by the pool. Though summer was officially over, it lingered on in the balmy temperatures. Rebecca, wearing shorts and a loose blouse, sat more upright than Logan with a notepad on her lap and a pen in her hand. Logan had a notepad, too—she'd given it to him. The difference being that his was lying on his face to block the light.

For a man who was reported to work intensely seven days a week, he was currently a picture of relaxation.

"I'll want you with me at my father's ball," she said, doing her best to ignore the expanse of muscled torso hinted at beneath the T-shirt that stretched across his shoulders and chest. *Unfair,* she'd wanted to protest. That, too, was a difference between him and the men she'd dated, this lean purposeful strength that looked to have been honed over a lifetime of activity. He even had a couple of small, intriguing scars, one on a bicep, another across a knuckle. She clenched her hands. She did *not* wonder how her fingertips would feel on those scars or the contours of his chest…

He lifted the notepad from his face and looked at her as he shook his head. "That's too far away. I'll be back in the States by then. I'm speaking at a charity fund-raiser the day before."

"I want you with me at my father's ball. Can you come back for it?" He watched her closely, frowning slightly as he appeared to consider her request. "That's my deal breaker. Remember, Logan—" she smiled as she quoted his own words "—it has to be a win-win for both of us."

"Okay," he said slowly then lowered the papers back to his face, "I'll come back for it."

"These things you want to be seen with me at." She scanned the list, which, as well as dinners at elite restaurants and high-profile gatherings, included black water rafting—she didn't even know what that was—and a polo match.

"Mmm-hmm."

"They're not my usual type of thing. I generally live as quiet a life as I can outside of royal commitments."

"If we did your usual thing no one would seriously believe I was dating you. But you can add your *things* to the list, bearing in mind there's only so much of the orchestra and inane cocktail parties that I can stand." He sat up, placing his feet on either side of the sun lounger, and suddenly he was intense. "Are we doing this or not? Because if it's not, pleasant as this is, I have other places to be. And you, doubtless, will be wanting to come up with another plan to put your father off. Unless of course you want to start working your way through his list?"

He held her gaze. The lesser of two evils? Suddenly she wasn't so sure.

"It's a good plan," he said.

Rebecca swallowed. "I'm in." And with those two tiny words she committed herself to the unknown.

# Four

Logan had had some bad ideas in his time. He hadn't thought this was one of them.

Until now.

He dragged his gaze from Rebecca's curves as she wriggled into the full-length, skintight wet suit and reached behind her back for the zipper. He'd known that beneath the sleek lines of her tailored outfits she had a good body. But the wet suit wasn't tailored.

It clung. Like a second skin.

And it left nothing to the imagination. He was, he admitted, floored. *Good* was a completely inadequate word.

Suddenly he wanted her back in something—anything—that disguised the curve of breast and waist, and flare of hip, the length of her slender legs. Failing that, he wished their guides, standing close in the sparsely furnished briefing room, were a mile away because he'd seen the appreciative glances the young men had directed at her, even as they were explaining the seriousness of their safety procedures.

And that was before the wet suit.

It wasn't that he was being either possessive or protective, it was just that…she seemed to have no idea. Not of how she looked or of how others looked at her. She thought they saw only the princess—not a woman.

The black water rafting—floating on inner tubes through an underground cave system—had been his idea, in part because he'd figured that it would be something completely different for her, something a little out of her comfort zone. And he didn't want her thinking she was the one in control.

Now she was the one making *him* uncomfortable.

She turned her back to him and stepped in front of him. "Can you finish pulling my zip up, please." She sounded exasperated. The zipper rested in that hard-to-reach spot between her shoulder blades, revealing a deep vee of pale skin.

Logan closed his eyes and swallowed. Opening his eyes, he rested one hand on the curve of her waist as he slid the zipper up, closing the vee, sealing away the skin with a mixture of relief and regret.

"Thank you." She stepped away and he let go of the breath that had stayed trapped in his lungs.

He forced his attention back to the guides as they explained what to expect during their trip.

Ten minutes later the four of them stood at the top of a short drop into a dark, watery cavern. The first guide jumped in, landing with a splash. Rebecca, who was supposed to jump in next, took off her headlamp hard hat and fiddled with the adjustment for the chin straps before placing it back on her head.

Was it his imagination or was she looking paler than she had earlier? Logan moved to stand in front of her. He shifted her cold, fumbling fingers out of the way and fastened the strap for her, his fingers brushing her throat and beneath her chin. "Are you okay?" he asked quietly. "We don't have to do this if you don't feel good about it." He'd wanted her out of her comfort zone, but he hadn't meant to frighten her. And fear was what he thought he read in her wide gray eyes. He had to remember that she was sheltered and probably pampered—she was nothing like his brothers, relishing challenges, relishing the chance to vie for superiority. Never backing down.

Not meeting his gaze, she stepped away from him and smiled. But it was a royal smile. Brittle and practiced. "I'm fine." Before he could say anything more she took hold of her inner tube, took a deep breath and stepped off the ledge.

Maybe not so dissimilar to his brothers.

Only much better looking.

She bobbed, seated on her inner tube and floating out of the way as Logan jumped into the frigid water after her, followed by their second guide.

In the quiet, watery darkness, they drifted together through the caves, holding on to one another's inner tubes as their headlamps played over the vaulted caverns adorned with ancient stalactites and stalagmites. The only sound was the occasional drip of water falling from the ceiling above.

They passed through a narrow opening and into a much larger cavern. And on the lead guide's instruction turned off their headlamps. Beside him, Rebecca gasped.

He shared her wonder. The darkness would have been complete but for the tiny lights of thousands of glowworms dotting the unseen limestone surfaces and reflecting in the ink-black water. As it was, he could see nothing of the hand he held up inches from his face.

It was like floating in the night sky.

Rebecca shifted her grip on his inner tube and her hand bumped into his. When she would have shifted her hand away again he took hold of it. He couldn't make out so much as her outline. But the joining of their hands, palm to palm, was a warm point of human contact amid the silent wonder. They maintained that wordless contact for the next twenty minutes of their trip.

It wasn't until they floated out of the darkness and into the light and warmth of day that Rebecca eased free of his grip.

They reached the point where they got out of the water. Logan went first and again held out his hand. "Did you enjoy it?" he asked.

She let him help her from the water. "It was certainly the most unusual first date I've ever been on."

"But did you enjoy it?" he persisted, not accepting her evasion. "It's not a contest, Princess, you don't lose anything by telling me you enjoyed it."

She sighed. "It was amazing. Thank you. I never would have done it otherwise." Gratitude, and traces of their shared wonderment, shined in her eyes.

"You were frightened? At the start?"

"I was…uncomfortable."

Was that princess-speak for terrified? "I'm sorry. I didn't know."

She smiled at him, her regal best. "You weren't supposed to."

Admiration wasn't something he'd expected, or wanted, to feel for her. Nor, he admitted, was the attraction that had him thinking extremely improper thoughts about the very proper princess. The admiration couldn't hurt. The attraction, on the other hand, could well lead him into trouble.

Three days later Rebecca sat with Logan in the plush cabin of his private jet as they flew to San Philippe. News had filtered through to the media that she had been spotted with a mystery man, so they were expecting something of a photographers' welcoming party. She'd even been reported on one site as "cavorting with her new beau at an island retreat." Rebecca, who knew better than to get upset by anything in the media, had taken exception to the use of the word *cavorting.* She never cavorted, and walking along the surf's edge with someone, as she'd done with Logan twice at George and Therese's place, hardly counted as such. Next thing they'd say was that she'd been canoodling.

She finished reading through her notes on her next week's schedule and looked at the man reclining in the armchair across from her as he worked at his laptop, large fingers moving surprisingly deftly over the keyboard, a frown of concentration etching two vertical lines above his nose.

There was no cavorting or canoodling when they were in private. Their relationship was, as agreed, strictly business. In fact, he barely spoke to her. Occasionally she caught him looking at her but his expression revealed nothing of what he thought. And occasionally she caught herself looking at him. Sometimes in an effort to try and figure him out. Sometimes in reluctant fascination.

Upon landing they would part ways and she'd see him

tomorrow for the ballet. Something he'd made clear he wasn't looking forward to. The jet taxied to a halt and Logan shut down his laptop and looked at her. "Are you ready for this?"

"Not really." It didn't feel right. On so many levels. "I've never tried to trick people before."

He stowed the laptop in its case and stood. "What, you've never pretended you were happy when you were actually seething mad, or pretended to look interested when you were bored out of your skull? Never pretended you were fine when you were frightened?"

"Well, yes, but this is different." She made no move to unfasten her seat belt.

Logan nodded at the novel open in her lap. "How long do you think you can hide out in the jet for?"

Reluctantly, she closed the book and slipped it into her tote. "I'm not usually the center of media speculation. That's traditionally been Rafe's role because he was the one getting into scrapes, or Adam's because he's heir to the throne."

He held a hand toward her. "Come on, Princess. I've seen you work vast cheering crowds."

She looked at his hand.

He followed her gaze. "You may as well get used to it." The fact that she *was* getting used to it was part of her problem. He offered his hand with such unthinking ease, as though it were a perfectly normal thing to do. Just another sign of the differences between them. In her world nothing could be done, or said, without thought for the consequences, for the appearances, for the interpretations and implications.

She took the offered hand—still there was that little frisson of sensation that ought to have gone by now—and let him help her to standing, and they walked toward the door. "This'll be a cinch," he said. "We get off the jet, we smile, we wave. A quick kiss. We get in the waiting car together but it drops you off at the palace and takes me to my hotel. We don't see each other again until I pick you up for the ballet."

Rebecca had been analyzing—again—how it felt to rest her hand in his. It was different, but not unpleasant. His firm, dry grip was certainly more appealing than Eduardo's somewhat clammy grip. "Back up a second. What did you say?"

"You go to the palace, I go to my hotel. And then I'll pick you up tomorrow night for the ballet."

They'd reached the open doorway at the top of the stairs and as predicted a crowd had gathered behind a roped-off area.

"That wasn't the bit I meant."

"You meant this, no doubt." He smiled and waved at the crowd and then he slipped an arm around her shoulders, pulled her toward him, bent his head to hers and kissed her—stealing her breath, along with rational thought and the strength in her knees.

Heat.

It scorched through her. His lips were gentle and seeking and in that first surprised instant she forgot to pull back, forgot to analyze, and instead gave herself to the kiss, let herself experience it, the touch of his lips to hers an intimate joining. His warmth surrounded her. His arm around her back shielded and supported her. And held her close. She let herself enjoy—

Enjoy? No.

She pulled back and recognized the sound of a cheer from the crowd. What on earth had she just done?

Logan's gaze sought hers. Something serious in those dark eyes quickly transformed into amusement. He winked.

"Not so icy after all, Princess. In fact, not bad for a first kiss. You tensed up a little at the end, but we can work on that."

"First and last. We won't be *working* on anything." She searched for the *ice* he accused her of. Her refuge. Her armor. She was desperate that he not know that inside she was a shaken mess and anything but icy.

He took her hand and together they descended the steps.

"Last? That'll never convince anyone. I can't let you be right about that."

"The cavorting was bad enough," she said, relieved that the words came out with just the right touch of distance. He laughed, just as he had when he'd first realized her outrage over that word. "I have a reputation and an image to maintain, both while you're here and after you've gone. And I don't think—"

He kissed her again, quick and hard, and came up smiling broadly. "Good. Don't think. Some things are better that way." Dimly, she heard another cheer from the crowd. "That's tomorrow's papers taken care of," he said easily. "I have a reputation to consider, too."

She couldn't push him away, that wouldn't look right at all, and she definitely couldn't touch her fingers to her lips. She withdrew her hand from his, lifted her chin and continued to the bottom of the stairs, Logan at her side.

And she just knew he was smirking.

The chauffeur shut the door behind him and Logan waited. The princess sat on the far side of the seat from him—as far as she could get in the confines of the luxury car. Her gaze—part irritation, part contemplation—was fixed straight ahead as she fed the strap of her handbag back and forth through her fingers. A small frown drew her finely arched eyebrows closer together.

Logan leaned back, crossed one foot over the other and laced his fingers behind his head. Doubtless she'd have something to say about the kiss.

Finally her fingers stilled. She pressed the button that raised the privacy screen and turned to him. "About that kiss."

He smiled.

"It wasn't funny."

"No. It definitely wasn't funny. Intriguing, I would have said. There was distinct potential." And though he was deliberately trying to needle her, he spoke the truth. The kiss, her flash of response, the taste of her, had hit him harder than he could have imagined, had tempted him, had him wondering. "I think with a little practice you'll—"

"We agreed we were going to be seen together. We didn't talk about kissing." Her tone was wintry and controlled, as though at any moment she was going to issue a royal edict banishing him to the Arctic or wherever people from San Philippe got banished to.

"You want people to believe we're in a relationship, don't you?"

"Yes, but…" She looked away, suddenly uncertain.

"But what?"

"Surely we can achieve that without kissing."

"No, we can't. I'll look like your bodyguard or a brother. And that's not the look I'm aiming for."

"We could hold hands and look lovingly at one another."

"We'll be doing that, too."

"Though the looking lovingly is going to be a struggle," she said with feeling as she glared at him. Nothing remotely loving there.

"We'll manage. Listen, Princess. I didn't enjoy it any more than you." At least, he knew he shouldn't have.

Her frown deepened. Clearly she thought he ought to

have enjoyed it and only she had the right to complain. "It's one of those tasks we'll have to endure."

Her jaw worked for several seconds. "Then there need to be some parameters."

"Such as?" He turned more fully toward her. "This ought to be good. Royal kissing rules."

"Only in public."

He nodded. "Fair enough."

"And there should be a time limit."

"Makes sense. Forty-five seconds? A minute?"

She turned to look at him. "Good gracious, no."

His gaze dipped to her lips—the lips in question. Today they were a soft pink that matched the silk of her blouse. Silk that had shifted beneath his hands as he'd held her shoulders to kiss her. "Too short. You'd like more? I guess I can work with that."

"This is no time for joking. I was thinking a maximum of five seconds."

"Now who's joking?"

"I'm perfectly serious."

She certainly looked it, her wide gray eyes intent. But she had to be having him on. "Who kisses for five seconds? I've seen my grandparents kiss for longer. Though," he added, "it was an image that stayed with me for a disturbingly long time."

She said nothing.

"Seriously. Who kisses for five seconds? Your first kiss behind the bike shed at school maybe." But then again she'd probably been to an all-girls school that didn't have a bike shed. Just a limo parking area.

Her gaze went to the window and her fingers again began working at the strap of her handbag.

"Who was the last man you dated, Princess?" Now he was curious. It'd be easy enough to find out. Doubtless there were entire gossip columns devoted to the subject. "Some namby-pamby royal hanger-on?"

"My dating history is nothing you need to know about. You're getting sidetracked. I'll go as high as ten seconds. No more."

"I can have you begging for more."

"You flatter yourself, Logan. Ten seconds will be all I can stomach and I'll be counting every one of those."

"Is that a dare, Princess? A challenge? I've told you how seriously the men in my family take a challenge."

"It was a statement of fact. I'm just warning you. Don't take it as anything else."

"Ten seconds is scarcely enough time to get started."

"You seem to be forgetting that we'll only be kissing to perpetuate a myth. It's not as though we'll really be kissing."

"And when we're eating together are we only going to pretend to eat the food? Pretend to enjoy the food?" he asked.

"No. Of course we'll be eating and if it tastes good…"

"My point exactly."

"But if we're not enjoying the meal we still have to look like we are," she said, desperately trying to regain ground in this conversation. "And we won't prolong meals unnecessarily."

He slid his arm along the backseat of the car, slipped his hand beneath the fall of her blond hair and ran his thumb along her jaw. She tensed beneath his touch, sat a little straighter. "I'm not sure whether you're just trying to fool me or whether you're fooling yourself, as well. I've been watching you." Again he caressed her jaw with his thumb. He waited to see whether she'd move away from his touch. She didn't, but she was doing her best to ignore it. Maybe it was only him who was struggling. Her skin was so soft it invited touch. "You're more tactile than I'd first thought. You like to touch things, textures and shapes. I saw you in that art gallery in New Zealand and in the gift shop afterward. You felt the silks, ran your fingertips over the pottery, you closed your eyes when you sniffed the soaps. And I'm guessing there's a far more sensual nature beneath the cool exterior than you let on."

"You're wrong. I'm naturally cool and reserved and I like it that way."

"I'd say you're naturally passionate and sensuous and you've trained yourself not to reveal it. You keep your thoughts and feelings hidden, but that doesn't mean you don't have them."

He had to stop. He didn't want to be thinking about her as passionate, it was easier—necessary even—to safely categorize her as the cool, reserved woman she categorized herself. Haughty even, that was how he'd thought of her since he'd first met her. Remote. Unfeeling.

But there'd been nothing haughty about the way she'd clung to his hand in the caves, and *haughty* had been the furthest word from his mind when he'd seen her in that full-length wet suit, seen the sensuous curves that were usually hidden beneath tailored skirts and blouses like the one she wore now.

And there had been nothing remote or unfeeling about their kiss.

If he wasn't careful he'd find himself orchestrating public occasions at which to kiss her. And he'd take every one of his allotted seconds. And more. Though who'd be being taught a lesson, her or him, he wasn't entirely sure.

He withdrew his hand from the vulnerable curve of her neck, and dropped it to the seat. Strictly business, he had to remember that, focus on the ultimate goal, buying the subsidiary he needed. That was what mattered here.

The car eased to a stop beneath the hotel's portico.

As the doorman opened his door Logan saw a posse of photographers standing in waiting. "See you tomorrow, *ma chérie*."

"Don't—"

He touched a finger to her lips, then replaced the finger with his mouth, felt her soft, made-for-kissing lips part with a yielding gasp of surprise. So much more mobile than when she was arguing with him.

He didn't have time to savor the taste or feel of her before he lifted his head. "Five seconds." Or thereabouts. He'd lost count after one second but had definitely kept it short. "Short enough for you? I'll work on the getting-you-to-beg-for-more kisses later."

He exited the car, waved to the photographers and strolled into the hotel.

# Five

The tower clock chimed the hour as Rebecca stepped into the blue room at the palace and stopped. Logan, his back to her, stood in front of the window that overlooked the manicured gardens.

She'd had time to gather her thoughts after their... encounters on the steps of the plane and in the car. And she knew he was toying with her. Yes, he was more experienced than she was, but she was no fool.

Slowly, he turned and they surveyed each other. He wore an expertly tailored tuxedo that highlighted a physique that needed no highlighting. The change, after the jeans and T-shirts of the past week, was an intriguing, almost breath-stealing contrast. If she were the sort to have her breath stolen.

As if in defiance of the refinement of the tux, his bow tie dangled untied around his neck and a five o'clock shadow darkened his jaw. He didn't look like any man she'd ever dated.

Or any man she'd ever known.

A raw masculinity always lurked beneath the surface.

He dominated the room, seeming to dwarf the antique furnishings, making them look flimsy and overly ornate. But it was more than just his size—he had a presence, a sheer force of will that cloaked him. He would never blend in or fade into the background as some people did. She'd once walked in on Eduardo in this same room and taken far too long to realize he was even in it.

Yet she couldn't let Logan exercise that will on her or she'd find herself trampled. Most people kept their distance from her, and she relied on that fact. Logan seemed to want to push boundaries. It was in his nature. But now that he'd made her aware of that with his kisses, she was better prepared to deal with him. The kisses had caught her off guard. That was the only reason she'd found herself responding, almost…wanting. His arm, powerful yet gentle as he'd swept it around her shoulders, pulling her to him, against him, had made her feel—

"Princess." Logan nodded.

Her thoughts snapped back to the present and the decision she'd made to maintain her distance from him, to show him she was in control of herself, at least. She'd quickly realized she'd never have a hope of exercising any control over Logan. "Are you always going to call me that?" She hated the formality of that label coming from him, carrying, as she knew it did, his unflattering sentiments on royalty.

"I thought you'd ruled out Sweet Thing and Punkin?"

She met the challenge in his dark gaze. "I was thinking *Rebecca* might do."

"Or Becs or Becky?"

"Or just Rebecca," she said, patiently refusing to react.

"No."

"No?"

"It's not right. I'm not sure what is. I'll let you know when I figure it out."

"How can you tell me my name's not right and that you'll let me know when you figure out what is? It's *my* name. Who are you to say otherwise?"

"My apologies." He paused. "Princess. Forgive my presumption." One side of his mouth quirked up in a grin. He was enjoying himself immensely, getting pleasure from riling her.

"I'll *let you know* when you're forgiven." She couldn't help but respond to that grin. "In the meantime we ought to get going."

Logan crossed to her and held out his arm.

"Your bow tie." She gestured to the dark strip of fabric that dangled around his neck. "Do you want me to call someone to tie it for you?"

His eyes narrowed on her and he lifted his hands, buttoned the top button of his dress shirt and with practiced movements began tying the bow. "Is there a mirror in here?" he asked when he was all but done.

"No."

He finished the knot. "Is it even?"

"Almost. You just need to tug that side—" she pointed to left of the bow "—out a little."

He adjusted it but unbalanced it the other way. He looked at her and she shook her head.

"Could you?" he asked. "It's tricky without a mirror." She could see in his eyes that he expected her to refuse.

Rebecca hesitated then stepped closer. Apparently she was little better than his brothers at turning down an unspoken dare.

He'd helped her with her chin strap at the rafting, this was no different. Only then she hadn't been quite so aware of the breadth of his chest or his scent. He hadn't been wearing the cologne—citrusy and subtly spicy—that he wore now.

Nor, then, had he yet kissed her.

So she hadn't been thinking of his lips, the precise full shape of them. And she wouldn't now. She reached up, the back of her hands brushed the underside of his jaw and she felt the gentle abrasion of hours-old beard. She pulled her hands away and stepped back, ignoring his grin.

"Perfect," she said, focusing her gaze on the black bow tie.

"Thank you. You're not too bad yourself."

"I was referring to the bow tie."

"And I was referring to you. You look…beautiful."

Rebecca opened her mouth, suddenly lost for words at the sincerity in his voice and eyes.

She'd spent an inordinately long time deciding what to wear this evening. As a princess her dress was scrutinized at the best of times. But tonight she had to send the right message to the public and be careful not to send the wrong message to Logan. She didn't want him to think she'd dressed for him. After trying on innumerable outfits she'd gone back to her first choice—a simple ice-blue gown beaded with tiny crystals. It had a scooped neckline at the front and at the back it dipped rather more daringly. The slim-fitting skirt fell to the floor with a slit in the side— nothing too revealing—that allowed her to walk.

"Thank you," she said quietly. Please don't let that be a blush she could feel heating her face.

He held out his arm. "Shall we?"

Rebecca hesitated then looped her arm through his, felt the fabric of his suit shift over the muscles of his forearm.

"You spoke to my father this morning?" she asked, as much to distract herself from his nearness as anything else.

"Yes. And he warned me, very diplomatically, that if I hurt you in any way I'll suffer the consequences of his enduring wrath."

She nodded. "He has that talk with anyone who wants to date me."

"It's very effective."

"You're not…"

"No. It'd take more than that to scare me off."

"You wouldn't be the first one." Several relationships she'd had hopes and dreams for had faltered at that hurdle.

He glanced at her. "Then the ones who were scared off weren't worthy."

"Thank you. But you do remember that for our plan to work I need to look heartbroken. Dad could turn people against you."

"I remember. But our breakup will be mutual. You'll assure him of that. And I'll be just as heartbroken as you," he said lightly. "Though of course I'll hide it better."

She sat in the Ferrari's passenger seat. "I usually have a royal car take me to formal engagements like this one."

"And I prefer to drive. I like the control."

"Figures."

His lips twitched.

What it meant for Rebecca was that rather than being the width of a broad seat away from him she was the width of a gear stick away. And dependent on him. On the plus side it meant that, with his hands occupied with the steering wheel and gearshift, he couldn't slide his hand behind her neck as he'd done yesterday in the car. Couldn't disconcert her that way.

He pulled to a stop in front of the royal theater house.

A valet opened her door and Rebecca got out. It was also harder to exit a low-slung Ferrari with the appropriate royal dignity than it was a limousine. But she managed.

Logan tossed his keys to the valet and approached, his gaze narrowed intently on her, seeming to focus on her lips, and a smile played about his eyes.

"Don't even think about it," she whispered as he stopped in front of her.

"About what?"

"You were going to kiss me."

Dark eyebrows lifted. "Actually, no, but if it's what you want."

Had he not been intending to kiss her? Was that her imagination? "It's not what I want," she insisted. "We've already kissed enough."

"Was that in the Royal Kissing Rules, frequency as well as duration? I'm sure I don't remember."

"You remember."

He reached for her hand, and interlaced his fingers with hers. An intimate joining, his larger fingers stretching hers apart. "A curious question, Princess. So if I understand it—" they began walking the stairs to the grand, arched building "—in your world, lovers kiss for no more than five seconds and no more than once a day?"

"No, but…we're not lovers."

"It's what we want people to think, isn't it?"

"No," she said more abruptly than she'd intended, something like fear making her blurt the word out.

He stopped walking and turned to her. "No?"

"They can…wonder, they can perhaps guess or assume but…"

He leaned closer. "So they can wonder if when I get you home—" his words were low, barely more than a whisper "—I'll be peeling this beautiful dress off your exquisite body, baring your pale skin to the moonlight and touching my hands, my lips—"

"Stop it."

Behind a cordoned-off area flashes were popping wildly as they stood halfway up the stairs having a conversation in which she was completely out of her depth.

"What is it that frightens you, *ma chérie?*" As if sensing her desire to run, his hand tightened around hers. "No one is close enough to hear."

Out of her depth and getting deeper. "Nothing frightens me," she lied.

"Nothing? Oh, to be you."

"Logan." She tugged at his hand. "Now isn't the time or the place."

"Perhaps not."

Slowly he turned and Rebecca used the opportunity to disengage her hand. Which only meant that as they reached the top of the stairs and approached the door he could lift his hand to her back, rest warm, blunt fingers along her spine. The images that she'd conjured in her mind—Logan peeling off her dress, touching her skin with those large calloused hands—returned, sending a bolt of unwanted yearning through her.

The ballet was... Rebecca couldn't say what it was. She barely knew which ballet was being performed, and she couldn't say whether it was being performed well. It was the royal ballet company so one could make assumptions, but her lack of focus had been complete. Logan—his words, his actions, his proximity—prevented coherent thought. Though she'd refused to look at him through the first act of the ballet, all her thoughts were on him, the way he disconcerted her—deliberately—as he'd done tonight. The way he took what should have been ordinary conversation and twisted it. The way he made her think thoughts she didn't want to think. The way just his fingers interlaced with hers made her think of other joinings and interlacings.

He had her—usually serene and in control—tied in knots, and she didn't know how to manage it, how to untangle herself, or her thoughts.

At a small sound beside her she turned. Logan sat low in his seat, his head tipped back and his eyes…closed! The sound had been a gentle snore. It had also caught her sister-in-law's attention. Lexie, sitting on Logan's other side, looked from Logan to Rebecca and then, suppressing a grin, returned her attention to the ballet. Lexie might think it funny but Adam, here with the Swedish ambassador's daughter, would not. He took his duties seriously. Some would say too seriously, the weight of his future responsibilities already weighing heavily. It had been a long time since she'd heard her brother's laughter and the last thing she wanted to do was call down his censure on her now.

Rebecca elbowed Logan in the arm. Slowly, he opened his eyes, then narrowed them on her. "What was that for?"

"What was it for? You were sleeping," she hissed. She'd never hissed in her life.

"I wasn't sleeping. I was reliving one of those beautiful earlier moments in my head."

"You were snoring."

Even in the dim light of the theater she could see the amusement in his eyes as he feigned interest and asked, "So, this new lead dancer…what do you think of her?"

Rebecca turned back in her seat.

"Nice legs."

"You're not supposed to be looking at her legs."

"I meant yours."

She looked down to see that with her twisting in her seat the side split in her dress had ridden up and parted, revealing a glimpse of her thigh. Which was still vastly more than she wanted Logan looking at. She rearranged the dress so that it sat properly.

He leaned closer. "I'm still imagining taking it off you."

Maybe she shouldn't have woken him.

At the intermission he took her hand and walked with her to the royal lounge. When he would have approached a cluster of people that included her brothers and Eduardo she steered him instead to a quiet corner of the room.

Still holding her hand, he turned to her. "You want to make out? Here? Do you think that's really appropriate?"

He took far too much pleasure in needling her. "It'd be more appropriate than me killing you. Here." She tried to slide her hand from his but his grasp tightened.

"So you do want to make out?" His gaze dropped to her lips then flicked to the split in her dress before coming back to connect with hers. Deliberately provocative. He rubbed his thumb over the back of her hand.

"No. But I do want to kill you," she said, smiling sweetly for the benefit on any watchers.

"Because?" His thumb probed gently between her fingers.

And Rebecca had to fight to keep her focus on what she was saying and not on what he was doing. "You fell asleep. And you made me hiss."

"Bet I can make you sizzle, too."

"Be serious." She didn't want to contemplate that assertion for fear that he might be right. "We're talking about you falling asleep during the ballet."

"And that's a capital offense in San Philippe?"

"I'm a patron of the ballet," she said in a low voice.

"I'm so sorry."

For a moment she almost believed he was sincere in

his regret. He took two champagne flutes from a hovering waiter and passed one to her.

"That must be awful for you. Do you have to come very often?"

"I love the ballet."

"You do?" For the first time this evening she knew she was hearing genuine sentiment—surprise—in his question.

Eduardo appeared at Logan's side. She'd been so intent on Logan that she hadn't seen him approach. "Rebecca." He nodded and gave a small tight smile. "Logan."

She knew the two men had met previously. She just didn't think they'd got along. Even looking at them now, and even both good-looking and dressed in tuxedos, they were polar opposites. Eduardo lean and fair, Logan with his darker coloring and more powerful build.

"How are you enjoying the ballet, Logan? I wouldn't have thought it was your thing." Eduardo had been raised in the same circles she had, privileged and cultured—a world away from the blue-collar background Logan had told her a little of, and of which he was so proud. Eduardo was basically a decent man when things were going his way, but he could be cold and calculating and could, at times, be a complete and utter prat. She had the feeling now might be one of those times. She'd refused his offer to accompany her to this very ballet.

Logan darted a glance at Rebecca, amusement in those dark eyes of his, and she tried to convey with her gaze that she needed him to take this seriously. Her family and friends, many surreptitiously watching, needed to be convinced that they really were in a relationship. That they had things in common.

"I'm enjoying it almost as much as I'm enjoying Becs's company." Hopefully only she knew that meant not at all.

"Becs?" Eduardo repeated disapprovingly, echoing Rebecca's surprise. Logan moved so that he stood beside her. He lifted his hand and touched the bare skin of her back, sending a shiver coursing through her. She couldn't step away from the touch without destroying the image they wanted to create. And a part of her—a small rebellious part—didn't want to. His fingers were warm and gentle. His touch possessive. Rebecca took a sip of champagne.

Eduardo looked intently at Logan for long seconds. "I heard you two were an item," he said. "I'll admit I didn't believe it until I saw you here together."

"We ran into each other in New Zealand. Becs hasn't been able to tear herself from my side since." His fingers trailed up and down her spine. He couldn't know the strange effect that movement had on her, causing heat to coil and swirl low within her. She tried to ease just a little away from him, but he spread his fingers and pulled her in closer. She felt the imprint of his palm and of each fingertip. She couldn't be certain but she thought perhaps those fingertips had slipped beneath the edge of the back of her dress. And again, that image that he'd planted outside on the steps, of him peeling her dress off, came back to her. Those large calloused hands of his that she knew, from watching him at his laptop and tying his bow tie, could also be deft and clever.

Rebecca swallowed another sip of champagne and marshaled her errant thoughts as she tried to force the heat from her face. "He's joking, of course. Logan does so love to twist things. He's the one who can't seem to let go of me. I was scarcely aware of him until he invited me to dinner that first night."

"Ahh, but you're aware of me now, aren't you, *ma chérie?*" His thumb circled slowly.

Far too aware.

Rebecca's gaze latched on to the distant entrance to the restrooms. She hadn't hidden out in a restroom since her early, awkward teenage years, but the thought of doing so at this instant was infinitely tempting. But, she took a deep breath. Logan was watching her, testing her, seeing how far he could push her and she wasn't going to give him the satisfaction of running away. She looked over her shoulder at him. "You're certainly impossible to ignore." Her comment could be interpreted as a compliment…or not.

Her deliberately ambiguous response seemed to please him because he smiled. A smile that crinkled the skin around his eyes. She found herself smiling back and holding his gaze for the longest time, losing herself in the depths that were as tempting and sinful as chocolate. There was something so different, so…invigorating in the way he teased her, and the way he allowed and encouraged her to tease him back.

Eduardo cleared his throat. "How are the leBlanc negotiations coming along?"

Logan's smile vanished and he swung his gaze to Eduardo. "I never discuss business when I'm on a date with a beautiful woman."

"Of course not," Eduardo said, something smug and unattractive in his eyes. "And I'm interrupting." With a small bow he excused himself.

Logan dropped his hand from her back.

Rebecca stepped a little away from him, needing more air, more space. "Shall we go back in? I don't know that I'm ready for more performances like that." She put her champagne flute on a passing waiter's tray.

"But you're a natural. If I didn't know better I would

have thought there was real warmth, almost heat, in that gaze."

Rebecca lifted her chin. "Then it's a good thing you do know better." His laughter was quiet and deep as he offered her his arm and they began walking. Beneath her palm she felt the solid strength of a powerful forearm.

"What's Eduardo's interest in leBlanc?"

She lifted a shoulder. "Probably his new stepfather."

"Who is...?"

They reached their seats and she slid her hand from his arm. "Theo Summerfield."

"Damn."

"That's a problem?"

"No. But I should have known. I hadn't made the connection." He stood while he waited for her to sit in one of the plush red seats then lowered himself beside her.

"Theo is Eduardo's mother's fourth husband. And Eduardo is the son of her second. It's not easy to keep track of."

"No. But it's the sort of thing I do like to keep track of."

"Know your opposition?"

"Exactly. For instance, I did know that you and pretty boy—"

"Eduardo."

"That you and Eduardo were once an item."

He knew her dating history? Not that it required extensive research or even a particularly good memory. In stark contrast to what she knew of him, her list of suitors was short. "Not an item. We went out. Twice." She really should have learned after the first time. All Eduardo had wanted was the kudos for dating a princess. He still did. He had political aspirations. And from what she knew, his stepfather was currently in the process of seeking "By

Royal Appointment" endorsement for his line of breakfast foods. He too wanted her to date Eduardo.

"It's beginning to make sense," Logan said.

"What is?"

"The 'once a day and for five seconds only' rule you have."

She wanted to disagree with him but maybe he was right. The rules she'd tried to establish with Logan had been based on her previous—limited—experience. She'd only dated men who didn't push boundaries, who respected—too much—her position, failing to see who she was inside. Men who neither tempted nor taunted her.

But the thought that Logan had *researched* her was disconcerting on several levels. "Does this interest you appear to have in my social life mean you see me as the opposition?"

He leaned closer. "No. Not the opposition. But I make a point of knowing how things stand with the people I'm… dealing with. We're allies now, remember."

"Now, yes. Uneasy allies, I might add."

He shrugged and slipped his arm behind her shoulders, the fabric of his suit brushing against her skin. "But allies nonetheless. And I'm starting to think things might not always be uneasy. That in fact, some things might be very easy and enjoyable."

"That's right. The things that don't require us to talk. As I recall I'm allowed to sit next to you and whisper in your ear at the rowing regatta."

"There are other things that wouldn't require us to talk." His thumb moved slowly over her shoulder.

And the heat she'd thought she'd tamped down…stirred. "This is all some kind of game to you, isn't it? Like chess and you see me as a pawn."

"That's one way of looking at it. But I'd have to see you as the queen, don't you think? Do you play?"

"Not if I can avoid it. Chess is more Adam's game. I used to play with him but I didn't look far enough ahead and kept falling into the traps he'd set." The stray notes of the string section of the orchestra retuning violins and cellos sounded. "Do you play?" Did he set traps? Was she walking unwittingly into one?

"Occasionally. It's not really my thing, either. Takes too long."

"You played with your brothers?"

He nodded, offering nothing further. For some reason his upbringing, his brothers and the relationship they had intrigued her. Probably because she knew it would be so utterly different from her own experience of family life—brought up in a castle, largely by nannies and then a private all-girls school. The lights dimmed and the curtain rose.

"What about your parents?" He'd mentioned brothers several times but never a mother or father.

"Shh. It's starting."

"And you don't want to miss a thing?"

His lips stretched into a grin as he slid a little lower in his seat.

"What are you doing?"

"Getting comfortable."

The delicate strains of flute music twirled through the theater. "Don't you dare fall asleep," she said quietly.

"I wouldn't dream of it."

"You might not dream of it but you might actually do it."

He smiled, a glimpse of white teeth. "Help me stay awake then."

"What do you want me to do?"

"Too innocent." His smile widened as he raised an eyebrow and his gaze dipped to her legs, and the glimpse of thigh revealed by her dress.

Rebecca tugged her dress down a little. "Be serious."

"I was. I'll be fine. Just hold my hand."

As the dancers pirouetted onto the stage she slipped her hand into the one he held out for her, too enamored as always by that simple touch, so different than any other.

Logan drove back to the palace in silence. Floodlit gravel crunched beneath the wheels as he pulled to a stop in front of a discreet entrance to the towering west wing. Discreet it might be—but only in comparison to the main entrance. The armed, uniformed guards at the door were a whole new spin on Daddy waiting up in the porch rocker with a shotgun across his lap. Daddy might not be here in person but his eyes and ears and his firepower were. Logan grinned. He'd had his share of encounters with protective daddies. None quite of the caliber of Rebecca's father, though. But he'd never been one to back down in the face of a challenge.

Making sure the doors were locked—he didn't want an enthusiastic valet, or overly suspicious guard interrupting—he turned to her. Read and relished the uncertainty in her eyes. It didn't take a genius to figure out that she may not have had the same level of experience as he did. Conflicting urges surprised him. The urge to protect her vied with the urge to show her a world he suspected she knew little about, to show her things about herself she might not even know. And, of course, there was the urge to explore further what they'd begun on the steps of the plane.

She averted her gaze. "Thank you."

"Thank you?" So polite. So royal. So challenging. Logan slid his hand behind her neck. Lustrous hair caressed the back of his hand, silky skin lay beneath his fingers. A world of sensation at his fingertips.

If they had, as she'd suggested, taken a royal car they would have had the entire drive back and the entire comfortable width of the Bentley's backseat.

She glanced at him but then looked back out the windshield, her delicate throat moving as she swallowed. "For coming to the ballet. I know it wasn't—"

He did what he'd wanted to do the entire drive home, the entire evening actually, since the moment he'd first seen her in that dress. He dropped his other hand, slipped it through the split in her gown, the split that had worked its way to midthigh. He touched sleek skin only a little above her knee and still had to suppress his groan even as he enjoyed her breathless gasp.

She turned to him, her eyes wide with surprise and something more. Curiosity? Temptation?

She opened her mouth and he covered her lips with his before she could say anything. Captured her words, her breath. She was too full of questions and protests and analysis. Too reluctant to trust in the obvious. The simple. And the obvious and the simple were the heat that flamed right here and right now as his tongue found and teased hers. As he felt her tentative return exploration. Not just her tongue but the hand that snaked around his neck, pulling him closer, threading into his hair.

Kissing her was like kissing a dream, effortless perfection, no awareness of anything other than their simple joining and sharing, mouths that fit as though made only for each other. She sighed into him, deepening the kiss. Drugging him with her taste, her scent.

They had something.

Something far more potent than he'd even thought to consider.

*She* was far more potent to him than he'd thought to consider. He, who liked to think through all the possible scenarios, had bought in to the carefully constructed portrayal of her as someone without spontaneity, without passion. The Ice Princess.

How wrong he'd been.

The Ice Princess currently had him heading toward fever point. And it wasn't just him. She moved beneath him, arching and pressing. Her body soft and yielding against his and yet straining to get closer. Her mouth beneath his, supple and seeking, her leg beneath his palm, moving ever so slightly away from the other, inviting access. Another gasp escaped her as he slid his hand farther up the soft skin, his thumb finding the thin silken barrier, pressing against it. He wanted it all—her surprise, her passion. The taste of her, the feel of her. Only after lifting her hips to press against him in return did she seem to realize what she was doing. Her legs snapped back together, trapping his hand in the velvet warmth between them in an exquisite prison.

Logan lifted his head. The shock and desire in her parted lips and in her wide eyes reflected his own.

Who knew?

He lifted a corner of his mouth in as much of a smile as he could manage right now. While his heart still pounded and blood still rushed in his veins.

"How did you do that?" she whispered.

"That wasn't me, sweetheart, that was you." He curved his palm where it lay blissfully snared against her thigh. Then, regretting the necessity, he withdrew it.

"No."

He nodded.

"No." She refused to believe. "That was you. It had to be. Because if it was me it would have…"

"Would have what?"

"Happened before," she said with a confused frown. "I have to go." She reached for the door handle.

"Leave it. I'll get your door." He couldn't tell her that the plunge into the conflagration that just touching his lips to hers had caused was new and different for him, too. He'd been there before. But not like this, blindsided by the chemistry, insensible to anything else.

"It's okay." She raised her hand. About to signal a doorman? "One of the—"

"I'll get it." He cut her off. "It's what I do when I bring a woman home from a date."

"Oh."

Though she was like no other woman and this was like no date he'd ever been on before. He was out and walking around the front of the car before she could change her mind. Opening her door he reached for her. She didn't take his hand. "Afraid of me, Princess?"

She straightened to her full height. Even in her heels she was only somewhere between his chin and his nose. But somehow she managed to look down her nose. "Yes, Logan. I think I am." A gentle breeze swept a tendril of hair across her lips. She reached for it before he could and tucked it behind her ear, denying him that excuse of touching her further.

Her candor surprised him. He'd expected her to bluff her way out with royal composure. Not to admit that she was unsettled. Afraid of him. He reached for the hands she'd kept from him. "Don't be." Soon they would be someplace where they had time to explore what sizzled between them. Where he had time to explore *her*.

"I don't see how I can't be. That…" She inclined her head toward the car, the jerky movement a far cry from her normal gracefulness. "That. You. What happened. The way I forgot about everything."

"That's what's supposed to happen when you kiss someone." Admittedly it didn't always. And almost never so completely and so quickly.

"In books."

"In life." There was a faint tremor to the hands he held. Again the conflict. Soothe away the tremors or make her tremble all over? For him.

"Not to me."

"Ever?"

She shook her head. Her eyelids dropped, shielding her gaze. In the distance the tower clock chimed.

That it hadn't happened before, but had happened with him, pleased him inordinately.

"I stay in control. It's who I am. It's everything." She said the words with a vehemence that was perhaps meant to convince herself as well as him.

He waited until she looked back at him, caught and held her gaze. So serious, so wary. "I can respect that. I like control, too. But there are times when it's overrated and times when it's just plain wrong." He dropped his voice. "Like when making love." Her eyelids lowered. And he knew that, like him, she, too, was imagining what that might be like between them. He'd never expected things to get this far this fast between them, like fireworks bursting into life at the touch of a match, flaming gloriously, belying a simple exterior.

She took a step back from him, gave a small shake to her head, but tellingly left her hands in his and her eyes on his face—searching for something. Confirmation, reassurance, promise? He didn't know which or how much of any he could give her. He just knew that against reason and judgment he wanted—almost desperately—to make love with her. And when they did there would be nothing controlled about it.

Dropping one hand, he led her to her door and she turned to him. "Good night." She was struggling to put back in place the barriers they'd broken through tonight. She might not know it but they were broken for good. Some fences couldn't be mended.

"Good night? You're not inviting me in?" He kept his tone light, teasing. He didn't want to frighten her with the sudden intensity of his desire for her, and he didn't want her to realize his weakness for her. She still had some figuring out to do. For that matter, if he was sensible, so did he.

The crown prince's warning and his concerns for his daughter rang in Logan's ears. If they took this further the potential for hurt grew exponentially. And the last thing he wanted to do was hurt her.

"No." Her eyes darted to the various staff standing discreet distances away, and doing their best to appear invisible. "It wouldn't be appropriate."

He leaned in and brushed his lips over hers. Kissed her jaw once. Then whispered in her ear, even as he inhaled one last breath of her scent and spoke on impulse, "No. I'd make sure it was anything but appropriate."

# Six

Rebecca finally had it figured out by the time she finished her shower the next morning. She ought to have—she'd spent enough hours tossing and turning through the night thinking of Logan and their…situation. His kisses and what they did to her. She dried herself off, hopping as she patted the towel beneath her foot. He was so unlike any other man she'd known that he kept her off balance.

Planting her feet firmly on the cool marble she looked sternly in the mirror, willing conviction and strength into her expression. Sometimes you just had to look like you were in control to convince other people you were and even to believe it yourself. It wasn't, however, a strategy that was working today.

Because of the unpredictable impact Logan had on her thought processes, on her senses and even on her body, she would have to keep him at a distance emotionally. Which shouldn't be too hard because he didn't strike her as the sort to encourage deep emotions.

She dropped the towel and reached for the body lotion. In their remaining weeks together, an insistent voice whispered, maybe he could teach her...things, show her...things. Things that weren't deep and meaningful or emotional, but things that were shallow and physical. Things no one had ever thought to show a princess and things a princess had never thought, or dared to ask. They would have their scheduled dates and there would be private moments.

Like last night.

She could ask him to...tutor her.

She smoothed the scented lotion on her legs and remembered the touch of Logan's palm on her thigh in the darkness. Gently abrasive and fiercely seductive. Banishing the recollection she pulled silk underwear on— and was reminded again.

She caught her reflection, the uncertainty on her face, in the full-length mirror. She turned to the side, stood straighter. It was a long time since she'd really looked at herself. She wasn't tall and willowy like the model girlfriends her brother dated or the type of women Logan had gravitated toward when she'd watched him socially. But there was nothing overtly wrong with her, nothing that makeup and well-tailored clothes couldn't compensate for. And she had to hope that within the confines of their agreement, what she could offer him in return was enough.

She pulled her hair back into a ponytail and examined the effect. Maybe she could pretend for a time to be normal, to be the type of woman a man like him, who, despite phenomenal financial success, still enjoyed life's simple pleasures, might go out with.

Because clearly the woman she actually was, a princess

whose life was governed by rules and protocol, was not that type of woman.

She tried to imagine herself in jeans and a T-shirt.

She'd always been curious about what life outside the confines of her role might be like. Logan, more than any other man she knew, could give her a taste of that. If in doing so she kept her father's matchmaking at bay and helped Logan achieve what he wanted in San Philippe, then it was, as he'd called it, a win-win situation.

Her phone rang. Logan's number showed on the screen. As if she'd conjured him. Had he been thinking of her?

"I need to see you again," he said when she answered. "Soon."

Her heart gave a girlish flutter at his use of the word *need.* Ridiculous. She wasn't a teenager. She was supposed to be mature and dignified. At all times. Rebecca looked away from the bright hope in her reflection. Away from the fact that she wore only her underwear while she was speaking to him. A concept that seemed almost scandalous and, well, just a little bit exciting. As were his words.

"We could go out to dinner tonight," she suggested.

"It needs to be something your father will be present at."

The glimmering bubble of delusion burst. Rebecca turned away from the mirror. "Ah."

"I have an unscheduled meeting with leBlanc Industries next week. And one of the members of the board of directors and the main opponent to leBlanc signing with me will be there. He's an ardent royalist believing firmly in tradition and connections. If I've been seen with you *and* your father, it'll help my cause."

She was a means to an end for Logan. She had to remember that. This was business for him. "He's careful about being seen to sanction individuals."

"But he'd do it for you?"

"He might, yes." He would if she asked.

"I'm not asking for an audience with him, just to be seen with you, at something he's at."

This was their agreement. Rebecca pushed aside her disappointment and mentally sifted through what she could remember of her schedule, specifically events at which her father would also be present. "There's not much coming up that you could attend."

"I don't care what it is. It just needs to be soon."

Walking through to her bedroom, she called up her schedule on her organizer. "There is one thing on this Thursday afternoon, and it's semipublic so my father won't be too concerned about you being there," she said hesitantly, "but I don't know that it's your kind of thing."

"Whatever it is. Count me in."

"Thank you. I think." Logan spoke the words through partially gritted teeth and Rebecca smiled.

He sat by her side under the white silk canopy shading the temporary stage. A "new rose" walk in the San Philippe botanical gardens was being dedicated today and each of the seven rose breeders who'd developed one of the feature roses in the walk had been invited to explain the genesis and naming of each flower. They were passionate about their craft and their blooms. And each one of them strove to outdo the others, to demonstrate his or her depth of skill and knowledge, part science, part art, part magic.

But all seven of them speaking, it was too much, even for her. Most of the guests did their best to look riveted but many were fidgeting. And those were just the ones Rebecca could see from her elevated position. Doubtless there were those fighting sleep in the back rows warmed by the sun and lulled by the speakers.

Which reminded her of Logan. Worried, she glanced at him. His eyes were open though a little glazed. Sensing her scrutiny, he leaned closer, his shoulder brushing against hers. His scent tempting, beguiling, making her want to close her eyes and inhale deeply. "What are you thinking about?" she asked.

"I was wondering how the Cubs will do this season."

Figured he wouldn't be contemplating the subtleties of rose breeding. Not that she blamed him. She'd like to see a baseball game one day. See what all the fuss was about. She imagined sitting next to Logan at a game as opposed to the opening of a rose walk, and didn't need any special knowledge to know it would be an entirely different experience, *he* would be a different man. Keyed up, sitting forward in his seat. "If it keeps you from snoring I guess it's a good thing."

"What do you think about, Princess, when you're trying to look interested in something that holds no interest for you? What are you thinking about now?"

Him. His shoulder so close to hers. His jaw, strong and masculine. "I try to find something of interest in what I'm supposed to be doing. It's usually possible." Usually. But not always. Occasionally the distractions were too great.

He nodded toward the podium. "I take it there would have been bloodshed if just one of the esteemed rose breeders had been given the privilege of addressing a royal audience."

"You have no idea."

"Isn't it taking political correctness a little too far?"

"This is nothing," she said quietly. "The royal secretaries devote significant portions of their days, their lives even, to making sure people are treated evenly. That no one is seen to receive undue favor without warrant, and that those who warrant it are given it."

The scent of roses drifted on the warm breeze. The third speaker was an internationally respected expert but he was no orator, his voice an unfortunate monotone.

"It's a challenge, isn't it? One of those impossible fairy-tale tasks set by kings in order that no one actually be able to win the hand of his daughter. Given the choice I'd rather brave the fire-breathing dragon. This one feels more like trying to drain the undrainable well."

"The worthy ones always managed it." As a young girl she'd daydreamed about her own knight in shining armor, someone who'd slay dragons for her or tirelessly drain the well.

Logan slid his sunglasses on and settled a little deeper into his seat. Speaking of daydreams... She leaned closer, caught a hint of his scent, far more tempting than that of roses. "Do not go to sleep again. It's broad daylight."

He tapped the side of the sunglasses. "No one will be able to tell."

Maybe he was teasing her; after all, this was supposed to be important to him. The trouble with Logan was that she couldn't be sure. She nudged him with her elbow, hoping the movement was subtle enough to avoid detection by anyone watching. "It'll be over soon."

"Not soon enough. Are you a patron of the rose breeders' association?" He settled lower still.

"No." She nudged a little more forcefully.

"Then it doesn't matter so much." He crossed his long legs in front of him at the ankles.

"It matters. It always matters."

He shook his head. "How do you do it, sit through these things so serenely? So...awake? Forty minutes and I'm more than ready to make a run for it."

"Coffee and training. Don't forget you insisted on attending. And trust me, if you fall asleep you'll definitely make the papers but not for the reasons you're wanting."

He sat a little straighter, but then shuddered as the speaker droned on. "How do you bear it?"

"It's my job."

"And you can't even quit."

No. She couldn't quit. Though the thought had never occurred to her. It was who she was. You couldn't quit being yourself. It left you purposeless. With no identity. Didn't it?

"We're definitely going to be doing something off my list next. The ballet and a rose garden back-to-back is too much like torture."

"You wanted this."

"I know. That makes it worse," he said with such feeling she almost felt sorry for him.

"Next is polo. That's yours."

"Better. Horses, competition, sweat, noise. It couldn't get much different."

"The rose breeders are fiercely competitive. There have been accusations of theft and sabotage in the past."

"Now, that would be more interesting." The speaker sat down to polite applause. Another stood. "How much longer will this go on?"

"It'll get faster now. The next few speakers aren't quite so fond of the sound of their own voices."

He stifled a yawn. "That woman in the front row, the one with the enormous hat."

Rebecca knew instantly who he was referring to. Her hat, smothered in apricot silk roses, was possibly the largest sun hat she had ever seen. And she'd seen a lot of hats. The two people seated on either side of her were leaning subtly outward to avoid hitting it. "Mrs. Smythe-

Robinson. She loves all things royal, knows more about us than I do even, and her second love is gardening."

"I thought maybe she was planning on making a run for it, that the hat was camouflage. You know, crouch down amongst the bushes and tiptoe for the exit."

Rebecca stifled her smile at the thought of the portly Mrs. Smythe-Robinson, a stickler for protocol, doing any such thing.

"But if she's not going to use it, I say we do. I'll create a diversion, you get the hat, it's big enough for both of us, and we make a run for it."

Laughter hiccupped within her. She oughtn't to be laughing. These things were not supposed to be funny. But it was such a change to be sitting with someone who didn't take them seriously and didn't even pretend to.

"I thought you needed to be seen with my father."

"Photographers snapped us arriving together. Your father's here. The right connections will be made." A slide show, set to orchestral music, began playing on the screen to the side. "What do you say? On three?" he asked.

She focused on her duties, her responsibilities—now was not the time to let him distract her. "There's a ribbon to cut."

He sagged back into his seat. "The ribbon cutting is your job, I take it?"

She nodded. "It's a hereditary role." And she didn't need to ask how insignificant that would look to someone who ran a multinational corporation he'd founded after dropping out of college. "I took over after my mother died." The mother whose grace and warmth had added elegance to whatever she did. The mother who'd died when Rebecca was a child.

His hand closed around hers. Was that sympathy? "So

you're pretty handy with knives and scissors," he said half a minute later.

"Just some of my many talents. Timing is very important."

"Don't belittle your skills or responsibilities. I know you work with schools and hospitals and that both the local fashion and tourist industries credit you with their recent upsurges in business, and that The Princess Foundation has raised a huge amount of money to benefit many charities."

"I do my job."

"You do. And you do it well. And I owe you an apology."

"An apology?" She smiled. "That's not a word I'd have thought would often pass your lips."

He matched that smile, his own wry. "It's not. Because I try never to be in the wrong. And generally I'm successful. But I came here with preconceived notions of royalty and I let them color my opinion of you. I even said as much to you. Which you took with remarkably good grace. Which made it all the worse as I came to realize how wrong I was. So, yes, I apologize."

"Thank you." What else could she say?

"There's that good grace again. The one that almost makes me feel worse. You could try gloating?"

"Gloating's not really my style."

"I've noticed. It's one of the many things I admire about you."

"Are you up to something? Is there an agenda here I'm not seeing?"

Logan laughed. "Not at all. It's just…you're different from any other woman I've known. And I have to admit I like those differences. The whole serenity thing you have going…it's nice to be around. Very tranquil. I don't have a lot of tranquility in my life."

"So tranquil you fall asleep?"

His smile flickered. "That wasn't a reflection on the company. What I meant was that when I'm with you the things that drive me ease. They just don't seem quite so important. It's almost a relief."

"I'll add that to my list of skills."

"There are other skills and talents I'd like to explore further," he said a few moments later. The hand around hers tightened. His thumb stroked. Now that he'd given up fantasies of escape apparently he'd turned to other fantasies, other ways of disconcerting her.

The innuendo was clear. But she had no *other* talents. Not of the sort she thought he was referring to. But perhaps she could learn. As she looked away she became aware that the press photographers were paying at least as much attention to Logan and her as they were to the man at the podium. She smiled at him, hiding her uncertainty, and then returned her gaze to the speaker. Though she kept part of her attention on Logan, aware of his hand, aware of the potential for him to drift to sleep. And wondering whether she had the nerve to put the exhilarating idea still percolating in her head to him.

He, she was certain, was more than talented.

Twenty minutes later she'd cut the ribbon—precisely—and the guests were finally permitted to stroll the new walk. The small crowd stood with an enthusiasm that owed as much to being allowed out of seats that had become progressively more uncomfortable as it did to the desire to see and smell and enjoy the blooms and the walk. And, of course, to be seen in return.

As she and Logan meandered the cobbled path, he maneuvered them so that they fell a little behind the main group clustered around her father and the rose breeders. They strolled up a gentle rise and paused. Not too far away a lake glittered, and several small rowboats wended their way across its surface. "It looks so serene," Rebecca murmured. "I watch the boats every time I come here."

"Ever been in them?"

"No. It's not really the thing."

"The thing?"

"The right look."

"But you'd like to?"

"Maybe. I've never rowed a boat. It looks fun."

Mrs. Smythe-Robinson detached herself from the main group and puffed back up the path toward them. "Speaking of fire-breathing dragons," Logan whispered.

As she approached, the older woman pointed to a rose-bush covered in apricot blooms. "This is the one Spriggs developed. I'm not sure it's his best."

"The floribunda," Logan said with creditable enthusi-asm.

Rebecca hid her surprise. He'd been listening?

"No, no. It's a grandiflora."

"You're right, of course." He deferred politely to her.

Mrs. Smythe-Robinson smiled, set her sights on some-one else and bustled away. Rebecca and Logan walked on. "Was she right?"

"Not according to what Spriggs himself said less than half an hour ago," Logan said.

"Very diplomatic of you."

"She didn't look like the type of woman I'd want to argue with. No chance of winning regardless of the rights and wrongs. And with some people even when you win you lose."

"You know who she is?"

"As it happens, yes. Her husband heads the government committee on foreign investment in San Philippe."

"And won't you need that committee's approval?"

"I already have that committee's approval. But she still didn't look like the type of woman I'd want to argue with."

"There's a type?" She pulled away from him on the pretext of smelling a luscious cream bloom. In reality she needed distance so that she didn't lean in instead.

"Most aren't worth the effort."

She looked up from the bloom. "Shall I take that as a compliment because you have no problem arguing with me?"

He offered his arm and she slid her hand over it. "Yes. But arguing with you has other benefits. I like seeing you get heated up, you make this indignant little huff. It's discreet, and kind of cute, but still a huff." He placed his hand over hers, holding it in place.

"I do not." She tugged at the hand but it was clamped against unrelenting muscle.

"See. Just like that one. And there's a most entrancing lift to your breasts when you do it."

"I did not huff." She kept her voice calm despite wanting to grit her teeth. "And even if I did, you shouldn't be looking at my breasts."

"I've tried not to. Believe me, I've tried. But like I said, they're entrancing. And I like seeing the conflict within you, the repressed passions. Even when you sound calm, like now, your eyes give you away. They flash silvery fire. A fire that could be better directed. A fire that must be all-consuming when you make love."

She did her best to hide the reaction he so clearly watched and waited for. It wasn't easy. Curiosity about what making love with him would be like flared. And Logan talking about making love, here, was too much.

"Enough." Finally she freed her hand. Now she just needed to wrest control of the conversation back. "You've had your fun but you can't say that type of thing here. No matter how bored you are." Because he was entertaining himself at her expense. She was sure of it.

Logan guided them down another narrow side path farther away from the small crowd.

She spoke quietly. "One of the things you need to learn about royal—"

With a hand on her shoulder he turned her to face him and covered her lips with his and what she'd been about to say fled her mind. Her awareness slid into the sudden vortex of sensation, the feel of his lips against hers, soft and warm and seeking, his hands on her shoulders anchoring her close to the hard strength of his body. He'd been talking about making love and now his lips were on hers and her traitorous body primed by his earlier words and the images he'd sown leaped in response as his tongue teased. His grip on her tightened, something in this kiss changed, heat flared. And that quickly she knew there was nothing academic about her desire for him to tutor her. It was all physical. A compulsion that sprang from the repressed passions he'd alluded to.

Her sun hat tumbled to the ground. And still it was several seconds before Logan broke the kiss and stepped back. His gaze darkened, then he blinked and bent to sweep up her hat, giving Rebecca precious seconds to regroup before he was again looking at her. "You were saying?" he asked.

She could read nothing in his gaze. Nothing of the confusion that assailed her. Nothing of the arousal that flooded her. She bit her lip. Hard. "Why did you do that?" she asked, watching his lips, full of sensual promise.

"Stop so abruptly? Because we were at our five seconds." The lips quirked.

She was losing control. She had to focus. Not on his lips but on his words. She looked at his ear instead. "Not stop. Start. When I was in the middle of trying to say something to you." Darn it, he even had nice ears, curving ridges and hollows that invited touch.

"Because I thought it was going to be a lecture, and—" he winked "—because I can." How real was his nonchalance? The teasing light in his eyes that she'd grown accustomed to wasn't there. And there'd been something far from nonchalant in the kiss. But she had so little to compare it to, and was far from trusting herself to interpret Logan's state of mind. "It's been the best part of the day so far," he said easily.

"Oh." Had it? Would that it had anything like the impact on him that it did on her. She knew she'd relive it later tonight. Maybe then she'd be able to sort out what it had meant to her.

Liar, a little voice whispered. The kiss had, without a doubt, been the best part of her day, too. And it had promised so much more. A promise that called to her, pulled at her. Logan was a window of opportunity. A window to another world.

He glanced ahead to where the approved press photographers lurked. "And it'll make a nice shot for the papers. We may as well give them something they can use, something that works for us, otherwise they'll find something of their own that may not suit our purposes so well."

"Like you yawning?"

"Precisely."

It was all about his plan, his goals, nothing more. He was so much more focused than she was. So much more in control. But perhaps that was a good—safe—thing. "Warn me next time."

"Why?"

"So I can be ready." So she didn't melt unthinkingly into his arms.

He appeared to give her request some thought then shook his head. "I prefer the element of surprise. I like the way you're kissing me back before you even realize what you're doing."

He was standing so close still. She ought to step away. Ought to, but connection, or maybe fear, or maybe desire, held her there. She wouldn't examine which.

"Besides," he said, "I was completely within the rules. Less than five seconds. And there haven't been any others today."

Rules. Rules and plans and appearances. How real was anything they shared?

He lifted her hat, placed it on her head, studied her for a second and then adjusted the angle so it was more to his liking. His arms framed her face, creating a strange intimacy between them, shutting out the rest of the world. She was about to thank him, politely, when he swooped in and planted another kiss on her lips—quick but gentle. "Technically that one may have been outside of the rules." He stepped back, took her hand and they started walking.

If no real sentiment was engaged didn't that mean her own secret plan was even more viable?

Thoughts and possibilities pursued her. For five minutes they walked in silence. All her life she'd been schooled in how to comport herself in public. But she'd had no guidance in private matters.

A father and two brothers had been a great help in all things royal. But that was where their help ended. Hearts and hormones weren't discussed—at least not in front of her. She'd become good friends with Rafe's wife, Lexie. But it was still a relatively new friendship. Not the sort of deep sisterly connection she hoped they'd one day share.

No, any next step into the unknown was hers alone.

Could she ask Logan for more? Ask for an amendment to their agreement. A special clause. Because she wanted to know so much more. And Logan was the one who could teach her. He certainly had the...skills, and he wasn't from here, wouldn't be staying here. "Do you..."

"Do I what?"

"Do you...like...kissing me?" It wasn't the question she'd been going to ask, but it would lead her to the answer she sought without revealing too much of her vulnerability.

His eyes narrowed, as though suspecting some kind of trap. "Far too much."

"It's not just for the press?"

He shrugged. "It's for the press and for the public. But remember what we said about how we didn't need to pretend to enjoy a meal if it was a good meal?"

Yes, she did. So he enjoyed kissing her? As much as she enjoyed kissing him? Though she wasn't entirely sure that *enjoy* was the right word, it was too uncomplicated, too tame almost. Kissing him thrilled her, confused her, made her want...more, made her uncertain of herself even as it gave her pleasure. So many things, too much for something as uncomplicated as enjoyment. But still he was only kissing her because of their arrangement. He didn't need or want anything further from her than the appearance that they were in a relationship. That could work in her favor.

"I get to kiss you and enjoy it. Like tasting a delicacy that has you craving more. A definite win-win situation."

Somehow his words stirred an element of loss, too. She couldn't quite identify it. Somewhere along the line this had become something far more important to her than it ought to be. Not just showing her father that she was a woman capable of making her own decisions and controlling her life. But about showing herself that she was a woman. Not a princess.

Logan reached for a delicate dusky pink bloom, ran a blunt fingertip between the petals. "Do you know what these velvet petals make me think of?" Still teasing, still trying to disconcert her. He knew this type of conversation, this subtle flirtation, wasn't her forte.

"Stop it. It's a flower, nothing more." The rose breeders would slay her if they heard her say that.

"Or how I have visions of laying you down on a bed of rose petals?"

"Logan. Don't." How had their conversation taken such a sudden swerve? How did he so easily plant images in her mind, or bring to life the images that she'd already allowed to grow?

"Or what?"

"Or I'll call Mrs. Smythe-Robinson back over."

A honey bee landed on the rose, collected pollen. "We can talk fertilization with her. I'm sure she'll have an opinion on the subject."

Ahead of them there was a burst of laughter.

"Can I ask you something?"

"You can ask me anything you want and I'll answer, but only something you actually want the answer to, because I'll be honest."

She believed that much of him, but she pressed her lips together because her thoughts flashed back to last night and this morning.

"Go on. One question. Anything. I dare you."

Ah, the Buchanan dare, she could hear the cockiness in

his voice, the expectation that nothing she could ask would throw him. "What if I asked you to…"

Her request faltered beneath the sudden intensity of his gaze. It was so easy to say things in her head. *Teach me pleasure. Teach me how to be myself when I'm with a man. Teach me what men like.*

"Go on." He couldn't possibly know what she'd been about to ask but there was a sudden wariness to his tone as though he at least knew it wasn't going to be a flippant request. Although maybe she could phrase it that way. *Teach me how to make pancakes for breakfast for the man I've just spent the night with.*

"Teach me—"

Those liquid brown eyes held her still, urged her on.

"Your Highness, there you are. We thought we'd lost you." Mrs. Smythe-Robinson bustled toward them, her program for the day's events in her hand, a small posse of enthusiasts behind her. "Can you can settle something for us? Was your mother's favorite color apricot or lavender?"

Relief washed through her at the interruption because she'd been suddenly afraid of Logan's response. He wanted her on his arm in pictures to further his company's goals. He had no need or desire to help her learn what she wanted to know. He had scores of willing women who needed no teaching whatsoever. She allowed herself to be drawn into settling the supposed debate.

Once, when looking at a child's artwork, her mother had exclaimed that the apricot crayon used was her favorite color. From that moment on she had been deluged with apricot-colored gifts. She had confessed to her family, but to no one else, that her favorite color was in fact blue. It had been a lesson for her mother, who had only been trying to be diplomatic. A lesson she had ample time over the fol-lowing years to contemplate.

One of her father's secretaries approached her. "You're needed for the photos, ma'am."

She turned to Logan, realized that at least now with her question rightfully repressed she could look him in his lovely brown eyes. "This may take a while. And then I have to go straight on to a meeting of The Princess Foundation. I'll see you for the polo match tomorrow."

"Your question?"

"It doesn't matter now." She was hardly going to ask it with royal staff standing nearby no matter how much they pretended not to be listening.

He reached for her wrist before she could turn away, anchoring her to the spot. Heat snaked up her arm, slithered deep inside her. He held her gaze, his eyes serious, and gave a single slow nod. "Yes. I'll teach you."

# Seven

Rebecca sat in the car given to her for the evening by the chief of security. It wasn't one she'd driven before. And never before had she sat so uncertain for so long.

Out of a desire to preserve the architectural heritage of San Philippe, there were no true high-rises in the city. So it was easy enough to look up at Logan's riverfront penthouse apartment.

But what if Logan's *yes* hadn't actually been in response to the question she'd wanted to, but hadn't quite asked? What if his *yes* had been "yes, I'll teach you to row a boat." He hadn't called her or made any attempt to contact her to discuss her question. Admittedly, it had only been a matter of hours since she'd asked it but if she didn't act now she'd lose her nerve. His windows revealed nothing. All she could make out was that lights were on inside. She looked from those uninformative windows to the phone clutched in her hand.

Spineless. Time to either go through with her plan or go home.

Men were supposed to like the hunt, the thrill of the chase. She knew that much. Desperate women who threw themselves at men were *desperately* unappealing. Then again, she didn't need Logan to like her, she just needed him to…help her.

On the ancient bridge spanning the river, couples walked hand in hand. Women leaned heads on partners' shoulders, so trusting, so gently intimate. Two looking almost as one. And here she was sitting alone in her car.

Following the photo session and then the meeting, her father had wanted a private conversation with her this evening. But she'd figured she'd face an inquisition over Logan so she'd cried off, explaining she'd already arranged to see Logan, knowing that her father would be in Switzerland for the next couple of days. She was becoming quite adept at evasion, at telling…things that weren't quite the truth. In her head she could almost hear Logan challenging her to call it what it was—a lie.

The only person she was practiced at lying to was herself. For so long she'd pretended she didn't have wants and needs of her own. In the time she'd known Logan he had made her far too conscious of her self-deceit. And more than anything else he made her conscious of those wants and needs.

She lifted her phone then closed her eyes and doubt flooded in.

She couldn't go through with it. What was she even doing here? What had she been thinking? She was not, and never would be, a normal woman. She'd never walked with her head resting on a man's shoulder. Because she couldn't depend on a man like that. She couldn't trust Logan—or any man—like that.

Because if you didn't trust someone they couldn't betray you. Trusting someone gave them power over you.

And Logan was too much an unknown quantity. Too unpredictable. Too uncontrollable. She had too much to lose.

A light rain began to fall, refracting the light on her windshield, obscuring the world outside, making it shimmer.

Home. She would go home where she was safe and knew the rules. They had a plan. A good plan. Safe, if not completely sensible. All she had to do was stick to it and pretend to date Logan for the allotted weeks. No more. No less.

The phone cradled in her palm vibrated and rang, making her jump. Logan's name lit up on the display. He needn't know anything. "Hello," she answered, keeping her voice casual, a little curious.

"What are you doing?" His voice was almost all curiosity. Curiosity with a hint of something knowing.

The knowing could only be her imagination, her guilt. "Reviewing the minutes from the foundation's meeting," she said with a bored sigh. But her lack of skill at lying shined through and she spoke a little too quickly, her voice a little too high.

"In your car?"

"Sorry?" She pretended she was confused, that she hadn't quite heard or understood a question that ought to make no sense. In part she *was* confused. He couldn't possibly know she was outside his apartment building. She looked around to make sure. There was no one near her car, no one paying any attention to it. The windows were darkly tinted.

"That is you, isn't it? Parked along the riverfront. Near the street lamp."

Her face heated in the darkness. Clearly he could, and did, know.

Part and parcel of being no good at lying was being no good at extricating herself from a lie. "I…I…have to go. I'll talk you later."

"You're sure you wouldn't rather see me sooner?"

"I have another call coming through. I think it's my father. Bye." She jabbed at the off button and let her head fall back against the headrest. But only for a few seconds while her heartbeat slowed. Anyone else in the world would surely have handled that better than she had. And she was a princess. She was supposed to be adept at handling delicate situations. Time to get a grip. She turned her key in the ignition and flicked on her lights. Illuminated in their beam, a tall, broad-shouldered man, his dark hair rumpled, walked toward her, his long, easy stride eating up the distance. Rebecca tapped her forehead against the steering wheel. She'd had extensive training in defensive, and evasive driving; hand-brake slides, high-speed escape maneuvers. But none of that would be any help to her now. There was no dignified retreat.

He tried her door. She pressed the button to unlock it and cut the engine. As he opened her door he held a hand toward her. She focused on that hand rather than his face and held on to it only until she stood. Eventually she had to look up. A frown creased his brow, not irritation but…concern? As his gaze traveled over her, assessing, the frown eased. His breathing was rapid but controlled. As though he had raced to get here? His button-down shirt was untucked and the first few buttons undone. He started walking and Rebecca had little choice but to fall into step beside him.

He asked no questions. She volunteered no explanation,

no excuses. Their footsteps sounded in quiet unison on the damp cobbles.

He walked slowly, strolling, when the part of her that wanted to escape her foolishness would have strode as though she could leave it behind. The more distance she put between her and her car, the more she could pretend she'd never parked on the road in front of his apartment, never been caught.

They crossed the pedestrian bridge that arched over the river. Balmy night air wrapped around them. Light shimmered and reflected in the inky water and on the damp cobbles. Ahead of them a couple walked hand in hand, their mingled laughter barely audible. And somewhere in the unseen distance the rapid, fluid notes of a Spanish guitar sounded.

Still she waited and mentally prepared for Logan's request for an explanation, or his mockery. She would be regal. She owed him no explanation. And she could rise above his mockery.

Neither came.

They just walked. Side by side. And she didn't feel regal. She realized, after maybe ten minutes, that this might be what it was like to feel normal. She could be with a man and not be compelled to make polite conversation. She could just...be, soaking in the sights and sounds and sensations.

His shoulder was close to her head. If she had the courage she'd reach for his hand, she could tilt her head, rest it on his shoulder like the couples she'd watched earlier. She did not have the courage. They passed beneath an ornate street lamp.

"Jeans?"

It was the last thing she'd expected him to ask. She'd

almost forgotten them. "I was trying to be normal. You know, not a princess. For an evening."

They walked on. His silence perplexing.

"What do you think? Of the jeans?" They both knew she could pretend but she could never be normal. Leopards and spots and all that.

"Nice." His hand swung back and patted her butt. "Very nice."

Nobody had ever patted her butt.

Rebecca smiled.

Logan lifted his arm and settled it around her shoulders, pulling her gently against him. And her head nestled against his shoulder as though designed to fit there. Sensation surged within her. She recognized it as happiness. Maybe she could walk like this all night long, circling the old parts of the city.

The sounds of the guitar grew clearer as they approached a strip of waterfront cafés and restaurants. "Have you eaten?" he asked.

"No." She'd escaped the palace rather than have dinner there.

"Neither have I." He steered her down a side road then stopped to open a door beneath a small green awning. "The view's not the same as on the waterfront, but it's quieter and the food—"

"Is divine?" she asked with a smile, remembering his previous descriptions of food.

He matched her smile. "It's simple but good. I think you'll like it."

They walked down a set of narrow stairs into the small restaurant redolent with aromas of Mediterranean cooking, olives and tomatoes and garlic. A short, balding man hurried up to them, arms held wide, his gaze and his smile lighting first on Logan, then freezing momentarily as he noticed Rebecca.

"Stefan," Logan said, "a quiet table, please."

"Of course." Stefan led them past the tables in the busy restaurant. The hum of conversation died away, to be replaced by whispers as diners realized who she was. Stefan showed them to a small corner table partially screened from the main restaurant. "I hope this will be suitable."

Stefan seated her. Logan sat opposite. A low candle flickered and danced between them.

She watched him, wondering when it was that Logan had changed from an irritant to the pearl.

Gradually the noise level resumed its initial volume.

Logan leaned back in his chair, watching her. And all the reasons this might not be such a great idea returned. The primary one being that now there was no escape for her, no avoiding his questions. Stefan placed a basket of assorted breads on their table. Rebecca smeared pesto on a small wedge of bread and waited. And waited. Until she could bear it no more. "I suppose you're wondering what I was doing outside your apartment."

"Actually, I was wondering what it must be like to have people fall silent just because you walk past them. To have people stare."

No one had ever asked her that. "It's just how it is, how it's always been. And it will undoubtedly help give you the profile you're after." She tried to keep the hint of hurt from her voice.

"Undoubtedly. So, you're here with me for my benefit?"

She didn't need the hint of sarcasm. "No. To be honest I'm not sure why I'm here with you. It seemed like a good idea to drive to your place. I know my father keeps tabs on me, that it will help convince him we have a real relationship. He has doubts."

"Smart man. And that was your only reason."

"And," she said and took a deep breath, "partly I just wanted to see you."

He hesitated for just a second. "And the other part?"

She waited while Stefan poured two glasses of ruby-red wine. But by the time he'd backed away her resolve was gone.

"The other part doesn't matter anymore."

"It always matters."

Rebecca took a sip of her wine. "Try this. It's divine."

And Logan laughed, recognizing her use of his own distraction techniques. She'd never met anyone whose laugh was quite so deep, quite so warming. It was one of the things, if not *the* thing, she liked best about him. There was such an appealing openness to his laugh, a complete lack of pretension. And it stirred a warmth within her, made her want him more. Made her wonder what it would be like to wake up to that smile, that laughter.

One of the other things she liked about him was his patience, though she knew that he could probably wield it as a weapon. He didn't press, seemed content to enjoy a meal that was as he'd predicted very good. She'd never heard of Stefan's, never eaten at a place like this in San Philippe. How much more was there for her to discover in her own small country?

She watched Logan's hands as he buttered bread, his lips as he sipped wine, the vitality in his eyes as he talked. Did he have anything like her level of awareness of him?

And she thought about those eyes watching her, those hands touching her, those lips kissing her.

Forbidden thoughts for a princess. She'd never before had trouble controlling her thoughts. It was what she did.

But Logan with his indifference to royalty made her keep wondering what it would be like not to be royal. Foolish notion. She couldn't, and wouldn't want to, change who she was. There was no point wondering.

No point in wondering, or wishing, for just a few weeks of anonymity. A few weeks when everything she said and did, or didn't say and do, wasn't scrutinized, reported, speculated on. A few weeks when she did something real. Her work with charities and schools and the arts was appreciated and did, she knew, benefit others. But sometimes she daydreamed about being a gardener, or a cook, or a painter—not an artist, but someone who painted walls and fences. Someone who at the end of the day could stand back and see what they'd achieved, other than neatly bisecting a ribbon or attending meetings.

And then she would berate herself for her daydreams because she knew that a good portion of the rest of the world daydreamed about having her life. She should be nothing but grateful.

"You have a very expressive face."

Rebecca's grip tightened on her fork. "Expressive?"

"Thoughts and emotions seem to flit through your eyes, even while you're looking far away."

"I do sometimes get a little caught up in my thoughts."

"A man could find it less than flattering."

As if he needed flattery from her. From anyone for that matter. "Doubtless women fawn all over you."

"Less, I expect, than men fawn over you."

"Actually, they don't. They tend to be intimidated."

"The threat of beheading, no doubt." It must be something to do with the candlelight, the way it glinted in his eyes.

Rebecca smiled. "No one's been beheaded in San Philippe in centuries."

"The dungeons?"

"They've been converted. Lighting. Heating. Part's even a gymnasium. You'd never guess their history." And despite her joking she knew it wasn't the nonexistent prospect of royal incarceration that kept suitors at bay. Though it was generous of Logan to give her that out. "No. I think I intimidate them." It was only men like Logan with an agenda—to make it into royal circles—who were prepared to overlook "her" and the glass bowl of her life in order to get what they sought. But at least Logan had been honest about that, which gave her leave to be honest in return.

"You're a princess. I can see how that might throw a man off his game, so to speak."

"But not you?"

"A person's a person. Regardless of what they do for a living, or where they live."

"Not so many people think like that. But it's more than the princess thing. I can be reserved." And sometimes she came across as remote, cold even. And the more uncertain she was the more reserved she became.

"I noticed," he said agreeably. "And haughty."

"No. Just reserved."

"Especially when you enunciate so clearly."

Like she just had. Years of elocution lessons were almost impossible to recover from. The princess persona was all of her training. All of her security. "Is it bad?"

"I was teasing you, Princess."

"That's another thing. I'm not always sure when people—and you in particular—are joking. And I don't want to not laugh if they've made a joke, but on the other hand I don't want to laugh if they weren't making a joke."

"I'm sure you're making this a whole lot harder than it

needs to be. How about you laugh if and when something strikes you as funny?"

She shook her head. "Too risky."

They lapsed into silence as their dessert arrived, a rich decadent chocolate tart, along with two spoons. The chocolate melted into her mouth, almost seeming to soak into it. They watched each other eat. Surreptitious glimpses and other more openly appreciative glances. And the liquid heat that she'd come to associate with Logan, as though her insides were following the example of the melting chocolate, filled her.

"Do you analyze everything?"

"Almost everything."

"Must be hell on your lovers."

Rebecca swallowed. "I wouldn't…I don't…analyze that. Only things about myself. Public things."

"I'm relieved to hear it."

Because? The question almost slipped out. Because he might think there was potential opportunity for her to analyze him, or merely because he believed in male solidarity?

He watched her over the rim of his wineglass, a frown clouding his expression. "There have been other lovers, haven't there?"

Relief, at the clarification—he did know what she'd asked of him, and had agreed to the same—warred with embarrassment at having this discussion here and now. For long seconds she looked at her wine, the red so dark it was almost black in the candlelight.

Then she looked up, met Logan's gaze. "Yes. But my experience is limited." He hadn't asked for numbers. "And I wasn't analyzing, not at the time, but I've come to think there might have been room for improvement."

One man, not much more than a boy really, at the end

of her first summer home from college. They'd met a few times over that week. It was a time she'd be happy to forget. It hadn't been, she suspected, earth-shattering for Ivan, either.

"It always gets better as lovers get to know one another's bodies."

She looked around the restaurant. "I'm not sure that this is a conversation we should be having here." No one was sitting close enough to hear, but all the same.

He nodded. "I just wanted to be clear."

"Would it have been a problem if there hadn't been others?" Why, when she was the one who didn't want to be having this conversation here and now, did stupid questions slip out? But she had no idea how men thought, not about things like this.

"Not a problem as such, but…" He shrugged.

How would it change things, she wanted to ask, but finally had the good sense not to.

Logan tipped his head back and looked for a moment at the ceiling. At the curving brickwork of what had once been some kind of cellar. He looked back at her. "Do you know how hard this is?"

"How hard what is?" she teased, quietly pleased with the flirtation and double entendre she was usually so appalling at.

She was rewarded with the flash of his grin. He leaned forward, resting his elbows on the small table. "How hard it is to sit here discussing this with you when from the very moment you asked me that question at the rose gardens, and if I'm honest from well before then, I've been imagining you naked and beneath me. How if we weren't in this restaurant I'd have hauled you against me and—" He looked back at the ceiling again, exhaling roughly.

His words thrilled her. She'd thought he was so in control.

Logan stood. "Let's go."

He took her hand and led her from the restaurant. They crossed back over the river to head in the direction of her car. And his apartment. There was still a voice, a royal cautionary voice, in the back of her mind insisting that she didn't know what she was doing. That she was making a mistake. It was the same voice that dictated her behavior day in and day out, year in and year out. That voice was saying run, get in her car and get out of here before she got into something she was ill-prepared for.

But the louder voice came from the hunger that stirred and swirled whenever she was with Logan, whenever she thought of him, the clamoring hunger that said this man could both inflame it and satisfy it.

This man who'd insinuated that she analyzed things too much.

She forced her mind to still, to focus on the here and now. They neared her car. "Thank you," she said. "I don't know when I've enjoyed a meal so much." It was true. The meal, eating with Logan, just being herself had been a rare pleasure. The sensual currents had heightened everything. A new and delicious experience.

"I could say the same. And although the food was good, it was the company that elevated it. You're an intriguing woman, Rebecca."

They were almost opposite her car when Logan paused in front of the wide, gold-lettered, glass doors of his apartment building, the oldest and most exclusive in San Philippe. He turned to her and lifted an eyebrow in inquiry.

And she knew what he was asking.

No discussion, no pressure, no expectation. That in

itself was a novelty. Her life was usually nothing but pressure and expectation. The decision was hers alone. She thought—hoped—that he had a preference as to her answer. He was, after all, issuing the invitation.

This was *the* moment. The fork in the road. And, for all her angst, it was a surprisingly easy decision. She wanted this. She wanted it academically for all sorts of reasons that made sense in her head but she wanted it physically, as a woman. She wanted it inside and out. And deeper still there was a yearning in her heart for this connection with Logan.

He held her gaze, his searching and utterly serious, as she nodded. In turn, Logan nodded to the doorman who opened the door and ushered them through. The sounds of the street outside were silenced as the door closed behind them.

# Eight

Inside Logan's apartment, Rebecca crossed to the mullioned windows overlooking the street. Logan came to stand beside her, his shoulder a whisper away from hers, his scent subtle and warming. Down below, her car sat clearly visible on the far side of the road. Nothing covert about it. A nearby street lamp dimly illuminated the interior through the front windshield. She closed her eyes. She hated it when she was an idiot. He would have had little trouble identifying her. How long had he watched her before calling her?

"Give me your keys and I'll park your car in one of my spaces below the building."

"Oh. Thank you." She handed him the keys. Their fingers brushed. A small current of desire sped through her. He felt it, too—she saw it in his eyes. He closed his hand around the keys and strode toward the elevator.

She crossed to the couch to sit. And then, unable to sit

still, stood. She took the opportunity of his absence to look around his apartment. The sparse furnishings were at odds with the ornate interior and symbolic of a man passing through. The clean modern lines of the couch and single angular armchair contrasted with plaster moldings and a crystal chandelier and rich red velvet curtains. An acoustic guitar leaned against the couch. The instrument was the only personal touch in the whole room, the only thing that gave any clue as to its inhabitant. A low coffee table was pulled close to the couch. She could imagine Logan sitting on the couch, feet on the coffee table, guitar in his arms.

With him gone, the apartment was quiet and still and she had further opportunity to doubt the wisdom of her decision to come up here. She curled her hands into fists. It was the right decision and she would go through with it.

He would leave San Philippe once he had what he wanted. That was what made it—him—safe.

Rebecca was still staring at the battered instrument when he came back. She turned to see him standing on the far side of the living room watching her. "What sort of music do you play?"

"Whatever takes my fancy at the time."

"I'd like to hear you."

"Some other time, maybe."

It was nothing personal and she shouldn't take it that way. Some people didn't like playing for others. She looked back toward the view and the glittering city outside. This was all feeling too planned, too academic.

Warm fingers touched her jaw, turned her head. Her eyes met warm deep chocolate. A hint of a question lingered there along with a hint of intent. His lips were a serious, straight line. "Rebecca—"

She stepped in close, rose up on tiptoes and pressed her lips to his, needing to silence whatever he'd been going to say or ask. Yes, she knew what she was doing, she was sure. And yes, she most definitely did want this.

She felt his lips curve into a smile as his hands went to her shoulders and he pulled her closer still. His lips parted and moved with an assurance and pleasure her own lips had quickly come to recognize and her body had quickly come to respond to. Suddenly nothing felt planned or academic. There was only now, his lips on hers, his body against hers, his hands framing her face.

And there was no need for words or questions. But need aplenty for this. Just this connection.

Again no pressure, no expectation. In their stead, enjoyment, delight.

And heat.

He gave with his kiss. Gave of himself. Gave pleasure.

Sensation sang through her body as she let herself take. She wanted his touch and the taste of him. She wanted the wonder of his exploration, the delight of her own discovery.

Her hands found his chest, fingers splaying over powerful contours, relishing the warm silk over hard muscle. So male. So intriguing. So infinitely tempting. And beneath silk and muscle the beat of his heart. So human. She slid her hand beneath his shirt so that his skin all but scorched her palm where it came to rest on his chest. His heart seemed to beat right into her hand, as though if she curled her fingers she would be able to cradle it.

And all the while lips and tongue tasted and tempted, dared and challenged and invited.

She accepted the invitation, kissing him back, discovering the secrets of his mouth. Those lips that so often quirked in amusement were now hers for the taking and claiming hers in return. He angled his head, deepening his kiss. The hint of his beard gently abraded. There was something restrained in his kiss, she felt it and thought maybe she should be grateful for that. Maybe she was. But, then again, maybe she wasn't.

Her second hand joined the first, exploring the breadth of his torso, over sparse hair and small nipples, sliding around the hard strong back. Everything so male, so different. And everything feminine within her thrilled and leaped in response to what he was doing to her, to what she was doing to him and to the sensations possessing her.

She pressed harder against him, pressed her hips against his. She felt the shape of him.

A low masculine groan resonated somewhere between chest and throat and that sense of restraint she thought she'd felt shattered as the kiss became fiercer, hungrier.

He broke the kiss, bent and scooped her into his arms, striding through his apartment to his bedroom, setting her down gently on her feet beside an enormous bed.

Enough silver light from the city outside filtered through the windows to illuminate the angles of his face and a jaw set with determination, lips full and skilled in arts she knew little of but hungered to know more. His brow was etched with concentration as he worked at the small buttons that ran down the front of her blouse. When he had enough undone he pushed a shoulder of her blouse aside, pressed those lips to heated skin. Rebecca shuddered with savage delight.

He jerked his head upward and pulled back, and she knew a pang of loss caused by the distance. Had she done something wrong—responded too freely, not responded enough?

"I want you." He said the words he'd once said so clinically. This time his voice was a rough growl threaded with need. "Tell me," he said, "that this is what you want.

Tell me now." He gripped her shoulders, ready to either set her away or pull her closer. "I need to hear the words."

The raw edge to his voice thrilled her, his suave control was gone—for her. She lifted her hands to cup his jaw, tilted her head to meet the fierce expression in his eyes. "This is what I want," she said quietly. "You are what and who I want."

His Adam's apple moved in his throat. But that was his only movement. Her heart thumped as she waited at the brink of a precipice, not quite knowing how to force a leap from it. Why was he holding back? She knew he wanted this. It was there in his kisses, it was there in the rapid tattoo of his heart, the shallow breathing. She recognized the mirror of her desire.

"Think of it as a royal command." She kept her gaze on his as she dropped her hands to the remaining buttons of her blouse, picking up where he had left off. Then she tossed her blouse to the floor.

Those lips that so fascinated her quirked in a flicker of a smile. "I'm yours to command," he said as his head lowered to hers and as he eased a bra strap from her shoulder and kissed the spot where it had lain, then nipped her. And that quick gentle press of teeth on her skin arrowed need through her.

She knew with a fierce satisfaction that this moment, this thing between them was just that, something between the two of them alone. He was a man and she was a woman. Not a princess. Just a woman. Filled with a feminine power and feminine needs that only he could satisfy.

And then her bra was gone. Logan stepped back. Looked, admired, then lifted his hands to her breasts, rubbed thumbs over pebbled nipples. Her insides tightened with need for him, her legs almost gave way as she leaned in to his touch.

The imbalance in their dress seemed unfair. Rebecca reached out to undo his buttons, and pull his shirt off him.

And then she stilled.

His body, what she could see of it, which wasn't yet enough, was…beautiful. He had a broad sculpted chest with a light covering of hair, a lean hard abdomen. There, too, a faint trail of hair led her gaze downward to the snap on his jeans.

He stepped in, scooped her into his arms and set her gently on the bed. With tender haste he peeled what remained of her clothing from her as though unveiling a long-sought treasure. Raising her arms above her head, he anchored them there with one hand, trailing fingertips and kisses over her body—her face, her throat, breasts and arms, and each of her fingers. He explored as though he wanted to learn every inch of her. He pressed velvet soft kisses behind her knees, the soles of her feet, parts of her that should not be so sensitive but that were aflame at his touch. She writhed and rose up to meet him. And then he began the slow journey back up again.

And when he pressed his kisses between her thighs she could no longer keep her arms above her head, and instead plunged her fingers into the rich silk of his hair as her body jerked with the sensations that jolted through her.

Surely it was wrong to feel this intensely. Wrong and so wonderfully right. The rational part of her, hanging only by a thread, slipped away so that there was no thought, only exquisite pleasure. Her head thrashed with clamoring need for something she couldn't quite reach.

And then she reached it. Or rather it reached her, sweeping through her, wracking her body. She tried to suppress the cries of surprise and passion but they escaped.

And then Logan, broad shouldered and fierce, rose up above her. He sheathed himself and slid inside of her, the length of him stretching and filling her. So that where she'd thought it couldn't be possible to feel more, she felt so very much more.

They moved together, skin against skin, slowly, beautifully, moving as one, desire quickening, until they melded into a powerful, crashing rhythm, something desperate and primal. Until once again she cried out. This time her cries mingled with Logan's raw groan as he drove into her, nothing gentle or refined, pure naked desire and need fulfilled.

# Nine

Logan woke with a princess in his bed. Definitely a first. An X-rated fairy tale. His own new spin on *Lady and the Tramp*. He studied her face, softened and vulnerable with sleep. And he remembered the passion that flared between them last night. Perhaps he should have treated her with more respect, more reverence, but that choice hadn't been one he could make, nor had it been one she seemed to want.

Who knew that someone so quietly elegant could inflame and return such need and desire?

When she'd first hinted at her question yesterday in the rose garden, he'd known an onslaught of emotion. Recognized it for the double-edged sword it was, full of possibilities and pitfalls. When it looked like she might turn away he'd known there was only one answer. Any other would be unthinkable.

She had chosen him. He was humbled yet wanted to beat his chest and roar his euphoric victory.

From the time of her question, he'd been consumed by thoughts of her. Not that she hadn't already taken up an undue amount of mental space. Not that he hadn't already had fantasies. But suddenly the possibilities were real and imminent. And the pitfalls enormous.

She stirred beside him, her lips full and gently curving as though her dreams were pleasant.

Last night as he'd sat alone, he'd played his guitar—it was what he did when he needed to think. He had time to consider, to wonder—the whys of what she was asking, and whether she knew what she was getting into, and whether she was as innocent and guileless as she seemed or was in fact toying with him.

He almost hoped it was the latter. That would be simpler.

He'd put down his guitar and strolled to his window. And instead of the city view he'd seen her car. She sat in it for the longest time and he watched for the longest time, and smiled as he imagined her arguing it out with herself. She'd come this far, would she take that final step?

In the end, it occurred to him that there could be other reasons for her presence there, troubles or concerns. His mind had been so firmly on its single track that it had taken too long to think of that. So he'd called her.

Gone to her.

The sweet guilt and uncertainty on her face had given him her reason for being there.

And so they'd walked. He didn't want her feeling guilty, and he didn't want her uncertain. Because what was about to happen would change things between them, complicate them.

And as much as he ached to know her, he didn't want to

lose what they already had. More than an understanding, closer to friendship. She was a glittering jewel and she sparkled for him. She was like no one he'd known before.

He looked at her now and could only hope that she woke with regrets, agreeing that it shouldn't have happened and adamant that it couldn't happen again. That they would do their best to carry on just as they had been. It might just be possible.

They could have no future, they didn't belong in each other's worlds.

Somewhere in the night she'd talked about going back to the palace. He'd pulled her toward him and convinced her that his bed was a far better place to be.

But that was then.

He made to slide from that same bed, thinking for the first time in hours with his brain, and one that wasn't completely addled with desire.

This could be awkward. Mornings after a first time always held that potential. Particularly when it was a liaison that could have no future.

A delicate hand flattened itself low on his abdomen. Her lips curled softly upward and her eyes opened, something shy and vulnerable shining in them. Hopes and dreams. And expectations. He was going to have to hurt her. They had to wind back the clock. And he had to be the one to tell her.

She'd said only that she wanted him to teach her things and he'd agreed. He'd never have been able to refuse because hell, she turned him inside out with desire. But she was a princess. It kept coming back to that. That and the fact that, for all the royal hauteur she displayed, inside was someone far more vulnerable, someone who might think she only wanted to learn the ways of desire, but someone who deserved, and he suspected needed, to be cherished. One who believed in fairy tales and happy ever afters.

Her hand slid tentatively lower.

He had to tell her. Now. His throat ran dry.

Long lashes dropped to screen her eyes as the hand slid lower still to wrap around the hard length of him. And he knew that he was a thousand kinds of bastard because he couldn't stop himself from reaching for her. She rolled toward him.

He was so doomed.

He wanted to watch her in the soft morning light. He wanted to see her naked beauty, her hair swinging, her eyes glazing over with passion, he wanted to grip the curve of hips as she rode him.

He wanted to satisfy her, to give her this one simple pleasure.

And so he said nothing. And then as she moved over and onto him knew that in the onslaught of sensation speech wasn't possible.

But he could give her tenderness, and completion, this woman of beauty and uncertainty who deserved so much better than him.

She lay pressed against him, her hair draped across his shoulder, spilling onto the pillow, and he could have sworn their hearts beat exactly in tune, gradually slowing. He had no idea what she was thinking, probably that was for the best. He hardly knew what he thought himself, other than the awareness that he'd gotten into a mess from which he needed to extricate himself. But it was the most divinely blissful mess he'd ever been in.

"I'd like—" she said quietly, then said no more.

He turned his head. She was watching him and before he knew it he'd pressed a gentle kiss to her softly parted lips, then pulled back. "What would you like?" Right now he'd give her the world.

She caught her bottom lip in her teeth. "I'd like to make you breakfast."

That wasn't what he'd been expecting. "Sure."

"But…"

"But what?"

"I haven't done it often. You might have to help me. Which I know sort of defeats the purpose. Only this one time, though. After I've done it once I'll be fine for the next time."

Just like last night.

And then as though realizing what she'd said she caught her lip again, looked away.

A woman in his bed, and not just any woman but a princess, and not just any princess, but Rebecca, and she wanted to cook for him—with his help. Maybe other magic had gone on last night than that which had occurred between the sheets.

"Sure." Breakfast, and then he'd tell her.

"I'll just shower first. Will you wait for me?" She waited for his nod and then slid from the bed. His gaze stayed glued to the pale length of her back, the sweetly rounded behind as she walked from his room. She glanced back over her shoulder and a slow sweet smile curved her lips.

He didn't wait for her. He joined her in the shower. Joined with her.

Bright morning sunlight gleamed on the kitchen's dark granite surfaces and shined in Rebecca's hair as she measured ingredients into a bowl, humming to the song playing on the radio. Logan sat at the breakfast bar watching her. She'd had a change of clothes in her car, claiming that a princess was always prepared. He'd brought the bag up for her this morning. A blue sleeveless top in some kind of silky fabric and the jeans that she really ought to wear more often. She had a figure made for jeans.

She didn't want him to do anything to help her. Except tell her how to do everything.

She'd sought…instruction last night, too. Asking him what pleased him, seeming almost uncertain about what best pleased her even, but taking delight in finding out. A quick and enthusiastic learner.

She'd wanted to make pancakes, like they'd had their first breakfast together. Logan sipped the coffee he'd made. There was something wrong with the concept and it took him a while to figure out what was sending the whispers of unease along his spine.

The domesticity, the remembrance of their first breakfast, it spoke of something more permanent than either of them had signed up for. Fear shafted through him. Fear that he could like this too much, that it filled something in him he hadn't realized was empty.

But she seemed so happy, so relaxed, that he wanted her to have this morning. Besides, she knew, just as well as he did, what they did and didn't have.

And if he was honest, he wanted it for himself, too.

Frowning in concentration, she measured ingredients.

The fact he wanted it, too, was what convinced him to move out of the kitchen. He opened his laptop on the dining table, forcing himself to read through emails and check the markets rather than watch her. Watch her hands, watch her face, watch everything about her.

She didn't understand, wouldn't because she'd had so little experience of relationships, how they worked and how they ended. How you had to not let yourself be drawn in. You had to keep a part of yourself separate and walled off. A part that watched, from a remote—safe—internal distance.

"Who taught you to cook?" She looked over her shoulder, a smudge of flour on her jaw.

"I taught myself."

She threw a puzzled glance his way. "Are your parents both still in Chicago?"

"In a manner of speaking. They're buried there."

"Oh. I'm sorry." She rested the wooden spoon in the mixing bowl and took a step toward him, her face crestfallen.

"It's okay." He held up his hand in a stop gesture. "I don't need your sympathy." And when he saw her stiffen ever so slightly at his words, he had to try to soften them. "It was a long time ago."

She turned back to the bowl, began stirring. "How long?"

"I was nineteen. My brothers were seventeen and fifteen."

"But you have three brothers."

"The twins were fifteen."

She stopped stirring. "What did you do? What happened to you all?"

"Jack and I were old enough to take care of the twins. And we had my grandparents close by." Though to be honest his grandparents had been more of a hindrance than a help—always criticizing, always negative. It was, he knew, their way of trying to help. It just hadn't been a particularly helpful way. "Anyway, my mom had done all the cooking when we were growing up and I mean all of it. She loved cooking, saw it as her role. It was her way of showing her love for us. Consequently there was a steep learning curve including lots of disasters and as many take-out meals as we could afford. But we got there."

"So, you're close to your brothers?"

"Yeah." It was something of a cliché but they'd made it through the tough times together, not without their share of drama, but those same tough times had brought them closer, made them stronger. They didn't live in each other's pockets, apart from the twins, but they were all there for each other. He watched Rebecca ladling batter into the pan, hoped she was done with the personal stuff and started thinking about ways of distracting her if she wasn't. He had to pull his own thoughts back into line. The here and now. That's where they should be. "When bubbles form and burst, you can turn them," he said.

"Do you want children?" She didn't look up.

Okay. Not done with the personal stuff. Not by a long shot.

She looked up now, biting her lip. "Sorry. I should never have asked that. It's like because we've…" She waved her hand in the air. "I've forgotten where the boundaries are." She turned back to the pan, a delicate pink blush rising up her cheeks. "And just so you know, it's not like I was thinking that because we…slept together I'm now wanting to be the mother of your children or anything." She glanced at him again. Biting her lip again but this time it looked like she was doing it to stop from laughing. "I'm making this worse, aren't I?"

He nodded because for a moment dread had welled up. But his first reaction, before the dread had swamped it, had been a flicker of something more primal, something almost the opposite of dread.

"Honestly, don't worry, and stop frowning. Once you're gone and things get back to normal and Dad gives me the space to live my own life, I'm going to find my own nice man and do with him all the things we—" She pressed elegant flour-dusted fingers over her lips. "That's so not the thing to say, either. What have you done to me?"

Apparently only things she was already planning on doing with somebody else. "It's no big deal," he said, trying to get this conversation back to a semblance of normality, trying to be okay with the thought of her with another man. "Yeah, I'd like kids someday. When I'm not so driven by the business, when I meet the right woman and the time is right." And that was enough talking about him and some imaginary future. "How about you?"

Rebecca set plates on the counter. "I used to think, no. That I didn't want to bring children up the way my brothers and I were brought up—by a succession of nannies and staff, no matter how kind and well-educated they were, and constantly in the public eye, but…"

"But?"

"Since Rafe married he's been finding ways to keep out of the limelight when it suits him, which is more and more often these days. And Lexie's pregnant. Which is great news for them but for me, too, because it means that instead of third in line to the throne, I'll be fourth. And then if they have other children and Adam marries and has children I get further and further down the line of succession."

"You don't mind?"

"Mind? No, I've been looking forward to it for years. It means that interest in me—what I'm doing and wearing and saying, and who I'm seeing—will fall off. My life will become more my own. And I sometimes wonder if then perhaps I can be a mother. A normal one. If maybe I could have children and they could have a chance at a life that approaches normal. We could cook pancakes together." She smiled, but the smile dimmed. "But I'm not even sure I'll know how to be a mother. I have so few memories of my own. And—" she looked up "—that's way more than you wanted to know. I'm sorry. I shouldn't have dumped all that on you. I don't even know where it all came from. What I should have said was, yes. Just yes, or maybe. One day. What's really weird about all of this is that usually I know the right things to say and, more importantly, I usually know when to stop talking."

She looked suddenly uncomfortable, this woman in his kitchen with a dusting of flour on her lips. "Strikes me that any kid would be lucky to have you for a mom." Even luckier would be the man who got to make those babies with her.

"Thank you." She frowned at the pancakes. "I shouldn't have talked so much about myself, though."

"Why not?"

"It's not good manners, it's not good conversation. I should have asked more about you."

"Because it's good manners?" he asked, offended.

"Yes. Tell me about—"

"Don't you dare ask me something just because it's good manners. I'd far rather talk about you. I'd far rather talk to that woman I just got a glimpse of. The one who's a person with fears and insecurities and not a perfect princess."

She smiled. She really had a beautiful smile. It lit her whole face. "If it's fears and insecurities you want I can give you those by the bucketful." She turned back to the pan and flipped a pancake.

He wanted to kiss her. Wanted to cross to her and take her in his arms, take her back to his bed. Which made him want to kick himself. They'd transitioned from what they had—something safe—to this, which he couldn't quite define, but which felt like the slipperiest of slopes.

He glanced at the screen in front of him. He'd pulled up the home page of the *San Philippe Times.* It was covered in photos of the two of them at the rose gardens. "The press are taking the bait." It wouldn't hurt to keep to the forefront the fact that this was a charade. Admittedly one with benefits.

"Oh." She didn't look up from the pan. "Great."

He scrolled through the photos on-screen. The two of them at the rose garden, sitting close, leaning slightly toward each other. The two of them walking, looking at each other—the heat clear to see. The two of them kissing and then finally… "Damn."

"What is it?"

"A photo of your car on the road outside. They got it before I shifted it."

Rebecca lifted one slender shoulder in a shrug. "It wouldn't have been difficult. It was out there for a while."

"I should have shifted it sooner. I'm sorry." The politeness and awkwardness was creeping in. He should welcome it, not regret it. Not want to take them back just half an hour to when they were in bed.

"It was hardly your fault. I drove here. I parked it there. Besides, ultimately my life will be easier with just a smidgen of tarnish on my reputation. The whole Perfect Princess thing is pretty hard to live up to. So long as I ultimately get that engagement ring. The fake one," she added quickly, as though to reassure him she wasn't still thinking futures and babies. "Everything will be fine."

He kept his focus on the screen, annoyed nonetheless. "There are some things the whole country doesn't need to know about." Their private life for one thing, because what they'd shared last night, for all that it had a purpose and limits, was private. It had been between them. Not to further either of their causes.

"The thing with publicity is that while you can influence it, ultimately you don't get to choose." She flipped another pancake.

"I know."

"They'd be thinking it anyway," she said carefully. "And it is what we wanted, isn't it? We have this intense relationship, we get engaged, we break up."

"True. But it should have been better planned, better controlled. And I'm not sure you realize that once the tarnish is there it's hard to get rid of."

Rebecca all but rolled her eyes. "You're seriously trying to explain to me about reputations?"

"Preaching to the choir?"

"The millionth sermon on the subject."

"I just feel bad for your lack of privacy. That you can't do anything without people knowing about it."

She shrugged. "When you don't have a choice you do it. Probably you would have said when you were eighteen that you weren't able to raise three brothers but you did. This is just how my life is. Besides, people need to think things are progressing fast and well between us so that our engagement is believable and so that they're on my side when it ends."

"So, you're just using me?"

She smiled. A man could grow to count on those smiles. "Yes. I'm using you."

"If that's being used," he said, "I'm all for it." He returned his attention to the computer screen. He had to, otherwise he'd be out of his chair and letting her use him all over again.

"You were very good, you know. I enjoyed it. A lot."

"Rebecca."

She looked at him.

"You're not analyzing, remember." All the same he

knew that together they had been much better than good. It was a definite chemistry thing.

She smiled. So sweet. So unbelievably sweet. "Seems like, if somebody gives you a gift, you should say thank you. So I'd just wanted to say—"

"Don't. Don't you dare." Because if there were thanks to be given it wasn't her who should be giving them.

He read a couple of the captions and some of the accompanying text. "They're definitely going to be on your side if what I'm reading is anything to go by. They're happy that their 'lonely' princess has found love." He almost stumbled over that last word. That was exactly what they wanted people to think, but to see it in black and white and applied to him and Rebecca, it seemed wrong. The fact that this was indeed playing out exactly as they'd wanted seemed wrong.

"I don't know why they're always insisting I'm lonely."

"That's the bit that irks you?"

"Being on your own does not make you lonely." Her hands fisted on her hips. An irate, beautiful chef/princess in his kitchen. Almost all too much to process. His brothers would laugh their heads off.

Speaking of which, he'd undoubtedly have to let them know something was up. They hated reading stuff about him in the papers before he'd told them. Although they probably wouldn't credit this particular story for a while, writing it off instead as the media getting things utterly wrong again as they so often had in the past. In fact, the whole affair could be over before any of them picked up on it.

His phone rang. He considered ignoring it but so few people had his personal number he picked it up instead. Besides, he needed to remember this was just a charade. They didn't need cozy, intimate mornings in his kitchen.

If they weren't making love, or being seen in public, he told himself, then there was no good reason for her to be here. And then he felt like a prize jerk for even having that thought.

"Logan," he snapped into the phone.

"What's eating you?" a deep voice retorted.

"Jack?" Logan picked up his coffee and strolled to the window, preparing himself for the inevitable. Sunlight glistened on the slow moving river. "That was quick. I thought you guys would ignore the papers for a while."

"What was quick? What's in the papers? I haven't seen them in days."

Which wasn't unusual for Jack. He lived in a cabin in the foothills of the Sierra Nevadas, thriving on shutting himself off from the world. He could have an in-depth conversation with Rebecca about how being alone did *not* mean you were lonely. But at least for now Logan had a reprieve. "Nothing. But if it's not the papers why are you ringing?"

"Because I want you to let me in. I'm downstairs."

It took a moment for that to sink in.

Logan watched Rebecca watching him as he turned from punching the access code to allow Jack entry. "We've got company."

She tensed and took a step back, though how far she thought she could get in the confines of his kitchen was a mystery. "The papers are one thing." She shook her head as she spoke, her gray eyes wide. "Who?"

"My brother."

The tension lifted from her face, to be replaced by curiosity. Logan headed for the marbled foyer as the elevator door slid open. He could hardly block his brother. Wouldn't actually want to. But for all that, his timing sucked.

"What are you doing here?" he asked as the doors opened.

Jack strolled past him. "Good to see you, too." He walked into the apartment. "I had a meeting in London. I thought I'd call in seeing as I was in the neighborhood, so to speak." He dropped a duffel bag to the floor and walked farther into the apartment. "You don't mind if I crash here for a while." He tossed a jacket onto the couch. "And did you know there's a photographer outside taking pictures of your place?" He turned for the kitchen and stopped when he saw Rebecca. "And I'm guessing you know there's a woman in your kitchen."

Rebecca gave a tentative smile and lifted the spatula in a greeting.

"Yeah. I had noticed," Logan said, quelling his own smile as he watched Rebecca. A hint of color climbed her face. Sweet. It was intriguing the way she managed to keep surprising him. So few women did. "Rebecca, this is my brother Jack. And Jack, this is—" He didn't know if there was a way he was supposed to introduce royalty, but he'd never been one to follow protocol and he wasn't going to start now. "Rebecca."

Jack studied her. "You look familiar. Did you ever live in Chicago?"

"No."

Jack shrugged then looked at Logan, speculation and a question in his gaze. "I should go, right?"

"No," they said in unison. She sounded almost as relieved as he was to have Jack here. Which was weird given than she'd instigated the whole let-me-make-breakfast routine.

"In fact," Rebecca said, "I should go."

This time it was Jack's turn to protest, but it was Logan she watched so he added his denial to his brother's.

"Rebecca's a fine cook." She raised her eyebrows and shot a worried glance at the fry pan then whirled with a gasp.

"Smells…interesting," Jack said.

And there was, Logan admitted, a definite hint of charcoal in the air. "Second batch always turns out better than the first," he said as he stepped into the kitchen, effectively blocking her exit when it looked like she might bolt. He held her shoulders. "Ignore Jack." He tipped the burned pancake into the trash, set the pan back on the stove and gestured to the bowl of batter. "Second time's a charm."

"I'll just take a shower," Jack called, then turned and walked away.

"I really should go." Rebecca looked past Logan.

"No."

She stiffened. "Are you telling me what I can and can't do?"

"The royal outrage is cute, Princess, but I'm telling you you're not leaving now. If that's what you're asking."

"But—"

He shifted her hair to expose her neck then kissed her, and though he hadn't yet gotten to her lips he'd effectively cut off her words. It was the only way he could think of to silence her protests. But just for good measure he found her lips, too. Let himself savor the gentlest of kisses. And effectively derailed his own train of thought, as well. One moment he was thinking only of soothing the panic that looked about to bloom into royal hauteur, and the next moment the taste of her, her soft warm mouth beneath his, had him remembering all the things they'd done together last night. All the things they could do again and the things they had yet to do. He'd need—not a lifetime, never that—but it could certainly take all of the remaining weeks they had left.

# Ten

Rebecca sat at the table with two big and largely silent men, both intent on eating. If there was anything wrong with her pancakes, they were doing a good job of hiding it. That much about this morning gave her a sense of satisfaction. She rarely cooked for herself. Living in the palace it just wasn't necessary. There was something elementally satisfying about watching Logan and his brother eat.

But she couldn't dwell on the satisfaction because this was all wrong. She should have left last night. She'd wanted Logan to share the benefit of his experience with her—which he'd been more than generous in doing. So much so that she hadn't been able to leave. She'd been enthralled. But there had been no talk of mornings after. She had what she thought she'd wanted. She should be content with that and go. Except he'd stopped her when she'd tried. Good manners only? She didn't know and could hardly ask.

"So, Jack. Logan never mentioned he had a brother coming to San Philippe."

Jack set down his fork. "Logan always plays his cards close to his chest. But in this case it's because he didn't know. But more importantly he didn't mention to me or either of our other brothers that he was seeing a beautiful woman. Which is a perfect example of what I mean about the cards and their closeness to his chest. Very secretive, my brother. Hates people knowing what he's doing."

"Feel free to address your questions and observations directly to me," Logan muttered.

"Thanks. How long have you two been an item?" Jack asked.

"Oh, we're not really—"

"A few weeks," Logan said. "I was going to let you know."

Jack shrugged. "I'm not surprised you haven't. You two clearly had other more important things to do."

Rebecca turned her attention to cutting a slice off her pancake. People—other than Logan—didn't usually make such blatant innuendos around her.

"Jack." Logan's voice was a low warning. Another hint of that unexpected chivalry, the one that had surfaced when he'd been concerned for her reputation.

Jack looked up, genuinely surprised. "What? There's a woman in your kitchen cooking you breakfast, both of you look like you had a damn fine night. You have that glow about you. The one I haven't had in far too long. What else am I supposed to think? Since when did you get so prissy anyway?" Jack reached for his coffee.

"Since I started dating a damn princess is when."

Jack coughed, trying and failing to contain the coffee he'd just sipped. He reached for a napkin to mop up the table.

"I don't expect people to change for me," Rebecca insisted.

Jack studied his brother. "A princess. I knew you were moving in high circles but how did that happen?"

Rebecca looked to Logan for the explanation. She didn't know which version of their story he wanted to give his brother. The spin or the truth?

Whichever, Logan wasn't looking thrilled with his brother. "We met here a few times and then I ran into Rebecca in New Zealand."

"You'd been visiting the Coromandel properties?"

Oh, great. He'd really had business in New Zealand. She'd all but called him a liar over that.

"Yes." Logan winked at her, enjoying her discomfort. "And it turns out we have a few things in common—" he shrugged "—and one thing led to another and so here we are."

So, a version somewhere between the spin and the truth.

"Here you are," Jack said slowly. "Can't hurt with your plans to expand into Europe."

"No."

Jack looked at Rebecca. "No matter what success he achieved at home he always wanted Europe. Always wanted to prove a point to the old man, our grandfather," he explained, looking at Rebecca. "Nothing any of us ever did was good enough for him. And being German, Europe was the acme of achievement. I think maybe dating a princess would impress even him."

"Good to know I could be of use," Rebecca said mildly.

"It's a bit late, he's dead now," Jack added, "but the conditioning lives on."

"And I really do have to get going." Rebecca stood. Logan and Jack both stood, too.

"Nice meeting you, Rebecca." Jack smiled and shook

his head. "My brother and a princess. Never would have seen that one coming. Does this mean I could have a nephew who's king of San Philippe one day?"

"No," Logan said. "Because San Philippe is a principality not a kingdom."

"There's a difference?" Jack asked.

Logan shook his head in mock despair. "Kingdoms have kings, principalities have princes. Look it up."

"And," Rebecca continued, "because your brother is just using me for my connections and I'm using him for his body. There's nothing permanent." Her version of the truth.

"I'm not sure that you're getting the better half of that deal." Jack laughed and puffed out a chest as broad as Logan's, folding his arms so that his biceps bulged against the sleeves of his gray T-shirt. "Now if it's a fine body and a fine mind you're after…" He winked.

Rebecca laughed though Logan didn't look to find his brother as amusing as she did. She linked her arm through his, an arm that had held her so tenderly last night. "I'm pretty satisfied with my side of the deal so far."

"I'll walk you to your car. Say goodbye, Jack."

She extricated her arm. "Just give me a minute. I need to freshen up a little and get my bag."

In Logan's bedroom she barely spared a glance for that big, big bed where she'd spent the best night of her life. Instead she gathered up her things and dropped them into her bag. In the bathroom she tidied herself up, put on a little makeup. Outside, she could hear low voices. They weren't exactly arguing but there was definitely a discussion of sorts going on. As she left the room she caught Jack's voice. "What are you trying to prove to the old man? He's dead anyway."

"It's not that."

"Come on. This need of yours to always be the best. Doesn't get much better than royalty."

"Keep out of it, Jack." Logan's voice was low and serious. "She's not royalty. She's a woman."

Rebecca was oddly touched by the distinction.

"I can see that—"

Rebecca didn't know what Logan said or did but Jack stopped speaking for a moment. "Oh. So have you given her the I-can't-let-a-relationship-interfere-with-business speech?"

"No. This is different," Logan said abruptly, clearly not enjoying the conversation.

"Okay. Wow. Sorry. She must really mean a lot to you."

"No." His denial was quick and emphatic.

"You're not fooling me. Your guitar's out. You never play for other people."

"I didn't play for her. She doesn't mean anything to me."

Rebecca walked around the corner. She would have stopped and waited if she'd known those were the words she was going to walk around to.

Both men turned to look at her. Only one of them, Logan, cursed. "I'm sorry. I didn't mean—"

What? He didn't mean that? He didn't mean to say it? Or he just didn't mean for her to hear it? She'd never know because he didn't finish the sentence. Her lover of last night, the one whose words alone had lit fires within her, seemed lost for words.

But she was a princess so it was okay. Because she could smile through anything, look dignified through anything.

"Jack, it's been a pleasure meeting you. Logan, I can see myself to the car. Please stay with your brother."

She turned to go. Regal, refined, letting no emotions show. She could do it. Though she'd never had to fight quite so hard for calm before, to walk serenely when she wanted to run, to smile over the gasp of pain that had threatened to escape.

Logan caught up to her. Stepped into the elevator with her before she could shut the doors.

"Rebecca…" Her name on his lips resonated with remorse.

"It's okay, Logan. I'm not supposed to mean anything to you. Though you could have at least waited until I left the apartment. It kind of ruined what had been a very nice night." There was the understatement of the year. Two of them. *Kind of* ruined and *nice.*

He faced her, turned her to face him. "It scared me when Jack said you must mean something to me because I don't want you to mean anything to me. I don't want what we have to mean anything. Because it's going to end. But whether I want it to or not, it does mean something. It means a lot. You have to know that. You don't spend a night like last night with someone—and I'm talking about all of it, the walking by the river, the meal and the making love—without it meaning something. And this morning."

She wanted so desperately to believe him. She just didn't know if she could. "I'll have to take your word for it. You'll have noticed that my experience isn't quite on the same plane as yours."

"Then do take my word for it."

"Thank you. I will. You're very kind."

"Hell, Rebecca, stop that."

"I'm trying to be gracious."

"I know. That's what I want you to stop."

"You'd rather I ranted and raved."

"Yes."

She studied him a moment, silencing the part of her that

could too easily rant and rave. She was better than that. "Well, you don't get what you want. Not this time."

"And you've never said something you wanted to be true even though you knew it wasn't. Something like, 'That didn't hurt Logan, those words didn't cut. I'm not upset.'"

"Can we stop this?"

"No. Not yet. Not until you believe I didn't mean what I said to Jack."

The elevator stopped and the doors opened to the parking garage and Rebecca stepped out. "It doesn't matter."

Logan walked with her. "It matters."

"In that case I do believe you. And I'm not just saying that to placate you or saying something I want to be true even though I know it's not. Because last night meant something to me. And although it can't possibly have meant as much to you, it had to mean something. Didn't it?"

They stopped at her car. Logan stood in front of her door, blocking her escape.

"It did." He said the words so simply. His gaze open and intense, as though he was willing her to look into his eyes and believe him. He shouldn't be allowed to have such beautiful eyes. "It. *You.* Mean a lot more than just something."

A terrible sadness welled within her, threatened to break loose.

She leaned forward and kissed him, a touch of her lips to his just because she could. And because she couldn't not. And then she stepped back. "See you at the polo." They could go on from here. Go on with their deal. She would keep seeing him in public. She might even kiss him in public. But that—what she'd just done—was their last private kiss. She could almost wish it had been longer so that she'd have more than the memory of a fleeting taste of coffee and maple syrup, of firm lips, of fledgling warmth.

"You're okay? You'll be there?"

"You flatter yourself, Logan, if you think just one night with you could be so affecting that it would change everything."

So who was lying now? The voice of honesty taunted her.

He reached for her, gripped her shoulders and lowered his head to hers, gave her more of a memory, beguiled and enchanted her with his kiss as he seemed so effortlessly able to do. She, on the other hand, had to make an effort. An effort not to melt into him, not to wrap her arms around him and hold him close.

He pulled back, his hands had slipped up to frame her face and he held her head still while he studied her, held her gaze. "You mean more to me than is good for me."

Finally he released her and stepped aside to open her door.

She got in, put her key in the ignition and forced herself to think clearly and without emotion or sentiment. They'd get engaged—and she would not let it mean anything—and then they would break up. That time couldn't come soon enough. Because if this morning's debacle had taught her anything, breaking up with him was not going to be easy. At least not for her.

He closed her door and she lowered the window and looked up at him. It had to be said. "I wanted to say thank you."

"Thank you?" He practically growled the words. "Don't you dare."

"Good manners dictate it." She glanced at his fingers tightening on her door frame. "I made a request of you. And you more than satisfied that request."

"You think that's the end of it?"

"It has to be."

He stepped back and folded his arms across his chest. And for the first time since she'd heard him talking to his brother, a flicker of the amusement she was so used to flashed in his eyes as he shook his head. "See you at the polo then. But just so you know, that's not the end of it. Not by a long shot."

# Eleven

Rebecca stood at the front of the royal enclosure. Usually she loved watching polo, the drama of the thundering hoofbeats. And she'd seen Logan play before. He was a natural horseman with an uncanny ability to read the game, to be in the right place at the right time. He'd told her how he'd learned to ride working vacations on a relative's ranch but that he'd come to the game itself comparatively late.

Today she had to split herself in two to watch the match. She had to appear to be fascinated because she needed to convince the throng of people in the marquee that Logan captivated her. In particular she wanted to convince her father, holding court in the enclosure, and the bachelors here from his list who were trickling into the country.

The impromptu ball was fast approaching. She needed her relationship with Logan to look solid, she needed to look infatuated. But at the same time she needed to not be infatuated. Infatuation being a state that might well be easy to slip into. So she watched with determined detachment. And though she tried to concentrate on her brothers, who were both on the team, it was Logan who drew her eye. *I will not admire his skill. I will not admire his seat, in either the equestrian or the bodily sense of the word.* Detachment. She practically had to repeat the word like some kind of mantra.

He had phoned her last night, his voice warm and gentle over the line. He'd called, not to ask anything of her, not to rehash the mess the morning had turned into. But just, he'd said, to hear her voice, to know that she was okay.

She had wanted to go to him. To ask him to come to her. She had wanted the balm of being in his arms. But she managed to keep those needy words at bay, and to just bask in the warm cocoon that had surrounded her. That, she'd decided was his skill, the ability he had, even over the phone, to establish a connection that felt exclusive as though he thought only of her.

The opposing team scored a goal, leveling the score.

Various people—too many of them male and eligible— tried to claim her attention. But that wasn't what she wanted, either. So she positioned herself close to Lexie, who, like the boys in the team Rafe coached, cheered raucously, focusing intently on every play of the game.

Standing on the other side of Lexie, watching with no enthusiasm but looking stunning, was Adam's latest date, a young Hollywood actress.

Logan sped around an opposing player, swung his mallet and scored a goal, turned and cantered past her. She couldn't help but watch him, irritated with herself that his wink seemed just for her, threatened to warm her. She could feel what was happening and she wouldn't let it.

She would not fall for him. Something that one-sided would be sheer stupidity.

Lexie nudged her arm. "I didn't think he was going to get that last goal, he spends so much time looking over at you. But I guess that gives him all the more incentive to try to impress."

"He doesn't need to impress me."

"Because you're already impressed?"

"No. Because he's not the sort to try to impress, and I'm not the sort to be impressed by sporting prowess."

"What about by a fine body?" Lexie nudged again, drawing out a smile.

"Maybe a little." She watched that fine body as he rose up in his stirrups, lean-hipped, in nicely fitting whites. She sighed and dragged her gaze away.

Lexie's eyes danced in knowing amusement. "Great seat."

"How's the pregnancy going?" Rebecca asked pointedly, eager to change the subject.

Lexie leaped on the change. "I'm feeling terrific." She pressed her hand to her abdomen. "We're going to announce it soon." Lexie turned when one of the boys from Rafe's team approached her.

Rafe's whirlwind courtship and marriage to Lexie had surprised everyone, including Rafe. But the fact that the two of them were deliriously happy was plain to see. And Rebecca couldn't be more pleased for them. But she also couldn't help wondering whether she'd ever find that kind of soul-deep love, that kind of happiness. She looked over at Logan—to whom she meant nothing—and looked away again. Her heart sank further as she saw Eduardo walking purposefully toward her.

"Things going well with you and Buchanan?"

"Good game, don't you think?" She gestured at the

field. Eduardo was the last person with whom she wanted to discuss her relationship with Logan.

"I've seen better. There's another board meeting next week, the main purpose of which is to discuss the sale of the subsidiary."

Why was he telling her? "I didn't realize you had an interest in leBlanc."

Eduardo affected boredom. "The new stepfather. Wants to do a little father-son bonding. Wants my opinion on Buchanan's character. That sort of thing."

"Oh, look. Another goal." Rebecca clapped.

Eduardo glanced at the game. "You know he's using you to further his business interests? I thought you should know."

Eduardo ought to know. He'd wanted to use her, too, to further his political aspirations. "Thank you for thinking of me. That's really very sweet of you."

Eduardo's mouth tightened. "He's not right for you."

Rebecca hid her surprise at Eduardo's intrusion into her privacy. He was usually more subtle. Warning prickled along her skin.

"He's never going to fit into the kind of life we lead. He doesn't understand it. Doesn't approve of it. And he doesn't play by the rules."

It took effort to keep her voice neutral, to not leap to Logan's defense. "Thank you for your opinion. You are, as always, right." What he failed to understand was that was part of Logan's appeal, and Rebecca couldn't like any "we" that bracketed her with Eduardo. "Now, if you'll let me watch the match."

Eduardo's eyes went cold. "I apologize for my interruption. I was only trying to help. We've been friends for a long time. And I'll still be here after he's gone."

"We have been friends for a long time. So please don't spoil it."

"I'd do anything not to spoil it. But I need to talk to you. And for your boyfriend's sake it should be before the board meeting." There was something about the way Eduardo was speaking that chilled her, made her think that she hardly knew this man she'd known for most of her life. A couple of members of one of the visiting polo teams approached. Eduardo leaned closer and spoke quietly. "I need to talk to you in private. Soon."

"Make an appointment with my secretary."

Eduardo, displeasure curling his lip, nodded then turned and strode away.

Five minutes later the final chukker was over and still she watched Logan, surrounded by well-wishers, people wanting to congratulate him on the winning goal, wanting to revel in the reflected glory, to share in the team's jubilation. She kept her distance and chatted with other spectators. She caught his gaze a couple of times when he looked her way, both times as he'd looked at her his smile had faded. He left with his teammates to shower and change. She would have gone then, too, if it hadn't been expected that she'd wait. She'd be being watched, analyzed. They were supposed to be a couple. And if she was a true girlfriend, one who meant something—she couldn't help the mental aside—she would stay. An early departure would draw attention. The wrong sort.

She was still speaking with the polo players when she felt a familiar tingle along her spine and turned to see Logan approaching, his gaze intent on her. And then he was at her side, smiling as he apologized to the players and various other people wanting to speak with both of them as he led her away.

She let out a sigh and wasn't sure whether it was relief at escaping the artifice or pleasure at being with him.

The worrying thought was it might be the latter. She liked being with him too much. It was something beyond logic, beyond control. It just was.

"Watch the Argentinean player. Number eight. He's a player in all senses of the word," Logan said.

"But charming to speak with and he has quite the sense of humor. Slightly wicked but very funny nonetheless." She could look after herself.

Logan sighed.

They walked past the hospitality marquees brimming with guests sipping champagne and around to the players' side of the fields. Horse trucks were parked in long rows; beside them grooms brushed down tethered polo ponies and unwound and deftly rolled up the protective bandages from their legs.

She'd always liked the smell of horses, warm and earthy. Now it combined with the scent of the freshly showered man at her side, one of soap and spice.

They walked side by side, not talking. Arms occasionally brushing. He caught her hand in his.

"I'm glad you came," he said finally.

"I said I would."

"I thought I'd ruined it yesterday." Regret tinged his voice.

"You did. But I needed the warning." She was trying to show him that she had things in perspective, even if she wasn't sure she did, and she was trying to assure him that she wasn't upset. They could continue with their charade like two rational adults.

"Dammit, Rebecca."

She glanced at him and raised her eyebrows. It wasn't like him to curse in her presence. But still it gave her a small sense of satisfaction that he'd lost some of his composure. "Dammit? Really?"

"And don't get all prissy on me."

"I'm not getting *prissy,* I just thought we'd lifted our game when we started dating a princess." She knew her use of the royal *we* would irk him. But hadn't he said as much to his brother? And hadn't she insisted she didn't expect people to change for her?

"You're driving me nuts."

"It's mutual." They strolled up a gentle rise and stopped under the shade of an oak tree, turning back to watch the activity around the horse trucks a short distance away. "We can call an early end to this whole thing if that would suit you better?" She needed to put that option out there for him.

And suddenly his arm was around her shoulders and he swung her in close and kissed her. Angry and hungry and wanting. And—dammit—she needed his kiss so badly. Needed it because it pushed through all the barriers between them. It said he did feel something for her, even exasperation was better than nothing. She leaned into him, let his mouth claim hers, let his tongue tease hers, and did her share of claiming and teasing in return. Her eyes closed so that apart from the sounds around them, her only sensations were physical—the press of him against her, his arms around her and his lips on hers. The taste and flavor of him. His warmth, his strength.

She missed what they'd lost. Craved this feeling of being in his arms, of being close, the certainty that what was between them was important, was in fact the only thing that mattered. But as soon as the kiss ended the surety evaporated.

Just yesterday she'd made a resolution to not kiss him

in private anymore. She looked about. There were people not too far away, so this kiss had definitely been allowed.

He stepped back, just a little, breathing hard. "No. It wouldn't suit me better."

Still partially dazed from their kiss she had to think back to what her question was, what wouldn't suit him. Oh. "I suppose you still need board approval. But maybe after the board meeting…"

He closed his eyes for a second, and when he opened them again he was utterly serious. "No. It still won't suit me after the meeting. We have an agreement. Our relationship lasts until after the ball." His eyes narrowed, his gaze intent on her. "What do you know about the board meeting?"

Rebecca considered telling Logan about Eduardo, but what had he really said? Only that Logan was using her and that Eduardo would be around after Logan had gone. Both facts that were out in the open. She lifted a shoulder.

"Just that it's the meeting you talked about. The one that meant you needed to be seen with my father." And look where that had got them.

"I saw you talking to Eduardo."

"Yes." She lifted her chin. "Not just the other polo players. But as far as I can recall our agreement didn't stipulate who we could and couldn't talk to."

He leaned closer, put his lips near her ear and murmured, "Prissy."

And Rebecca laughed. "Maybe just a little. But I'm allowed. It's in my job description." In so many ways Logan was good for her. She took herself too seriously sometimes. He made sure she didn't. He seemed able to ease a tension she didn't know she carried, making her laugh. And then there were the other ways in which he was good—very good—for her.

He was still close. Close enough that she could practically count the dark spiky lashes framing his eyes. He held her hands in his, touched his forehead to hers. If only this moment, the one simple connection that wasn't about anything other than just being here with him, could last forever.

Where was the distance she'd promised herself? The cool reserve?

"There's something disturbingly appealing about you when you do the royal thing, all clipped and precise with that haughty tilt to your chin. It's such an act. I can't believe more people don't see right through it."

Neither could she. But most people had no idea. It seemed only Logan saw through it. Which meant Logan was the one who saw her insecurities. But with him at least she knew they were safe.

"There you are." A booming voice interrupted. "I see you've finally taken your foot out of your mouth long enough to do something useful with it. Your mouth, that is. Not your foot."

"Yes. And you're not helping." Logan glanced at his brother. "Go away."

"Can't yet. I just met a delightful—"

"Then we will." He looked at Rebecca. "Are you ready to leave?"

She nodded, all the while knowing that she was far too ready to do whatever this man wanted of her.

Photographers snapped shots of them as they headed for his car, walking purposefully, Logan holding her hand. She couldn't imagine it would make interesting viewing for anybody.

"Where are we going?" she asked as they pulled away.

"Somewhere we can get some privacy," he said through clenched teeth. "There's something I want to do with you."

That they weren't followed, Rebecca put down to the increasing speculation about Lexie's possible pregnancy. Press hopes were for a shot of a baby bump or even a public announcement. Though there was some gossip about a potential engagement between Logan and her, theirs was perceived as the less likely and less imminent news.

But privacy with Logan? Something he wanted to do with her?

She thought back to the last time they'd had any real privacy. She looked at the line of his jaw, the small vee of tanned chest revealed by the undone top buttons of his shirt, his competent hands on the wheel, hands that had touched her so intimately, so lovingly, so…magically, and knew that he could too easily undermine her resolve to maintain a degree of physical and emotional distance.

"I don't think your apartment's a good idea."

He raised an eyebrow and a grin quirked his lips. "That's not what I had in mind."

She wanted to kick herself. That simple assumption had revealed too much about the paths her thoughts took. She might not think his apartment was a good idea, but that didn't mean it wasn't where the less sensible part of her wanted to go. "So, where?" she asked casually.

"You'll see."

"You really do like to play your cards close to your chest."

He stopped for a traffic light and brushed a knuckle along her jaw. "And you really don't like not being the one in control. Just wait. I think you'll like it."

# Twelve

Half an hour later Rebecca stood smiling on the small dock as she looked at the pretty white-and-red rowboat Logan had hired for them. She glanced down at her dress and shoes, a well-coordinated ensemble in cream and beige, the shoes with the cutest heels, perfect for the polo, not so perfect for a rowboat.

"You'll be fine," Logan said, breaking into her thoughts as he came to stand beside her. "All you have to do is sit." He passed her one of the matching straw hats and then handed her into the wooden boat, and once she was seated, climbed in and sat facing her on the front seat. He nodded at the man renting them the boat, who then disappeared into the small brightly painted shed on the dock and returned a few seconds later carrying…a guitar? He handed the instrument in its soft case to Logan, who set it behind him in the boat. Logan was going to play for her. Her heart soared foolishly. The boat owner gave them a firm push off from the dock.

Logan began rowing. Here, the river, overhung with willows, moved slowly. He rowed with long, smooth strokes, taking them upstream. Sunlight sparkled on the water. The only sound was the quiet rhythmic knock of the oars in the rowlocks.

"This seemed like the best way of getting you away from the people who want to talk to us," he said as he rowed, "but we're in public, it'll still count toward the occasions we've been seen together."

In the distance visitors strolled through the rose gardens. "And very romantic-looking, too," she said, trying to sound as though she was thinking purely analytically, while not sounding cynical. "It'll definitely look good."

"Exactly."

For the sake of the balance of the boat she sat directly opposite him, her feet in their impractical heels firmly together but placed between his widely spaced feet.

She leaned over the side and trailed her fingers in the cool water, mainly to avoid looking directly at Logan. Though she couldn't help the occasional glance. For all that this ought to be relaxing, he didn't look relaxed. Didn't look to be enjoying himself any more than she was. "Can I row?" she asked.

His gaze narrowed doubtfully.

"Princesses aren't helpless, you know."

"I never thought they were. Actually, I've never given any thought to it, but I've never assumed anything of the sort about you. Quite the opposite, in fact."

"Oh. Thank you."

"Swing around to sit beside me, then I'll shift to your seat."

They completed the maneuver. Logan took the guitar

with him and Rebecca began rowing, glad to have something to do, something other than Logan to focus on. Her unpracticed efforts were clumsy at first, but Logan placed his hands beside hers on the oars, helped her get a feel for the rhythm of rowing and the placement of the oars.

He unzipped the guitar.

"You don't have to." It was enough that he'd thought to bring the guitar. A gesture she appreciated.

"I know I don't have to. I want to. You are the only person on the list of people I would play for. It's private. But this is so you know that you mean something. That what you heard me say to Jack couldn't have been further from the truth." The intensity in his gaze and the sentiment behind his words almost made her want to weep, so desperately did she want to mean something to this man.

Looking away, he settled the instrument on his thigh and began playing, his fingers moving assuredly over strings and frets. He glanced up. "Just don't expect me to sing." His smile flashed.

Rebecca rowed slowly, overhanging willows occasionally brushing the boat, and listened. His soft strumming was the perfect accompaniment to their afternoon.

Too soon he stopped and slid the guitar back into its case. "It wouldn't be right to let you do all the rowing."

"I was enjoying it. Your playing. And the rowing."

"But still. Besides, there's something we need to talk about." His voice was suddenly serious.

Rebecca concentrated on keeping the oars even, dipping them into the water simultaneously, pulling back evenly. "Is everything all right?"

"I've never done this before."

"Sat in a boat while a woman rowed?"

"Not that." Logan slid a hand into the pocket of his

trousers, pulled out a small jeweler's box and leaned toward her. "I think we should get engaged."

Her left oar skittered across the surface of the water, the boat swerved, she overcorrected and the boat spun the other way. Finally she got it back under control. She rowed with long strokes, trying to find a rhythm that suddenly eluded her. "I guess." Somehow, after the guitar playing, the offer of engagement felt like a letdown.

He still held the small velvet box in his hand. "I didn't know if I should have had you with me to choose the ring. I wasn't sure what you like. But this one appealed. I could imagine you wearing it."

Long even strokes. That was all she had to do. This wasn't a proposal. Logan wasn't asking her to marry her. Even if he had imagined her wearing the ring he'd chosen. This was just a temporary symbol of their temporary arrangement. "It doesn't really matter." She spoke the words as much to convince herself as him.

"It does matter. I want you to like it. You're the one who has to wear it."

"Makes sense," she said casually. "But it's only for a couple of weeks. Then you'll get it back." Something tightened in her throat.

"I don't want it back," he said, the words clipped, almost angry. "What am I going to do with an engagement ring?"

She glanced back over her shoulder to make sure her direction was true. And to avoid meeting Logan's gaze. "Give it to someone else? Sell it?" It wasn't easy to stop herself from looking at either Logan or the ring but she managed. She looked at her hands on the oars, the water, the riverbank. She hadn't cried in years. She wasn't going to now. She didn't even know why the sudden urge was there, tightening her jaw. It was as though this expected *proposal* had spoiled a near perfect afternoon. And yet this was precisely what they had agreed upon. But the voice of the girl she'd once been—idealistic and full of dreams—wanted to refuse, because suddenly this wasn't enough. She wanted more.

Just this morning over breakfast her father had been so relaxed, the lines that creased his brow almost permanently had eased. He'd expressed his satisfaction with her relationship with Logan.

She couldn't throw it all away now.

And besides, Logan needed her for his negotiations. To help his dreams come true. Which was precisely why he was sitting opposite her holding a small box out for her. "Are you even going to look at it?"

"Of course. If you'd like." She pulled the oars toward her, sliding them through the rowlocks so she could rest them on the edge of the boat.

When she'd run out of excuses to not look at him she lifted her gaze to his glare. This was not how engagements were supposed to happen. Even fake ones, surely.

"Of course, we'll need to talk to my father. Royal protocol and all that."

"I've spoken to him. Asked his permission. It seemed like the thing to do."

"When?"

"Yesterday afternoon."

"What did he say?" Though she knew what her father must have said, given his contentment this morning.

"I'm here, aren't I? Although he didn't say much at all. First I got one of the longest silences I've ever had to endure."

Rebecca smiled. She could just imagine it. "He's good at that."

"Very. And then he asked if I thought I could make you happy."

"Oh." She suddenly knew the answer to that, too. She looked at the peeling paint on the bottom of the boat. Logan did make her happy. Being with him was unlike being with anyone else.

"For a while there I didn't know if I could go through with it. The thought of lying to your father wasn't a good feeling. But the funny thing is that when I finally said yes, it wasn't a lie. Sometimes I think I do make you happy, when I'm not making you sad by saying stupid things to my brother. You do something…similar for me. So that bit wasn't a lie. When I told him you're the most amazing woman I've ever met, that wasn't a lie, either. It was just the wanting-to-marry-you bit that wasn't exactly the truth. But after a couple of reasonably dire threats about what will happen if I fail to make you happy, he gave me his permission. So, given what I've had to go through already, you could put an end to the torture and at least look at the ring rather than the floor of the boat. As fascinating as it is."

She looked up and met his gaze. There was something both teasing yet utterly serious in the depths of his eyes. She reached for the box, and eased open the lid. An exquisite sapphire surrounded by diamonds sparkled and glinted, full of promise and beauty. Her heart seemed to rise up in her chest, blocking her throat even further. "It's beautiful," she said.

"Do you really like it?" His voice had gentled, and contained an unfamiliar uncertainty. "I thought of you when I saw it."

Rebecca nodded.

"Can I put it on you?"

She nodded again, still looking at the ring and the

wooden floor of the boat beyond it and out of focus. She didn't know when, if ever, she'd been quite so lost for words, quite so certain that if she said something it would be utterly inadequate, or worse, utterly unintelligible.

Logan eased the box from her fingers, lifted the ring out and slid it onto her left hand. Rebecca stretched her fingers out. The ring caught the sunlight and sparkled, full of false promise.

"I can change it if you don't like it. We could choose something different together."

"No. It's beautiful."

The boat bobbed on the water. Rebecca didn't trust herself to say anything more. Because she knew, in her heart of hearts, that she had somehow fallen in love with the man opposite her. The man whose ring she was wearing. The realization appalled her.

"Shall I row?"

That might be a good idea. She nodded and they swapped seats. Logan turned the boat downstream.

"If we announce it at the official dinner tomorrow night it ought to help your chances at the board meeting."

"That's not why I did this now." He dug the oars into the water.

"Then why?"

"I had other reasons. Not all of them quite so selfish."

"I wasn't accusing you of being selfish. I was just trying to look at the positives."

"Because otherwise it would be a negative?" He pulled hard on the oars.

"No. That's not what I said, either."

Logan heaved a sigh. "Next time I propose to a woman I'm going to do a much better job of it."

"I hope so." She managed a smile, though the thought of Logan proposing properly to a woman he loved and wanted to spend his life with did not please her. If anything quite the opposite. She bit her lip.

Logan stopped rowing and pulled in the oars, letting the boat drift with the current. His legs bracketed hers and he leaned forward, slid his hands along her jaw. His thumbs stroked over her cheekbones, and for long seconds she just looked into his beautiful brown eyes, and then he pulled her closer to kiss her. And his kiss did what it always did— broke through the maze of barriers, to something simple and lovely.

There was a kernel deep within her that ached for this to be real, for Logan to love her, to want to spend his life with her.

He ended the kiss and, after searching her face, started rowing again and Rebecca decided that sometimes it was best if they didn't speak. If she didn't let the feelings— insecurities and hopes—that she wasn't supposed to have bubble to the surface.

On the dock ahead of them a small group of photographers gathered. She sighed and Logan glanced back, scowling when he saw the pack. "Either we were followed or the boat owner must have called."

"My reputation," she said as pieces started to fall into place.

"What about it?"

"That was your other reason for getting engaged now. You wanted to protect my reputation after that photo of my car at your apartment."

He again looked back over his shoulder to the photographers. His face darkening.

"That's sweet. Thank you."

His strokes slowed. "This is supposed to be good for both of us. So far it seems to be working mostly in my favor."

"I don't know. It's doing what I need it to. And there have been other…benefits," she said, thinking, as she did far too often, of how they'd made love, knowing he'd know that was what she was thinking of. She'd hoped to make him smile with the reference. She didn't succeed.

They neared the dock.

"Once the news is released there will be questions." She pointed out the obvious.

"Like, when's the wedding going to be?"

She nodded.

"In ten months."

"You sound certain."

"I had to talk your father down from eighteen months. He insists that at least that much time is necessary to arrange a proper royal wedding. And after Rafe and Lexie snuck off for theirs and cheated him and the country of that celebration he is insisting on a proper royal wedding. But I wanted to be convincing, which meant I needed to stick as close to the truth as possible. If we really were getting married I'd want it to be as soon as feasible. I wouldn't want to waste another day not being married to you."

He would have had no difficulty convincing her father. He almost had her convinced—so badly was she blurring the lines between reality and fantasy.

Logan flicked another glance at the small group on the dock. "As for where we're going to live I don't see why we can't spend half the year here and half the year in the States. If your father and your adoring public would allow it. And if you wanted to."

"Sounds perfect." Almost too perfect. They may as well get their story straight.

"Babies?"

"Eventually," she answered, letting herself believe the

fantasy they were weaving. "We'll want some time together alone first."

"Long evenings when we can make love."

"And you can play the guitar for me."

"Definitely. And you can make us pancakes for breakfast."

"Definitely." She looked at her hand. The ring that represented so much and so little, sparkled.

# Thirteen

The ring still sparkled but in the space of a day everything else had changed. Yesterday afternoon Rebecca had—for a blissful time—willfully indulged in the fantasy and allowed herself to be happy, even though it was all a pretence.

She didn't even have that now.

Now she was both executioner and victim.

Wearing a vibrant glittering red dress, a far cry from the somber mood that gripped her, she sat at Logan's side for the official dinner, her head swimming, her heart heavy.

As Eduardo had requested, she'd made time to speak with him. Just two hours ago.

And everything had changed.

She'd then spoken with her father. And her father had had to call in his aides to let them know of the changes in the dinner plans.

Usually these evenings dragged. But tonight the pre-dinner

socializing, and the dinner itself, sped by. She hadn't had a chance to be alone with Logan, who wore a tuxedo better than any man she'd ever met. And she'd wanted and needed that chance desperately, while at the same time hoping it would never come. She'd hoped to delay doing what she now had to do.

It wouldn't hurt him, she told herself. It wouldn't even hurt her. He'd get what he'd wanted and so would she. She was just speeding things up a little. So why did she feel so wretched?

Her father stood to make his after-dinner speech. Logan reached over and squeezed her hand, his thumb swept over her fingers. Frowning, he dropped his gaze to her bare left hand.

His beautiful ring was back in its box, making a small bulge in her evening bag.

"You're waiting for the official announcement?" He glanced at her father as the prince began speaking then back at her.

Rebecca bit her lip and shook her head. "There's a change of plan. Our engagement isn't being announced tonight."

Doubt clouded his eyes. They sat through the announcement of Lexie's pregnancy. She got the feeling it was as difficult for Logan, knowing something was wrong, as it was for her to join in the air of excitement and joy. Her father sat down to rapturous applause. Animated conversation erupted around the room.

Logan's gaze rested unnervingly on her. "Where can we go to talk?"

"I can't leave the dinner. Royal protocol." A protocol she was choosing to follow when, if she really wanted, she could arrange to slip out. But she couldn't be alone with Logan right now. She wasn't strong enough to do what she had to if he was questioning her, pressing for an explanation.

Music, an upbeat waltz, began to play. Couples filled the dance floor.

Logan sat stock-still at her side. "Is this about what I said the other morning?" His voice was a low whisper beneath the sound of the music. "About you not meaning anything to me. I thought we sorted that out. You know it wasn't true."

She could not let him believe that. Not now. "No," she said, "this is about me not wanting to go on with this charade." Her own words tore at her. She reached for her evening bag and felt inside for the small velvet box. Her hand closed around it and she clutched it for just a second before drawing the box out. Beneath the table, she slid it to Logan. His hands stayed clenched into fists on his thighs. She took a breath and called up the awful, gut-wrenching words she'd rehearsed as she'd dressed. "I don't want to pretend to be engaged to you."

Quite the contrary. She'd realized when she'd spoken to her father earlier, telling him not to announce their engagement, that what she wanted more than anything was to make what she had with Logan real.

That she loved him.

In an awful irony the lie she'd had to tell her father was not that she loved Logan when she didn't, but that she didn't love him when she did.

His hand closed around hers and the small box within it. "Put it back. I'm not taking it from you."

As Rebecca slipped the ring back into her bag, the man seated on her right leaned in to speak. Logan got in first. "Excuse us, please. We're about to dance."

He led her to the dance floor, pulled her in close to him with the hand that curved about her waist.

Dancing with him was effortless. He moved with such assured grace, his body in tune with hers. As she should have known he would be. As she'd never get to experience again. She gave herself a few stolen seconds, stored away the sensation. She could lean her head on his shoulder now, all too easily. Now when she wouldn't let herself. The seconds were exquisite torture.

"What's going on?" his low voice whispered in her ear.

She swallowed. She had to do this. She'd known that what they had would end. But not like this. Not by her own hand. And not so soon. She pulled back from him a little and smiled brightly, aware of the brittleness of her expression. "Nothing's going on. I realized I don't want to go through with this." She spoke dismissively. "That's all."

"This?"

"The charade of an engagement."

He leaned back enough to watch her face. "What's wrong?"

The concern in his gaze, a concern that was all for her, nearly undid her. He wasn't buying her indifference. And she knew he'd try to find a way to push and probe until he uncovered the truth of what was happening. If he knew she was doing this for him he wouldn't let her. That was how he was. He'd insist on honoring his side of the bargain. A bargain that felt more hollow than ever.

So she said the only thing she knew would make him back off. "I had time to think after we got back from the lake and I've realized there might be other men I'd like to date. Men from my own social milieu." She lifted her fingers from his shoulder and waved to an imaginary friend across the room. She swallowed again and lifted one suddenly cold shoulder in a shrug. "My father's list might not have been so terrible."

"That polo player?" he asked through gritted teeth.

Rebecca tried for a playful smile, as though she wasn't breaking her own heart, shattering her own dreams. "Amongst others. He wanted to take me to the opera next weekend. I thought that might be nice. And I know you don't like the opera."

"Nice?" Logan stopped dead, his jaw hard, a muscle working high up, near his ear. He studied her as though he'd never seen her before in his life. The music still played, dancers swirled around them. For a moment she thought he might walk away, leave her standing alone on the dance floor.

But his grip on her hand, and his hold at her waist, tightened. His gaze narrowed and darkened. "Will you come outside with me, somewhere where we can talk properly, and tell me what's really going on?"

"I can't leave the dinner," she said blithely, looking up at him. "It's just not done. And really, there's nothing I can add." She had to lock her knees to keep her legs from trembling.

"That's it?"

"It's for the best. No one was seriously going to believe we were a couple. I told my father not to announce our engagement because it was over between us. But it's been…fun. Thank you." She didn't know how she stood for so long smiling through his scrutiny. People moved around them, glancing curiously at them. Finally he lifted her hand and pressed his lips to her knuckles in the gentlest of kisses. A kiss that nearly undid her. Then he led her from the dance floor, dropped her hand and kept walking.

Rebecca didn't call out to him to ask—beg—him to come back, and she didn't run after him. Nor did she give in to the urge to flee and hide where she could lick her wounds, give in to the sobs that tried to force their way from her chest. She didn't do any of the things she wanted to do. She watched his back as he cut a swath through the milling guests, watched the top of his dark head until he was gone from her sight and then she returned to her seat and made polite conversation with the guests at the dinner. It was what she was trained to do.

Never had she needed her training more.

Two mornings later, Logan strode into the reception area of leBlanc Industries. This opportunity, he reminded himself as he looked around at the old world elegance, was all he'd wanted in establishing himself in this country. It was his entrée into the rest of Europe. The continuation of the expansion that had fueled his dreams for almost as long as he could remember.

Rebecca, who had left a gash in his heart, had been a means to that end. But not the only means. She'd been window dressing. He could do it without her.

He still didn't understand how he'd misjudged her and everything between them so badly. Still couldn't make sense of her sudden U-turn. Or his reaction to it. The loss of sleep that had nothing to do with a loss of business opportunities, or the bleakness of a day that held no promise of seeing her, hearing her voice, touching her.

He unclenched the hands at his side. He didn't need her. He'd bought in to or taken over numerous businesses in the past, all without her at his side. This would be no different. He looked to his future, a future with no place in it for a princess.

A personal assistant arrived to lead him to the boardroom. A dozen formally suited board members sat around the massive mahogany table, their smiles and body language receptive.

An hour later he strode out and boarded a plane for Chicago.

They'd offered him everything he wanted.

# Fourteen

Rebecca fingered the thin gold chain around her neck as she skirted the crowded dance floor. All she really wanted was to escape the ball being held in her honor. The ball that had been intended to help her choose a suitor.

Tonight only Adam was fulfilling their father's expectations, dutifully dancing beneath the glittering chandeliers with almost every hopeful female attending, though none more than once.

Rebecca had danced with no one.

Because she had driven away the only man she wanted.

She had set herself the challenge of staying until midnight, but the minutes and hours had dragged. Soon though she would be able to leave. Alone. She had just one thing to do first.

Eduardo had been avoiding her since their last meeting.

The day Logan had walked out of her life and gone back to Chicago.

Eduardo's practiced smile dimmed and grew wary as she approached and unclenched her jaw enough to ask him to dance.

This was the only way to guarantee he would talk to her, to guarantee that she would keep a rein on her emotions and guarantee a specific end point to their conversation.

Their plan—hers and Logan's—had worked even when she'd wanted it not to. Despite her efforts to conceal her despair, her father had sensed its depths and offered to cancel the ball. He said he'd seen how upset she was over the end of her relationship with Logan. But she had insisted the ball go on. Because *upset* didn't even begin to describe her desolation.

That she'd done the right thing was little consolation.

When Logan had left she'd needed to rant and rave and so in the privacy of her bedroom those first nights she'd given vent to her heartbreak and grief and it had made her laugh and then cry harder to think that Logan would be proud of her for yielding to her emotions, for allowing herself to be overcome by them. As if she'd had a choice.

She walked to the dance floor with a tellingly silent Eduardo.

It was duty that had kept her going. She'd thrown herself back into work even as she'd felt like a hologram of herself. She had filled every hour of every day in a fruitless attempt to ensure she had no time to think about Logan, to dwell on him, to compare the emptiness of her life now to its fullness while he'd been in it. But no matter how busy she kept herself, thoughts of Logan underscored or overlaid every single thing she did. There was always time to think about him.

She dwelled.

Compounding her misery over the loss of him was the hurt of knowing how badly he must be thinking of her.

His good opinion mattered more than anyone else's in the world. And she had lost it. He believed she'd coldly reneged on their agreement and their relationship because she wanted to see other men.

As if any other man could compare.

She dwelled while she'd sat on boards, and attended openings. While she drove to kindergartens and hospitals. She dwelled when she fell into bed at night and couldn't sleep. She imagined him back in Chicago. Wondered what he was doing. Whether he thought of her.

And the pain and heartache had all been for nothing.

For which she blamed the man with whom she now danced, resenting every second of the touch of his hand to hers.

There was a wretched part of her that knew she should probably thank Eduardo. He had merely precipitated the inevitable and preordained conclusion. If her time with Logan had gone on longer, the trauma of the end, as overwhelming as it was, would have been even more devastating.

When she thought she had mastery over her voice and the storm of anger and grief within her, she spoke. "You broke our bargain." Her voice was gratifyingly steady. "I never thought you'd stoop so low." She wasn't yet ready to thank him. "You couldn't seriously think I would ever go out with you again, no matter how well that would reflect on you or how much political capital your stepfather would gain from the association."

Eduardo frowned and stiffened. "I kept our bargain."

Rebecca gave an unprincesslike snort of derision. "Our bargain was that Logan got the approval he needed if we weren't together."

"He had the board's approval. He turned it down."

"*He* turned it down? I don't believe you. It was everything he wanted."

"He turned it down flat and walked out of the meeting. And don't look at me like that. It was nothing to do with me. The board members were as perplexed as you."

"But…"

Eduardo moved and spoke stiffly. "Whatever happened, and for whatever reason, I still say no good—for you or the country—could have come from a relationship between you and Logan Buchanan. He was wrong for you. Utterly wrong. In time you'll see that."

"I doubt it."

"Then you're not the woman I thought you were."

She disengaged her hand from his and stepped away. "I've never been the woman you thought I was." The only man who'd ever seen the woman she really was had gone. She turned and walked back to her seat.

Midnight was only minutes away. Then she could leave and seek the sanctuary of her quiet, dark, Logan-less room.

She tried her best to be attentive to her table companions, to play her part.

A couple of times she caught Adam, in the arms of one or another beautiful woman, frowning at her. He would have to do his royal duty for the both of them. It didn't look as though it was too much of a hardship for him.

Finally, finally she heard the slow distant chime of the tower clock. As politely as she could—hiding her desire to flee—she excused herself.

She made it outside, to the top of the broad sweeping stairs, and closed her eyes on the welling tears. She drew in a deep, shuddering breath just as the twelfth chime of midnight sounded on the air. Her fingers sought the chain about her neck. And despite knowing better, despite the futility, she couldn't help but wish that she could wind back the clock and do everything differently. That she could have one more chance with Logan.

She'd never told him she loved him. The love that in a different lifetime would have been a joy was now her burden.

Footsteps approached. She waited for them to pass. She needed just a moment before she faced her life again…

"You're going about this all wrong." A deep, low voice sounded by her ear. And even though she tried to tamp down the vicious flare of hope, because Logan had gone back to his life in Chicago, she whirled to face the speaker. Daring to hope.

And her heart soared.

Logan searched her face, just as she drank in the angry, beautiful sight of him, as though it had been an eternity, not a handful of days since she'd last seen him. She catalogued and savored his features, the hard line of his jaw, the tense set to his shoulders and the smoldering depths of his eyes. And the roughness to his breath, as though he'd just sprinted the dozens of stairs. His bow tie dangled undone about his neck. His presence, so longed for, felt almost like an apparition, like the unexpected granting of her deepest wish. So surreal that she feared at any moment he might vanish.

She longed to reach for him, to touch his face, to throw her arms around him. But the foreboding in his gaze held her still. "I thought you were in Chicago."

"I was. I had commitments there."

"But you've come back?"

"Because I have commitments here, too." He lifted his hands to her face and she saw in his eyes, and in the dark shadows beneath them, something of her own torment. His gaze dipped to the chain around her neck.

"If you want to get rid of me," he said, "the very last

thing you should tell me is that I'm second choice. It just makes me determined to win."

No words came as he watched her, waited for her response. "That was what you were trying to do, wasn't it? To get rid of me?"

And despite the fact that the denial and explanation stayed trapped in her throat, he lowered his hands and looped his arms around her waist to pull her close. As though he craved the connection of touch as desperately as she did.

She ought to pull back.

Instead she clung. She took pleasure in his nearness and his touch, in his scent and his warmth. She closed her eyes and breathed deeply, trying to inhale the very essence of him.

In spite of the tension vibrating from him she dared to hope.

He had come back.

To the music that drifted from within the great hall, he began swaying with her. He edged them away from the wide doors, away from the guests coming and leaving.

The voice of doubt and self-preservation wouldn't give up. She couldn't jump to conclusions just because this was what she ached for. He'd come back, but why and for how long? "You didn't buy the subsidiary."

"No." He held her tighter.

"But it was everything you wanted. Everything you'd worked toward."

He stopped moving. "*It* wasn't everything I wanted. I don't take well to being manipulated. And I don't need your charity."

She pulled back at the accusation in his tone. He loosened his hold only enough that she could see his face. "Manipulated? Charity?"

"I won board approval only after I told them our relationship had ended. They were prepared to award it *because* you and I were no longer an item. And the man behind it all, the one looking the smuggest, was your old friend's new stepfather."

Rebecca gasped. "You didn't take it because of pride? You threw away everything you'd worked toward because you were miffed?"

"No."

"Then, why?" The words hiccupped in her throat, caught behind a sob. So much pain and for what?

"Because I needed to prove something."

"Point scoring? With Eduardo and his stepfather?"

"No. With you."

"I don't understand." Her anger was beginning to rival the one she sensed in him.

"Answer this. Why did you send me away?"

"I wanted to give you what you wanted. Eduardo guaranteed you would win the bid, but only if we were no longer together. I did you a favor."

"And you didn't trust me enough to tell me what your so-called friend had said, let me find a way around it?"

"I knew you'd think you had to honor your side of the bargain and give me the public engagement we'd agreed on. But it would cost you what you wanted. You could at least appreciate the sacrifice."

He stilled. "So it was a sacrifice? Ending what we had?"

He lifted both hands to her jaw, tilting her head up, forcing her to meet his gaze.

"Yes. But it was the right thing to do. And I'd do the same again. We were ending anyway."

"Were we?"

"That's what we'd agreed." That simple agreement seemed like a lifetime ago.

"Yes. It was," he said gently. "But when the end came, it turned out to be not at all what I expected. Or wanted."

"That's why you didn't buy into leBlanc? It doesn't make sense."

Something softened in his gaze. He lowered his hands to loop them behind her back again and began moving slowly with her, not waltzing, just swaying. Together. "Nothing about us makes sense on the surface. But here," he brushed his fingers over his heart, shifted them to where hers pounded with hope, "here it makes sense." Then he scooped a finger beneath the chain that hung around her neck, dipping below the neckline of her dress. Lifting the chain, he pulled up its secret treasure. The ring that hung hidden against her chest. She couldn't wear it on her finger but she had wanted it close, wanted to wear it somehow.

"You're wearing my ring."

There was no response she could give that wouldn't incriminate her. She'd tried but hadn't been able to give up the ring, had needed to keep it close. So she opted for full-on incrimination and whispered, "Always."

"The reason I didn't take the opportunity you so nobly offered was because I needed you to know that when I came to you to tell you I love you and ask you to marry me, that I was doing it for you alone. *You* are everything I want."

Logan reached behind her neck and undid the clasp of her chain then removed the necklace and let the ring slide into his upturned palm. He picked up her hand and, holding her gaze, his eyes seeking permission, he waited for her nod before sliding the ring onto her finger.

"I want you, Rebecca Marconi. I want you in every possible sense of the word. Forever. I love you and I want you to share my life and I want to share yours. Whatever

I have to do to make that happen, whatever sacrifices and compromises are necessary will be worth it. Because nothing is as important to me as being with you." He paused for breath. "Will you marry me?"

Rebecca nodded as tears welled in her eyes. "Yes," she whispered. "Because I love you, too."

And then, finally, he kissed her.

# Epilogue

Rebecca sat on the balcony and watched as the sun rose above the sea, turning the ocean golden, seeming for a moment to light it on fire. At a slight sound, she turned to watch Logan stroll out carrying two steaming mugs. He handed one to her before pulling a second chair close to hers and sitting down, resting his arm along the back of her seat.

"You were right about coming here."

"I knew you'd admit it eventually," he said with a wink.

Because he knew her too well. When he'd suggested coming back to New Zealand for a break, she'd argued against it. Their wedding was only two months away and the preparations were gaining pace, almost frenetically so. But that, he'd said, was precisely why she needed the break. Despite the occasional unnecessary panic by a staff member, everything was under control back home. Her schedule had been rearranged. She could be spared for a week. All the major decisions had been made long ago and the small ones could be dealt with by other people, or when they got back. And leaving the rain drenched fall back home for a crisp, sunny spring was a bonus, too. The hillside behind them rang with a chorus of birdsong.

Rebecca looked back out at the sunrise and breathed deeply. "Everything's so beautiful," she whispered, awestruck. "So perfect."

"Especially you," he answered, sounding just as amazed. She turned to see him studying her. She never got tired of the way he looked at her, and her body never ceased to respond—whether they were alone like this, or in the midst of a crowded room at a royal function. She lit up for him like the ocean had for the sun. And he knew, and used shamelessly, the effect he had on her.

But the balance of power wasn't all in his favor. She had the same effect on him. She'd been able on more than one occasion to distract him from what he'd claimed was pressing business. She delighted in that power.

Today he wore faded jeans and a dark T-shirt, the same as he'd worn that first morning they'd both been on this same deck of Colleen's B & B. So male, so appealing. Despite how good he looked in a tuxedo, the jeans and T-shirt combination was her favorite. Other than when she stripped that T-shirt, and then the jeans, off him.

"Come and sit here." Logan patted his lap and grinned. She went to him—she always did—and sat, reveling in the feel of his broad chest behind her and his powerful thighs beneath her. He wrapped his arms around her, held her to him. "Have I told you I love you, today?"

"Yes." And she had told him the same.

She leaned back against his chest. "You're sure I'm not too heavy for you?"

Behind her, she felt him shake his head and then press a kiss to the side of her neck. "Never."

"Never?"

"Never." He kissed her again.

"What if I was pregnant? I don't think I'd fit."

"You'll always fit. There will always be room for you." She heard the hint of curiosity in his voice, and the arms that had held her tight shifted. He moved his hands till they rested over her abdomen, still flat beneath her jeans. "Especially when you're pregnant."

They'd been planning on having children soon after they were married and had been careful. But there had been occasions when enthusiasm overrode care.

His hands shifted again, and he lifted and turned her so that she sat sideways across his lap rather than with her back to his chest. "Are you trying to tell me something?"

She nodded. "I saw my doctor yesterday."

Logan's jaw dropped and myriad emotions flitted through his eyes and across his face. For the first time since they'd known each other, she saw a hint of tears in his beautiful eyes.

He placed a hand over her stomach again, gentle yet possessive. "When?"

"Just over eight months. It's very early yet. Too early to tell anyone else. Especially because the first trimester is the most tenuous."

"The flight?" he said, a note of panic in his voice.

"Pregnant women fly all the time. It's fine." She slipped her arms around his neck, loving how this man, so confident in every aspect of his life, looked suddenly uncertain. But gradually that uncertainty faded from his face and was replaced by joy and pride.

"I won't even be showing in my wedding dress. But people will be able to do the math once he or she is born."

"Who cares?"

"You don't mind that it's so soon?"

"Mind? After your 'I love you' and your 'yes' to my proposal, that's the most wonderful thing I've ever heard you say." His eyes drifted closed as he held her to him, one hand still on her stomach as though trying to sense the life they'd created growing there.

He opened his eyes. "How will your father take it? The timing?"

"Initially he'll be a little put out. He does like things to be done 'properly.' But hard on the heels of that reaction will be joy at another grandchild. What with Bonnie already with a stranglehold over his heart he won't stand a chance." Rafe and Lexie's little girl was the light of her father's life. Time and again she'd watched her father turn from being a reigning monarch to a sappy, doting grandfather the moment he set eyes on Bonnie. "All it needs for Dad's world to be complete is for Adam to find someone he loves."

"How's Adam going with that?"

"He's giving it his best shot. Doing everything he ought. But…I don't know. Adam's always been too academic about things, thinking he can analyze and then control how life ought to unfold. I'm worried he'll pick someone because she meets a list of criteria he's drawn up for himself rather than someone who gets beneath his skin and into his heart even though on paper she might not be right for him."

"Like you did to me," he said. His hand shifted from her stomach to her thigh.

"And you to me."

"Adam's a smart man. He'll figure it out."

"Not so smart about everything."

"He'll figure it out. Besides, he's got Rafe and Lexie and now us showing him how it ought to be done."

"Maybe you're right."

"You know I am. But I didn't bring you here to talk about your brother." His hand curved around her thigh. "Do you remember the first time I saw you in jeans?"

How could she forget? They'd made love that night for the first time. "Yes." She brushed a kiss across his lips.

He reached for her head, brought it close again so that he could return the kiss, deepening it.

He pulled back and she looked into his beautiful eyes, watched his lips curve into the smile she loved so much. With one mind they stood. Leaving the sunrise, and their drinks on the table, they headed back inside.

\* \* \* \* \*

# LET'S TALK
## *Romance*

For exclusive extracts, competitions
and special offers, find us online:

 facebook.com/millsandboon

@MillsandBoon

@MillsandBoonUK

**Get in touch on 01413 063232**

# MILLS & BOON

## THE HEART OF ROMANCE

## A ROMANCE FOR EVERY READER

**MODERN**

Prepare to be swept off your feet by sophisticated, sexy and seductive heroes, in some of the world's most glamourous and romantic locations, where power and passion collide.

**HISTORICAL**

Escape with historical heroes from time gone by. Whether your passion is for wicked Regency Rakes, muscled Vikings or rugged Highlanders, awaken the romance of the past.

**MEDICAL**

Set your pulse racing with dedicated, delectable doctors in the high-pressure world of medicine, where emotions run high and passion, comfort and love are the best medicine.

*True Love*

Celebrate true love with tender stories of heartfelt romance, from the rush of falling in love to the joy a new baby can bring, and a focus on the emotional heart of a relationship.

*Desire*

Indulge in secrets and scandal, intense drama and plenty of sizzling hot action with powerful and passionate heroes who have it all: wealth, status, good looks…everything but the right woman.

**HEROES**

Experience all the excitement of a gripping thriller, with an intense romance at its heart. Resourceful, true-to-life women and strong, fearless men face danger and desire - a killer combination!

To see which titles are coming soon, please visit

## millsandboon.co.uk/nextmonth

# JOIN US ON SOCIAL MEDIA!

Stay up to date with our latest releases, author news and gossip, special offers and discounts, and all the behind-the-scenes action from Mills & Boon...

 @millsandboon

 @millsandboonuk

 facebook.com/millsandboon

 @millsandboonuk

*It might just be true love...*

# GET YOUR ROMANCE FIX!

Get the latest romance news,
exclusive author interviews, story
extracts and much more!